'Clinical
a wealth
note-wor   ho-
logical ve

'Voodoo
crackles a   ing
fan base
Good Re

'This is a   s,
and winn

'I suspect   *ald*

'Plumbin   as
an air of
nasty and
GQ Aust

'There's a   at
suggests i   res
deeply ab

'Giarrata
your atte
describin   vith
flaws tha
need, layi
www.crimedownunder.com

'Particularly nasty crime fiction that threatens to keep you awake at
night can always be dismissed with that hoary old chestnut "It's only
make-believe" . . . No such comfort with a debut book by Leah
Giarratano.' Lucy Clark, *Sunday Telegraph*

Also by Leah Giarratano

Vodka Doesn't Freeze
Voodoo Doll

leah
giarratano
black
ice

BANTAM

SYDNEY AUCKLAND TORONTO NEW YORK LONDON

Galiano Island
Community Library

A Bantam book
Published by Random House Australia Pty Ltd
Level 3, 100 Pacific Highway, North Sydney NSW 2060
www.randomhouse.com.au

First published by Bantam in 2009
This edition published by Bantam in 2010

Addresses for companies within the Random House Group can be found at
www.randomhouse.com.au/offices

National Library of Australia
Cataloguing-in-Publication Entry

Giarratano, Leah.
Black ice.

ISBN 978 1 74166 813 1 (pbk.)

Drug abuse and crime – New South Wales – Sydney –
Policewomen – New South Wales – Sydney – Fiction.

A823.4

Cover illustration by SuperStock
Cover design by Blacksheep-uk.com
Internal design by Midland Typesetters, Australia
Typeset by Midland Typesetters, Australia
Printed in Australia by Griffin Press, an accredited ISO AS/NZS
14001:2004 Environmental Management System printer

10 9 8 7 6 5 4 3 2 1

The paper this book is printed on is certified by the © 1996 Forest Stewardship Council A.C. (FSC). Griffin Press holds FSC chain of custody SGS-COC-005088. FSC promotes environmentally responsible, socially beneficial and economically viable management of the world's forests.

FSC
Mixed Sources
Product group from well-managed
forests and other controlled sources

Cert no. SGS-COC-005088
www.fsc.org
© 1996 Forest Stewardship Council

For Joshua George. Semper Fidelis.

This book is dedicated to Aunty Nancy.
And Beetle.

In vino veritas.

Prologue

Monday 1 April, 4 pm

Seren ignored the sting of the fly sucking blood from her ankle. She pushed her lips into the salty skin of her knees, pressing the sobs back behind her teeth. This is the last night, she told herself. The last night with her back to the wall, shrunk into the corner, praying for morning. Whatever happened tonight, it would be the last time she slept with the lice scrabbling for purchase on her near-shaved scalp, and nesting in her pubic hair.

She'd walk out or they'd carry her out. And if they carried her, it would be to an outside hospital or to the morgue. No way would she spend even a single night in the prison hospital. She had a six am release and she was going to keep it, one way or another.

In the meantime, she waited for Crash and Little Kim.

One of the screws had told her that Crash got her nickname at age four when her father threw her through a plate glass door. Apparently her little brother had mimicked the noise it

1

made, and her family had thought it cute. Broke the tension while they waited for the ambulance.

Seren couldn't figure how Little Kim got her name. The only little thing about Little Kim was her eyes, her facial features blurred and contracted by Foetal Alcohol Syndrome.

Hek – probably the most respected screw in the Silverwater Women's Complex – had tried to help Seren understand why they disliked her so much. He told her she shouldn't have made such a big thing out of the letters she got from her son.

'Their kids don't write to them,' he had explained a couple of months ago while she had been sweeping the yard.

'Their kids can't write,' Seren had retorted.

She'd felt like a bitch as soon as she said it, but since the smacking she'd copped from Little Kim the day before, her top lip split every time she smiled. Not that she did that a lot in here.

'What's even worse is that Crash and Kim can't read. You make them look stupid,' he'd told her.

'*I* make them look stupid?' Seren had snorted, and her lip had split again. The whole left side of her face throbbed. 'Don't make me laugh, Hek.'

'Besides,' he'd said, 'they don't really hate you. Little Kim seriously hated her last cellmate.'

'I heard,' Seren had said, eyes on the broom.

'We know everyone knows what happened,' Hek had said, 'but no one will make a statement.'

'Would you?' Seren had asked.

Rhonda Whiteman, Little Kim's previous cellmate, had died in the shower block, stabbed thirteen times in the back. When she was found, the shiv was still protruding from her right kidney, jammed in up to the handle. So Seren knew she could've had it much worse. Angel, who got to sweep in the nurse's office, told her that Little Kim's weight was listed in her med file as 128 kilograms. She could've snapped Seren's neck her first night there. Seren suspected that Angel was the reason the girls hadn't hurt her too bad. Everyone loved Angel.

2

But she knew they were really mad now. She was going home. Six months early, because her appeal had come through.

'And how is that fucking fair, bitch?' Crash had asked her at breakfast this morning. 'We don't get to go home. You get everything you want, don't you, you pretty little slut?'

Yeah, Crash, Seren thought now, crouched on the filthy mattress. Life has been *real* good to me so far. She pulled her knees closer to protect her stomach. Hek had warned her at lunchtime that she was going to get a goodbye flogging. Maybe that was true. But no one was going to hurt her badly enough to keep her from seeing her son tomorrow. She reached behind her back and pulled the broken broom handle a little closer.

One filament in the ceiling light above her popped and fizzed, dying. She stared at the door, her eyes seared with the waiting. Suddenly she slapped hard at her leg. The fly dropped, broken, onto the mattress.

Seren pushed her back further into the corner and waited for Crash and Little Kim.

1

Monday 1 April, 4 pm

Madame Truelove gripped her cigarette between her lips, pushed a greying lock of hair back from her forehead. Her other hand cupped Sergeant Jillian Jackson's fingers, palm up. She squinted through the smoke trickling from her mouth and removed the cigarette. She turned her head away and exhaled hard.

'I'm sorry, sweetie,' said Madame Truelove, turning back to face Jill, 'I've forgotten your name again. Was it Kristen?'

'Krystal,' said Jill, momentarily taking her eyes from the fire twirler performing in the middle of the Fairfield street mall in front of her. From this angle, despite the crowds surrounding the other three sides, she had a perfect view of the young woman wearing multicoloured tights, dreadlocks and a lime-green tutu.

'That's right. Krystal. Beautiful name, how could I forget? Krystal: a seer's name. Do you ever receive messages yourself?'

'I don't know, I guess I am pretty intuitive,' said Jill, happy to

4

extend the conversation so that she could hold this position for as long as possible.

'Yes, yes, I can see that here in your hands. And you're after some more adventure in your life, aren't you, dear?'

'I guess my life has been a little dull,' said Jill. Yeah, right.

'With the exception of your love life, Krystal.'

Jill gave the palm-reader another quick glance. 'You see that there?'

'Yes, yes. You're torn. You don't know which way to go. Do you go backwards to find true love with a man from the past, or should you move forward into uncertainty, perhaps danger?'

A group of laughing kids surrounded the fire-twirler. Hyped up on fairy floss, snow cones and the carnival atmosphere of the street festival, they were torn between tearing around madly to see everything and standing still, transfixed by the woman spitting fire from her mouth. They settled for jumping from foot to foot, squealing.

'Actually, do me a favour and give me the answer to the love life question, will you?' said Jill.

'Ah, Krystal, that is not my role, my love. It is for you to determine your own destiny. And you know the answer, deep in your heart.'

Yeah, sure I do, thought Jill. Well, what did you expect, Jackson, that this woman could give you serious advice?

She noticed that the small, dishevelled huddle of adults watching the performance had grown, and she recognised some of the regulars from the streets. Given the press for space, a generous perimeter surrounded the group, as parents, office workers and children instinctively steered clear of them. She tracked a hand gesture from one of the group to a man and woman approaching from the other side of the mall – Skye and CK. So this was definitely going down soon.

Jill watched the couple approach. CK, in a grotty white tracksuit and runners, coughed, raising a hand to his mouth. Skye, much taller at five foot ten, flinched, her hand flying up to protect her face. With the movement, her lank, auburn hair fell back and

Jill noted the angry scabs pocking her cheeks. Jill had seen too many kids around here with faces like that – gouges they'd tear themselves when gripped by ice psychosis, convinced worms had burrowed into their flesh, gnawing muscle, hatching eggs just under their skin.

As the fire artist sprayed a final jet of flames into the sky above her, the punk rock band on the stage to her left screeched into sound, and the kids shrieked their way over to them. A crowd of teen Goths had already claimed the area in front of the podium and they thrashed around industriously, all wearing the anarchist's uniform: eyeliner, piercings and frowns.

Madame Truelove raised her voice without commenting on the din. 'You are worried about someone in your life, Krystal, and you have good reason for your concern.' She flicked at a long cylinder of ash that had crumbled from her cigarette onto the back of her hand. 'The matter will soon come to a head and you will find that you are needed.'

'It's nice to be needed.' Jill kept her eyes on the mall outside the tent.

The fire artist was packing her belongings slowly. The assembly in front of her had now swollen to around twenty or so people. CK and Skye formed part of the cluster. The group spoke among themselves, but seemed otherwise uninterested in the carnival. From inside Madame Truelove's marquee, Jill could see but not be seen.

'You must be more vigilant, Krystal.' Madame Truelove's words were intoned mechanically. Jill wondered fleetingly what the woman was actually thinking about – perhaps shopping for dinner tonight? 'Betrayal and danger await you if you do not take care. Fortify your defences and gather close your friends. You will have need of both in days to come.'

'That sounds ominous,' said Jill, trying to peer around the backside of a man standing in front of the tent. Just when she thought she'd have to relinquish this position, the man moved on, tomato sauce on his chin, oozed from the hamburger clutched in his sausage-like fingers. She figured he was off to find a seat – you didn't get a body like that by walking around too much.

Jill saw that the fire artist had packed all of her equipment into a huge silver carry box. Her dreadlocks whipped around as though alive as she hefted it up and headed for a tent that had been set up for the performance artists. With Jill, the people in the group watched her every move.

'You don't need to be too alarmed, Krystal, but I *would* recommend that you consider some angel-work,' said Madame Truelove. 'We need to summon your guardians and ask them for their guidance and beneficence at this time.'

'That sounds like a plan,' said Jill. Skye had separated from her friends and was following the performer.

Jill stood to leave.

'Wait!' admonished Madame Truelove. 'I haven't finished your reading, Krystal. And I need to let you know about the angel-therapy I can perform for you. I'm usually booked out months in advance, but –'

'Twenty, wasn't it?' Jill dropped the cash onto the table.

'Twenty-five.'

Jill threw the old woman a hard look and flung a ten-dollar note down next to the twenty. She moved out into the cacophony of music and shouting. Wearing sneakers and a denim mini-skirt over black, footless tights, she blended in fairly well, but she pulled the hood of her white sleeveless sweatshirt up over her blonde ponytail and angled her face to the pavement anyway. She kept her eyes on the fire-eater's tent. When she lifted her hand to her face to cover a feigned coughing fit, the scales-of-justice tattoo on her deltoid stood out on her pale skin; a young mother almost steered her pram into a bin to avoid her.

Three other members of the group had joined Skye at the performer's shack – CK, a hand-rolled cigarette stuck to his lip; a young Aboriginal male – Jill hadn't seen him around here before; and Abigail. Ah, Abi. Aged fifty-five, with a thirty-year heroin habit still going strong, she was known as 'Mum' to half of Fairfield, and legitimately so for a good eight to ten of them.

Jill found a doorway. A beautician's, closed early for the festival. She drew into the recess and leaned back to watch.

The fire-eater, a black tee-shirt now covering the top of her tutu, emerged from the tent. Around her waist sat a utility belt – a large, pocketed 'bum-bag' – from which she pulled a bundle of flyers. From a pocket in her jacket, Jill withdrew a still-shot camera the size of a matchbox.

Individually, or in groups of two or three, the small crowd Jill had been watching came to collect a flyer from the performer. She observed each of them carefully inspect the leaflet, front and back, and then hand something back to the woman, which went into her utility belt.

Jill spoke into the phone hidden in her hand, and then took some more photos with the camera. Squinting down at the tiny device, she searched for the button to forward the photos.

'Haven't got fifty cents for a phonecall, have you, love?'

She snapped her head around to face the speaker, a skinny girl of Asian appearance. Jill hadn't noticed her around here before. What had she seen? She palmed the camera.

'Nah, I can't help you, sis,' said Jill. 'I need to get some more money myself before I can get something to eat.'

'No worries. Take it easy.' The girl shuffled towards the next pedestrian.

Jill dropped the camera back into her pocket and made her way towards the temporary stage where the crowd frothed and writhed. The four boys on stage still screeched unintelligibly; the lead singer had not let go of his balls once as far as she could tell. Please God, let him need to take a piss, she thought. Maybe then they can take a break for ten minutes.

You're getting old, Jackson, she told herself.

When she reached the edges of the throng, she stopped and glanced back towards the performers' tent. A commotion of a different kind had erupted. Cops swarmed out from behind the structure. The fire-eater swung her legs wildly, suspended in mid-air by Grojan, the probationary constable who'd made the Olympic weightlifting team. She saw Clarkson and a young uniformed female officer take CK down to the concrete; Skye screamed and tried to bite another cop, who had her in cuffs.

Clarkson caught Jill's eye, and she inclined her head slightly.

As a few people around her became aware of what was going on behind them, Jill turned her back on the scene. She couldn't risk one of the cops making too much eye contact with her; she didn't want any of the crowd guessing that she had had anything to do with the police making the bust.

Jill pushed through the crowd and went in search of something to eat.

2

Monday 1 April, 5 pm

After securing the deadlock and dropping the iron bar into place, Jill took a final peek through the spyhole on the door of the unit. What did CK call this lock the other day? She tried to remember: pig stick, pig lock, something like that. Gives a prick a bit more time to flush the stash when the pigs come to call, he'd said.

Huh.

She dropped the takeaway containers onto the linoleum of the kitchen bench and tried hard not to think about the number of germs that would be living in those cracks.

At least the food was delicious in Fairfield. She pulled from the plastic bag a fragrant tom yum soup, a container of garlicky fried tofu and one of steamed spinach in thick oyster sauce. The smells left her salivating. She could dine in a different part of the world every night. With the immigration detention centre close by, pretty much every nationality was represented in this suburb.

She reached into a cabinet for a big bowl and her mobile sounded. Work phone. Hmm.

'Jackson,' she said.

'Jill, this is Lawrence Last. Are you clear to talk right now?'

'Yep, good to go, sir.' What's this about, she wondered.

'Are you well, Jill?'

'Yes, sir. I'm fine.'

'I'm sorry to call you today, Jill. I know we weren't supposed to touch base again until later in the month, but I'm afraid I'm going to have to ask you to come in for a meeting.'

Jill took the phone away from her head and grimaced at it. She put it back to her ear.

'Is that absolutely necessary?' she said.

'Afraid so. You know I have to seek approval for another three months for you to stay undercover. Well, the Commissioner has said he won't automatically okay these things anymore. They want you to see the psych and we're going to use the opportunity to review your progress over the past couple of months,' said Superintendent Last. 'You really have done a remarkably good job.'

'Thank you, sir.'

'Is the apartment all right, Jill?' said her boss.

She stared around at the pockmarked walls and second-hand furniture of the second-floor, one-bedroom housing commission unit. She mentally pictured her spotless, sunny two-bedroom apartment overlooking the ocean at Maroubra Beach, and sighed. This place smelled perennially of bleach from her best cleaning efforts, but still she found herself washing her hands compulsively and she showered three or four times a day.

'The unit's fine, sir,' she said.

'I can't tell you, Jill, how much we value having you out there. The operation this afternoon was flawless. We have five in custody. The main offender is involved in a joint criminal enter-prise to supply methamphetamine on an ongoing basis. We have hopes that we may be able to encourage her to testify against her conspirators. She's a young mother, and is already asking how she might be able to reduce her sentence. We seized eight thousand in cash and the drugs are sixty-five per cent purity. Three months

11

from now, I will be using all of my influence to recommend you for promotion – should you apply, of course.'

'Thank you, sir,' Jill said. She took a deep, tired breath. 'So how are we going to do the meeting?'

'Same as last time,' he said.

'What. Now?'

'If that's okay with you.'

'That will be fine, sir,' she said. 'Ah, Superintendent Last?' She sniffed morosely at the fragrant steam rising from the bench.

'Yes, Jill?'

'Have you got anything to eat in there?'

Jill undid her ponytail; she checked her reflection in the door of the microwave and fluffed out her blonde hair. She scooped up a forkful of the salty, sticky spinach and then put all the plastic containers away in the fridge. She took a quick swig of mandarin juice from a bottle on the shelf and recapped it.

She waited for the knock.

'POLICE! Krystal Peters! This is Fairfield police. Open up now, please!'

'Hang on a fucken minute!' she screeched. 'What the fuck do you pricks want?'

The walls in these units carried every howl, sob, scream and crash. Most of her neighbours were out at this hour, but she heard Mrs Dang open her door.

And then Ingrid started up. 'Oh, what the fuck now?' Jill heard the door across the hall slam open. 'Can't you leave people the fuck alone? She's not even home!'

'Just stay where you are, Ms Dobell, or you'll be coming in too.'

It was Adam Clarkson. He'd found it fun arresting her the last time. 'Open this door now, Peters, or we're coming in,' he bellowed.

Jill leaned against the doorframe, studying her nails.

'Okay, okay.' She made sure her voice was loud enough to carry across the hall. 'Can't you give a person time to put some fucken *clothes* on? You bastards all just want to cop a free feel, don't ya?'

She heard her neighbour's hard bark of laughter. 'You take your time, Krystal. I'm a witness,' she heard Ingrid shout.

Jill figured she should open the door before they tried to kick it in again. The police department still hadn't paid her back for the locks she'd installed last time.

3

Monday 1 April, 4 pm

Byron Barnes surreptitiously licked a finger, and rubbed at the splodge of white stuff smeared on the leg of his jeans. The mark spread. He rubbed the heel of his palm against it, frantically, and then stared in dismay at the mess he had made. His hand balled into a fist that pretty much covered the smudge. He left it there.

Byron's other hand hovered over a gleaming granite board-room table that stretched three metres to a wall of windows at the other end of the room. Byron had never seen a view like it in his life and he avoided looking at it now. Everything shone so goddamn much. Sunspots pulsed red and black across his field of vision. Sydney's eastern suburbs from thirty floors up was too bright for Byron's hangover. He wanted to rest his head on the table and wait for the others, but he didn't dare even put his arm down. His denim jacket had already smeared something gluey across the mirrored black shine. His eyes reflected up at him from the inky depths, warning him: don't fuck this up.

Byron saw them walking through the lobby beyond the heavy glass doors. Heading this way. He sat straighter in the high-backed leather chair. Please God, just this once let me get off, he prayed.

The door swung open.

Byron tried to keep his eyes off her tits, but it was friggin' hard, man: they entered the room a fair way before anything else. They belonged to the sort of girl who always looked right through him. Like, they knew he was there staring straight at them, but they couldn't see him at all. Just once, Byron thought, I'd like to fuck a girl like that. She waited for the men to reach the table before she chose a seat, and, yep, it was like she'd entered a completely empty room.

When Christian Worthington strode around to Byron's side of the table with his hand outstretched, it finally occurred to him that he should be standing and he jumped to his feet.

'Byron,' said Christian.

Byron stared up at Christian, and in the hundred-dollar haircut and thousand-dollar suit he saw everything that he was not. His mouth formed 'Hello', but nothing came out.

'Byron, I want you to meet Ray Whitmont and Stephanie Tyler. Ray's new around here and he's going to be helping me with some of the legwork on your case. Stephanie's my legal secretary and she's the person I'd have been billing you a couple of hundred dollars an hour if you were paying us for this.'

Byron checked her out again and figured he could find two hundred dollars for that. He smiled at his shoes. Thing is, he knew it'd also cost two-fifty an hour for Ray in his shiny suit, and fuck knew what Christian Worthington would charge to keep a prick out of gaol. Thank God he didn't have to try to find that kind of money.

Whitey and Damien still wouldn't believe he had Worthington running his case. Nothing he said would convince them.

'Haven't you heard of pro bono work, you dumb cunts?' Byron had asked them last night, playing pool.

'Pro bono work? You're doing some work on his bono is what I'm guessing, you poofter.' Whitey had stretched his hand across the table to slap Damien's, who'd missed the easiest shot with his shout of laughter at Whitey's comment.

'Now that's the spirit, Byron.'

Byron snapped his attention back to the too-shiny boardroom to find Christian Worthington frowning at him.

'I tell you you could be looking at two years and you find that funny?' said Worthington.

'Nah, man, that'd be terrible,' said Byron. 'Can't you get me off?'

'Well that, Byron, is why you're here. In fact, that's what we're all doing here. But we're going to have trouble with this thing unless you concentrate. Can you do that, Byron?'

Fucking ADHD. Concentrate, you dickhead, Byron told himself. You're not going to get another chance like this.

'Really, Christian, why do you take on people like that?' Stephanie Tyler sat opposite her boss, packing up the notepads and pens used during the last couple of meetings. She hated these charity cases. She noticed the greasy smear at the place that had been occupied by Byron Barnes and recoiled, her nose wrinkled in disdain. She left the pen he'd used right where it was.

'Steph, we've all got an obligation to do some work for the people who'd ordinarily never afford us, you know that,' said Christian.

'Yeah, but he's a *drug* dealer, and she's a shoplifter. Could you not find someone else to defend who's maybe even a little less . . . scummy?'

'Stephanie! She could be back any minute. Would you be careful?'

'What! Isn't the meeting over?'

'I told her we'd walk her downstairs and point her in the right direction for the train. She got lost on the way here.'

Stephanie noisily exhaled.

Christian Worthington leaned back against the leather chair and swivelled to face the view. Hands behind his head, he smiled down at the brilliant ocean vista. Stephanie, watching him from behind a lock of straight blonde hair, tugged a little at the front of her blouse, exposing just a smidge more cleavage. Her boss appeared not to notice and stood when his last client slouched back through the doorway.

Looking for something to steal, I bet, Stephanie thought.

'Take an early mark today, Steph,' said Christian. 'You've earned it. Christ knows I have. I'm out of here.'

'Anything special on tonight?' Stephanie tried not to sulk as she stood and hurried to keep up with him. She had never run after a man in her life until she met this one.

'Just a bit of a gathering with Cassie, nothing much. I think it's an exhibition or something.'

Cassie Jackson. Skinny. Model. *Bitch*.

'Sounds great, Christian. Don't stay out too late. Remember you've got that breakfast meeting with Arlington at seven-thirty.' At least there's that, she thought. She'd told Professor Arlington it was the only time Christian could meet and vice versa. The more time she had with Christian away from Cassie Jackson, the better chance she had.

All men could be corrupted. Stephanie was certain of it. At least, she had been until she'd met Christian Worthington.

When the car jerked to a sudden stop, Jeremiah Dylan glanced up from his Nintendo DS. Ordinarily, he'd keep his eyes on the screen. After all, he only got fifteen minutes a day with this thing – just the time it took to get from his private school in Bellevue Hill to his tutor's house in Bondi Junction. But his mother, Judita Dylan, rarely swore, and Jeremiah's eyes shot up reflexively when he heard her curse.

'Sorry, darling,' she apologised. 'Nothing to worry about. Missed the lights again, that's all. We don't want you to be late.'

Jeremiah sighed. Frankly, he'd be happy to be late, but he

would never tell his mum that. She'd be quietly pained, and that night there'd be a sit-down with his father. Another talk. About the value of education, the discipline required to make it to the right university, the obligation and responsibility he had to make the most of his privilege in this world. Their speeches would be eloquent, sincere; they'd each up the ante to verbally out-perform the other. In spite of himself, even Jeremiah would be seduced. The adored only child of a supreme court judge and a surgeon, he could find nothing to rebel against – his life had been so carefully crafted and was so comfortable and reasonable.

Jeremiah smiled at his mum in the rear-view mirror and glanced out the window.

Fuck! An AUDI R8; this year's model. Not too many of them in the country yet. The driver looked pretty young, too. With the driver's face angled down slightly, his hair hid his eyes a little. His lips moved, like maybe he was speaking on a hands-free.

Heterosexual, privileged and intelligent, even Jeremiah Dylan was not spared the adolescent drive to admire and desire the more attractive members of the species. The man in the Audi brushed his hair from his eyes and Jeremiah gave a low whistle.

'Hey, Mum,' he said. 'Isn't that Christian Worthington? That guy Dad had around for dinner last week?'

Judita Dylan glanced to her left and smiled; she fluttered her fingers at the man at the wheel of the car next to them.

Good-looking fellow, she thought, as she motored her Mercedes across the intersection with the green light.

Hot car, thought Jeremiah Dylan, bending back to his Nintendo. I guess that's one reason I should get enough marks to study law, he thought. I can get myself a car like that.

Thus occupied, Jeremiah and Judita Dylan did not witness Christian Worthington pressing his hands firmly down into his lap.

They didn't hear the words he groaned to his last client for the day.

'Good girl. Stay there, now. Suck harder.'

4

Monday 1 April, 4.30 pm

The blatt of the siren signalled muster – it was time for head-count. Still intently watching the cell door, Seren reached behind her back and tucked the broom handle down between the wall and the lip of the filthy mattress.

They must be waiting for lights out, she thought.

She dropped from the bed to the floor and hurried out to the corridor to take her place against the wall. Crash watched her approach, leaning into Little Kim, the huge woman's chin resting on the top of Crash's dark head.

'Hey, baby,' said Crash when she approached. 'Ready for your last sleepy-byes?'

Seren ignored her, and nodded at Angel.

More than once Seren had whispered a prayer of thanks that Angel had been assigned to her on her first night. She'd never say it out loud, but privately she figured that her dad was up there somewhere, sending people to help her when she needed it most. It'd be just like him to send her an angel if he could.

Angel had given her the tour, shown her the routines, gone through the 'Rights and Responsibilities of Inmates' document with her. Most importantly, Angel had taught her the unwritten rules of life in gaol.

'It's pretty much simple, Seren,' she'd said, stirring sugar into the jumbo mug of tea that everyone here seemed to have glued to their hand unless showering or asleep. 'Keep to yourself. Little things you can find to help people, you do. But you don't have to have friends. It could be easier if you don't. You see, your friend in here might've robbed someone out there, and next thing you know, this chick from outside steps off the truck and you're sharing a cell with her. Now you're *her* enemy too.'

Angel knew everything. At forty-five she was a veteran. Although she'd only done five years inside, she'd done twenty in a war zone, being beaten bloody daily by her 130-kilo ex-boxer husband, Danny.

Both eardrums perforated by years of blows to her head, Angel hadn't heard the cops arrive when they'd come to investigate Danny's disappearance. They'd found Angel freezing in the rain, sitting on the grave she'd dug herself, a half-empty gin bottle keeping her semi-warm, waiting to join the ten or so bottles surrounding her.

'What'cha doing there, Angel?' the cops had asked.

Angel told Seren that the local cops knew her well. They'd carted Danny off to gaol countless times, and these two constables, Kerri and Karl, had carried her out to the ambulance at least twice.

'Just talking to him,' she'd told them.

'Danny hasn't signed in for a couple of days, Angel,' Kerri had said. 'We know he's stuffed up his bail conditions before, but he hasn't been seen at the bottle-o either. You don't know where he is, do you?'

'Been meaning to come tell you guys,' Angel had told them. 'Danny won't be signing in or out anymore.'

Angel had told Seren what she'd told Karl and Kerri that night. That she'd warned him. That she just couldn't take any more. That he should stop, or let her leave, or just go away himself. He'd broken her nose for the third time that night and when he'd finally dropped onto the lounge, piss in his pants and bourbon on his breath, she'd buried a ball point hammer in his skull. She stopped after the third strike; with the hammer no longer meeting any resistance from bone, her hand had slipped into his brain.

Took a whole bottle of gin to stop the slimy feeling, she'd told Seren. Feels like soup. Have to live with it in here, she'd said, wiping her hand against her gaol-issue pants.

Seren loved the story, and she loved Angel.

Thank God Angel would be out the day after her, thought Seren; she needed someone she could rely on out there. They could hardly believe it when they'd discovered the timing of their releases.

Now, in the hallway, Angel leaned in closer to Seren and her cellmates.

'Gonna be a big night for you tonight, ladies,' Angel said.

Seren stared. Was Angel geeing them up? She knew Crash and Kim had it in for her!

'Got a new one coming in,' Angel continued. 'They're putting her in the cell next to yours.'

So that's it, thought Seren. Maybe that would distract them a little. Everyone loved a new playmate.

'Poor little rabbit,' said Angel. 'Just a tiny little thing, but she's out of control.'

Little Kim combed Crash's hair with her fingers, while Crash watched Angel intently.

'Yeah? What's her problem?' Crash said.

'Gotta be ice,' said Angel. 'She's been sent straight from the Sydney cells, and she's coming down hard. They give them nothing over there. Word is she bit one of the cops when they put her in the truck and so the screws hate her already.'

'Whoah! That'll teach 'em.' Crash's eyes were alight.

Angel clucked her tongue. 'And her file says she's Hep C, too.' She shook her head.

Crash sniggered. 'So she's causing some shit over there?'

'You could say that,' said Angel. 'Poor thing. That ice sends them crazy, I tell you. She's been in the observation cell for three hours and she hasn't stopped screaming once. Seems she reckons they've put radio waves in the light bulb and they're fucking with her brain. She's made it her mission since she got in there to rip the light off the roof.'

'Ha. Good luck with that,' said Seren.

Kim and Crash laughed. The observation room was a dry cell, designed to be indestructible. The light was enclosed in a cage, the walls were completely bare, and there was nothing in the cell that could be lifted, torn or thrown.

'You'd think she'd have no chance, hey?' said Angel. 'Thing is, the little bugger's gone and ripped the cage right off the ceiling, light fitting and all. No one can figure out how the hell she did it.'

'Cool!' said Little Kim, staring down at Angel.

'So, what'd they do to her?' asked Crash.

'Sent the squad in,' said Angel. 'Suited up. Poor little bugger, they flattened her, but she went down screaming. I'm telling you, that ice gives you some strength.'

'No shit,' said Crash. 'All this talk is making me hungry. Think you could bring me some of that back in when you come to visit, princess?' She stared hard at Seren.

Hek walked by, finishing the headcount, and Seren didn't answer. No way I'm ever coming back here, she promised herself.

5

Monday 1 April, 5.30 pm

'I'm sorry you had to get dragged in here, Jill,' said the psychologist.

'Literally,' said Jill.

The other woman gave a sympathetic smile.

Jill stood near the seat diagonally opposite the door, despite the fact that the psychologist's notepad and pen sat on the table next to the chair. Well, it's not as if it's her office, thought Jill; she knew that the woman had been sent out from Central specifically to speak to her. And she did like to take the seat that faced the door. Good feng shui.

'I know. I'm sorry,' said the therapist. 'It's got to be one hell of a life you're living right now. Look, Jill, we haven't met properly. My name's Helen Levine. I'm a clinical psychologist. I do a lot of work with the New South Wales Police.'

They shook hands.

Helen retrieved her notepad and gestured to Jill to take a seat. She took the other chair.

'So you don't work for the department?' asked Jill.

'No. I'm in private practice,' said Helen, 'but I should tell you straight up that this isn't your regular counselling session. This is more of an assessment to make sure you're okay, Jill, and I have to tell you that what we say in here is not confidential.'

'Who're you going to tell?'

'I have to report back to Superintendent Last, and a copy of my report will be annexed to his application to the Commissioner to have your undercover duties extended.'

'Okay.'

'So, if it's all right with you, Jill, I'm going to record our session to help me with my report.'

'You're going to record it.'

'If that's okay with you?'

Jill curled her feet up onto the chair and wrapped her arms around her knees. She was under constant scrutiny out on the streets, and in here, where she was supposed to be safe, she felt under siege again.

'Whatever . . . You're going to report everything I say anyway,' she said, resigned.

'Let's get going, then,' said Levine. She fussed briefly with a voice recorder on the desk and then came back to her chair. 'So what made you want to do undercover work, Jill?' she asked.

'Actually,' said Jill, 'Last asked me to do it. I was between assignments at the time, so I thought I might as well.'

Helen gave a short laugh. 'You thought you might as well? That's a pretty risky job to just jump into for the hell of it.'

Jill shrugged.

'You'd been working on that home invasion case last year. What did they call the killer – Cutter? How did you pull up after that?'

'Fine.'

'You were shot, I believe.'

'Not really. Blowback. My partner shot the offender. I got a bit of a graze on my cheek.'

'Your partner,' Levine glanced down at her notes, 'Gabriel

Delahunt. A federal agent. Do you have much contact with him now?'

'I don't have much contact with anyone at the moment,' said Jill.

'Oh, of course. Obviously,' said Levine. She read a little more. 'The offender in that last case died in your arms, is that right?'

'You seem to know the story.'

The psychologist smiled. 'You've had a remarkable career, Jill,' she said. 'Really. It's quite exemplary. Your superiors are full of praise. There have been some very difficult moments over the past couple of years, though. I think it was only *just* over a year ago that you were involved in another fatal. You killed the man who had been the leader of an organised paedophile network.'

Jill didn't speak.

'I shouldn't say this, Jill, but congratulations. That must have felt great.'

Jill exhaled. 'You have no idea,' she said. The man she had killed, Alejandro Sebastian, had abducted and raped her when she was twelve years of age. She had killed some of her nightmares with him.

'You were working over at Maroubra then, weren't you?' Helen Levine looked down at her notes again. 'That's right. With Sergeant Scott Hutchinson. You're a long way from Maroubra now.'

'Tell me about it,' said Jill. This was great. Every subject she didn't want to think about, raised within the space of ten minutes. Cutter. A sexual sadist. When she closed her eyes, she could feel her face on his neck when he died, shot dead by Gabriel. She remembered listening to him die, her mouth full of his blood, sounds muffled and distorted. Her hearing had returned slowly, although doctors had since informed her that she had lost some range of sound because of her proximity to the gunshot blast; the shot that had prevented Cutter slashing her throat. Gabriel had saved her life.

Gabriel. Was he safe? He'd been pulled back into counter-terrorism intel immediately following that case. She knew that a cop had been shot arresting one of the suspects Gabe was investigating.

And Scotty, her previous partner. Never far from her thoughts, especially whenever she thought of Gabriel, Scotty understood that she was officially incommunicado, but she knew that he would expect her to call him anyway.

She shifted in her seat, antsy, wanting to be out of there, to get back to work, to do some training, to do anything, really, other than sit exploring her feelings with a stranger like this. Jill turned, expressionless, towards the woman speaking. Can we just get this over with, she tried to tell her with her eyes.

'I believe,' said Helen Levine, 'that the operation you're currently involved in aims to try to clean up some of the Fairfield methamphetamine trade.'

'Amphetamine type stimulants generally,' said Jill. 'Ice, speed and ecstasy, basically.'

'Your last case was just over in Liverpool. Aren't you afraid that a drug dealer from Liverpool might see you in Fairfield?'

Thanks again, Jill thought. You're making me feel a hell of a lot better, Helen.

'I didn't do any work on the street in that case,' said Jill. 'And they reviewed the media footage from the case. There was really only one shot of me in which my face was visible, and I looked pretty different from the way I present myself now.'

'Yes, I have to say, I couldn't have picked you as a cop,' said Levine.

Jill smiled tightly. Her job was done: she'd disguised herself from being recognised by some university-educated white girl. Yay.

'How did they train you for the undercover work?' asked Helen.

'There's a two-week course,' said Jill.

'That seems quite brief.'

'I've been doing this job for fourteen years, Helen. And I've been UC before – in Wollongong. That should be in that file you've got there.'

'I know. I didn't mean to . . . It's just that undercover work can be very stressful on cops. You don't get your usual social and professional supports. You don't work with a partner. You're out in the street. I believe they've rented you an apartment locally?'

'Nothing but the best,' said Jill.

'Have you been lonely?' asked Levine.

Jill studied her hands. Did this woman really expect her to be frank? Probably not, she realised. But if she said she was fine, and she one day claimed psychological injury, she could bet that the tape of this interview would be produced pretty quickly.

'I'm fine,' she said.

Levine paused. 'I don't really know how to ask the next question, Jill,' she said.

Jill waited. She didn't either.

'I believe,' continued Levine, 'that there's general acknowledgement that undercover operatives may have to take drugs at times during covert operations in order to divert suspicion?'

Jill said nothing.

'Have you had to do that?'

'No,' said Jill. She'd been told to lie if asked that question in court. She wasn't in court now, but she was being taped. She uncurled her legs from the chair and sat up straight. She'd had enough. 'Helen,' she said, 'I'm really hungry. I've been working all day and it's, what, six o'clock? Is there a lot more we have to do? I've still got to report in to Superintendent Last.'

The psychologist read the top sheet of her notepad, then flicked the page over.

'Actually, Jill, they were the most important questions. I understand that you're tired. Thank you very much for your time.'

Jill stood.

'Before you go,' said Levine, 'could I just give you my card? I'd like you to call me if you need any help, or even if you just feel like talking.'

Jill took the card. 'Will do, Helen,' she said. She moved to the door of the office and waited.

The psychologist stood, uncertain.

'Could you please open the door for me, Helen?' said Jill. 'This is going to have to look as though I'm still under arrest.'

'Oh, of course, I forgot.'

Helen Levine opened her office door. Adam Clarkson stood there, grinning. The hall was otherwise empty.

'Alrighty then, Krystal,' Clarkson said to Jill. 'Let's get you over to the booking room.'

'Ready when you are, pig,' said Jill.

The door closed on Helen Levine's somewhat startled face.

Jill dropped the card into the first rubbish bin as Clarkson steered her down the corridor.

6

Monday 1 April, 6 pm

'All right, if I could ask you to take a seat, please? Most of us are due to knock off now, and I know people are keen to get home.' Superintendent Lawrence Last stood at the front of the booking room, his grey suit and face rumpled with the day. Jill figured that when he'd reached adolescence and his height of six foot seven, he must never have felt the need to develop any brash aggression or male bravado. He towered over most of his colleagues in the police force, and with his height and his hushed, serious tone of voice, he could settle hostility in both cops and civilians faster than anyone she knew.

The other four occupants of the room took seats in front of their commander. Jill sat closest to the wall, with Adam Clarkson to her right.

'First up,' said Superintendent Last, 'I would like to offer congratulations and my gratitude for a superb job this afternoon. The operation was flawless, and that is due to the professional way in which all of you conducted yourselves.'

Last turned towards Jill.

'A special thanks to Detective Jackson here. Her status remains undercover, and although I know it's unnecessary to say this again in present company, I will do so. While Jill is in this building, she is Krystal Peters, today being questioned in relation to items stolen from the Priceline chemist. She will be released without charge this evening, immediately following this meeting.'

'What'd ya steal, Krystal?' said Clarkson. 'Some make-up? You could use some; you're looking a little rough tonight.'

Jill smothered a grin. Clarkson had asked her out three times. She liked him. But not that much.

'Nope, treatment for my lice,' she said, and reached out with a hand to lightly brush his shoulder, as though flicking something off.

'Okay, okay, let's get on with it, please, people.' Last spoke quietly and the banter died quickly. 'I'm preparing an application to extend this operation for another three months. This meeting will serve as an operational debrief for progress thus far, and the notes will be included as part of the application,' he said. 'Before we review the paperwork, I'd like to point out that the covert monitoring has been highly successful so far. In addition to the drugs seized, raids have netted two shotguns, a .22 handgun, a thousand dollars in counterfeit cash, and ammunition. Remember that Jackson's brief is to observe and befriend people with the aim of netting us the major dealers where possible. We don't bring anyone in unless we can get them under the Trafficking Act.'

Last handed Jill a slim bundle of papers. 'Please take one and pass it on,' he said. 'Obviously, these cases have yet to go to court, so the verdicts and sentences have been left blank, but this will give you an idea of our progress to date.'

Jill reviewed the typed table in front of her. It looked pretty impressive and she stifled a private smile as she bent over the paper. She read along as Last went through each case.

**Drugs – Amphetamine/ Methylamphetamine – multiple
supply: s.25A.*s.25A(1) Drug Misuse and Trafficking Act 1985
(NSW) – supply prohibited drug on 3 or more occasions during
30 consecutive days – maximum penalty 20 years***

Case	Drug	Amount	Priors	Facts
Acardi	s.25A	.37 g .49 g .86 g 26.7 g	Priors including drugs	Engaged in small-scale, but systematic, business of supplying drugs from garage. Small amounts typically sold, but informed undercover police officer he was prepared to sell larger amounts if required.
Lam	s.25A	13.53 g 27.6 g 27.4 g	Prior convictions, including drugs	Sold amphetamine to undercover police officer on three separate occasions during one-month period. Drug of very low purity.
Vrancic and Fencott	s.25A Four related offences	26.24 g 63.38 g (85% pure) 9.13 g	Vrancic: Lengthy record, including possession and supply, and assault	Vrancic: Eleven separate sales worth $30,000. Drug equipment found at premises. Fencott: A runner.

Jill zoned out at some point during the review, lost in memories of
the things she'd had to do and say to aid in these apprehensions.
The work was satisfying and exhilarating, but she also felt
saddened by the plight of many of the users she'd befriended in

the line of duty. From her years in the job, she knew their stories well: many of the women were incest survivors who'd escaped home with the first man possible. A man whose possessiveness seemed adorable to begin with – a true sign of his love. But the months would wear on and she would find herself increasingly estranged from friends and family; trying desperately to please this person who was now never happy, who had taken to belting her when she dropped a glass, or arrived home a little late from the shops. She'd just have to try harder, of course, she'd tell herself, but he was so angry when she had no money for speed, and she'd taken a liking to the goey too. When he pissed off with her best friend, there'd be another man, more violence, and the speed was no longer enough. Valium, Serepax, pot, and the piss of course, but if she fell in love with heroin, as many of these women did – so good for making everything feel like nothing – then DoCS would take the kids and she'd take up with a pimp.

Jill understood that everyone has choices, but she was also aware that some have more options than others. Although she was hardly a true friend to these women, she knew that what she was doing was right. Drugs screwed people's lives and she was making it harder for the poison to get around.

When the meeting wrapped, Jill left the station – theatrically spitting on the pavement out the front for the punters – and walked back the couple of blocks to her unit. She tried not to be dispirited by the sight of some of her new neighbours – a filthy couple screaming at each other in front of the takeaway shop, a youth on the nod at the bus stop. Every day gave her another chance at pulling in someone big, and in the meantime she was putting a lot of mid-level dealers out of action for a while.

7

Monday 1 April, 9 pm

'Would you listen to the little bitch?' Crash strode the confines of the cell, each pass by Seren's bed causing her to contract involuntarily. At any moment, the woman could swing and strike. She'd done it before, and God knew Seren was long used to blows beginning for no reason, with no warning. She shrugged a little closer to the wall.

'Je-sus, honey, it's not like we can hear anything else, is it?' Little Kim sat spreadeagled on the toilet, her fat, white thighs parted, picking at an ingrown hair on her shaved vagina. 'The little whore just won't shut up.'

The screaming ranged in pitch and tone, but the volume rarely dropped. From piteous wailing to screeching fury or shrieking terror, the woman in the cell next door was living in her own kind of hell, locked somewhere inside a mind deranged by drugs. Seren had watched a couple of people coming down off ice before, but it had never gone on this long. On the outside, junkies were never very far from a dealer, and a pension cheque, a hot sat-nav stolen from a four-wheel drive, or a quick blowjob in a car park would get them what they needed to shut the demons up for a while.

'Fucking bitch! How are we supposed to sleep?' Crash's gaol-issue tracksuit pants sat low on her hips; she'd pushed the bottom of her tee-shirt up through her bra so her flat, dark-brown stomach lay bare. She'd rolled the sleeves up too, exposing chiselled shoulders and the mostly gaol-drawn tatts that covered them. She passed Seren's bed again and stopped at the cell door.

'Shut the fuck up, cunt!' she yelled. 'You wait till this fucking door opens!'

Seren put her head in her hands when the screaming intensified, magnified by the shouts of the other inmates, inflamed by the cries in the night. Little Kim chuckled quietly on the toilet, at home in the din, desensitised to the soundtrack that had played her whole life.

It wasn't like Seren hadn't also grown up with the screams and the threats, the sobbing and begging. It's just that she'd never grown used to it. She tried now to take herself back to the time when the nights had been quiet and she'd fallen asleep to the sounds of *Neighbours* on TV and her mum and dad talking quietly. She dived into the world of her past, each sight, sound and smell rubbed raw from use. This was where she came to try to stay sane when the world around her howled with madness; back to twenty years earlier, when Serendipity was five.

Little Seren Templeton tiptoed barefoot in pyjamas down the corridors of her memory. Soft flickering colours flared and vanished from the TV in the lounge room as she padded away from the tinkle of Mummy's laughter. Sometimes she wondered whether it had really happened, if Daddy had really existed and Mummy had smiled all the time. There was nothing left to prove it had been real.

There! It *is* there. Soft, deep breathing. She walked, mesmerised, towards the crack of blue light at the end of the corridor. Bradley's room. She pushed at the door softly. The breathing stopped. Seren shuffled towards his bed, her eyes adjusting to the dim light. She could see the yellow baby blanket that used to be hers, hear his soft chortle, like a smile set to music, and smell the sweetest, warm scent, better than lollies.

And there. His hand! A chubby little star, reaching out from the sheets, smooshing at her nose. But she could never see his face.

Little Bradley. Daddy. A mummy who smiled. Serendipity Templeton. Had they ever really existed?

On the hard mattress in Silverwater Women's Correctional Centre, Seren didn't know for sure, but she wrapped the memory tight around her to try to make it through another night.

8

Monday 1 April, 9.15 pm

Cassie Jackson straightened at the bathroom vanity, the remnants of a few deep-fried canapés sliding down the drain in front of her. She blasted the refuse with a spray from the cold tap and washed the offensive food from her life. Holding her hair back in a ponytail, she ducked her head under the tap to rinse her mouth. She checked her teeth in the mirror. Perfect.

Wiping at a smudge of charcoal eyeliner, Cassie searched for that crease under her right eye. She'd spotted it a week before, but it had been only intermittently present since, mostly when she woke up, typically late in the afternoon.

Must see Dr Teo about that, she told herself. Fuck knew it was already hard enough battling the fifteen-year-olds for jobs without showing up at a shoot looking like a wrinkled old bat.

Cassie grinned at herself and her eyes glittered. The woman staring back at her was hardly an old bat. What had that reporter called her hair colour last week? Burnished toffee, that was it. A new, heavy fringe hung over her kohl-rimmed green eyes. The

36

scattered freckles across her turned-up nose were a trademark feature and never hidden by the make-up artists. At thirty, she was still booked eight months in advance and got more work than ninety per cent of her peers.

Her body got her the jobs, but her friends kept her there. She'd had to call in favours a few times too often recently. She'd turned up late, sometimes with bloodshot eyes, a cold sore and even a black eye last month. Nothing that a little blow shared around wouldn't cover. Plenty of people in the business searched their letterboxes daily for one of Cassie Jackson's inspirational greeting cards. The cards were always beautiful – cherry blossoms on fragile silk from Taipei; heavily embossed fabric from Milan; ochred desert scenes on hand-pulped paper from Darwin – but the little snap-locked baggies inside the cards always brought the widest smiles.

Speaking of which . . . Cassie took a quick glance at the bathroom door and reached into her clutch bag. Her hand found the small crystal vial immediately. Looped around the neck of the petite, stoppered bottle was a thread of gold chain securing a minute golden spoon. Cassie smiled as she held the pretty little object up to the light. Along with its contents, it had been a perfect gift from Christian. She scooped the white powder up with the spoon, raised it to her nostril and snorted.

Lovely.

Ready now, Cassie took a last long look over her shoulder at herself in the mirror and sauntered from the bathroom.

9

Monday 1 April, 9.15 pm
'Now this is gonna be one for the road, okay, Templeton?'

Crash pulled her tee-shirt over her head and began to peel off her tracksuit pants, all the time staring hard at Seren. Crash, it seemed, had never been taught the basics of hygiene; Seren could smell sweat and worse from the other side of the room.

No. No way. I'd rather take a bashing, Seren promised herself. Bad enough she had to listen to these two sucking and moaning every night – she was not going to join in now.

She got up on her haunches, ready to fight, and scanned the room. Little Kim still squatted on the toilet, but her close-set eyes now focused on the scene in front of her.

The wailing from the cell next door continued. The screws wouldn't come running to anything tonight.

'Fuck off, Crash. That is not going to happen,' said Seren, one hand behind her back.

'Oh, it's going to happen, Templeton, and you're either going to enjoy it, or you're not.'

'If you come near me, I swear to God I'll kill you.'

'You can swear to God, Allah and the freakin' Buddha for all I care, bitch. This has been a fucked-up night, my head hurts from that screaming cunt next door, and you're going home tomorrow. You owe me.'

Crash threw her dirty bra into the corner of the cell and walked naked towards her. Seren's eyes darted around wildly. Suddenly, she became aware that something was different. Little Kim. Ordinarily the big woman would've been right behind her girlfriend, ready to step in should Crash have trouble with one of her victims.

Little Kim hadn't moved.

At that moment Crash seemed to notice this too.

'Come on, babe,' she called over her shoulder. 'You gonna come get some of this?'

Nothing.

Seren tried to think. Her sight was pinpoint-focused on the threat in front of her and her heart scuttled madly in her chest. She tried her voice. 'What? Little Kim not good enough for you anymore, Crash?' she said.

Intent silence from the toilet.

'Shut up, bitch. Don't you go starting trouble now.' Crash stopped walking. 'Come on, baby.' She turned to her girlfriend. 'You know you like some three-way.'

'Why her?' Little Kim spoke.

'What do you mean? She's here. We're here. Why the fuck not?'

'I thought you didn't like her,' said Little Kim.

'What does like have to do with it? Come on, babe, don't act stupid. Let's all just have some fun over here. I'm tired, all right?'

Crash moved again towards Seren's bed, reaching a hand out to touch her. Seren slapped it away. Crash laughed.

'Don't call me stupid.' Little Kim stood up from the toilet, her pants still around her ankles.

'What? What's your fucking problem?' Crash straightened at the foot of the bed and turned to face Little Kim.

'I said. Don't. Call. Me. Stupid.'

'What? What are you going to do?' Crash stood with her arms out, staring down the huge woman opposite her. Seren made herself small on the bed.

'Why you gotta go near that skank? Aren't I good enough for you?' Little Kim obviously wanted an answer to Seren's question.

'Look, babe. This has never been an exclusive thing, you and me. You know that. And you're pissing me off over here. You know I don't like people telling me what to do.' Crash's tone was menacing.

'You're always telling *me* what to do.'

'Who keeps you out of trouble in here, huh? Now do me a favour, Kim. Either sit the fuck back down, or come over here and make me real happy like you do.'

Seren briefly considered that the woman in the cell next door must have invented some new kind of language. She crowed with madness. Crash turned back towards her and put one knee on the bed. Seren almost dry-retched with the musky stench caused by the movement. Time to move. She pulled the broom handle from behind her back at the precise moment that Little Kim said, 'I'm offering you out.'

Seren froze.

Crash whipped her head around. '*What*? You are *what*?'

Seren couldn't believe she'd heard right. Offering you out: prison slang for a challenge to a fight. Seren pushed the handle back between the mattress and the wall, but kept it close.

Oh, fucking hell. Little Kim was going to fight, and that hadn't happened since Rhonda Whiteman was shanked thirteen times in the shower block.

And Seren was stuck in the same cell.

10

Cassie knew that every eye was tracking her as she stalked across the foyer of the gallery. Even the outrageously gay artist exhibiting tonight took his eyes from his artwork to follow her movements. Doesn't she know the cat suit is so last century, he inwardly sniped, knowing full well that by the next season half the women in the country would own one, even though most of them would never wear it out and the rest of them shouldn't.

Cassie wore no underwear and the lush lycra acted as a second skin. Although sheathed neck to toe in black, she was more naked than had she been wearing the most minuscule dress.

Used to the attention, Cassie had her mind on only one thing.

Christian Worthington watched her approach from the other side of the room, a small smile playing on his lips. Although he'd just arrived, everyone in the room knew this woman would go straight to this man. It was natural selection. There was no one else present she would stride to with such purpose. Well, except perhaps the aged Western Australian mining magnate in the corner who'd previously been the most fascinating person there. But the Barbie doll he'd arrived with, with the trout pout and the silicon, would go to the mat pulling hair if this woman came anywhere near him. Half the men in the room would have paid plenty to watch that happen.

'Drink, darling?' Christian brushed Cassie's cheek with his lips, his fingers touching the small of her back. 'Fuck me now,' he whispered into her ear.

'Yes *please*, darling,' she said.

'Red, white, or sparkling?' he asked.

'Tequila.'

'Back in a moment.'

Cassie felt the cocaine rushing through her body and it felt like love. Hell, maybe it is, she thought. She knew she felt great when she was with Christian. He treated her right and he had his own money; not like her last boyfriend, Aidan, who'd left her with a debt to their dealer and a black eye when she'd told him it'd been real, but see ya. She and Christian shared many of the same friends; he had a beautiful home and a nice car and he was absolutely gorgeous to look at. Top all that off with the fact that he seemed to be able to get the best blow and anything else she fancied, and Cassie thought that perhaps she'd hang on to this one for a while.

She glanced around the room, and just for kicks gave the mining magnate a luscious smile. When his date stood and blocked their eye contact with her tits, Cassie laughed out loud. A waiter offered crayfish hors d'oeuvres, but she simply smiled and declined. She waited on her man and her tequila.

Although not comparable to Sydney Harbour, tonight Darling Harbour was a jewel, throbbing and glittering, pulsing with colour. From the darkened balcony of a sixth-floor penthouse apartment, Cassie Jackson stood, completely naked, staring out over the bay and city skyline. Red wine sloshed from the oversized glass in her hand as she tiptoed towards the balustrade of the terrace.

She thought she could fly.

Cassie took another deep sip from the glass and set it down carefully on the lip of the balcony. The pills and the wine had smoothed the hard wire of the coke and she felt fluid, sedated, liquid, like a part of the sky. She leaned forward into the night, the April breeze bathing her overheated skin. She boosted herself up a little, tilting further forward. If she could just . . .

Cassie felt Christian's hands on her back, smoothing and stroking, moving around to her belly, her breasts. She leaned back into him, reaching her arms over her head, revelling in his hands on her body, gliding down now over her ribs, her hipbones. He turned her face to meet his and his lips found her mouth. Christian turned Cassie around and led her by the hand back to the lounge room. He pulled her down onto the thick carpet, the only light in the room washing in from the city skyline. He bent over her body and continued to stroke her skin, reaching everywhere, until it felt as though his hands were all over, all at once. Cassie moaned and reached her arms wide, her throat exposed, like a cat at full stretch. He nudged at her legs with his hands and she opened herself completely to him.

Christian reached across to a low table beside them and brought out a small package. With her eyes closed, Cassie did not feel him sprinkling the cocaine between her legs, but she certainly felt him licking it off.

When Cassie stopped shuddering and he felt her breath relax into sleep, Christian rolled her onto her stomach and knelt behind her. Shaking a little more of the powder into his palm, he rubbed the tip of his cock with one hand and used the other to spread the cheeks of her arse.

11

Monday 1 April, 9.20 pm
The thing is, when the worst of the damage is being done, it doesn't even sound that bad. Seren knew that the moments in between the screaming and crying were the most dangerous. Of course, you could still hear it. Like now – a dull splat, like a raw steak dropped onto a kitchen bench. And a whoof and sigh. And again, a wet clap. A moan.

Seren wanted to close her eyes and put her pillow over her head like she used to. But she forced herself to watch the scene playing out in front of her. Little Kim had tried to retreat several times, not because she was losing, but because she'd already hurt Crash so badly. The white bone of Crash's forehead shone where her left eyebrow should have been, and blood streamed from the gash. Seren had watched one of Crash's teeth float along in the rivulet of blood and come to rest in the nook of her collarbone.

Stay down! Can't you just pass out? Seren wanted to scream. But when Little Kim tried to move away, Crash would pull her back by her hair, or launch herself onto the mountain of the other woman's back.

The cells were otherwise silent. The new arrival next door was finally sleeping or too hoarse to be heard. A dreamy stupor began to overtake Seren. For her, the fight had morphed into some macabre ballet. Little Kim had finally kicked off her pants and her huge fleshy thighs were mottled pink with exertion. Crash fought like some tribal warrior, her breasts slick with blood.

Surely, I'm not here, Seren thought. This can't be real.

The feeling was familiar. At night, when Bradley had gone and Daddy was dead, she'd stuff herself into her wardrobe with her toys. In the dark, with her winter parka and her skates, she'd pretend to be on her way to Narnia, ready to step out into a winter wonderland. Once, the fantasy so compelling, she'd snuck out of the wardrobe – the screaming must be part of the battle with the Ice Queen for Narnia, she thought – her friends needed help. She'd stolen down the corridor, Humphrey in hand, on her way to the adventure.

Her stepfather faced the other way, thank God. But Mummy could see her. Mummy was crying. She always cried now. He had hold of Mummy's hair. He pushed her head down there. Mummy talked to her, only she didn't speak. Her eyes told Serendipity that she should go away. Her eyes said Serendipity couldn't help Mummy and Mummy couldn't help her. Please, Serendipity, her mother told her silently, you've got to go.

Serendipity left that night, and Seren remained. She'd stayed in the house until she'd turned fifteen, for as long as she could take it. But Mummy had been right. Seren couldn't help her, and no one could help Seren.

12

When the remains of the cocaine conquered the oxycontin in her blood, Cassie Jackson rolled over and woke.

Christian sat naked on the lounge, his skin painted blue by the videogame he played on the huge plasma TV. The volume was low.

'What time is it?' she murmured.

'Ah, three, I think.'

'Don't you have to work?'

'Yep, breakfast meeting. Might as well stay up now. Hungry?'

'Not really.' She sat up and winced, feeling a dull ache in her bottom. She searched for the memories of what she'd done before passing out, but everything was a big smudgy blur.

'You ever done shabu?' he asked.

'I don't *think* so.' Cassie stared at him. 'Do I *look* like I smoke ice?'

Christian laughed. 'No. Do I?'

'So *you* use ice?'

'Oh, every now and then. What do they say – sometimes when you have lobster every day, you feel like a little hamburger?'

Cassie reached for a cigarette and the remainder of Christian's wine.

'Oh, what the hell. Could be fun,' she said. 'So, what do we do?'

'Oh no. Can't you find someone else? I've just done eight hours.' Gabriella Marmon leaned her head against a partition at the nurses' station, the phone cradled on her shoulder. Her buddy, Georgia, made faces at her from the other side of the desk. 'But you know I hate the graveyard shift . . . yes . . . and there's no one else . . . okay, then, all right, yeah.' She slammed down the phone.

She stared daggers at Georgia, who capered about. 'Don't you start.'

'It'll be fun. We've ordered pizza.'

'Fun. I'm exhausted. And you look like one of the bipolars, dancing around like that. You better stop it before Radisson sees you.' She picked up her nurse's badge and pinned it on again, dropped her bag back into the drawer at her feet and locked it. 'So where's the pizza?'

Gabriella stood to begin her second shift for the night. Four am. They could be lucky. Even though it was St Vincent's Hospital, Sydney, it was only a Tuesday morning, and Tuesday was usually the quietest night of the week.

And then she heard the screams from the end of the corridor.

'You coming?' asked Georgia.

'Yeah, I guess. Just tell me when the fun starts.' She walked tiredly from behind the nurse's station and followed her friend down the hall.

'Hey, Gary, what have we got?' asked Gabriella, moving forward to help the ambos restrain a young woman who was struggling in his arms.

'No idea. We found her down near the truck out the front.' The tired-looking man moved calmly, but he used full force to restrain the girl. She wore a man's business shirt and nothing else, and she was screaming at the top of her lungs.

'Another one dumped.' Gabriella and Georgia stepped aside as two orderlies rushed to take over from the ambulance officers. When they threw the girl into a wheelchair, the screams died down to a low moan and, as they strapped down her arms and legs, Gabriella leaned over and shouted, 'What have you taken?'

The patient opened her eyes, stared straight at Gabriella and screamed hysterically.

'Hell, I don't look that bad,' Gabriella said to Georgia, who was trying to take the girl's pulse. 'My name is Gabriella,' she tried again. 'Can you tell us your name?'

'They'll kill me! Let me GO! LET ME GO!'

'Can you see any ID?' she asked Georgia.

Georgia rolled her eyes. 'Can you?' The shirt could not cover the woman's body completely as she thrashed and struggled, and Georgia and Gabriella had already seen every part of her.

'I'll order the blood work,' Gabriella said.

'Already done. Gary called it in on his way out,' said Georgia.

Georgia suddenly gasped. 'Don't look now, honey,' she said to her colleague. 'I told you you were going to be glad you worked tonight. Guess who's coming down the hall?'

'He is *not!*' Gabriella blushed.

'Yep. Sergeant Scott Hutchinson and he's heading our waaay.'

'What's he doing here?'

'On the job, I'd guess – unless he's coming to see you, of course.'

Gabriella quickly smudged her finger across the front of her teeth and surreptitiously flicked out her hair. Within a couple of strides, Scotty was by their side, beaming. Gabriella's smile was pretty wide too until she saw the look of horror cross Scotty's face.

'Oh my God!' he said. 'That's Cassandra Jackson!'

13

Tuesday 2 April, 10 am

Seren sat on her hands in the waiting room of the parole office, staring straight ahead. She'd been out of that hellhole for just an hour, but the view wasn't much better yet. Posters on the wall advertised free needle exchanges and women's cottages for survivors of domestic violence. The only reading material on the pockmarked coffee table consisted of a Bunning's hardware sales catalogue, a flyer for the latest Maserati, and a discarded Streets Cornetto ice-cream wrapper. She couldn't afford any of those things at the moment. She had a cheque for her first week's rent, a fifty-dollar Salvation Army food voucher, and fifty dollars cash, for which, she had been told at the gaol, she had a debt to the Department that she would have to pay back from her first month's pay.

A floor-to-ceiling metal partition separated the waiting room from the balding man behind the desk in front of her. At least I'm not the one in the cage anymore, she told herself.

Needing to stretch, she stood and walked over to the water

dispenser in the corner of the room. On a wall above the unit was a fly-speckled mirror. Seren filled a plastic cup slowly, staring into the reflection of her eyes.

The woman who stared back always surprised her. At twenty-five, with a ten-year-old-son, she half expected to see the image of a forty-year-old in the mirror. At other times, she imagined the glass would reflect back the little girl she remembered from her dreams. But instead, she saw this person.

She'd always worn her platinum blonde hair short, but this was the shortest shave yet. Other than the slightly bloodied abrasion above her beestung lips, her skin was flawless. Her huge blue eyes appeared clear and unguarded. Although she stood barefoot at five eleven, her rangy body and open countenance made her seem smaller somehow, childlike. That helped and it hindered where she came from. Men wanted both to save her and punish her for her innocence, and women wanted her far from their men.

There was one man Seren was going to find as soon as she could. And when she did, he was going to pay. She walked back to the couch and sat, wanting to concentrate fully on her revenge fantasies.

'Mr Dobell, I know I told you to do Carson's file first.'

Seren turned towards the voice.

A thick-set woman stood over the man at the desk, although only just: although the man was seated, the dark-haired woman's face was just a head above his own.

'I had to finish the draft report for the meeting.' The man stooped his head a little, as though afraid to be hit.

'And I told you to do what?'

'Carson's file, but –'

'And you did what?'

'I'm sorry. I'll do it now. I don't need to go to lunch today. I brought something . . .'

The woman stared at the crown of the man's head a moment longer as his voice trailed away. He seemed to scrunch lower in his seat.

The woman looked up. At Seren. Staring straight at her, she lifted the folder in her hands as though to read from it. Seren could see her name lettered in thick, black ink.

Without looking at the file, the woman called to the otherwise empty waiting room, 'Seren Templeton?'

Seren smiled, and walked towards the desk.

'Seren Templeton?' the woman repeated.

'Uh, yes. I mean, present. That's me,' Seren said.

The woman stabbed at a button on the wall and Seren heard the click of the door to the partitioned area. The door swung outward and the woman used her body to hold it open. She wore a knee-length chequered skirt and an egg-yolk-yellow silk blouse that could not contain its contents; Seren could see flashes of bra and skin between the buttons. A big silk bow tied at the neck did its best to regain some propriety.

As she approached, Seren realised how tall she was in comparison. The woman had to tilt her head backwards to address her.

'Ms Templeton. My name is Maria Thomasetti. I will be your probation and parole officer for the next twelve months. You may call me Ms Thomasetti and I will call you Ms Templeton. Follow me, please.'

'You have some rights and you have some responsibilities out here, Ms Templeton,' said Ms Thomasetti from behind the desk in her office. 'I see that this was your first time in gaol, and so this is the first experience you will have had with Probation and Parole. You need to understand a few things very clearly.'

Seren alternated between wanting to sit up straight in the swivelling computer chair, and to slouch down so that she wouldn't tower over this woman so much. She settled for stooping her head somewhat, but she kept her hands in her lap and her eyes intent on Ms Thomasetti to indicate attentiveness.

'Firstly,' Ms Thomasetti continued, 'we can send you back to finish your sentence at any time. Your twelve-month probation is a privilege. You effectively remain in our custody and must prove that you are a fit and proper member of the community.'

She pushed a sheet of paper across the desk to Seren. 'Can you read?' she asked.

'Yes,' Seren told her.

'Can you write?'

'Yes.'

'Humph. Well, you should get to know these four points right here on this paper especially well. They stand between you and the cell you left this morning. Number one.'

Ms Thomasetti pointed with a pencil at a numbered line halfway down the page. Seren focused hard to distract herself from the dark moustache above Ms Thomasetti's lip. 'You will provide a supervised urine sample in this office each week. The presence of any non-prescription drug will send you back to prison to serve the remainder of your term. Do you understand?'

'Yes.'

'You were incarcerated for possession of crystal methamphetamine, Ms Templeton. That is an especially addictive drug. I would recommend that you attend an NA meeting as soon as you leave my office. A list of meeting locations is provided in this folder.

'Number two,' she went on. 'You must not consort with known felons. This is a discretionary point, Ms Templeton. We understand that you may have neighbours who have also been in trouble with the law. This cannot be helped. If, however, we feel that you are associating too closely with known felons, and we suspect that you are at risk of engaging in criminal enterprise, you will return to Silverwater to serve the remainder of your term. Do you understand?'

'Yes.'

'Number three. You are to remain employed at all times. The Department has found a job for you. If you do not maintain this job, which includes having a satisfactory attendance and perform-ance record, you will return to custody to serve the remainder of your term. Do you understand?'

'Ah,' Seren began.

'"Ah" is not an answer, Ms Templeton. Do you understand point three, or do you not?'

'Well, you know that I have a son – Marco.' Seren couldn't help but smile with anticipation. 'I can't wait to see him,' she said.

Nothing.

'I just want to make sure that I'm around to look after him when he's not at school. I need to know that I'm not doing night work or anything. You see, I don't have any family or friends who can look after him for me.'

'You didn't think much about that when you got yourself incarcerated, did you, Ms Templeton?'

'Hey, hang on a minute. I love my son.'

'And where has your son been for the past twelve months, Ms Templeton?'

Seren's eyes burned. Just speaking about Marco left a fist-sized knot of tears in her throat. It had been two weeks since their last visit. He'd had his tenth birthday out here without her. He'd been in two foster homes, sleeping in two different houses with people she'd never met. Over the twelve months she'd been inside, Marco had gone from clinging to her so hard that an officer had to intervene when the visit was up, to leaning away from her when she tried to hug him. This woman's comments were a knitting needle jabbed into her heart.

Ms Thomasetti pressed her. 'Where has your son been these past twelve months?'

'In foster care.' Seren scraped out the words.

'And why is that, Ms Templeton?'

A pulse began to beat in Seren's neck. Her nails made blood-red crescents on the palms of her hands.

'Can you hear me, Ms Templeton? I think we need to address this issue.'

'You know why my son was in foster care,' she said. 'You know why because that's why I'm sitting in here.'

'And you, Ms Templeton, need to say it. Why did your ten-year-old son spend the last twelve months of his life in the care of the state?'

'I was in gaol.'

'And why was that, Ms Templeton?'

'Look, I don't have to do this.' Seren tasted acid at the back of her throat. 'Why should I sit here and listen to this? You've given me the paperwork. I know what I have to do, now can I just get out of here? I need to see my son.'

'Actually, Ms Templeton, you do have to do this. I'm your probation and parole officer and I tell you what to do. And you do what I tell you to do, or you go straight back to . . .'

'Yeah, yeah, I know. I go straight to gaol, do not pass go, do not collect two hundred dollars.'

'. . . Silverwater.' Ms Thomasetti completed her sentence. 'Now, I do not like to be interrupted, Ms Templeton, and the interruption will not divert our conversation. You will come to learn this.' She tugged a little at the hem of her skirt, trying in vain to cover her white knees. She gave up and tapped her pencil three times against the desk. 'Now, Ms Templeton, let's get back to it. What did you do to cause you to go to gaol, resulting in your son having to spend the past year in foster care?'

Seren drew herself up to her full height and drilled a five-second stare into the rolls of fat around Ms Thomasetti's knees. She smiled inwardly when the woman brought the folder down to cover them.

'Although I know you have it in that file right there, Ms Thomasetti, I will tell you again anyway. I was locked up for possession of ice. What you don't know, Ms Thomasetti, is that the ice did not belong to me, and that I hadn't used drugs for eight years before I was busted.' She stopped speaking aloud, but the rant continued in her head. You also don't know that the person to whom the drugs belonged was supposed to love me. That even when I was caught he promised he would never let me spend a night in gaol. That he told me he'd be my lawyer but didn't ever register, and didn't even bother showing up at my court case.

Ms Thomasetti made a smile that looked as though she had a toothache.

'Do you know, Ms Templeton,' she said, 'that I don't think I've ever seen a woman in here who was guilty? Isn't that peculiar? All of you, to a person, sit there and tell me how it was someone else's fault. And I think that's why so many of you end up right back where you came from. Denial, Ms Templeton: you'll learn about it in NA, if you bother to go. Unfortunately, attendance at the meetings was not made one of your bail conditions, so I have no way to compel you to attend, but I would urge you to seek help for your addictions.'

Seren smiled sweetly. And you should try Weight Watchers, she said with her eyes.

Ms Thomasetti tapped her pencil again on the paper.

'And the final point. Number four,' she said. 'You must adequately care for your son and you must maintain your rental unit properly. The Department has obtained an affordable private rental apartment for you. This point, point number four,' she continued, 'includes – and this is vitally important, Ms Templeton – never missing a rental payment. Should a rent payment be overdue, you will have violated your parole conditions and you will return to prison. Do you understand?'

'Yes, Ms Thomasetti.'

'Very good, Ms Templeton. Now, please sign here.'

14

Frances Jackson plucked at the dressing gown she'd draped around her daughter's shoulders. The man's business shirt had been removed, and under the robe Cassie wore the thin, shapeless hospital smock used by patients preparing for surgery. The pale blue of the smock was a deeper shade of the bruises under Cassie's eyes.

Cassie slept, or pretended to.

Robert Jackson, Cassie's father, sat in the chair recently vacated by the psychiatrist, Dr Lambton. Jill stood behind her father, leaning against the wall, her face hidden from the door by the currently unused monitoring equipment next to her sister's bed.

'At least she won't need any further treatment,' said Frances.

'Well, she needs some sort of bloody treatment,' said Robert.

'What I mean is that we get to take her home,' said Frances.

'I'm not sure that she should be at home at all,' Robert stated. 'We're going to have to try to find her some sort of rehab clinic.'

'Do you really think that's necessary?' Frances asked.

'Are you bloody serious?' Robert's voice carried, and Jill winced. 'They pumped her stomach, and she was having some sort of psychotic episode when she got in here. Naked. I can tell that nurse is not convinced she wasn't trying to kill herself.'

'Of course she wasn't!' said Francis.

'She had enough drugs in her system to kill her easily. You just heard the shrink say that, Frances! I think this is the bloody problem,' he said. 'You've mollycoddled her all along. You make excuses for her all the time.'

Frances leaned over Cassie. From where she stood, Jill saw that her mother was trying to hide her tears. Still trying to protect them all.

'I can get you some numbers,' Jill said. 'Places she can go. There are two types,' she added. 'Pretty cheap, with huge waiting lists – if you can get on a list – or God-awful expensive.'

'We'll get her the best, if she wants to go,' said Frances.

'Oh, of course we will,' said Robert. 'We're made of bloody money, after all. Even though we're retired now, and on a fixed income, but if Cassandra needs to go to some special resort for junkies . . .'

'*Robert!*'

'Mum. He's right.' Jill's voice was as cold as the stainless steel splashback behind the bed. 'Cassie earns plenty of money, and she got herself into this mess.'

Jill's mouth tasted sour. She couldn't believe that her sister, who had every opportunity life could afford a woman, was lying in the emergency department simply because she could deny herself nothing she wanted, even if what she wanted could kill her. The words: *pathetic, degenerate drug addict* ran through Jill's mind as she stared at the bed. What the hell did Cassie have to run from? A jetsetting life travelling the world, photo shoots that often netted her Jill's yearly salary, a face and figure that had made people stop and stare since she was fifteen years old.

The ferocity of her thoughts caught Jill by surprise. She gazed down at the sad, beautiful face of her little sister; watched their mother bending over her, appearing older than she ever had in her life, and her eyes brimmed with tears. She was ashamed of her thoughts, and lifted her hand to reach over to the bed. At that moment Cassie's eyes opened and she stared straight into Jill's.

'So compassionate, big sister,' said Cassie. 'I can hear you, you know. I'm not in a bloody coma. And no one asked you to be here. I got myself into this mess, after all.' She parroted Jill's last sentence in a singsong snarl.

Jill's tears dried instantly. She opened her mouth to retort, to comfort, to scream at her sister. As usual, at times like this, nothing came out.

Frances clutched Cassie's hand, but Robert's face turned to the floor, his spine ramrod straight. Cassie stared Jill down, her eyes spitting venom.

And then Scotty walked through the door.

Scott Hutchinson. Jill hadn't seen him for three months, since the day she'd started this assignment. The doctor had told them Scotty identified Cassie last night, but Jill hadn't thought he'd show up again this morning. She wasn't ready to see him – not now, not here.

Scottie wore a big smile that animated only the lower half of his face; she recognised his worried eyes. Carrying an enormous bunch of pink oriental lilies, he walked right into the middle of the tension that seemed to further chill the frigid air of the hospital room. His stride faltered and the smile dropped with the outstretched flowers.

'Jacksons,' he said.

Frances burst into tears.

Jill scrabbled for something to say. Got nothing. Bolted from the room.

15

'This place will be great, Marco, you'll see,' Seren enthused as she dropped the box she carried and hurried to take another from her son's arms.

'Yeah, great,' he said. He looked folornly around the empty unit, blue eyes blinking behind his glasses. She almost shook with the effort it took not to run to him, lift him into her arms, and sob into his silky black hair. When he'd pushed her from him, hard, at the Department offices, it had felt as though someone had rammed their hand down her throat and ripped her heart from her chest. She wasn't sure she could take that rejection again.

'I know there's nothing in here yet,' she said, 'but we'll go shopping. I've still got some money in the bank, and they told me to come up to St Vinnies to get some new things.'

Marco shot her a withering look. She didn't blame him. If he knew that a lot of the money she had in their bank account had been used on storage fees for the few possessions they owned, he would probably have been even more cynical. He would never

59

know of the plans she had for every remaining cent. Shopping for their new home would have to wait until her first pay cheque; the money in her account was earmarked for revenge.

'And tonight,' she continued, 'if the truck doesn't get our beds here on time, we'll camp out!' Her smile stuck to her teeth as she considered the state of the threadbare carpet in the cheap rental flat. Her skin started to itch just thinking about trying to sleep on it.

Together they walked through their new home. The tour took five minutes, the unit consisting of a combined lounge and kitchen area, two dark bedrooms, and a dingy bathroom with an outlet for a washing machine. Without speaking they made their way back to the kitchen. Seren could hear a baby crying somewhere close by.

'I'm hungry,' said Marco.

'Me too,' she said. 'Let's go check out the shopping centre. I've never been to the shops in Eastlakes.'

'I've never been to Eastlakes,' Marco mumbled.

Seren grabbed her handbag from the floor and walked towards the door. 'Come on baby, what do you want to eat?'

As she unlatched the front door, a hairy arm pushed through. Seren recoiled.

'Hey!' she said, instantly manoeuvring Marco behind her.

A barrel chest and oversize belly stood in the doorway, blocking her exit. Seren smelled the beer that had helped the body get that way. A roaring sound filled her ears. The man wore gaol ink and his meaty hands and face were crossed and pocked with scars. He remained between her and the door.

'I saw you guys moving in,' he said, smiling a gap-toothed leer. 'Wayne Treadmark. People call me Tready. I'm in 612.'

'Okay, Wayne,' she said, heart thudding. 'Well, pleased to meet you, but we're actually on our way out again, so –'

'Where are you going?'

'My son is hungry.'

'Hello there, mate. Come on out and say hello to Tready. Don't be a little poofter, hiding behind your mother like that.'

Seren felt Marco make himself even smaller behind her back. She reached behind her and gripped his upper arm firmly. With her other hand she held her bag in front of her stomach; she straightened her back and walked directly into the man's chest. Caught by surprise, he stepped backwards and out of the flat. She let go of Marco, pulled the door shut and grabbed her son again. She began to march him along the external corridor that would take them to the lifts.

'Hey. I could go something to eat,' Tready said, following them. 'You going down the plaza? Just let me grab me smokes and wallet and I'll be right with you.'

'Actually, we're going to meet Marco's father,' Seren lied. 'And he doesn't like me speaking to strange men.'

Tready was silent a few moments, taking his time to look her up and down.

'Well, I'm not a stranger no more,' he said, finally. 'We're neighbours. And youse are going to get to know me real well.'

16

The thing about undercover work that got to Jill was that there were no routines.

Pillows completely surrounding her body – she'd slept in this illusory fortress every night since the kidnappers had let her go – Jill decided she would never get used to the lack of structure. She could wake when she wanted, go to bed whenever. Probably most people would love the freedom, she imagined, but for her, structure meant control, and control in Jill's life was like a sentry with an Uzi nine millimetre keeping the hell-people at bay.

Although right now, at ten o'clock in the morning, with the sound of rain coursing through gutters outside, she decided she should at least try to sleep a little more. The building complex beyond her front door smelled like a homeless wet dog, and she was bunkered safe in bed. Her sheets were Kmart cheap, but no one would guess that inside the covers nestled a premium duck-down doona and pillows. She huddled her head in deeper and let the feathers envelop her face. She hadn't had nearly enough sleep.

But it was no good. Her body simply could not get used to sleeping at ten in the morning, even if she'd only gone to bed at four.

She sat up and stretched, sighing. Another day out here. She stood and crossed the lino to the kitchen. At her insistence, the unit had no carpet – lino could be bleached and scalded with boiling water. Even so, with her boy-leg briefs and singlet she wore socks: she couldn't get the floor that clean.

She opened the fridge and leaned in.

When she'd started this assignment, she'd promised herself she would never let anyone else into her unit, but the rule had since been broken a dozen times. People here had few boundaries and her neighbours had gaped at her, offended, when she didn't ask them into hers, or pop around to theirs. So to fit her cover, that meant No-Frills food in the fridge. Well, sort of.

She pulled a carton of eggs, some butter, milk, and tasty cheese from the refrigerator, as always astonished by the four-litre cask of chardonnay at the back. Her neighbour, Ingrid, had stared hard at her when she'd come in to Jill's unit for the first time and seen the contents of the fridge.

'Where's your wine?' Ingrid had asked, one hand on her hip, the other on the still open fridge door.

Jill met her look blankly.

'Ah, I'm out,' she'd managed finally. Was it even lunchtime yet? She'd glanced at the clock on the oven. Nope.

'Well that's no bloody good, is it, Krystal?' her neighbour had said. 'Come on, we'll go round to mine for a couple.'

Ingrid had the cask bladder unpacked from its box, luridly silver, wobbling right there on the shelf in the fridge. She'd held the bag full of wine over a coffee cup and squeezed down hard. The pale yellow liquid jetted from the plastic spout like a horse taking a piss. Jill stared down into the cup when Ingrid pushed it over to her. It even frothed up like urine.

What a way to break the drought, Jill had thought.

After a year, aged fifteen, when she couldn't get enough alcohol, Jill hadn't had a sip until last October when she'd tasted a mouthful of butterscotch schnapps in the company of Gabriel Delahunt, her former partner. Despite her fears that once she started she'd never stop, she'd had only two glasses of wine since. Both were with Scotty, her other work partner. Each evening had left her feeling completely flummoxed and she hadn't found a reason to have a drink since.

Until that day at Ingrid's. Her neighbour had smiled at her, coffee cup raised, ready to toast. Alcohol was currency around here; wine the most expensive foodstuff in Ingrid's home. Jill couldn't refuse.

Now, in her kitchen, blinds drawn against the drizzle outside, she found an onion in the cupboard and took a small glass lemonade bottle from the shelf. Inside was grass-green extra-virgin olive oil, but it appeared pretty unspectacular housed this way. She diced half the onion finely and trickled a small amount of the oil into a pan, adding a thumb-sized knob of butter. When the melted butter foamed, she dropped in the onion and turned the pan down. She cracked two eggs into a bowl and flicked them together just two or three times with a fork. The secret to soft scrambled eggs – don't over mix them; Gabriel had told her during one of his out-of-the-blue cooking lessons when they'd been racing through traffic on the job a few months ago. She splashed just a dash of milk into the eggs, and slid two pieces of bread under the grill. Next, she grated some cheese into the egg mixture.

The onions smelled delicious, sizzling in the butter, and were just changing from opaque to translucent. She slipped the eggs into the pan, again swirling once, twice, with the fork. The buttery froth rose up around the eggs and Jill immediately turned the heat off and put a plate over the top of the frypan. When her toast was cooked, she slid the fluffy eggs over the top and smiled all the way back to her dining table. Thanks, Gabriel, she thought. These eggs were worth the extra couple of kilometres she'd run this afternoon.

Her sunny mood evaporated after the first bite when the guilt kicked in. She hadn't called her mum in a couple of days and had no idea how Cassie was getting on. That was the other thing about undercover work. The irregular hours meant that the times she would ordinarily have kept in touch with her family and friends were spent working – cultivating the networks that would lead to the next bust.

She picked her mobile up from next to her plate and scrolled for her parents' number.

The call was answered almost immediately. 'Hello, Frances Jackson.'

Jill was surprised. Her mum usually let her calls go through to the machine to deter telemarketers, picking up only when the caller spoke.

'Mum, hi.'

'Cassie?'

'No, Mum, it's Jill. I guess Cassie didn't stay with you guys then?'

'Hi, darling. No. She left the same day we brought her home. She let me drive her to her unit. I got her settled in, and she seemed okay. Very tired, of course.'

'Did she say whether she'd get some counselling?' asked Jill.

Frances sighed down the phone. 'Well, we talked about it for a little while, but she said she didn't need it. She said that she'd been stupid and learned a big lesson and would never do anything like that again.'

'Anything like what?' said Jill. 'Overdose?'

'Oh, you don't think it was deliberate, do you?' Frances sounded terrified.

'No, Mum. I really don't,' said Jill. 'I think Cassie just has too much money and too much time on her hands. She hangs out with too many people just like her, and they all think that the whole world is a big carnival and they should get on as many rides as they can.'

'I hope she's going to be all right,' said Frances. 'Anyway, how are you, darling? Is everything okay? It's not like you to call at this time of day.'

'I'm fine, Ma. Believe it or not, I just got up.'

'What's going on? Are you sick?'

'I'm fine. I'm eating scrambled eggs. I have to give you this recipe.'

'Hmm – sleeping in and eating properly. Whoever you are, could you put my daughter on the phone, please?'

'You're a riot,' Jill said. 'What're you doing today?'

'Groceries, bills, gardening, cooking. You know the drill. What about you? How's the case going?'

Jill's mother knew nothing about what she was doing, other than that she was working on something she couldn't discuss, and it involved living away from home for a while.

'Really well, actually.' Not a lot more she could or wanted to say.

'Any idea when you'll be working back at Maroubra?'

'Not in the short term.' If ever.

'It was nice to see Scotty the other day,' said Frances. 'Have you caught up again since?'

'I called him. We're going to meet up on the weekend for a bike ride.' Jill now wanted out of this conversation. Her mum's next questions would be about her feelings – for Scotty, about Gabriel – and she'd rather have a conversation with a speed dealer than go there. 'Mum. I have to go. I'm sorry. I'll give you another call soon.'

Jill cleaned away her breakfast and took a shower. That was the other thing she'd fixed as soon as she got in here – a new shower-head to ensure the water coursed hot and strong. She donned her uniform for the day – Playboy hipster tracksuit pants in baby blue, matching midriff hoodie, a white singlet, push-up bra and sneakers. Her hair went into a high ponytail, and she slicked on lots of black eyeliner. Sitting down on her bed, she picked up a cheap jewellery box from the nightstand and began pulling on the ten silver rings Krystal Peters always wore. She was not prepared to have any more piercings for this assignment – one in each ear was enough for her – but lashings of inexpensive rings and bangles seemed to help her blend in with her neighbours. Some spangly silver earrings completed her outfit. Ta-dah, she checked out Krystal in the mirror, as always bemused and a little shocked to see her standing there. She picked up her handbag and set off to wake Ingrid.

It had turned out that Ingrid Dobell – Jill/Krystal's new bestie, and her neighbour from across the hall – was hooked in with plenty of the speed and smack dealers in the Fairfield area. She didn't use herself – told Jill she'd seen the damage it had done to her father and brothers – but she'd grown up in the area and had a lot of friends. When Jill had moved in, supposedly on the run from a bad break-up with her man in Brisbane, Ingrid had come around to drop off a welcome pack: a shiny red laundry bucket packed with a bottle of no-name washing-up liquid, some Chux, a small jar of instant coffee, a roll of toilet paper, a package of shortbread biscuits and a carton of milk.

In her kitchen, Jill had unpacked the bucket, touched by the thoughtfulness. At ten-thirty the next morning, she'd gone around to thank Ingrid.

'Come in, come in,' said her neighbour, standing back from her screen door, waving Jill inside with the smoke from her cigarette. 'Don't mind the mess. Haven't got around to getting my place done yet.'

Actually, the unit wasn't terribly untidy. Some unfolded washing on the couch, a few dishes in the sink, shoes on the floor. Jill would have had to have typhoid fever to leave her place like that overnight, but she'd been expecting a lot worse of her new neighbours.

'I'm a carer for Mrs Dang, next door to you,' said Ingrid. 'Poor love has schizophrenia. I make sure she's taken her meds, had something to eat, and I tidy up a bit.' Ingrid took a seat at her kitchen table; with a bare foot, she pushed out the other chair for Jill. 'She's not too bad this morning. Only asked about her cat once.'

'Her cat?' said Jill.

Ingrid laughed and blew smoke towards the ceiling. 'Yeah, poor thing. She thinks the government took her cat to do experiments on it.'

'Where is her cat?'

'Never had one as long as I've lived here, and that's coming up for nine years now.' Ingrid laughed again. 'Doesn't worry me.

She's good fun, and I'm gettin' the carer's pension to look after her.'

'No shit,' said Jill.

'Yep. Not bad, eh? Mind you, she wouldn't cope on her own. I've been doing this shit for her for years anyway. She's fucked.' Ingrid finished her cigarette and looked around for another. 'Anyway, Krystal, what's your story?'

It was over the first glass of wine a week after they met that Jill had sounded Ingrid out for some contacts. She'd seen no drug paraphernalia around her flat, so she was a little worried about Ingrid's reaction, but she figured that she might as well try to get something if she was going to have to drink this crap.

'So, Ingrid,' she tried. 'You wouldn't know where I could get any shabu around here, would you?'

That had been three months ago, and Ingrid's initial introductions had led to others that had resulted in the takedowns Lawrence Last was so happy about.

Jill wanted more. Despite the busts of numerous clandestine laboratories, there was still a huge amount of crystal methamphetamine on the streets. Although her brief was to try to find ice and ecstasy dealers, it was the proliferation of dodgy ice cooks in particular that most worried the authorities. The manufacture of ecstasy was quite an art. Getting it right could be tricky, and production was most often a large-scale affair by professionals. Ice was another thing altogether.

Locking the door to her unit, Jill thought about the massive proliferation of this drug over the past five years. The problem with ice, she thought, is that half the country knows how to cook it. Theoretically. She knew that she could go to the internet today, and within five minutes collect twenty recipes. But most people manufacturing it were taught face to face by a friend. She knew that there were plenty of small operations making enough to service a local group of ice addicts, but large-scale production generally originated in Asia. The source ingredients required were tightly controlled in Australia, meaning that major meth production was rare. But there was certainly plenty on these streets, and Jill and everyone else around here knew that someone had a bloodline to a major supply. So far though, no one had been able to give her any useful links to the really big players.

Today, she would be meeting someone she hoped could hook her up to a bigger supplier. Jelly. Jelly owed her. Or at least he thought he did.

Jelly was a regular on the Fairfield street scene. An easy target, he was rolled regularly for his cigarettes, phone, and any money he had. Jill's best guess was that Jelly was aged around twenty-five, with the IQ of an eight-year-old. She was guessing some sort of hormonal abnormality accounted for his problems: Jelly seemed to be pumping too much oestrogen. Jill knew she could never hope to have breasts as impressive as Jelly's; the skin of his face was smooth and hairless, and when he spoke he sounded a lot more like a girl than most of the chicks he shared the streets with. As far as she could tell, Jelly didn't seem to have sexual proclivities that leaned either way. When left to his own devices, he was more than happy to swap dumb jokes, shoplift lollies – or any other food he could get his hands on – and attempt to skateboard. At six foot, and a hundred and twenty kilos, he looked pretty stupid on a skateboard, but Jelly didn't seem to realise that, no matter how often the kids at the skate park told him.

Even without the contacts he had, Jill would have kept an eye out for Jelly; he might as well have had a big red target painted on his rounded back. So, when she'd found him curled up in the railway carpark being battered by four youths obviously not from around the area, she'd jumped in. Actually, it had been kind of fun. She hadn't had a chance to practise her kickboxing for real for a long time, and discovering that she had lost none of the power from her roundhouse kick was gratifying. The melee had ended disappointingly quickly. The youths were evidently weekend warriors, fearless only when their prey couldn't fight back.

But Jill knew that Jelly had another guardian angel. Kasem Nader. The only reason Jelly hadn't long ago been kicked to death for sport was that most people around here knew that Kasem

Nader would come find them if they hurt Jelly too badly. Nader had had a long association with Merrylands police, dating back to his primary school years. Since then, he and his brothers had collected an impressive criminal portfolio, from stick-ups and standovers to weapons charges and abduction. Jill had heard that the boys now had an impressive meth lab up and running and were looking to expand their operations.

She had met Jelly for the first time one morning in Ingrid's kitchen, where he was trying to bake cupcakes. Ingrid told her that although he lived in a neighbouring unit block, he was in her flat more often than his own. Jill had peered into his mixing bowl before he poured the ingredients into some patty cases Ingrid had found for him at the back of a cupboard.

'Ah, what's in this?' Jill had asked, sniffing carefully.

Ingrid pushed her way between Jill and Jelly and leaned over the bowl with them. 'Fuck knows,' she said. 'You wouldn't eat any of that shit, anyway, Krystal. I just let him go for it. What'd'ya put in there, Jelly?'

Jelly showed them. Some of his special ingredients had come from the cupboard under the sink.

Twenty minutes later, with Jelly's batter grey-green and hissing in the drain, 'Krystal', Jelly and Ingrid had taken a hot batch of buttery cupcakes around to Mrs Dang's, and Jelly had been a loyal fan of Jill's ever since.

It was Ingrid who told Jill about the Kasem Nader connection. According to her, Jelly and his younger brother, Corey, had been sent to separate foster homes when their mother wouldn't quit whoring from her bedroom while the boys watched cartoons in the next room. Corey had grown up in Merrylands near the Nader brothers while Jelly had moved from home to home and ended up in the Fairfield area. Corey had been fatally stabbed in a brawl with some skinheads from Cronulla. Ingrid told Jill that Corey took a knife through the spleen when he jumped in to prevent Kasem being stomped to death.

Kasem had made a monthly trip out to Fairfield ever since.

And today, Jelly was due a visit.

17

Friday 5 April, 11 am

By eleven am Seren knew one thing for sure: she could not do this job for a second day. Not even to stay out of that hellhole in Silverwater. But with these thoughts, images of Marco swam through her tears and the pink-tinged water raining down continuously from the pipes overhead. Marco. Her son. Completely alone without her. What she'd sworn to him when holding his brand new body on her naked chest, she'd already betrayed: *I'll never leave you. I will always protect you.*

Seren swallowed the bile in her throat and reached out to grab a screaming chicken from the yellow crate at her side. Its warm body pressed into her palms and she felt its heart hammering wildly. Scrabbling with her gloved hand for one of its feet, she hung it upside down as she'd been shown at six o'clock this morning by her supervisor, and clasped each foot into the metal restraints; belly forwards, facing her. The terrified creature flapped its malformed wings, stunted by being raised in a box so small it had never been able to stretch; it swung its head wildly and its shining eyes met her own.

They begged.

I'm sorry, she told the bird, and snapped its neck with the piece of equipment designed by someone, somewhere, just for this job.

The dying bird's shit joined her vomit in the sink below the carcass. Seren pushed the button, and the conveyor belt took the body away.

Ten workers today. Fifty thousand chickens to be killed between them. I can't do this, she thought.

And then she remembered Marco being dragged from her by the DoCS worker, when the officer took her from the courtroom to the cells below.

She reached for another chicken.

Seren sat staring at the lunchroom table. Men and women around her laughed, bitched and ate sandwiches provided by their employers.

Seren didn't think she'd ever eat again.

'You'll get used to it, love.' The middle-aged man from the conveyor belt next to her offered her a Coke. 'Take it. It'll help settle your stomach.'

'How can I get out of that section?' she asked him.

He laughed. 'Not easy. You gotta be here a year at least to get into the packing section.'

'There has to be something else.' She turned her head to meet his eyes.

'There is. And it's worse. Believe me. I lasted a couple of weeks and begged 'em to put me back here,' he said. 'You're just lucky they put you on the line in the first place. You could have got sent straight to gutting.'

Yeah, that's me, Seren thought. Just lucky. Feeling faint, she lowered her head into her hands and tuned out the clamour around her.

For the first three months she was locked up, Seren had done little but cry. She cried for herself, alone in the world since fifteen, when her mother had died of breast cancer in Liverpool Hospital.

She cried for her mother, who'd lost all of her light when Seren's father had been killed, falling though a ceiling on a building site. She cried for her brother, Bradley, removed from their home by authorities; her stepfather charged for the 'greenstick injury' to his leg. Seren had always remembered that term and looked it up when she was twelve: she learned that children's bones are so new, so supple, that they do not snap like an adult's. Instead they bend when twisted, as a young tree branch might do. A greenstick injury. Seren had not seen Bradley since – fostered out for life, to give him the best chance.

Seren cried mostly for the little boy she'd had at fifteen. Marco, born two weeks after the state buried her mother. Alone. Out there, without her.

After three months crying, Seren had had enough. Enough of authority. They'd been involved in her life for as long as she could remember and where had it got her? Here. They owned her. She spent a month or so in and out of segregation, isolated from the other women for swearing at officers, being late for muster, refusing to complete the assigned tasks. All it took was cancellation of her visitor's rights for a month, though, and she had abandoned her rebellion instantly.

The fight left her, but not the rage. It boiled behind her eyes and seared a red-tinged image onto her retina.

The image of the love of her life.

The man she would make pay.

In the slaughterhouse lunchroom, holding her head in her hands, Seren Templeton worked through her strategy; honed her plans. She sent her thoughts out into the street, hunting him. The man she would make pay.

Christian Worthington.

At least the job finished in time to allow her to be there when Marco arrived home from school. At ten past three that afternoon she ducked her head out of the bus shelter and searched the road for sign of his bus approaching. The rain hung over the street ahead and she could see nothing but the cars immediately in front of her.

God, I wish we had a car, she thought. Safe inside a vehicle, there were fewer opportunities to be harassed. One day we'll have a car, Marco, she promised him silently.

Second day in his new school. She hoped it was better than the first.

The bus steamed to a stop in front of her.

'Hi baby. How'd it go?' she asked as he alighted, his second-hand school shorts bagging around his waist.

'Don't call me baby.'

'Oops, sorry,' she said. 'You're still my baby, though,' she whispered, bending to help him with his backpack. Two or three drops of rain spattered onto the lenses of his glasses.

Seren tried to hold the umbrella over Marco as they made their way back to the unit block, but he was always a step out of reach. The rain had decreased to a cheerless drizzle, so she folded up the umbrella and hurried a little to catch him up.

'Bad day?' she asked.

'Not really,' he said.

She kept her eyes on him, hardly heeding where she walked. She was hungry for the sight of him; she had missed him so much today. She watched his knobbly knees as he strode through muddy puddles. They cut through an ill-tended carpark, its concrete being reclaimed by the earth, fascinated by his dark hair slicked to his face like a helmet, his upturned nose.

'I think I made a friend,' he said to the ground.

Warmth filled her chest. Love and pain. Did they always go together?

'Yeah?' she said. 'What's his name?'

'Jake.'

'What's he like?'

'I dunno. A kid?' he said.

'He sounds fascinating,' she said. She thought she saw a smile.

They reached the group of buildings of their unit block and Seren tugged open the door that led to their stairwell and lifts. She waited for Marco to press the cracked button of the elevator. He always loved to press the buttons.

The lift smelled like piss and one wall proclaimed that Jonno gave good head.

'Get any homework?' she asked.

'Maths. I did it in class. I did all the stuff they're up to last year.'

'That's good. You'll know it twice as well. I'll have a look when we get upstairs,' she said.

When the lift bumped open at the sixth floor they got out and walked the short distance to their unit. As Seren unlocked the door she heard a shout.

'HEY, SARAH! Over here!'

Great. Tready. Shirtless, standing in his doorway down the hall, waving at them, beer in hand.

'Come over and have a drink!'

One of the neighbours did not appreciate Tready's yelling, asked him to keep it down: 'Shut up, you fucken drunk cunt!'

Seren bustled Marco through the doorway. 'So, you want a snack before dinner?' she asked him.

'That'd be great, *Sarah*,' Marco said, grinning up at her.

18

Friday 5 April, 11 am

At eleven am Cassie Jackson uncurled and stretched languidly in her king-sized bed.

That's the problem with having this mattress, she complained to herself. You just sleep too damn well on it. Shopping for a new bed for this larger apartment last year, she had remembered her mum's advice – don't pay a fortune for the bed frame, spend as much as you can afford on the mattress. When the salesgirl at David Jones had told her that this was the mattress she would buy if she won Lotto, Cassie had been interested. She always liked to have the best.

And then she'd seen the price tag.

'Eleven thousand dollars!' she'd exclaimed. 'Just for the mattress?'

'Try it,' the salesgirl recommended.

The new bed was delivered that same week, along with a couple of sets of one-thousand thread-count sheets, new latex pillows and the most deluxe doona the store could find her.

Now, nestled naked in the parchment-coloured fabric, Cassie bemoaned another broken pledge to get up at seven, eat a healthy breakfast and take a walk down to the beach.

She finally rose and shrugged into a slinky jersey dressing gown. She walked past the cigarettes on her dressing table – *your body is your temple*, she told herself – and stepped out onto her balcony.

From the nineteenth floor, even a drizzly Bondi Junction was delicious. She loved her view – a one-hundred-and-eighty-degree panorama between the Harbour Bridge and the lighthouse at Watson's Bay. After dark, Cassie's favourite time, the spectacle could bring a halt to any conversation.

She moved back inside and made her way to the kitchen, where two avocados on her benchtop accused her of being wasteful. Her mum had bought them for her, already ripe, three days ago now, telling her to eat them immediately. She had just been released from the hospital and had been determined to do as her mum suggested.

They sat there.

'You're fattening,' she told them. Her mum had told her repeatedly that avocados contained 'healthy fats'. No such thing in Cassie's book.

She opened the fridge. A package of prawns, purchased yesterday. Pure protein, no fat: her favourite lunch. But she felt like breakfast. An egg-white omelette? Revolting. She grimaced.

If she popped down to a café she could order something 'organic and healthy': read – low calorie. But this would be just the time that she would run into Tasha and the gang, and they'd want to know what she was doing tonight. This was the first weekend since the horror of the hospital and she was determined to make it through without drugs.

Cassie opened the freezer and found a package of frozen mixed berries. 'Yum, thank you, Sara Lee,' she said to her empty kitchen.

She rained the berries into her blender, whizzed them with some milk – skim – and yoghurt – fat free. Carrying her liquid breakfast in a tall glass, she gathered up a soft, toffee-coloured throw rug and went back out to the balcony, feeling positively virtuous. Curled up in the cushions on her day-lounge, feeling part of the heavens, she took a sip of her drink. Not bad, she thought. Although a splash of vodka instead of the yoghurt could have improved things.

Bad girl, she thought, grinning into her glass.

When she'd finished her breakfast, she considered the day before her. Next stop, the gym. Cassie knew that she really was one of those bitches who didn't have to work out. While she did use food deprivation to control her dress-size, a few really well placed curves remained without her having to do anything at all.

Nevertheless, her mate Bryce and his boyfriend, Nahid, former big-time party boys, had told her that they'd quit drugs using yoga and the gym. God knew, if they could do it, she could too. Bryce had been an absolute coke pig.

She slipped into footless leggings and a vintage Rolling Stones tee-shirt, threw gym shoes into her tote bag, and stepped into luscious heels – she hadn't worn sneakers out in the street since she was fourteen. She grabbed her leather jacket from the chair and her keys from the table in the entrance hall. Then stopped.

Most often she would pause here on her way out to check her reflection in the mirror. Today, the mirror was obscured by a profusion of colour: old-fashioned roses, two dozen of them, many of the assorted-colour blooms the size of grapefruit. She'd never have found a container big enough to hold the display, but this had caused her no consternation as they'd been delivered in a heavy, lead-crystal vase.

Christian, of course. She stepped around the corner into her study, adjacent to the entry hall, and picked up the card he'd attached from the wastepaper basket. She read it. Smiled.

As she left her apartment, Cassie tossed Christian's card onto the hall table, where it skidded to a stop against the exquisite crystal vase.

***

Cassie had no patience for the personal trainer the gym had recommended. Really, the little bitch tried to kill her on just the first machine! Instead, she watched people moving around the circuit, waited until they had finished, and hopped on each machine to have a go. A few reps was enough for each one. No point in being excessive in life.

On the pec deck she began to feel impatient, an internal itch she'd noticed arising around this time every day for the past four days.

Like something was wrong; missing. Something just beyond the corner of her awareness that she'd forgotten to do, that was troubling her, annoying her. She felt a sudden viciousness towards the chubby man working out on the machine next to her. His sweat was ugly and his tee-shirt horrid. Why did he bother?

She got off the lat machine and walked to the wall of windows overlooking the city. The clock on the wall told her it was three pm. On a Friday.

She stared down into the buildings that encircled the tower housing this gym, her eyes searching, seeking. They stopped. And something clicked. Cassie gazed, mesmerised, into the cityscape-oriented bar in the building next door, watching the beautiful people – her people – toast the end of the working week. Cocktails and business suits, straps and heels, cigarettes and champagne, lime and laughter, music, vodka, lip-gloss, tequila, flirting, texts, friends, pills, blow in the bathroom. She peered into her world like a newly ex-smoker watching someone light up. With lust, hunger, drive.

Cassie suddenly recovered her self-possession and stood straight again, turning away from the window. She moved towards the bathrooms.

Her handprint faded from the glass as she walked away.

She decided to take a shower here rather than wait to have one at home.

She picked up a towel from a pimply child at the desk and walked into the women's bathroom. In the communal dressing room, she stripped, used to being naked around a roomful of women. Two friends wrapped in towels stopped speaking for a few beats and then started again, their conversation more stilted, distracted, than before.

Cassie barely saw them. She threw her jacket and bag into a locker and took the key. She stalked naked into the shower, wrapping her long, honeyed hair into a knot on the way.

On her way out of the gym, newly made-up, hair sleek and shining, Cassie felt better than she had in ages. She thought perhaps she should just stop in at the shops and pick up something for dinner. From the window in the gym, she had spotted a grocery store in the complex next door.

Within moments of stepping into the gleaming granite building, Cassie was hailed by a girlfriend she had not seen in weeks. What was her name again? That's right, Adele Taha. She couldn't refuse a catch-up. It was Friday, after all; she'd really no excuse.

19

Friday 5 April, 3 pm

'Hey, Jelly,' said Jill.

Jelly watched the kids at the skate ramp, shuffling from foot to foot, waiting for his turn. Somehow he'd got his hands on another skateboard. Someone would have relieved him of this one by the end of the day, Jill was sure of it.

'Krystal!' he said. 'Got anything to eat?'

'No, but I'm hungry too, Jelly,' she told him. 'Let's go get some food.'

No point in asking Jelly where he wanted to go. Jill walked past an Asian food store – offering sticky, red duck; spicy satay noodles; steaming pork buns – past the Turkish takeaway, the windows full of fat pide stuffed with fetta cheese, spinach, nuts – and straight into McDonald's. At the counter, she ordered their usual.

'Pay you back next time, Krystal,' said Jelly, half his Big Mac gone in a bite. 'Kasem's coming to see me today.'

Jelly always had cash when Kasem left.

'Yeah?' said Jill.

'Yeah, silly. I told you the other day. You said you'd come meet him.'

'Oh, yeah,' said Jill. 'I forgot.'

'Well, you'd better not forget again, Krystal, 'cause Kasem said he wanted to meet you.'

'Where are you meeting him?' she asked.

'Orbit. Same as always,' said Jelly.

An hour later, Jill walked with Jelly into the dim den of Orbit, a computer gaming and snooker venue. She saw an unmarked detective's car across the road. She knew it had nothing to do with her; Orbit was always being staked out. The cops knew that countless drug deals took place in its shadowy interior every day. But cracking down with the cooperation from the management was out. The place was owned by Triad gangsters who dropped by from time to time in Bentleys and Mercedes to play a round or two of mah-jongg out the back.

Jelly jogged over to a pool table, holding his skateboard under his arm.

'Kasem!'

'Brother.'

Jill saw Jelly pulled into a brief embrace by a tall, swarthy male in a black jumper and dark denim jeans. As the man pulled away from Jelly, she quickly checked him out for other identifying features. Close-cropped black hair, a broad nose that looked as though it had been broken a couple of times and a ten-centimetre vertical scar close to his right eye. His chest was huge, and looked rock-hard from where Jill stood.

'Who's this?' the man said. Kasem seemed to be giving Jill just as thorough a visual evaluation. She stepped back a smidge.

'This is Krystal,' said Jelly. 'She's my friend. I told you about her. Say hi to Kasem, Krystal.'

'Hi, Kasem,' said Jill.

'*This* is the kick-arse hoodlum who saved your life the other day, Jelly? She looks too . . . sweet.' Kasem Nader closed the distance between himself and Jill and smiled down at her.

Although she would have preferred to walk out, or maybe arrest him, Jill smiled back at Nader, blinking her eyes a couple of times for good measure.

'I wanted to meet you, Krystal,' said Kasem, 'to thank you for helping out my brother, Jelly, here.'

'No problem,' she said. 'It was fun.'

Nader smiled. 'Yes, fun,' he said. 'You wouldn't happen to have caught any of their names, would you, Krystal?'

'Nah. Pussies pissed off pretty quickly.'

'That's a shame. You're sure, now?'

'Yep.'

Jelly wandered off to play his favourite arcade game with a handful of gold coins from Kasem, who watched him leave, smiling.

'Can you play pool, Krystal?' he asked.

'You could find out. We could have a bet.'

'There's a lot I wouldn't mind finding out about you, Krystal,' he said. 'What kind of money were you thinking about?'

'I've got five bucks left,' she said, pulling the note out of her bra and smacking it down onto the snooker table.

'Tell you what, Krystal,' he said, picking up the money. 'If you win, I'll double your money. But if I beat you, you come to a party I'm giving out at Merrylands tonight.'

Jill wasn't certain that she could have won anyway, but of course she threw the game. She was playing pool with Kasem Nader, and losing meant an invitation right into the heart of his world.

By eight pm, Cassie Jackson considered Adele Taha the best friend she'd ever had. Within ten minutes of running into her, she'd found herself in the very same bar she had spied from the gym. Sitting now, legs crossed, on a tall barstool right by the window, Cassie turned her head to look up at the gym. Not so much because she wanted to see it again – ugh, once was enough – but because she knew that her profile from this angle was killer, and the boy in the beautiful suit who was buying her drinks would be afforded an even better view.

Adele sat at the barstool opposite her. Another beautiful boy in a suit by her side. Cassie felt a kick under the table. Adele wanted her attention.

'Saxon, sweetie,' Cassie purred with a smile to the man at her elbow. She tilted her empty glass backwards and forwards in her fingertips. 'I'm *so* thirsty.' She watched him walk to the bar with his friend. Saxon. What a ridiculous name. At least she wouldn't forget this one.

'You wanted to say something, darling?' she said to Adele.

'Do you have anything on you?' asked Adele in a whisper.

Damn it. Cassie had been getting ready to ask Adele the same thing.

'Nothing,' she said. 'My body is my temple.'

Adele gave a snort of laughter. 'Oh, very good, darling,' she said. 'Well, I know where we can get some.'

'Some what?'

'Anything.'

'Well, what are we doing here, then?' said Cassie. 'Let's go.'

'What will we do with Blake and Saxon?' asked Adele.

'I'll give them my number. I'll let Saxon buy me drinks again another night.'

Cassie zipped up her leather jacket as they waited out the front of the building for their taxi. She didn't see the woman in the BMW driving past whack her husband on the arm when he almost mounted the gutter ogling her.

'Where are we going?' she asked her friend.

'To a party,' said Adele.

'Lovely,' she said. 'Where?'

'Merrylands,' said Adele, and laughed.

Cassie gaped at her.

'Merrylands,' she said finally. 'Can't say I've ever been there, but with a name like that it should be fun.'

Seren and Marco had his favourite for dinner. Again. Second time in the four days she'd been out. Smooshed-up tacos. Long ago, she'd figured that taco shells cost too much and that no-name corn chips would do just as well. She told Marco that the dish had been invented when a little boy dropped his taco and found it tasted even better all broken. They piled smashed corn chips, minced beef, shredded iceberg lettuce, chopped tomato and grated cheese onto their plates. Seren dolloped some plain yoghurt onto hers and Marco added tomato sauce.

Marco stirred the mess together and Seren immediately lost her appetite. The sauce looked like blood, and the smells and sounds of the slaughterhouse flared briefly in her kitchen. She pushed her plate away.

'Hey,' she said, shaking her head, trying to disperse the memory, 'do you remember Angel?'

'That lady from gaol?'

'Yeah. My friend. She ate with us a few times when you came to visit.'

Marco shovelled another forkful into his mouth. He stared at her. His hair was so dark, but he had her huge blue eyes, framed like works of art behind his spectacles.

'Anyway, she's getting out this weekend,' she continued. 'And guess what?'

'Nnnnfff?' Marco mumbled through a mouthful of cheese and chips.

'She got a unit downstairs. In this block. We arranged it while we were in there, so that we could hang out together now.'

'Okay,' he said. Then, 'Can Jake come over?'

'Of course. If it's all right with his mum. Does he live far away?'

'I dunno,' said Marco. 'I'll call him.'

'After dinner,' she said. Seren leaned back from the table and tried not to stare at her son eating. Things are going to be all right, she promised him silently. Things will be okay. She forced herself not to think about Monday morning and the world outside these walls.

20

Friday 5 April, 10 pm

There was no indication that a meth lab was being run from this place. Jill hadn't expected that to be the case anyway. She wasn't sure what she had expected, but it hadn't been the 1970s, two-storey, double-brick, family home that she walked into with Jelly and Kasem Nader later that evening. From the entryway she could hear male voices within. She peered around Jelly's bulk into a lounge area.

All around the room sat men around Nader's age, eating plates of food, watching TV and speaking in low voices. Even with the Cobra .45 tucked into a holster above her ankle, her adrenalin was a hot, thin wire coursing under her skin. As far as she could see, she'd be the only female in a room of perhaps ten males.

She stood near the entryway with Nader. Jelly, obviously comfortable here, immediately moved towards a buffet of food spread out across a table in the lounge room.

From the outside, the house looked more like she might have

86

imagined for the home of a criminal – a five-foot brick wall surrounded the property and there were bars on every window, but this seemed in keeping with the rest of the homes in the neighbourhood, as far as she could tell. On the inside, Italian-style furniture of the same era as the house blended somewhat uncomfortably with Middle Eastern rugs and paintings. An elaborate hookah pipe sat on a low coffee table; photos of children perched on sideboards and hung on the wall.

'This is my parents' home,' said Kasem, watching her check the place out. 'They're overseas. I stay here with my brothers sometimes.'

'So you throw a party while Mummy and Daddy are away?' said Jill. 'Aren't you a little old for that, Kasem?'

Nader smiled at her, but his eyes stayed flat. Jill resolved to tone down the sarcasm.

'Well, Krystal,' he said, 'I guess it's less of a party than a gathering of friends. These people here work with me or for me, and I trust them. There will be a few more people joining us, but perhaps I may have misled you a little. I'm not much into big, noisy parties. We'll all be having something to drink and eat tonight, we'll talk a little business, but that's about it. If you're uncomfortable, I can run you home now.'

'No, it's okay, I guess,' said Jill. 'I just thought there would be more girls here.' She smiled up at her host. Her firearm might extend only six inches, but it held ten rounds, and she reckoned she could make her way out of here any time she liked. 'I'm pretty hungry,' she said. 'And that food looks great.'

Cassie got out of the cab thinking she should probably have just swallowed her pride and gone and made up with Christian. All he'd really done was to drop her off at the hospital. Of course, he should have stayed with her, made sure she was okay, or at *least* come and seen her the next day. But he had sent the flowers, and he had left repeated messages. Still, she decided he could wait a little longer for forgiveness.

But the outside of this house did not look like her kind of party venue. She shot a look at her friend, who shrugged and smiled. She waited as Adele spoke into the intercom unit in the wall.

'Trust me, girlfriend,' Adele told her. 'You're going to thank me in ten minutes.'

Now, that did sound promising, Cassie had to admit. The gate buzzed open and she followed Adele up the pathway towards the front door. At least the place smells agreeable, she thought, breathing in the scents of spice and hashish. They waited for the front door to be opened.

The food was as good as it looked. Jill selected small morsels of tender chicken, which left her lips sticky with lemon, garlic and onion. She dolloped several of the colourful dips onto her plate – white bean; roasted capsicum; cumin-scented hummus – and a spoonful of the creamiest garlic aioli she had ever eaten.

'What is this?' she asked Kasem, who, somewhat disconcertingly, watched her as she ate.

'Tahina. Ground sesame paste, some other spices. My mum made it.'

Go figure. The mamma's boy gangster. Jill grinned, and went back for just a little more. A stuffed capsicum; a scrape of tabouleh. She scooped the food up with bread as everyone else was doing.

Jill surreptitiously observed her surroundings as she ate. The music was chilled and the sweet odour of marijuana began to fill the air. No one looked to be doing drugs of any other description, at least not out here in the open.

Kasem spoke to the others, but he did not leave the room. Jill was aware of him watching her, and each time she caught his eye he smiled. She observed the body language of the players: everyone deferred to Kasem, even the two men he introduced to her as his brothers.

Eight more guests arrived, and she was no longer the only woman in the room. There were now three other females, and, undercover in a criminal's house or not, Jill felt under-dressed. A blonde, wearing spray-on jeans and a one-shouldered, draping silver top, fired blistering looks in Jill's direction each time Kasem spoke to her.

Which was a lot, she couldn't help but notice.

'Krystal!' Jelly waved at her from the buffet table. 'Dessert! Come on!'

And then the impossible happened.

Of every person she could possibly imagine walking into this house in Merrylands, the very last would have been the newest entrant to this party.

As happened whenever she walked into a room, every head whipped around to stare at her little sister. Cassie. In Kasem Nader's lounge room. With his brothers, with Jelly, with Jill/Krystal, and the gun at her ankle.

Oh, fuck.

21

Seren, Marco and Angel sat picnic-style on a blanket on the floor of Seren's unit. Three boxes sat open in front of them. The pizza frenzy had died down, and only Angel was still eating, taking small bites now. Marco picked at some cheese on a slice and Seren frowned at him.

'Let me have a sip,' he asked again.

'You won't like it.' Seren handed her son the cup of red wine she held. She didn't even like it much, although it wasn't too bad for Chateau du Cardboard.

'Ew!' His little face wrinked. 'How disgusting.'

'And I told you what?' she asked him, smiling.

Hell, she thought, I just sounded like Maria Thomasetti. The name wiped her smile.

'Hey,' she said, turning to Angel, 'who'd you get for probation and parole?'

'Oooh, this lovely young bloke, looks like he's fresh out of school,' said Angel. 'What about you?'

90

'Ah, not him,' said Seren.

She leaned back against the couch, trying to relax. She was so relieved that Angel was out. Now it felt as though there was at least one other adult on the face of the earth who would watch her back. And a friendship tested in gaol had more weight than friendship forged with someone out here.

But while Seren wanted Angel as a friend, she *needed* her to help in a small way with her plans. Seren had to get to Christian, but she also had to keep her day job to meet her parole conditions. And that meant that she would have to find Christian at night. She could trust Angel to look after her boy while she was out.

Gaol had taught Seren patience. With all the time she'd had in there, she had come to see that killing him was a stupid idea. Running through the possible methods of murdering her former lover, Seren finally saw for certain that: a) she couldn't do it; and b) killing him wouldn't do her any good anyway. No, no. There were other ways to exact revenge, and Seren had had another twelve months with nothing else to do than to craft the perfect plan.

After a few weeks inside, she'd come to understand that Christian Worthington was not her only enemy. The more time she spent with her fellow prisoners, the more she came to realise that she had fallen foul of a much more powerful predator: destiny, fate – call it what you will.

For some reason, Seren and the women locked up with her had been cursed by fate. She realised that, sure, one day they'd all get out of there, but most of them would return to violent neighbourhoods and incomes below the poverty line. They could try to get out of their suburbs, get better jobs. But most of them had kids, and their children's lives were just beginning; they needed time too.

Seren had seen it before. Mrs Telomere, her neighbour growing up, had kicked her bludging husband out of the house and gone back to finish Year 12 at the same high school that her two sons attended. She'd worked nightshifts at 7-Eleven, and when she'd achieved her Higher School Certificate had enrolled at uni to study welfare. Then one day, about six months into her first year, word had spread around the neighbourhood in an hour: Mrs Telomere had been raped putting her garbage out, dragged down the alleyway next to her house. Seren hardly ever saw her come outside after that. The housing commission people found her a new place twelve months later.

But all low-rent suburbs were the same. And staying inside didn't help. Seren had heard countless stories of home invasions – or run-throughs as most people called them. You could be sitting at home, just eating tea, and three or four masked bastards would kick your door down and take all your stuff. The latest craze for the thieves was to bring a doona cover, make you help them shove everything into it, kids' toys and all. 'Reverse Santa', some smart-arses called it. If you were lucky, you'd just cop a quick flogging. Unlucky, and you'd lose teeth, an eye, your husband. Next day, you'd catch the bus with these blokes, or see them at your local chemist. Best to just nod and say hi, pretend not to know.

Of course, you could get out of there; move into non-subsidised private rental. Unless, of course, you had a criminal record, or a bad credit history, or an income from an unskilled job. Check, check, check. Everyone bunking down in Silverwater corrections with Seren was counted out.

So, Seren figured out that she had to do two things: pay Christian back, and get paid herself. Big time.

In gaol her plan had begun to come together. Now, she thought to herself, it's time.

Funnily enough, of the equipment that she would require, including a covert recording device and a laptop, what caused her the most consternation was her clothing. Seren had a few hot outfits put away in storage, but they had mainly been purchased by Christian; they were now a year out of date, and he had seen them all before. Seren knew that this would bar her entry back into the appearance-is-everything world he inhabited. She would need to gather a few things herself before she could make Christian contribute to his own undoing.

Sunday morning saw her waiting at the public library for the doors to open. She used their internet service to source a tiny camera and the most basic laptop she could find: it was only for downloading the audio-visual recordings she would make.

The hardware required a trip to the city, and as she bought her bus ticket she mentally calculated how much money she'd have left for the most essential purchases – the two items of clothing. In gaol, she'd gone over her first-meeting outfit options a hundred times. A glamour gown would be perfect, but impossible. She couldn't afford it.

In the end, she based it all around the shoes. The night before she had bought them had been one of the best nights of her life. The day after, the worst.

From the near-empty bus, Seren watched the suburbs dawdling past and her mind journeyed back to the first day Marco had ever seen the city; the day they'd met Christian Worthington. Marco's seventh birthday.

An appointment for Marco with an ophthalmic specialist had necessitated the trip, but she couldn't believe she'd never brought him before when she witnessed his awe and delight at the harbour, ferries and massive buildings seen for the first time. Seren would have loved to take him to the zoo, the aquarium and the Power-house Museum – places she'd never been either – but there was no money for things like that. She needn't have worried: Marco was so overwhelmed by the size and speed of everything that they'd had to regularly find places to just sit and be still, his huge blue eyes blinking behind his glasses. At such times, she'd just held his hand and waited until he could find a question.

The appointment had been for three-thirty at the Citibank building, forty storeys high. A concierge had pointed them to the correct bank of elevators. Heading in that direction, three lift doors had opened at once, and they'd stood, like rocks in the rapids, as a swell of office workers spewed forth. Seren remembered them both, her little boy in red, herself in blue jeans and a tee-shirt, surrounded by the grey froth of the city people. She'd suddenly wanted to go home.

Instead, they'd ploughed forward and entered the lift and she'd given gave Marco a look. No touching.

'Which floor?' The man asking had to look down at her, which didn't happen terribly often.

'Ah, thirty-one,' she'd said, reading from the card again for the twentieth time. 'Thanks.'

'Do you want to press the button?' The man had towered over Marco.

Marco nodded. Mouth open.

Before she had known what was happening, her little boy had been scooped up under the armpits, and set down again at her feet. Button thirty-one was lit up. Marco was smiling.

Seren smiled too when they left the lift, meeting the stranger's eyes for the first time.

The smile stayed until the snooty receptionist called their name half an hour later.

She'd always felt terribly guilty about Marco's eyes.

Although this specialist had also told Seren that Marco's eyesight problem was the result of a congenital abnormality that was likely passed down through her from one of her parents, she couldn't help but worry that her drug use during the earliest days of her pregnancy had caused the astigmatism.

Seren had been stealing beer from her stepfather since she was eleven, smoking pot since the age of twelve, and had tried speed lots of times by the time she was thirteen. She liked it a lot. But probably most of all, Seren had liked her mum's worry pills, the little white tablets she got from the doctor for her nerves. She'd managed to steal a couple a week. They made everything soft and smooshy, and they definitely worked. On the nights she took one she slept so well that that she didn't have to worry about the dull thumps and sobs from the room next door.

Seren believed she knew the moment that she got pregnant. She was fourteen and had just cut her hair off for the first time.

Her girlfriend, Alexandra, had been horrified. Seren's sheet of ice-blonde hair was legendary at their school.

'Don't even think about it!' Alexandra had said as Seren raised the scissors in front of the mirror.

Alexandra had screamed when the first snip hacked off the length of half of Seren's hair. The next cut evened it out, but she just kept going. Her mother's face was black and blue from the night before, and Seren figured if her mum didn't care about herself, why should she? She wanted to punish her mother, hurt her, wake her the fuck up. She wanted to punish herself. As the slivers of sunlight had rained from her head, Seren expected to soon resemble a monster – at least then her mother would notice her. But the more she cut, the more beautiful she looked, and Alexandra had watched her, transfixed.

With her face naked, she appeared unclothed and vulnerable. Seren had had to close her eyes to stop the lie that stared back at her. She felt filthy and besmirched; but she looked pure, immaculate. When her blue eyes blinked open again in the mirror, she could see straight through to the five-year-old whose giggles used to sound like bells.

Seren had left her bedroom with Alexandra right after, and gone driving with two guys they'd met the day before at the swimming pool. Seren had dived head first from the front seat to the back and fucked Todd, the boy back there, while her friend and the driver had pretended not to notice.

A week before her periods were due, she knew. She could feel him in there, waiting. Marco.

The next time Todd called, she told him to lose her number. She didn't even know his last name. She never saw him again.

Seren remembered that after the meeting with the eye specialist, she and Marco had walked back to the lifts. Both of them were tired; she remembered thinking that it would be good to get home.

The door had opened and he'd stood there.

'Aha! Button boy!' he'd said.

He must be a movie star, Seren thought when he smiled.

They stepped into the lift. Seren smiled back.

'This must be serendipity,' said the man.

'*What*?' she exclaimed.

'You know,' he said, 'serendipity – a lucky chance.'

Shaking herself from her memories, Seren alighted at Town Hall and headed towards Centrepoint Tower. The small store specialising in surveillance electronics was located along the way. Although she'd seen pictures of the audio-video recorder on the store's internet site just this morning, she was still astounded that the device was so tiny – the size and shape of a cigarette lighter. She popped her two-hundred-dollar purchase into her bag and walked into Pitt Street Mall.

She needed just two items of clothing – a white shirt and a bra.

She owned a pair of man-style black trousers that sat flat on her hipbones and fell, soft and full, down to the ground. At might-as-well-be six foot tall, Seren often had difficulty finding pants that were long enough. These trousers were the ideal length, well cut, and the fabric was gorgeous.

She searched through the major department stores, a few of the nicer chain stores, and then spotted the shirt she'd been dreaming of for a year, hanging in the window of a small boutique. Perfect. She knew she would find it. She could see herself in it right now; knew how it was going to look. She had to have it.

Seren entered the store and went straight to the shirt. She flicked a fingernail under the fabric and plucked out the price tag.

Double what she could afford. If she bought this shirt, she'd have no money left for the laptop.

'That would look great on you.' The sales assistant stood at her side, a look of approval on her face.

'I'll just try it on,' said Seren. Might as well torture myself, she thought. There's no way I can buy it.

The shirt was white, the supple Italian fabric an alternating matt and gloss white pinstripe. The effect was of a male business shirt, the cuffs worn long, falling to Seren's knuckles. But the resemblance to a man's attire ended there. The cut was for a woman's body; it clung to Seren's ribs, fell snug across her flat stomach. She fastened the shirt, finding the top button almost too tight across her breasts. That wouldn't be a problem, she thought, it wouldn't remain closed for long. With a heart-attack bra, the outfit would have liquefied Christian Worthington. Pity.

And that was without even considering the shoes. When she thought about the shoes, she sighed and carefully unbuttoned the shirt. She changed back into her own clothes and left the dressing room.

She walked towards the expectant sales clerk, an expression of deep regret on her face.

'I'll take it,' she said.

Seren sat on a courtesy bench in the food hall, watching diners lunching in a small café. She held her shopping bags close. Way to go, Templeton, she told herself. First day of the plan and you've already stuffed up.

A couple at a nearby table picked pasta and salad from each other's plates. Her stomach grumbled. Nothing for you, she told it. How am I going to get a laptop now?

The clinking of the cutlery sent her mind back again, remembering the night of her twenty-third birthday, dining at Altitude, an intimate dining room balanced thirty-six floors above Sydney harbour, a black velvet jewellery box open and spotlit beneath them. Even though she had then been dating Christian for almost six months, she didn't think she'd ever grow used to the hushed opulence of such restaurants.

She'd felt a flush in the hollow of her throat. Candlelight shimmered in Marco's eyes, reflected back from his glasses. He'd never seen anything like this. It seemed that every couple of minutes he stared down at his clothes in astonishment.

She doubted he'd ever even seen a child dressed as he was. Christian had taken them both shopping that morning.

She'd tried not to focus on her own gown. When she did, she'd experienced the panicky thrill of being virtually naked. Although the cream sheath fastened around her neck and dropped all the way to the floor, it left her back completely exposed to her waist. With her hair cropped close to her head, from behind every inch of her skin was exposed. When she moved even slightly, she felt the silk of the fabric slip across her nipples. Christian watched every move she made. She felt the flush at her throat spread.

She had never stayed the night before. Although Christian always paid for a professional sitter for Marco for the evenings they had spent together, he knew that she'd never leave her son overnight. So that night Marco's pyjamas, stuffed into his school backpack, waited in the boot of Christian's car.

Marco had fallen asleep at ten, drunk on the lights of Darling Harbour spread out beneath Christian's apartment, the Playstation console still in his hands. After Seren had tucked him into the spare bed, she'd gone to find Christian.

The next morning had been a blur. Leftover take-away Thai for Marco's breakfast; she'd have to be more prepared next time. Who didn't have bread and Vegemite in their house?

'Ew! Stop it!' In the car park at Central station, Marco had protested the parting kiss Christian gave her.

'Hang on, baby, before you go . . .' Christian had reached under his seat and brought forward a gift bag.

'No,' said Seren. 'Nothing else, Christian! You've already given me too much.'

'I'm going to be late for work, Seren, so we can't argue about it now. You're just going to have to take it.' He trailed a finger down her cheek, her neck . . . Stop it, she told him with her eyes, and pointed with her chin to her son in the backseat.

Her whole face a smile, she gave in and peeked inside the gift pouch. It contained a shoulder bag of the most velvety, yielding chocolate leather.

When she and Marco finally got out of the car, Christian cracked his window. 'There's a little something inside,' he said. 'Happy birthday, baby. Have fun shopping. I'll call you tonight.'

Ten one-hundred dollar notes.

When she had been around Marco's age, Seren had decided that every day she would deliberately expect something terrible to happen. That way, if nothing did go wrong – unlikely – she would have something to be happy about, and if a bad thing did take place, well, she'd have been ready. But every day for months now, only wonderful things had happened. Amazing things. Seren was beginning to believe it was time to develop a new policy.

She'd dropped Marco off at school and caught the train back into the city to do a little more shopping. She'd find something spectacular to make Christian's eyes light up. She was beginning to learn his taste.

The shoes had stopped her dead.

Syrupy patent leather, glowing like a just-rinsed blackberry. The heels were much too high. Ridiculous, really. Especially for a girl who'd never worn heels before meeting Christian. But he loved her to be tall, towering over all the other women. The shoes laced at the front like a camp parody of a man's business shoe. A cross between sensible schoolgirl and dominatrix.

The name of the shoes' designer clinched it. Christian Louboutin. Christian.

A sign. It had to be fate.

No price tag.

It didn't surprise her. She'd never set foot in a shop like this. A few months ago, she hadn't thought she ever would.

A uniformed security guard opened the door for her and Seren stepped inside, clutching her new handbag to her chest, using it both as protection and as proof that she had a right to be in a store like this. She had a brief glance around and then made straight for the shoes.

'Ah . . .' She cleared her throat, and tried again. 'Excuse me? How much are these shoes?'

For some reason it was so much more intimidating that the shop assistant was male. The suit and tie added to his daunting demeanour. He looked to have just stepped out of a magazine. Or Christian's office. The thought made her stand up straight and meet the man's eyes.

'The Louboutins?' he said.

She nodded.

'Nine ninety.'

What did that mean? It took her a couple of moments to comprehend the numbers and the realisation flared her pupils. Nine hundred and ninety dollars. For a pair of shoes.

Evil.

Nobody should pay a thousand dollars for one pair of shoes. Nobody should *charge* a thousand dollars for a pair of shoes. The store assistant dropped his eyes back to whatever had occupied him before she entered the shop. His studied, neutral stare very clearly stated, *Thought so.* He hadn't even moved from behind the counter.

Little prick, she said to herself. She looped the shoelaces around a finger and dangled the thousand-dollar shoes over to the counter. Dropped them in the middle of the open book in front of him.

'Got them in a ten?' she said.

And everything had gone to hell in a hand basket after that, of course. Her mother had always told her that pride comes before a fall.

The shoes were perfect. Freaking perfect. Even in her jeans. She towered over the shop assistant, who now seemed a little inclined to worship her.

It took him almost fifteen minutes to package them. An elaborate ritual of tissue, then a fabric slipper for each shoe, a huge, beautiful box, and, oh my God, the shopping bag! Focused on every step of the spectacle, Seren nearly swooned when he brought forward with a flourish the shining cardboard and ribbon carry-bag, expanding it with a crack and a flick of his wrists.

Her cheeks feverish with the sin of it all, Seren had felt almost loving towards the man at the cash register.

'And how will you be paying, madam?' He had smiled up at her.

'Cash.'

'Oh, of course,' he said. 'Very good.'

Seren reached into her delicious new handbag and pulled out the notes in a bundle. She handed them over to Eric, her new best friend.

'And all hundreds, too,' he said. 'Well, at least we won't be here all day.' He beamed at her and began to count. 'What the hell?'

A clear plastic snap-lock bag fell from the notes and landed on the counter. Several opaque pink-tinged rocks sat inside.

'That would be yours, I think.' Eric's voice had frozen.

Seren stared at the little bag. Fuck. What the hell was that? Nothing good. Her eyes darted from the bag to the store atten-dant, who now would not look her in the face. He flicked a glance over to the security guard.

Fuck. For fuck's sake.

She snatched the little bag up off the countertop, and dropped it into the carry case containing the shoes. She grabbed up the handles of the shopping bag and stared at the attendant expec-tantly. What else could she do?

He completed the transaction, his face a mask. They did not speak another word to one another. She left the store.

When she saw the uniformed cops waiting for her at the bottom of the escalators near McDonald's, Seren dropped her shoulders in resignation. Had to happen, she told herself. Shit was supposed to happen to her every day. Life had been stockpiling her daily dose for a good six months. This was going to be one crapload of faeces.

22

Since the day, aged twelve, when her parents had brought her home from the hospital after she'd been kidnapped, Jill didn't think she had ever again communicated anything effectively to her sister. So how the hell she'd been able to make Cassie understand, without saying a word, that she should behave as though they didn't know one another in Nader's lounge room in Merrylands, she would never know.

But that was what had happened. Fortunately, everyone at Kasem Nader's house had directed their total attention to Cassie when she had walked through the door. By the time Cassie's eyes had met Jill's and registered instant recognition, Jill had steeled her own expression. She had drilled her gaze in her sister's direction, a stare of desperate, deliberate focus. She had shaken her head slightly – no – as her sister's lips had parted.

And, unbelievably, Cassie's expression of shock had disappeared, her eyes had glazed, and she had continued her appraisal of the room, giving a semblance of being bored and slightly disdainful. Jill knew that look well. Had she not become a model, she was certain at that moment that her sister could have made it as an actor.

Jill had exhaled carefully, her heart thudding, and turned. Half the men in the room had moved forward, a few steps closer to the door, closer to Cassie. But one man stood still, his arms folded.

Kasem Nader had stared at Jill, who had slipped instantly back into her Krystal Peters mask.

From then, the night had progressed relatively uneventfully. Cassie and her friend had spent most of their brief time in the house speaking to one of Kasem's brothers. Jill had watched the three of them leave together, her stomach a miserable, acidic knot. Her sister had not again glanced in her direction.

What are you doing, Cassie? Jill wondered. What?

Jill stepped off the train at Bondi Junction station.

At Sunday lunchtime the platform was busy, but nothing like the crush of people here from six until nine in the evening every week day. She had never travelled to her sister's apartment by public transport before, and it took her a little time to orient herself. When she left the underground platform, she searched the skyline and spotted the apartment building relatively quickly. On the way there, she stopped at a deli and picked up some fat, black olives, five or six stuffed artichokes and some char-grilled red capsicum, shiny with olive oil. She didn't know what Cassie had planned for lunch, but this would go with most things. She added to her purchases a bag each of hazelnut-scented coffee beans and powdered sugar-dusted crostolli. At least Cassie would drink the coffee, she thought.

'Hey, big sis.' Cassie stood back from the door to her unit, welcoming Jill in. She wore a gauzy, transparent caftan over a bra and knickers. Barefoot and make-up free, her bronzed hair tousled, Jill saw now, as much as ever, why her sister made enough money as a model to afford this gorgeous apartment. She glanced down at her own jeans and black tee-shirt and inwardly shrugged. At least it wasn't a Playboy tracksuit today.

'Hey, Cass.'

They air kissed and Jill moved into the unit, dropped her groceries on the dining table and walked straight out to the balcony. She breathed in the view. She preferred the natural expanse of her ocean outlook, but she guessed she'd be able to get used to this, if she had to. She smiled. This apartment was worth three, maybe four, times her own.

'Salad okay with you?' Cassie moved around her kitchen, gathering up items.

'Great.' Jill came in from the balcony. 'Here, let me help,' she said.

'Got it all covered, sis,' said Cassie. 'Been slaving away over a hot stove all morning.'

Cassie placed a long French loaf and a platter of cold, poached chicken pieces on the white marble table. On her second trip from the kitchen she balanced a huge bowl in one hand and clutched a bottle of wine and two long stemmed glasses in the other.

Jill hurried forward and took the bowl. 'Cassie!' she said. 'You'll drop something.'

'I've got it,' said Cassie. 'You sound like Mum.'

Great, thought Jill. Good start. 'Yum,' she said, 'this looks gorgeous, Cass.'

'Rocket, pear, fig and blue cheese salad,' said Cassie. 'From Belgiovani's. Blonde chicken from Kim Sun's. Sauvignon Blanc from New Zealand – the Marlborough district, I believe.'

Cassie took a seat in a white leather dining chair and cracked the seal on the wine. She grabbed a glass and poured.

Jill walked into Cassie's gorgeous kitchen – she did so love appliances – and selected a white platter from a shelf. When she brought it back to the table a glass of wine waited at her setting.

Cassie gave her a cat-like smile.

Jill took her seat. Cassie knew that she didn't drink. At least she thought she didn't. Here we go again, she thought, using booze to break the ice. She took a sip of the wine and smiled back at her sister.

'Mmm,' she said, and laid out the food from the delicatessen.

They ate quietly for a few moments. Chill-out music drifted with fresh air through the apartment.

'So what were you doing there, Jill?' Cassie finally asked.

What were *you* doing there, Cassie? Jill knew the question she so wanted to ask was not the best way to get into this. She wanted this meeting with her sister to go well. For once.

'Cassie,' she began instead, 'thank you *so* much for not letting on that you knew me. You saved my arse. Seriously.'

'Yeah? I didn't know what you were doing there, but I could tell you didn't feel like a catch-up.'

Jill gave a short laugh and took another sip of wine. 'That's the understatement of the year,' she said. 'I'm undercover at the moment, and I was working.'

'No shit!' said Cassie.

Jill stabbed at a fig-half. 'Thing is, Cassie, I'm not supposed to tell anyone, even you and Mum and Dad, that I'm working this way. But because you saw me there, I had to explain. If you had blown my cover, I don't know what would have happened.'

'Oh my God. My sister's a super spy.'

'Yeah, yeah.'

The conversation stalled for a little with the unasked question hanging between them. *Why were you there, Cassie?*

'Seeing much of Scotty?' Cassie asked. A dangerous enough question, given that the last time they'd seen Scotty had been in the hospital after Cassie's overdose. The Scotty issue was always loaded for Jill anyway. She slid her glass forward when Cassie wiggled the bottle at her, an enquiry on her face.

'I thought I'd catch up with him today, while I'm out this way,' Jill answered. 'I hadn't seen him for ages before . . . the other day.'

Cassie sucked at an olive pit. One song ended. Another began.

'What about you, Cass? You still seeing Aidan?'

'Aidan. No. Loser. There's a new guy, a lawyer. I don't know, I thought he was great, but . . . Are they all losers, Jill?'

'Did you just ask *me* that question?'

Cassie laughed. 'Well, you don't seem to have too many man disasters,' she said.

'You mean, I don't seem to have too many men,' said Jill.

'There's Scotty. He's a big hunk of yum.'

Jill's heart somersaulted. No please, Cassie, don't turn your radar in that direction. But why not, she asked herself, surprised at the strength of her reaction. Why shouldn't Cassie date Scotty? Because I'd never stand a chance again, she answered herself. So I want a chance? Jill hit the mute button on the dialogue in her head and watched as Cassie scanned the table for a low-kilojoule morsel, her shiny fringe hanging in her green eyes.

'Yeah, well. I'm not too sure what's going on with Scotty,' Jill said. 'I prefer working. It's so much simpler.'

'Oh, definitely,' said Cassie. 'Simple. It does sound that way, Jill. What is your job again? New South Wales police detective pretending to be a gangster, or a gangster's moll, or a prostitute or something?' Cassie laughed. 'That was *some* tracksuit, sis.'

'Mmm, Playboy. I can lend it to you if you like.' Jill felt a little irritated; the volume of her sister's voice was increasing.

'Maybe,' Cassie laughed again. 'It might be fun to role-play a skanky drug addict . . .'

Cassie's fork froze halfway to her lips, as she seemed to realise what she had said. Her cheeks glowed. She dribbled the last of the wine into her glass, raised the glass to her mouth and drained it.

'Dead soldier,' she said, standing up with the bottle. Jill remembered that Cassie always referred to empty bottles that way. 'Same again?'

'I'm right, thanks, Cass,' said Jill, tearing off a chunk of bread. She needed something starchy to soak up what she'd already had.

Cassie returned to the table and cracked open another bottle of wine; poured some for each of them. 'So,' she said, leaning back in the chair with her glass, 'who were you pretending to be anyway?'

'I can't go into it any more than I have, Cass, sorry. But I probably should ask how you ended up in that house.'

'What? I'm supposed to tell you all about what I get up to, but it doesn't go both ways?'

'It's a different thing –'

'I'm just shitting you, Jill. It's no biggie. Adele's kind of got a thing for one of those guys. She met him at a club.'

'Which guy?'

'I don't know. Why? Has one of them taken your fancy? I did notice the big boy seemed pretty interested in you, tracksuit and all . . . What was his name? Casper or something?'

'Kasem.'

'That's the one. Yeah, I can see that he might be worth the hike out to the sticks. Bit of rough trade.'

'Cassie, please . . .'

'I might have made a move if he hadn't been so interested in you.'

'Cassie. Would you just stop for a minute!' Jill put her glass down hard and wine sloshed onto the table. 'Sorry,' she said, reaching for a napkin.

Cassie leaned back in her chair, a resigned, sullen look upon her face, waiting for the lecture.

'Look,' said Jill, 'I can't tell you what to do, Cassie, but these are not people you should be fucking around with.'

'I know what I'm doing, Jill.'

'Oh, of course you do, Cassie. That's why we got called to St Vincent's in the middle of the night.' Jill could feel her temper rising, wanted to reign it in, but the words spewed forth of their own accord. 'That's why you had a *psychotic breakdown*, for fucksakes. That's why you nearly died, overdosing on God knows what. What, so you smoke *ice* now? Coke doesn't touch the sides anymore?'

Cassie sat quietly, raised her glass to her eye and peered through the pale lemon-lime coloured liquid, as though studying it for judgement in a wine competition.

'You know,' she said finally, 'you're not Ms Perfect yourself.'

'Look, I'm sorry, Cassie. It's the wine. I'm not used to it, I shouldn't have said that.'

'Oh, you wanted to say it. For once in your life you might as well say what you want to say.'

'What's that supposed to mean?' Actually, I don't want to know, thought Jill, but it was too late.

'It means that you never say what you really think. That you avoid any kind of adult conversation, as though you're still some fucking thirteen-year-old. That you sit in judgement about others, but you live like you have OCD, or you're a fucking nun.'

Jill stood to leave. Had she scripted in advance the worst possible outcome for this lunch date, she could not have done a better job than what was going on now.

'That's right, run away again,' Cassie went on. 'Just like you've done ever since you got kidnapped.'

Jill whipped her head around and stared at her sister, stunned.

'That's right, Jill. You were kidnapped. We can say it out loud. Not that anyone talked about it ever again when you got home.'

I can't do this, Jill thought, searching for her bag.

'It wasn't just you who had a hard time after that, Jill.' Cassie stood too now, her face wet, flushed. 'Nothing was ever the same again. We all disappeared. You went up your own arse somewhere, and I became invisible too. Nobody spoke about anything real anymore. Can't upset Jill.'

Jill found her bag. She felt a muffled nothingness, as though she was watching this tableau from inside a glass bubble; the edges of the world were distorted with the sphere that surrounded her. She wasn't certain that, if she tried to speak, any words would actually make it out of the bubble, but somewhere, faintly, a pressure urged her to try; to give Cassie the message she'd come here to relay.

'Cassie,' she began, quietly.

Cassie leaned forward, her hands on the table, as though to brace herself for what her sister was about to say.

'If you listen to one thing I ever say in my whole life,' Jill continued, in an amiable tone, 'let it be this. If you say anything to any of your drug-fucked friends about what you saw the other night, you will get me killed.' Jill met her sister's eyes. 'Fucking dead. It will be on your head.' She walked to the door. 'Thanks for lunch.'

23

On the bus travelling home from her shopping trip, Seren considered the implications of not having obtained the laptop.

Every day for the past three hundred days, she had imagined this precise moment, this step in the plan, but in her imagination, she had been carrying four items: the camera, the shirt, the bra, the laptop.

She considered whether she could do without a computer. That would require capturing evidence of such irrefutable power that it would achieve her goal with just thirty minutes of data recorded – she hadn't been able to afford a device with more storage capacity. She'd been through the plan hundreds of times: she knew that she was most likely to capture numerous small indiscretions that she could use, cumulatively, to prosecute her case to Christian, to prove to him that he could not win this time, that he had to do as she asked. The likelihood that she'd be in the right place at the right time to get the one perfect scene was minuscule.

She'd have to try to take the shirt back.

Or, what if . . . Seren wondered whether she might be able to secure credit and pay a laptop off. It seemed every bloody schoolkid could get a computer. Loads of shops offered interest-free options. She suddenly kicked out at the seat in front of her. It wouldn't work. Obtaining finance required an employment history of a longer duration than three days. Should that not be available, some kind of guarantor was required. Seren could not see a way that she could get a loan.

Abruptly, the realisation that such a small misstep so early in the piece could derail the whole scheme shook her resolve.

If she could make such a stupid, ditzy move on the first day of the plan, how the hell was she going to follow this thing through to the end? The improbability of pulling it off weighed down on her and she leaned her head forward, resting her forehead on the back of the seat, staring down into her shopping bags.

Maybe it's time you just bloody grow up, Seren, she said to herself. You are out of gaol. You have your son, somewhere to live, and a job. She peeked at the handful of people on the bus around her. All of them appeared to be travelling home from some kind of work. On a Sunday.

See, you don't even have to work weekends and you're bitching, she berated herself. Life is not about restaurants, and units with harbour views, and thousand-dollar shoes. The handful of happy people who have those lives have been blessed by destiny; they as good as don't even occupy the same world you do. You think you're so special, Seren? You think you're better than all the people living in these houses by the bus route? Get a grip. You were a single mother at fifteen. You're an orphan, a parolee. You live in a shithole and you work in a slaughterhouse.

You are Seren Templeton. You are responsible for another person. A child. Your child, Marco.

Seren let the tears drop down into the grime on the floor of the bus.

It's his turn now, she told herself. You had your chance. Maybe if you don't fuck up his life, he can have a better shot at this crap.

A couple of stops passed before she lifted her face from the back of the bus seat in front of her.

Her shopping bags now just a burden rather than a magician's kit to get her out of this life, Seren leaned against the wall and stabbed repeatedly at the up button for the lift in her unit block.

Frigging thing took forever to get down to the ground, and once you were in there it was worse. She could have jogged the stairs faster – she had done it before – but she didn't have the heart today. She craned her neck up through the open lightwell to stare at her floor, six levels above.

Finally, she heard the pulleys of the lift complaining, straining to reach the ground. She stood back from the doors.

Along with the regular piss stench, beer fumes buffeted outward when the doors opened. Tready.

Not. Today.

'I saw you from up our floor,' he said. 'Where you been all day? It's a Sunday.'

Seren considered waiting down here, but she knew that this idiot would follow her regardless. She got into the lift. Tready stumbled a little and shoulder-charged the wall, trying to keep himself from falling. His piggy eyes squinted in concentration as he tried to remain upright.

'Whoa.' He steadied himself, and then with carrot-coloured fingertips put his cigarette back between his lips. The lift hadn't even moved yet. 'What'cha got there? Been shopping?' he said. As soon as the doors closed, he reached out and grabbed for her bags.

'Hey!' Seren held on.

Tready ripped the glossy cardboard of the bag from the boutique. The bag holding her white shirt. Before she could pull it away from him, he turned his back to her and snatched at the shirt. She heard him shredding the tissue that had wrapped it so carefully.

Seren saw the collar of her new white shirt in Tready's meaty hands and the world became silent. She stared into his sweating face as his mouth opened and closed, apparently saying something, then baring his teeth as he laughed. She watched him reach into one of the other bags – now slack in her hands – and draw out its contents. Her heart-attack bra.

Still no sound.

Tready's little eyes lit up, his mouth open in a big round O, teeth missing, yellow or blackened. With one hand, Tready unbuttoned. He lowered the zip of his fly. He pushed the bra down into his crotch and rubbed it all around, using it to polish his prick.

Seren finally heard something. A high-pitched whine in her head, which sounded a little like the conveyor belt that took the bodies of the chickens away after she had killed them. Except it sounded overloaded, like it was going to break.

Seren dropped her last shopping bag. She reached a hand forward and gripped a handful of the greasy red hair on the top of Tready's head, which was angled downwards as he pulled himself with her underwear. She swung her knee back as far as it would go within the confines of the elevator. Simultaneously, she yanked the hand holding his hair down as though ripping curtains from a window, and smacked her knee up to meet it. She visualised her knee smashing into her hand, as though nothing lay between them.

Her hearing working perfectly now, Seren heard the most pleasant wet crunch as Tready's nose was mashed back into his skull. And then the scream.

When he dropped, howling incoherently, she picked her shirt up from the floor. She retrieved her bra, leaving Tready's phallus flaccid against his leg. She stared for a beat at his groin, then lifted her sneaker and stomped.

When the door opened, Seren ensured that she had all of her purchases on her. She was going to need them. She stepped over Tready and left the lift.

24

Monday 8 April, 1 pm

Damien Rose shouted lunch. He sat with his three new friends in the Manning House eatery of the University of Sydney, and watched them devour hamburgers, hot chips and beer. Damien enjoyed his apple juice and a vegan falafel burger. They made them great in here.

There was a time when Damien would pass through here quickly, starving, while his classmates purchased lunch in this dining hall. For a student centre, the place was bloody expensive. He'd been surprised when he'd had to dip back into his wallet for another note, when the fifty wasn't enough for today's lunch.

Not that that mattered anymore. Damien sometimes couldn't fit his wallet into the pocket of his jeans. Shit, it was only this year that he'd even owned a wallet – well, not counting the Velcro surfie wallet he'd been given by a teacher as his only Christmas present one year.

Damien's family didn't do Christmas, or birthdays. That, and the Witnessing he'd had to do every Sunday until he'd turned fourteen and flat-out refused, had made him the local reject. Muslims, Catholics, Presbyterians, damn, even Buddhists, were all normal in Merrylands when he grew up. But Jehovah's Witness? That shit was just strange, man. At least that's what everyone thought.

And the suit. That was the worst of all. As far as he could tell, not one kid in their entire suburb, and probably the next five surrounding them, even owned a suit, let alone wore it to go knock on their neighbours' doors each week. How his mother could not figure out that this behaviour would cop him at least a weekly bashing, he would never understand.

Damien smiled and chewed, brushed his blonde fringe back from his eyes. Erin laughed at something Jacob was saying. Erin is so hot, he thought. Whitey had told him that he should have asked her out ages ago, but he'd never asked a girl out. Sure, there was Helen Chin from physics class at the Year 12 formal, but she'd asked him, so that didn't really count.

Whitey told him that by third year of uni, especially *this* year, he should have been getting laid at least every weekend. Whitey told him that he got pussy pretty much every day, and Damien now had no excuse.

'Ask her out tomorrow, man,' Whitey had said to him last night, 'or I'm gonna come out there on Tuesday and ask her myself. And I'll spoil her for life, man. She's not going to be able to come back to you after she's had Whitey.'

Whitey didn't hang around here much. He hadn't re-enrolled this semester. Damien had been scandalised.

'What are you doing, Whitey? Think of your future! Are you crazy?'

'Who needs that shit, Damien? We don't anymore. Anyway, no one's stopping you. You go and be a good boy and finish your degree. Shit, get your Masters if you want. You've got our perfect customer channel, and you might just learn some new tricks to really give our shit the edge.'

Erin and the others were getting close to finishing their food and he hadn't said anything yet.

'Where would I take her?' he'd asked Whitey. 'She's into clubbing and you know I can't dance.'

'Ask her round to our place.'

Five years ago, when Damien's mother had moved overseas to live in a Jehovah's Witness commune, Damien had taken over the rent of their three-bedroom fibro home. His night job at the servo hadn't been enough to make the repayments, so he'd asked Whitey to move in. He was the perfect roomie, really – Whitey never tidied his own room, but he'd help out with other stuff when asked. And he ate nothing – prick was thin enough to slip through fence palings.

'Oh, yeah, sure, Whitey,' Damien had scoffed. 'Like she'd want to come out to Merrylands from Newtown. Anyway, that would have been okay when we were just making the E, but now you've started cooking ice, the place smells like shit. That would be a great first date. Hell, *I* don't even want to be there.'

'There you go, then,' Whitey had said. 'Where do we go when we want to sleep somewhere that smells nice?'

'A hotel.'

'Exactly.'

'Exactly what? Seriously, Whitey. You've got to stop testing the product! I'm gonna ask Erin on a date to a hotel room? You've lost it, bro.'

'Listen, dickhead,' Whitey had said. 'We'll get a suite. On the harbour. Have a little private party. I'll take care of the music and the visuals. You won't have to dance. Your little Erin will be all over you.'

'What about you, Damien?' Jacob asked. Damien's attention snapped back to the university café.

Jacob and Brent were standing. They all stared at him expectantly.

'What? Sorry?' he said. Damn, he could never concentrate when he was nervous.

'What's your next class?' Jacob asked.

'Organic Synthesis and Reactivity,' said Damien.

'Have fun with that,' said Jacob and laughed as he and Brent headed off.

Damien knew that Jacob had enrolled in Medicine in his first year, swapped to Sports Science at the beginning of last year, and by July had moved to Arts, hoping to major in Philosophy. When Damien had asked why he'd dropped Sports Science, Jacob had told him he that he didn't like the campus he'd had to move to.

'Too many fat chicks,' he'd declared.

Erin hadn't left with Jacob and Brent, thank God. Damien got up and walked around to where she stood.

'Where are you off to now?' he asked her.

'Linguistics,' she said.

He grimaced. She smiled. He cleared his throat. She shuffled her feet. Oh for fuck's sake! Damien felt like any minute now a tumbleweed would roll through the dining hall between them.

'Um,' they both said, at the same time.

'You go,' he said.

'Well, it's about this weekend. I was wondering . . .'

Oh my God. It was going to be just like Helen Chin. She was going to ask him out!

'Well,' she continued. 'My friends and I – we really liked those pills you got for us last week, and I wondered if you could get us some more?'

'Oh,' he said. 'Okay.'

Damien didn't usually do the selling. They had Byron for that. Damien got to know people who'd want to buy, who were already buying, and would put Byron in touch with them. Erin and her friends had come to know that Damien knew Byron, and he'd hooked them up directly a couple of times.

'That's great, Damien! You're a darling.' And Erin reached up, put her arms around his neck, and kissed him. On the mouth.

'See you tomorrow, then,' she said. 'And thanks for lunch!'

She walked away.

Dickhead. Dumb. Mute. Tool. Could he do nothing right?

'Erin!' Damien called and started to jog after her. He skidded to a stop when he reached her side.

***

'Here, take these first.' Damien handed Erin two tablets and a bottle of water from the mini-bar.

'What are they?' She'd swallowed them before she'd even asked.

He stared. People had no idea what chemicals could do to their bodies.

She looked so gorgeous tonight. She had this stretchy white top thing on, cut real low, and, well, she was really, ah, big, up top. Damien had to look at his shoes when he answered.

'It's okay,' he said. 'It's just B6 and L-tryptophan.'

'Vitamins,' she said.

'Well, technically L-tryptophan is an amino acid,' he said.

'Are you shitting me?' Erin started to look worried.

'No, really. It's okay. For maximum effect, and to give your brain the best protection, I should have started you on a few things a week ago. These will both help increase your serotonin levels.'

'Isn't the eccy gonna do that?' she asked. She swept her eyes around the suite, like she had been doing every couple of seconds since she walked in. He didn't blame her. The Opera House glowed like their own private moon on the inky harbour directly beyond their balcony. He reckoned he could have just about thrown a rock onto the steps. Whitey had the music pulsing, but not loud; just a rhythmic throbbing that prodded beneath the conversations of the eight people in the room.

'Actually, the ecstasy draws on your brain's own serotonin, the chemical that makes you feel so great when you take it,' he said. 'It forces your neurones to release all you've got stored, so you're flooded with feel-good for a few hours.'

'And it feels so good,' she said. 'Are you going to roll tonight too, Damien?' Erin took a step closer and peered up into Damien's eyes. From this angle, his own private view eclipsed the Opera House any time. He had to drop onto the couch and grab a cushion.

'I don't use it,' he said.

She dropped down next to him. 'Someone told me that if you crush the tablet up and snort it, you get a better rush,' she said.

'Well, you can get the dosage in your bloodstream up a little more, up to around seventy-five per cent, but when it drips down the back of your throat it tastes terrible,' he said. 'I'm told,' he added.

'Some people shoot it up.'

'Some people are fucking suicidal,' he said. 'You'd want to be pretty sure about what the pill had been cut with before you started shooting it directly into your vein.'

'Ew. I wouldn't do that anyway.'

'You probably wouldn't like the other method either.'

'Which is?'

'Shafting. Inserting it into your arsehole. Up to ninety per cent absorption into the bloodstream.'

'Hmm. How revolting. Let's stop talking about this. It's killing the magic. Don't you think it's a beautiful night?'

Erin moved a little closer, brought her face close to his. She smelled like fairy floss. He licked his lips.

'You know a lot about ecstasy,' she said.

'Yeah, well, I guess I'm well read.'

She moved even closer. 'Anyone would think that you make it yourself,' she whispered. 'My own little chemistry boy.'

25

Monday 8 April, 1 pm

'Hey, chemical brothers!' said Byron when Damien opened the front door. He flopped down onto the lounge. It was back to the real world: Merrylands and the stench of their rented house. Damien moved back to the sink where Whitey was, trying to keep hold of the feeling from the hotel last night.

'Ah, we might have a problem,' said Byron.

'What?' Whitey and Damien spun around.

'Nah, man. It's all good. Nothing like that!' Byron laughed. 'Shit, you guys are tense,' he said. 'It's not the law.'

'What, then?' Damien turned back to the stove. He couldn't afford for this batch to get too hot. He'd had to start again once already this week, and it had cost a lot of time. He had two essays due on Friday.

'Well, it's not really a problem. We should think of it more as an opportunity,' said Byron.

Damien and Whitey continued to work.

'A business opportunity. A chance to expand, widen our networks.'

'We don't want to expand,' said Whitey.

'We're happy with our networks,' confirmed Damien. He smiled. Erin had called him three times today. He got a hard on every time his mobile sounded.

'That's probably where the problem part comes in,' said Byron.

'What are you talking about, Byron?' asked Whitey. 'Are you on the goey? You're making no fucking sense.'

'Well, you see, I've got a friend who wants to meet you guys. He wants to talk to us about collaborating.'

'Not interested,' said Damien.

'Forget it,' said Whitey.

'Yeah, but he's not going to just let it go at that,' said Byron. 'I think if you meet him and listen to what he's got to say it would be better for everyone.'

Damien ran some more water over the sides of the container to cool the liquid a little more. He added sixty-five grams of 3,4-methylenedioxyphenylacetone to the formahide and checked the temperature again. One-ninety degrees. Another five hours to go. He rubbed at his face and leaned back against the counter. 'Better for who?' he said. 'You? We told you, Byron. We don't want this any bigger. Haven't you got enough money? It's getting hard to spend all this cash.'

'I don't think you're listening,' said Byron. He stood up from the couch and jammed his hands into the pockets of his jeans. 'We don't have a choice.'

'The fuck we don't have a choice,' said Whitey. 'Who are you talking about, anyway? Who is this prick you want us to meet?'

'Kasem Nader,' said Byron.

Lying in bed that night, trying to punch his pillow into some sort of shape he could settle into, Damien could not sleep.

This is not good, he thought. This is bad. He should never have let Whitey bring Byron Barnes in on any of this.

When Damien had realised he had the know-how and access to the ingredients required to make good quality MDMA – ecstasy – he had at first kept it from Whitey. He knew Whitey would put it on him hard and not give up until they'd at least tried to cook up a batch. Damien knew this, because Whitey had been on about it since Year 11, when Damien had told him he was going to go for a degree in Medical Chemistry.

Damien didn't want to get involved in anything that hurt people, but he'd read up on the drug and been pretty surprised to learn that MDMA had only been made illegal in 1985, and that psychiatrists had actually used it therapeutically before then. He had downloaded the articles for two current studies being conducted in Spain and Israel using MDMA in an attempt to treat post-traumatic stress disorder.

The main danger, he learned, was when people used too much – chewed through all of their serotonin stores – which left them suffering chronic depression. And the other major problem lay with bad cooks: people who didn't know what they were doing, or who used dangerous substitutes for the chemicals that were hard to come by. That wouldn't be a problem for a properly trained chemist, he'd thought. And if people were going to be using it anyway – more than a hundred thousand ecstasy tablets every weekend in Australia – maybe it would be doing the right thing to make it properly.

Whitey had brushed aside the rest of Damien's concerns – like some recent findings about brain damage in animals – and within a month, they'd made their first press of pills. Whitey swallowed their first-ever tablet, washed down with a glass of six-dollar-a-bottle sparkling wine. Now, Whitey only drank Veuve Clicquot, but said that not even Veuve could improve on Damien's E.

But then Whitey had pushed the envelope. And Damien had been too much of a blow-arse to knock him back. It had begun as an intellectual exercise. Would he know how to cook meth, Whitey had wanted to know.

Damien knew that his weakness lay in his limitless curiosity for testing and chemical experimentation. He could admit to that flaw. He was also beginning to realise that he was easily seduced by flattery, especially when his ego relating to his intellect was stroked. He knew that Whitey could sometimes play him like a violin, and so, three months ago, Damien had cooked their first batch of ice.

And now this.

Damien had always known that the ice would be trouble. He'd figured on making just boutique quantities for a few very loyal and lucrative customers who wanted some product they could trust. Whitey hadn't pushed the matter. Very good of him, given that there was nothing that they could do to increase supply anyway. Sourcing enough pseudoephedrine to create what they made now flew them just under the radar of the law.

He had thought that the trouble would come in the form of one of the customers suffering a psychotic breakdown and coming to find him. Although Byron was their distributor, he was only one step removed, and hardly to be relied upon to protect them should some mad motherfucker or his family put the heavy on him.

Damien also worried about a possible explosion. He used the Nazi method to cook the ice, which involved reducing the pseudoephedrine using lithium and anhydrous ammonia – an air conditioner refrigerant – and the chemicals were highly unstable, even just in contact with water. He had nightmares about Whitey getting greedy and playing chef on his own one day while Damien was at uni.

And then there were Byron's current drugs charges. Although they were only for possession of pot – a pissy little charge that ordinary citizen could have thrown into a drawer with the parking fines – with Byron's history it meant automatic lockup if he was convicted. Last time he'd faced court he'd copped a suspended sentence – free to leave provided that he did not break any law during a two-year period. He seemed pretty positive that he was going to be able to get off his current charges with the help of some VIP lawyer. Still, Damien knew the cops could follow Byron here at any time. He knew everything he was involved with right now was risky.

But Damien had never considered that the threat facing him might come in the form of Kasem Nader. Had someone told him, on day one, that this would be the case, he would have lost his recipes and told Whitey that he needed to find someone else to live with.

Kasem Nader. Damien had always been grateful for the cred he got just growing up on the same block as the Nader brothers. His stories in Year 10 at lunchtime had helped him finally shrug off the 'godboy' and 'churchie' labels. He'd watched, relieved, as the school bullies had turned their consideration to the fat Asian kid who always smelled like rice.

No one ever got sick of hearing about the police busts at the Nader residence. They happened weekly for a while when Damien was in Year 10. He found he had a gift for setting the scene – describing Mrs Siham Nader running into the street in her nightgown, screaming at the cops who dragged her sons away.

And her boys never went without a fight. From his street-facing window, Damien watched the brothers being slammed by at least four coppers every time. The streetlights spotlit the faces of the arresting officers, orgiastic in their chance to bash a Nader. The boys were invariably thrown limp into the paddy wagon.

Except for Kasem. Brother number two. Loved or feared, often both, by everyone in this suburb, and many beyond.

Damien had perfected the art of watching. To have been spotted watching a Nader brother takedown and doing nothing to assist would have been suicide. He would turn off all lights in his bedroom and shove a towel in the crack under the door. He'd then create the tiniest chink in his aluminium venetian blinds, and stand up against the wall, still. Focus on the gap, peer through. With the lighting in his street, upgraded by the council when the Nader boys moved in, he could see just as well as if he'd sat on his porch with a Coke, watching the show.

And one night he'd seen Kasem in full flight. The problem, as far as he could tell, was that the bald probationary constable had shoulder-charged Mrs Nader when she clutched at Kasem as they'd dragged him across the lawn. Damien had stood, transfixed, as she'd tottered with the shove. She had reached out for her son, who couldn't get an arm free, and had then fallen onto the road, landing heavily on her backside, her hijab dislodging. She'd sat there, sobbing. Her other sons howled from their home, restrained, as usual, by the rest of the Merrylands cops on duty.

Damien hadn't bothered looking at the house. He watched Kasem.

Nader had seemed to go limp. Damien saw him have a word with one of his captors, perhaps a reasonable request – do you mind if I help my mum? Damien would never know whether the cops had briefly let him go to help his mother up off the road, or whether Kasem had broken away by brute force, but either way, when he moved, Kasem went nowhere near his mother. He exploded away from the officers holding him and sprinted towards the bald probationary constable. Although they stood at around the same height, Nader's king hit drove the cop's feet out from under him, and he smacked onto the road, the back of his head first, without even trying to break his fall. Damien thought he'd heard the crack from his room; he would always tell it that way, regardless.

Everyone in Merrylands knew that the cop never came back on the job. Some said it was stress leave, some said his parents had to shave and shower him now; shit, some said the prick died that night, right there on the road, and was buried at Rookwood. Damien had needed to know. He'd eventually learned that the cop was pensioned out hurt-on-duty and he now drove trucks interstate. His brothers in blue had a permanent hard-on for Nader, especially because he'd done only three months for the assault.

Damien swung his legs over the side of his bed and put his head in his hands.

He decided he wanted out.

26

Monday 8 April, 1 pm

The gutting supervisor signed on at twelve, and Seren knew that he was her best chance. She held herself together through the morning shift, somehow sickened that she actually was starting to get used to the killing. She had to get out of here. At eight this morning she'd almost thrown the job in again when two young blokes on the line had used as a handball an oversized tumour they'd found inside one of the birds.

She did not want to become accustomed to this.

She'd never melt her own supervisor, Maryanne. When the neck-snapping equipment failed or missed for some reason, and the line operator was struggling with a mutilated, terrified bird, Maryanne would approach and without a word kill the chicken with her bare hands, before moving on again.

But Zeko Slavonic, the gutting supervisor, was another matter entirely. Seren had seen the girls he presided over on his morning supervision shift; in the main younger than average, long, painted fingernails, dangly earrings. She'd seen the way Zeko watched her when she walked through his section on the way to the lunch-room. She knew men like him. Too easy.

It had at first seemed incredible to Seren that she would consider that pulling the innards from a dead chicken would be a great step up in the world, but after a week at the front line, with the live creatures, she couldn't wait to join Zeko's team.

There was not a lot she could do with the uniform – shapeless paper overalls – but she'd applied mascara this morning, and she slicked on a deep-berry lip tint in the washrooms before slinking through Zeko's turf on the way to lunch. This time when he tracked her sashaying across the floor, she waited until she reached the lunchroom entry and peeked back at him over her shoulder. Small smile.

He put his gloves down immediately and crossed the floor behind her. Hooked.

She reeled him in and, by two pm, she was learning the intri-cacies of disembowelling a fowl. Not the most pleasant way to spend an afternoon, but at least none of these chickens shrieked or begged.

Seren knew she'd made a new friend and a whole lot of enemies today. Zeko watched her with lust, his girls with hate, and when she walked into the locker room at knock-off time, she was unsurprised when the buzz of conversation ceased. The gift left in her locker was unexpected, though – the tumour-handball from this morning, wrapped up in her clothes.

A little parting pressie from Maryanne's team.

Standing barefoot in her bathroom that night, Seren smeared charcoal shadow across her eyelids, also smudging the smoky pigment under her lower lashes. Her clear blue eyes mocked her. In her mind, her face was always a contradiction: innocent, slut.

She planned her next move. Her job was bearable now. Just. But that was all right, she wasn't planning on building up a lot of superannuation benefits in that place. Moving forward with the plan was the only thing to do; she would worry about the computer later. Last week's pay had covered rent, shopping, and the small loan repayment back to the department; she had pretty much nothing left.

At least she had the outfit.

'You're going to go see him, aren't you?' Marco's voice came from behind her.

Seren spoke to her son's reflection in the mirror. 'Who, darling?'

'Why do you treat me like I'm stupid?' said Marco. 'I think you're going to see Christian. You told me they were his drugs that got you into trouble. Why would you go see him?'

Seren turned around. What could she tell her beautiful boy? Should she tell him the truth? He knew too much about the world already. She should just stick with the story.

'Marco, I told you,' she said. 'I'm going to be working most nights so that we can try to get ahead. Waitressing. Remember?'

'Yeah, Mum. I remember. Waitressing. Dressed like that.'

'It's a big hotel –'

'In the city, I know. You said that before.'

'Come on, darling. I'm sorry I have to go out, but Angel should be here any minute. She'll look after you. I'll get you ready for school when I see you in the morning.' She squatted down to his height, trying to get him to meet her eyes. 'I'm doing this for you, Marco.'

'Whatever,' he said.

There was a knock at the door and she moved to open it, relieved when she saw Angel standing there, carrying . . .

'What's that?' Seren asked.

'My laptop,' said Angel. 'Well, actually, it was Danny's. He won it in a card game. I don't know the first thing about how to use it, but I was hoping – ' she peered around Seren into the room, ' – that Marco could teach me some stuff. There are supposed to be some games on here.'

Huh.

'I thought,' continued Angel, 'that I could leave it here for a while, and Marco could practise and show me what he learned when I come over to babysit.'

Marco stood transfixed, still wearing his frown, but he hadn't taken his eyes off the computer.

'We've got them at school,' he said. Seren smiled – Marco used this careful nonchalance when he was at his most excited. 'I can show you a few things.' He kept his hands by his side, spoke again, 'But I'm not a baby. I don't need babysitting.'

'Oh, of course not,' said Angel. 'Just a figure of speech. We'll be hanging out while Mum's working. Is that better?'

Marco grinned, eyes on the computer.

Well, well. Seren's shoulders dropped a little. She watched her son closely; she always felt a rare sense of worth when she saw any indication of his happiness. Today hadn't been such a bad day. Maybe she was finally living up to her name a little.

She walked into her bedroom to finish dressing. Well, actually just to dab perfume at the base of her spine and to slip on The Shoes.

'Oh my God,' said Angel, when Seren came back to the living room. 'Are you sure you're going to be okay walking out of here like that?'

'I'll be fine,' said Seren. Tready would be in hospital for at least another couple of nights, surely. Her brow wrinkled and she turned around.

'What'dya forget?' said Angel.

Seren returned carrying a bigger handbag and standing a little shorter. 'You're right,' she said. 'I'll carry the shoes. A girl's gotta be able to run around here.'

Monday night happy hour at System. Christian hadn't missed one Monday at this club in the six months Seren had been with him. The idea was that you needed Mondays here to get over the first day of the working week, or to extend the weekend just a little more. A lot of Christian's friends considered that the weekend began on Wednesday night. Seren had discovered that although they still showed up at work Thursday and Friday, for these people, play nights began mid-week.

Christian had never pressured her to try anything, and he'd never used around her, but she'd been aware that he liked cocaine. He'd told her she could join him any time, but she had declined. She figured that if she'd gone almost ten years without a taste of anything, she'd be stupid to start again now. If she'd been honest with herself, she would have admitted that she found this part of Christian's life childish. She associated drug use with adolescent rebellion, and to see these affluent, educated adults out taking drugs every night seemed pretty pathetic to her. But Christian had been so great in every other way, and he never seemed to be terribly affected. In fact, she'd never really been certain when he'd taken anything.

After their first few dates, she had tended to avoid going to these clubs with him. She'd never grown used to the people who attached themselves to him, particularly the girls. And it was a lot easier to love him, to think of him as a father for Marco, when she didn't have to watch him dipping again and again into his jacket pocket.

'Look, it's no big thing,' he'd told her in the beginning. 'I have access to a safe source, and my friends know that. We're not the kind of people who are desperate enough to just hang out on a street corner trying to score. Everyone knows that I can get the best and I'd rather they came through me than get caught up in any trouble out there.'

Seren realised that she might not find him tonight. She was not particularly concerned. The best thing about her godawful job was the early starts – it gave her the afternoons before Marco got home to track Christian's movements; she would find him eventually. In the meantime, she would try his old haunts and see what she came up with.

She had her opening line down pat. He would not want to see her. Obviously. She imagined that he would have expected her to

sink back into the quagmire in which he'd found her, too humiliated to re-enter his world. Or that if she did show up, she'd be
hostile, aggressive, and he could pass her off as a jilted ex.

When she'd called him from the police station, hysterical, on
her twenty-third birthday, he'd been there in twenty minutes. Told
her he was so sorry, that it was all his fault, that it had just been a
little extra birthday gift he had thought they could enjoy together.
It will be fine, he'd told her. There won't be a problem. I'll be at
court, and we'll sort it all out. She had believed him, every word.
Of course, he would make it all better. That's what he did every
day. He was Christian Worthington, after all.

The social worker in the gaol had been called in when Seren
had been told that Christian would not accept her calls. The social
worker had called the psychiatrist, who had ordered intravenous
sedation.

27

Monday 8 April, 4 pm

Best thing she could do, Jill had decided after the disaster at her sister's the day before, would be to go back to work.

And she had. As soon as she'd arrived back at her apartment.

She had let herself in, dumped her handbag, added a few rings to her fingers, and left again. She went straight over to Ingrid's – who, thank God, had been at home. Jill had not wanted to be alone in her unit with nothing to do after the scene at Cassie's.

Ingrid had some mates over, as usual, and Jill had been quietly excited. She had wanted to grill these two for information for some time. Skye and CK were lovers, local meth smokers and small-time dealers. She'd never sent them up for dealing because they sold only to make enough money to use themselves. But word was that they had contact with some heavy suppliers and it was these men she wanted.

She'd gone easy on the wine, sipping very slowly, doing the refills for everyone and skipping her own glass whenever possible. People like these noticed when you took more than your share of anything, but under-serve yourself and that was sweet. As long as you drank something. Jill remembered an Aboriginal mother connected to a past case, trying to get her kids out of care, who'd been told that it would never happen unless she stopped drinking altogether. She'd told Jill that once her neighbours knew that she had quit, they'd shown up every day, free beer on offer, pressuring her to drink with them.

The headache this morning had been worth it. Jill had the names of two men she believed were up several levels on the meth supply ladder. Agassi and Urgill.

She had called Superintendent Last, and they had arranged to meet.

North Parramatta. McDonald's carpark. Four pm.

Jill caught a taxi from the station and now she sat, waiting, on the McDonald's car park railing, the wooden barrier hard on her backside, putting her legs to sleep. She stood and stretched.

'Krystal!'

At the sound of her undercover name, Jill glanced around. A man in a car just ahead in the car park. Oh my God! Is that . . . What the *hell* is he driving?

Grinning, she sauntered over to the 1990 Magna sedan; once red, the paintwork had washed out to an almost salmon pink, blasted by close to two decades of Australian sun and wind. She hooked an elbow over the driver's side door, facing the occupant, and kicked the hubcap-free front tyre. 'Sweet ride, boss,' she said.

Lawrence Last stooped over the steering wheel, his expression more morose than ever.

'Detective Jackson,' he greeted her. 'Should you not get in, Jill? I don't think I'd be recognised in this vehicle, but nevertheless . . .'

She strolled around to the passenger side, trailing a fingertip over the bonnet, eyes full of mock admiration, as though she surveyed a Ferrari. She yanked the door open and took a seat. As distinctive as the new car smell, the Magna reeked like a taxi close to retirement – cigarette-ash, sweat, farts and unwashed arses.

'Perhaps you will not be as amused, Jill,' said Last, 'when you learn that this is your new company car.' The corners of his mouth rose a little when Jill's face fell. 'Yes, as you can see, you have been richly rewarded for your service with the New South Wales police.'

'You're serious,' she said.

Last produced an A4-sized, yellow envelope, handed it over. 'Always,' he said.

Jill sniffed and grimaced. First thing she'd do would be empty a can of Glen 20 into this thing. She opened the envelope and flicked through its contents. Last had run the names and provided her with A4 photos of Agassi and Urgill, their sheets, names of known associates and last known addresses.

'So what's with the car?' she said. 'Why am I so lucky?'

'You told me that these men frequent a hotel in this neighbourhood. Now that your area of operation is expanding, I would prefer that you have some form of transportation other than trains and taxis,' he said. 'You may also find it useful for surveillance.'

'Thank you, sir,' said Jill. 'I promise I will ensure that no harm comes to it. You will get it back in the same pristine condition.' She glanced over at the back seat, its yellow rubber innards bursting forth in places, pushing through several splits in its velour skin.

'So what now?' she asked. 'Can I drop you somewhere, sir?'

'No need.' He peered through the windscreen and nodded his head. She followed the direction of his gaze and spotted a vehicle parked in a side street close by, recognising an unmarked police car. 'I'll just make my way over there.' He paused, and then searched her face. 'Is there anything else you need, Jill?'

'No thanks, Commander,' she said. 'This is great.'

'And you will call me at any time if you need anything at all.'

'Yes, sir.'

'You are doing a great job, Jill. But it's far more important to me that you are safe and you're coping emotionally.'

'Thank you, sir. I'm fine.' Well, she believed *his* words were true, anyway.

The engine turned over perfectly. That was the thing with a Department car. It might look like a junker, but mechanically the car would be sound. She knew that the Department would consider this car a 'paddock basher', at their disposal from the impound lot. When you had Lawrence Last's rank, the impound lot was a supermarket, although it did have its limitations. Full of confiscated goods that were the proceeds of crime, there was not always a use for much of the merchandise. There wasn't, for instance, a lot that a serving officer could do with a jet ski or a speedboat, undercover operative or not. Jill would have preferred one of the beamers she'd seen impounded, but 'Krystal Peters' couldn't exactly roll around Fairfield in a BMW.

She steered the car carefully out of the car park. As she drove down the side street adjacent to the restaurant, she noticed that Superintendent Last had waited to make sure she got away okay. Passing his vehicle, she shook her head and laughed. Adam Clarkson, the uniformed cop who'd 'arrested' her the other night in Fairfield, was Last's driver. He grinned at her through his windscreen, his thumb and forefinger forming a circle, indicating that her car was spot-on, perfect. Jill felt inclined to offer him a different finger gesture, but didn't consider it appropriate to direct that kind of message to a car containing her commanding officer.

She pulled out into the traffic on Church Street, and made her way to the other side of the suburb. I am definitely going to have to get this car detailed, she thought, when she pulled over adjacent to the Station Hotel. She cracked open the window. There was no way she was going to sit in this thing for hours on end when it smelled this way.

Jill opened the map book next to her; she would use it to cover her face if she was too closely observed. She'd parked just outside the cemetery, with a clear view of the entrance of the pub. This place was working class all the way. She didn't imagine the owners would bother spending anything on it to turn it into a yuppie establishment. She couldn't see the cocktail-set dining alfresco on a warm summer evening with this view over the graveyard.

If Agassi and Urgill were only mid-level crooks, they wouldn't advance a lot further with Skye and CK as friends, she thought. All she'd had to do the night before was mention that her ex was interested in buying five grand's worth of ice and they'd been so impressed that they'd even offered phone numbers. They'd told her all about these good friends: where they met them, their going rate. She'd learned that Mondays and Wednesdays were their business nights, out here at this hotel.

Ingrid had been more interested in her mentioning her supposed ex-partner. 'I thought you said he'd bashed you,' she'd commented.

'Well, not bashed, exactly . . .'

Ingrid was drinking wine from a lime-green coffee mug that could also have doubled as a soup bowl. Micro-fine spider veins rambled across her nose and chin; the rosacea of the alcoholic. The veins engorged when she had something to drink. Last night her whole face had glowed crimson.

'Krystal!' she began. 'That's denial talking, that is. And that shit can get you killed. I see it all the time around here. Girls leave their bloke because he flogs 'em and two weeks later he's been forgiven and it's all lovey-dovey again.'

'Well, he was good to me a lot of the time,' Jill had tried.

'Oh, you've got it bad, Krystal,' Ingrid had said. 'He'll be back on the scene soon,' she turned to Skye, 'you mark my words.'

'Enough of this bullshit,' said CK. 'Are we going to have another drink, or what?'

Jill had held up the empty cask bladder, a flaccid, silver sack.

'Time we was goin' anyway, love,' said Skye. 'People to see, places to go.' She had stood and swayed, held onto the back of the chair.

Now, out the front of the Station Hotel, in her salmon-coloured Magna, Jill thought about Ingrid's comments about boyfriends. 'Oh shit!' she suddenly exclaimed aloud. 'Scotty!'

She grabbed her mobile from the passenger's seat. She had told him she'd give him a call after she'd had lunch with Cassie, proposing that they meet up to work out. After the fight with her sister she had completely forgotten him. She opened the phone and scrolled for his number. She groaned in frustration and slammed her hand against the wheel. She *hated* these calls. The I'm Sorry call. The guilty feeling made her angry. Maybe she could just put it off. She was at work right now, after all. She felt a brief flash of relief at the thought of avoiding the call.

But she knew from experience that the longer she put this off, the bigger the problem would become for her. She had completely lost contact with almost all of her friends this way. She owed them a call, meant to call back, but had put it off, and then felt guilty. She couldn't bear it when people tried to rub in the fact that she'd been slack. The *very* few people she was close to never tried to guilt her when she contacted them unexpectedly after an absence of months or even years.

She couldn't lose touch with Scotty.

She hit the call button.

'Sorry,' she said, as soon as he answered. Got that out of the way.

'Yo, J,' he said. 'What? You didn't want to be humiliated again?' He thought he could beat her in every sport; they'd yet to find one where that wasn't the case, but she wasn't done trying.

'Lunch was horrible,' she said.

'Yeah?'

Jill leaned her head back into the headrest. 'Are you busy right now, Scott?'

'Good to go,' he said. 'So it wasn't the sister bonding session you'd hoped for?'

She groaned. 'I was awful. I pretty much called her a crackhead. Said her friends were all drug-fucked.'

'Whoa. What got into you?'

'Almost a bottle of wine.'

'For lunch?'

'It was Cassie's house, Scotty, what can I say?'

'Yeah, I get that with her, but that's not like you.'

'It's something I'm having to learn at the moment,' she said. 'When in Rome . . .'

'That's a worry, given the way you're earning a living at the moment, the people you're hanging around.'

'I've got it covered, Scotty,' she said. 'Anyway, I'm really sorry. I completely forgot I was going to call you. I just felt shocking, and I went straight home.'

'That's okay,' he said. 'What about a game of squash and a swim on Wednesday night?'

She'd be right here at the pub on Wednesday night.

'No good,' she said, 'working. Thursday?'

'I'm off to Goulburn Thursday morning,' he said. 'Gonna do some training down there for the recruits.'

'This is new,' she said.

'Gotta do something exciting,' he said. 'It's boring around here without you.'

'Should be fun,' she said. 'How long will you be gone?'

'Andreessen wouldn't let us stay the whole semester, so we're just doing a two-week course. Ethics in Practice. Can you believe it?'

Jill had a sudden premonition. 'Us?' she said.

'Yeah, me and Emma Gibson.'

'Well, isn't she industrious?'

Emma Gibson. Long raven hair, clear grey eyes. A man killer. And she'd wanted this man for as long as Jill had known him.

'Are you jealous?' he said.

'Are you crazy?' she replied.

'It's going to be like camp down there, you know.'

'And?'

'Well, you know, you get really close to your bunk buddies, that sort of thing.'

'Well, you have fun with your bunk buddy, Hutchinson. I've gotta go.'

'Wait! Jill. Don't hang up. I'm just teasing. I like it when you worry about other girls.'

'Emma Gibson is not another girl, Scotty. She's . . . oh, don't worry.' Jill felt stupid; she didn't know what she wanted to say.

'Don't *you* worry, Jackson. I'm gonna come home and we're going back to that beach.'

The beach where she'd tried to kiss him a couple of months ago. He'd stopped her, worried she would freeze him out the next day, blame her actions on the two glasses of wine she'd had that night.

'We'll see,' she said, 'and now I really do have to go.' She'd spotted the targets walking into the pub. She rang off.

Well, well. Jill pulled the map book up to her face and peered over the top. There, shaking hands with her suspects, was a new contestant in tonight's festivities.

Kasem Nader.

28

Monday 8 April, 9 pm

'Hey baby,' a whisper, 'got any blow?'

Seren had gone over a thousand possible ways to approach Christian and finally she'd gone with this. She figured that an addict like Christian would know that anything could be forgiven when you have to score. It was the only opening he would understand. He'd figure she was desperate, that she'd picked up some bad habits in gaol. He'd have control.

It worked beautifully.

Well, it was either that or the shirt.

'Close your mouth, sweetie.' She touched his face. 'People are staring.'

He drew her close and nuzzled her neck. 'Now, when are you going to get used to people staring at you, Seren?' he said, his lips barely touching her ear.

'I really thought you'd never talk to me again,' said Christian, an hour later.

The music was more mellow in the dining area of the club. Deep, velvet armchairs and retro lamps suspended just above the low tables aimed for the illusion that you were eating in a friend's lounge room. The table was spread with tapas, and a silver ice bucket at the side held a bottle of Veuve Clicquot.

'Well, you know that I do despise you, darling, and if I were you, I wouldn't turn my back while I'm holding any cutlery,' Seren said, 'but I figure, how long is a girl supposed to hold a grudge?'

'I'm so sorry, Seren. I just panicked at the last minute. The advice I got is that if I represented you and got caught, I would have lost my job. I wouldn't have been able to practise law again.'

'And it's not as if you could have got me off the hook, anyway, Christian. There's a mandatory sentence for that much ice.'

'Exactly, so we would both have gone down.'

'And what would have been the point of that?' she said. Fluttered her eyelids.

'I'm so pleased you're being reasonable about this, darling.' Christian covered her hand with his own. He turned on his megawatt smile.

She gave him hers. 'Oh, I'll be reasonable, darling,' she said, 'but we'll be taking up where we left off. Starting with dinner, at Altitude I think it was.'

He leaned back into the cushions and laughed.

'And next time, sweetie,' she continued, 'when you have a little gift like that for me,' she leaned forwards across the table, giving him something to think about when she left him tonight, 'do make certain that you tell me first.'

29

Monday 8 April, 9 pm

Damien typed a couple of words into his essay, highlighted them and hit delete. Fuck – he had to spend more time on this shit. You couldn't just fake your way through a paper titled *Synthesis of Biologically Active Cyclic Peptides*. He saved the document, closed the file and opened another Free Cell card game. With two fingers, he searched mindlessly for an easy game; his other hand raked through his blond hair. He exhaled noisily. The place stank of cat piss, an after-effect of the last meth cook.

He could just pack up and leave here any time; God knew he had the money now to rent somewhere else. When he'd told Byron earlier that he was having trouble burning through all the cash, he hadn't been joking. He had more than a hundred grand right now sitting in a safe deposit box in Martin Place. What the hell could you *do* with that sort of money? Plenty if it was legal. It would be a good deposit on a house.

But unlaundered drug money? Good luck with that. Damien wasn't stupid. He wasn't going to create any kind of goods or paper trail that could link him to this enterprise should it all go south. And that meant no cars, boats or Rolex watches. He could spend it on holidays – yeah, when? Between the drug shop and uni, he didn't have time to shit unless he took the trip with a textbook and a highlighter pen.

Whitey was churning through a bit on hotels and whores, but Damien couldn't get into it. A couple of times he'd been to Whitey's favourite massage parlour, but on both occasions he'd found himself speaking to the girls about how they'd ended up doing work like that. He couldn't force a girl to have sex with him, and, paid or not, it didn't seem like the staff at Sultan's Court had really had a lot of choice in how they ended up in their so-called chosen profession.

No doubt about it, life was becoming seedier by the day, and he was over it. What had started as an experiment to make some high quality happy pills had become nothing more than an immoral way to make too much money. Damien was a scientist. This wasn't the way he saw the rest of his life going.

His mouth twisted. It felt as though a hand had grown inside his gut and was squeezing it periodically; he just knew – this thing was going to end badly.

And it seemed like this was the beginning of the end. He didn't want Kasem Nader to have any idea who he was. And now this guy wanted to go into some sort of business with them? Nope, not going to happen. Damien would speak to Whitey tonight about shutting up shop. And if Whitey didn't like it, fine. He had plenty of cash, knew the recipes; he could get a new cook and move on with his life. Just not in this house.

Damien closed the card game and tried to get back into his essay.

30

Tuesday 9 April, 12 pm

Having the car was great, except that Jill woke up to find that everyone in the houso block suddenly needed a ride; had an errand they had to do today that couldn't wait. She needn't have worried about them not buying her story that her ex had given it to her, trying to win her back; apparently crap cars were an acceptable make-up present around here. Frankly, she didn't think they gave a toss where she got the car – a car was a car. She fobbed off half of the requests, but was happy to pick Jelly up from his unit in Merrylands and then drop him, Ingrid and Mrs Dang off at Westfield Parramatta, promising to pick them all up again in an hour.

She needed fresh air. She headed over to Parramatta Park, pulled in under a tree and hit the bike track. She ran for thirty minutes and got back to the car, winded. As she bent over the bonnet, she felt as though she was going to heave. You're out of condition, she told herself. The late nights and smoke-choked rooms were taking a toll. At two this morning, sitting on the side of her bed, waiting for it to stop moving, she'd looked down and found a roll of fat creased above her underpants. That had never been there before. But then, she'd never drunk sugar-soaked cask wine every night before either.

At least with the car it would be easier to get away to exercise, she thought. In this world, that was another behaviour that could put a target over your head. Exercise wasn't a high priority for most people around here, although Jill thought it should have been for most of her neighbours.

She took her mobile from the glove box and re-locked the car. She spotted a seat in the sun and made her way over. Although her body still thrummed with heat from the run, the days were shortening, and the shadows held their chill around the clock.

She scrolled through her stored numbers, wondered whether he'd answer. She hit the call button and waited to find out.

'Yep.' He picked up on the first ring.

'Gabriel?'

'Jill?'

'Hi, Gabe. Ah, how've you been?'

'Is that why you called?' Gabriel. Straight to the point.

'No, not really,' she said. 'Are you busy?'

'Designing a website,' he said.

'Is that for work?'

'Nope. I'm between assignments.'

'So what's the website for?' she asked.

A pause. 'Well, I don't know. Just thought I should see whether I could do it.'

As you do. 'Oh, okay,' she said. 'Listen, Gabriel, I wondered whether I could maybe get a little help with something I'm working on now. I wanted to get some advice.'

'Cool. I just put the lamb on. It will be ready about seven-thirty.'

What? She wasn't asking to come to dinner. 'Gabriel, it's twelve o'clock. How long are you going to cook the meat?'

'Seven hours.'

'What?'

'Seven hours. It's seven-hour lamb.'

Jill had forgotten their conversations had mostly been like this. She smiled and shook her head. 'Well, I guess I could come over if that's all right with you. It's probably better than talking over the phone. Thanks,' she said. A thought occurred to her. 'Actually, Gabe, that would be great. I know you've got access to a lot of databases. Would it be all right if I use your computers?'

'You can stay the night.'

Jill took the phone away from her ear, held it in front of her face. Stared at it. Hard. She brought the phone back to her ear.

'No. That's okay.' She spoke slowly, as though communicating with a lunatic.

'You're undercover,' he said. 'It'll be easier.'

Okay, first, how does that follow? And second, 'How do you know that?'

'We shouldn't talk about it over the phone,' said Gabriel, a little sternly, as if *she* had brought it up. 'So, I'll see you at seven.'

I give up, Jill thought. 'Great,' she told Gabriel. 'That would be great.'

'Don't forget your toothbrush,' he said. 'I've only got the one.'

Seren rinsed her hair a third time. Even though they wore paper caps, her hair always smelled like iron after work, the stench of blood and shit permeating everything, even her cropped locks. She towelled it off and stepped out of the shower.

Pay day. Rent day tomorrow.

She stepped into knickers and a bra and then kneeled at the side of her bed. She stretched a hand underneath. Further. Her heart shot to her throat. Where . . . Her fingers finally found the edge of the box and she dragged it towards her.

Just a box. Well, it was the Louboutin shoebox; the nicest box she'd ever seen, and in addition to that, it held her wages. She'd been told that the boss paid cash until you'd been there six months; eighty per cent of people didn't last that long, and that was all good to him.

Seren counted the cash. One more item of clothing was all she'd need to buy for herself, then she figured she could get the rest of her clothes free. After dinner with Christian at Altitude, she planned to hit him up for pressies. After all, he knew he owed her. He just had no idea how much.

Although it was only a Tuesday night, this was going to be tricky. Seren took eighty dollars from the box. That left just the rent. She prayed that Marco wouldn't need money for sport or an excursion this week. She mentally itemised the food she had for the week: potatoes and lettuce, flour, pasta, bread, cheese, eggs, butter, garlic, milk and Vegemite. That was it. So, sandwiches, omelettes, potato bake, pancakes, macaroni and cheese. Breakfast, lunch and dinner until next Tuesday. It would have to do.

She gnawed her lip. Was she seriously going to go and spend this eighty dollars on herself – on new *clothes* for godsakes – when she didn't otherwise have a cent to live on?

And what would eighty dollars get her anyway? Eighty dollars wasn't enough for a haircut in Christian's world; it was definitely nowhere near enough for a whole outfit.

Seren stood, and thought she caught another whiff of chicken blood. Maybe the stuff can soak into your skin, she thought, like a curse, a permanent reminder of the way she made a living – the slaughtered chickens' last revenge.

She made her way back to the shower. She had to come up with something.

31

Tuesday 9 April, evening

'What would be nice with lamb?' Jill asked the man behind the counter of the bottle shop. She had no experience with wine of any quality.

Fifteen minutes later, with the bottle and a block of dark chilli chocolate in hand, Jill pressed the intercom button at Gabriel's unit block in Ryde, located in Sydney's northwest. The buzzer sounded and the door lock clicked without Gabriel asking who it was.

Sloppy, she thought. For a cop. A federal cop at that. She climbed the stairs and knocked on his door.

'That's a piece of shit,' he said, smiling, when he opened it.

'Sorry?' she said. He couldn't mean the wine; it was in a brown paper bag.

'That car,' he said. 'What a shitbox.'

Jill shrugged. 'What are you gonna do? Company car.' She followed the gorgeous smells into the apartment, placed her purchases on the bench and glanced through the kitchen window. While the balcony of this unit overlooked a grove of native eucalypts, the view here, from the sink, was of the visitors' car park. She pulled down the blind, shutting out the sight of her Magna, illuminated brilliantly under a lamppost. Gabriel had obviously seen her drive in.

'Where's your stuff?' he asked.

She flushed. 'Well, I did bring a change of clothes. I left them in the car,' she said, speaking fast. 'It is a bit of a hike back there to Fairfield, and I figured that I should make the most of the time I can spend with your databases.' She moved her eyes in every direction but his.

'I meant your files,' he said.

Jill flushed. Had he been joking about staying over? Fuck! She felt like opening the sliding doors and scaling down the huge tree that mushroomed outside Gabriel's balcony. She couldn't speak.

'Ha! Just shitting you,' he said. 'It's good you're staying. I'm bored. We can get a lot done. I've been looking into this Kasem Nader.'

'What?'

'Nader. We've looked at him before, but only in connection with some of his associates. He's got some cousins hooked up with a group of gun runners from Melbourne and the UK.'

'How do you know Nader's part of my assignment?'

'Superintendent Last,' he said. 'We keep in touch.'

So much for a secret undercover operation, Jill thought. Still, she wasn't terribly disturbed that he was aware of the assignment. She realised that she trusted him. Wow. That brought the number up to around five adults on the face of the earth.

But trusting him didn't mean she felt comfortable.

She peered around the kitchen, looking for something to do, to fiddle with, until they could eat or start work. The bench tops were clear. She tugged at her top, a little unsettled with her uncharacteristic choice of clothing this evening. She wore a sheer black shirt over a black singlet. At the last minute, tired of the pants she'd been wearing most days since she began this assignment, she'd changed out of her jeans into black tights and a snug black mini-skirt.

He watched her discomfiture; then added to it. 'You look like some kind of comic book secret agent,' he said.

Probably she should just go home.

'Not in a bad way,' he continued. 'Just the black clothes with your blonde hair; maybe it's more a ninja look?'

'You having fun?' she said.

'Yeah. A little bit,' he said.

'At least I don't spend time designing a website no one's ever going to use.'

'Have you ever designed a website?'

'No, but . . .'

'There, then.'

Jill laughed. You couldn't win an argument with this guy. She didn't want to right now. 'The lamb smells delicious,' she said.

It was. After they'd eaten, they carried their dishes to the sink and Gabriel began to wash up. His little grey cat, Ten, sat on the windowsill above him, performing her own ablutions. It seemed to be a well-worn routine. There wasn't a lot of room in the kitchen to help out, and they seemed to have it covered, so Jill hoisted herself up to perch on the benchtop. She picked up her glass of wine.

'You okay that I'm sitting up here?' she asked.

'Why wouldn't I be?' he replied, as though she'd asked if it was okay that she turn on a tap. 'So what've you got so far on Nader?'

'Well, it was just word on the street until today,' she said. 'Plenty of people throw his name around like he's a big player. So, I got close to a friend of his. I suppose you'd call him a friend.'

'What's this person's name?'

'Everyone calls him Jelly. I haven't gone too far into his background. He's not a target.'

'Jeremy Simons,' said Gabriel.

'Yeah?'

'Yep. AKA Jelly. Agree he would not be a target; he's had IQ problems since birth.' Gabriel continued soaping pots. 'He came up as an associate when we were looking into Nader.'

'Anyway,' Jill continued, 'I got Jelly to introduce me to Kasem and I was invited over to his house in Merrylands.'

'The Nader house?'

'Yep.'

Gabriel gave a low whistle. 'What was that like?'

'Nothing remarkable,' she said. Except that my frigging *sister* was there. 'No sign of any criminal activity that I could see. Of course, that is his parents' house. They were overseas.' She kicked her shoes off and they dropped to the floor. Ten gave her a haughty look; went back to cleaning. 'So,' she said, 'I had nothing else until I got a little more intel from two small-bit locals. They say they buy their stuff from a couple of blokes named Agassi and Urgill. So, I followed it up and, yesterday, I see these guys at the Station Hotel, shaking hands with Nader.'

'So?'

'So, it looked like a business shake, if you know what I mean.'

'Yeah. Worth a look.'

Gabriel finished the last pot.

'Want a hand?' she asked. Big smile.

He threw a tea towel at her head. 'Let's go,' he said.

They moved into the lounge room and Gabriel took the armchair. Jill dropped down onto the couch. 'Aren't we going to do some searching?' she said.

'I thought first I'd give you what I have on ATS in the area.' ATS. Amphetamine type stimulants. The acronym used by those who worked in this field all the time.

'How do you know so much about amphetamines?' she said.

'I did some work with the ACC,' Gabriel told her.

Phew. The Australian Crime Commission, a statutory body headed up by the Commissioner of the Federal Police. The head honchos. Their brief: to draw together all arms of law enforcement and intelligence-gathering in order to battle organised crime. Jill knew that the ACC were conducting a special intelligence operation into Amphetamine Type Stimulant production in the Asia–Pacific region. She'd guessed that the findings from her current job would get back to these people eventually, but she knew she was just a grunt in the trenches to the ACC.

'So, you want some history first?' he asked.

Jill reached out to the coffee table for the bar of chocolate. She broke off a few squares and threw the rest over to Gabriel. She tucked her feet up underneath her and said, 'Go.'

'Well, believe it or not, ephedrine, the key ingredient in amphetamines, dates back to 2760 BC,' he said. 'It was used in Chinese medicine. Westerners cottoned on to it in the late nineteenth century; and when they got worried they'd run out of the natural supply, they synthesised it. Doctors tried it as a treatment for pretty much everything, but it got its biggest roll-out in World War II. All sides wanted their soldiers to have a little extra firepower.'

Gabriel ate a piece of chocolate. 'Anyway,' he said and then his face contorted in a grimace. He reached for a tissue and wiped his mouth. 'What is *that*?'

'Chilli chocolate,' she said.

'Oh,' he said, and snapped off another piece, popped it into his mouth. Jill smiled.

'When the war ended,' he continued, 'the supply was dumped into the civilian market. Japan was flooded with the stuff and they reckon up to one and a half million Japanese were abusing it. Governments around the world started cracking down, and made it prescription-only, but enough was still leaking out to make it uninteresting to major crime. There was the demand, but plenty of supply, therefore little profit. That was until the seventies, when the rates of amphetamine psychosis around the world were becoming a pain in the arse, and governments got serious.'

He reached for the chocolate and broke off another row. 'Good shit, this,' he said, wiggling his eyebrows. 'Anyway, you're as up to date as me with recent history. When supply dried up, organised crime got involved,' he continued, after swallowing. 'In Australia, it's mostly been about outlaw motorcycle gangs, as you know.'

Gabriel knew that Jill had received a promotion and a lot of cred when she'd been instrumental in shutting down a bikie meth lab in Wollongong.

'And your current corner of the world looks to be quite the hotspot,' he said.

'Yep, plenty to go around out there, that's for sure.'

Gabriel divided the rest of the bottle of red between their glasses. The merlot was spicy and delicious. Jill took a sip, savouring the wine. Her lips tingled from the chilli in the chocolate, and she sank back into the lounge. She felt relaxed for the first time in months.

Gabriel repositioned the lounge cushion behind him so that he could also recline a little. He swung his legs up over one of the arms of the chair and leaned into the crook of the other. 'We're predicting trouble at the moment with our neighbours,' he said. 'The AFP is pretty sure that there's a sizeable clan lab set up in one of the Pacific islands, supplying Australia with a great deal of a few of the precursors used to manufacture ice.'

'The Pacific islands?' said Jill. 'I'm surprised. I mean, I knew that Southeast Asia was a problem . . .'

'Yeah, didn't you hear about that clan lab busted in Fiji a few months back? One of the biggest ever found in the world,' he said. 'Enough precursors in there to pump out five hundred to a thousand kilos of crystal meth a week.'

Jill whistled.

'Yep, a shitload,' he said. 'It would have been devastating over here. We got another big bust in 2006 in Malaysia. It was in a shampoo factory. They could've cooked sixty kilos of ice a day. In each case, Australians were in on the syndicate. The crims know that Aussies are cashed-up and will pay a lot more than users in other parts of Asia, so big traffickers want in on this market. And because a lot of the Pacific islands have shit customs controls, they're perfect for factory-scale production.'

Jill sat up on the couch and put her empty glass on the table. 'It would make sense if there's a big lab in production,' she said. 'I mean, we're pulling in a lot of dealers, but there's just so much out there. Someone's got a big operation going on.' She paused, thinking about the addicts who lived near her. 'It does such a lot of damage,' she said.

'Even in ways you maybe wouldn't necessarily think of,' Gabriel agreed. 'I mean, did you know that the current rise of HIV in Australia is linked to amphetamine use? Everyone's loved-up and ready to party and they're doing it several times a night and never with a condom.'

'It's the little kids that get to me,' Jill said. 'Since I've been undercover I've had to call DoCS at least once a week. The fuckers get so violent when they're coming down off ice, and the kids are in the middle of it all.'

'It's gotta be pretty hard out there, huh?' said Gabriel.

'There's so much screaming,' she said. 'You wouldn't believe the shouting at night. Never fail, there's a major domestic every single night.'

'Yeah? You getting tired of it?'

'Well, I was tired of it the first day,' she said. 'But I'm not ready to stop yet, if that's what you mean. It doesn't feel right to.'

There was silence for a few beats. Jill let her hand drop, and absentmindedly stroked Ten, who punched her whiskery cheeks into her ankles, tail held high.

'You know,' said Gabriel, watching his cat headbutting Jill's hand, 'I worked for a while with a guy who got posted to East Timor. Good bloke. But he came back from deployment and couldn't settle down to things again in Australia. Told me he felt guilty just living life over here while people were suffering back there. In the end, he dropped out of everything. Quit the feds. Went back.'

Ten did some yoga poses on the carpet, angling for a tummy rub. Jill tickled her with a toe. She didn't speak.

'So what's with the drinking?' Gabriel said.

'With the what?'

'You and the wine. That's new.'

'A bottle of wine with dinner. Well, half a bottle. You drank the rest. What's with *your* drinking?'

'Why are you so defensive?'

'Why are you asking me these questions?'

'Just saying what I see. You're the one getting upset about it.'

'I'm not upset!' she said, standing and moving towards the balcony. When she slid open the door the night blasted in with a flurry of wind, billowing the curtains around her. The leaves of the huge tree outside churned and spun; the sound like a thousand rattlesnakes. The draught blew right through her and she hugged her arms around her waist. She slid the door closed, and turned to face Gabriel. 'I have to drink with them,' she said. 'A lot.'

He waited.

'I try to keep the amount down, but now I find myself looking for it.'

'How much?' he said.

'How much do I look for it, or how much am I drinking?'

'Whichever.'

'Well, I guess it's not that much, really,' she said. 'A couple of glasses a night, I guess. I try to go a day a week without any. It's just that I hate to be out of control with anything. I had a problem with alcohol when I was a teenager. I stopped completely, so I worry that even a bit is excessive.'

'Sounds like you're doing great,' he said after a pause.

'Why's that?' She lifted her head, looked him in the eye.

'Well, you are deeply embedded in a prime operational position, and you're doing excellent work, according to your boss,' he said. 'You are definitely out of your comfort zone, and you haven't gone crazy. Nothing terrible has happened.'

Gabriel was one of the very few people who knew that Jill had been kidnapped. She exhaled hard, realising she had been holding her breath.

'Thanks, Gabe,' she said.

'I made vodka affogato for dessert,' he said. 'But I probably shouldn't serve it to a pisspot like you.'

Who'd have thought it? An entire outfit for eighty dollars. Seren didn't imagine that many would consider a single blouse an entire outfit. She didn't either, really. But Christian would not be complaining.

The blouse had been on sale. Back at the unit, she shook it from its tissue-wrap and draped it across her bed. She stood back, arms folded and stared. Did she dare?

It was A-line, pale blue chiffon. The bodice was opaque, the long sleeves cuffed at the wrists, full and sheer. It fell to just past her bottom. It would look amazing with her black pants.

Seren slipped into her outfit for the evening. Underwear. The Blouse. The Shoes. Perfume.

Not a stitch else.

Thank God Marco was staying at Angel's tonight, where there was a DVD player and the biggest movie collection he'd ever seen. Seren wasn't sure that even a ten-year-old could believe a waitress would wear *this* to work.

'So what's your objective with the search?' Gabriel sat at one terminal, waiting for her answer. Jill perched in front of another. The overhead light was not switched on in Gabriel's computer room, but the space glowed regardless. Grey-green monitors waited, thinking quietly; deep-blue LED lights were spattered across every surface, as though flicked from a luminous paint-brush; winking red eyes oversaw everything.

Jill began typing on the keyboard in front of her. 'General fishing expedition,' she said. 'If you could gather up the stuff you guys have already collected on Nader, I'll go wide, find whatever else I can.'

'Sounds like a plan,' he said.

They worked quietly for a while, scanning the databases. Jill had learned on a previous case that she could gain access to more information in Gabriel's workstation than from the standard copshop computers. He had open access to records and systems that were off-limits to even detectives in the regular police force; at least without filing a crapload of paperwork first.

'Don't bother with his sheet,' said Gabriel after a ten-minute silence, other than the quiet clicking of their keyboards. 'I've just sent a condensed version to you. He's a great guy. We've got abduction, extortion, assault, standover charges. Zero for drugs. And in the past two years, it looks like nothing's stuck. There's not anything big pending, either.'

'Let's see if we can change that for him, shall we?' Jill said. She scrolled further through a site in front of her, and then called up another, highlighting text every now and then. 'You know what's interesting?' she said, her eyes still on the screen.

'What?' Gabriel asked.

'Well, I've just been looking at passports. Mr Nader was telling me the truth when he said that his parents are overseas at the moment. Lebanon. Been there once or even twice a year for the past ten, as far as I can see.'

'So?'

'Well, it seems Kasem's not so interested in his relatives.'

'Neither am I.'

'Yeah, but Kasem doesn't mind travelling, generally. It's just that he prefers other destinations.' Jill finally turned away from the screen, swivelled to face Gabriel, who watched her, waiting. 'Our boy's been taking *island* holidays,' she said. 'Papua New Guinea. Short stops, up to a week or so: five times last year, four already this year.'

'Shopping for real estate?' said Gabriel.

'Or a business,' said Jill.

32

Tuesday 9 April, night

Oh fuck. Fuck! Not a great way to begin.

The intruder balled the bleeding hand into a fist and wrapped it in the tea towel – the fabric that was supposed to protect it when punching out the window to Seren's flat.

The right hand, too. Useless now.

Fucken bitch. Another fucken thing to hate her for. Stuck up, pretty little slut.

The intruder stalked through Seren's shadowy unit.

33

Tuesday 9 April, night

Seren scrunched as far into the corner of the cab as possible, her bag covering as much of her bare legs as she could manage. Although she closed her eyes, she could still feel the cabbie gawking at her through his rear-vision mirror. She felt stretched, tissue-paper thin, as though one more set of hungry eyes would stab right through her skin, make her bleed. The attention tonight had been excruciating; feigning indifference to it, exhausting.

But it had worked. Christian had been enthralled the whole night. Her wallet was now full of cab vouchers – I don't ever want you on a bus again, he'd said. And she was to meet him in the city when she finished work tomorrow. Shopping. She'd just come out and told him: it'll be clubbing tomorrow night, and I need some new things. You don't mind, do you, darling?

She leaned her head against the headrest. So tired. She'd catch maybe four hours sleep before getting up for work again. A single tear made it out through her squeezed-shut eyes. She hadn't imagined how hard this would be. Smiling at him, kissing him, his hands on her. She'd once loved him. Now she hated him. She felt like a whore.

But one thing was certain. Seren snapped open her eyes and shot the driver a gaol-house stare that put his eyes back on the road. Cab vouchers and pretty clothes wouldn't buy her. Cocaine, lavish dinners, not even love would do it.

She would sell what she had to offer, but it would cost Christian a million dollars.

34

'Please, keep your voice down, Ms Templeton,' said the real estate agent.

Seren's eyes darted around the small office; people turned their heads away quickly, pretending they hadn't been watching the encounter. She hadn't realised that her voice had carried.

'I'm sorry.' Seren dropped into the chair in front of the woman's desk. 'It's just that this is a nightmare; I haven't had any sleep. I had to report the robbery when I got home and then I had to go to work.' She ran a hand through her hair. 'Look, I promise, if you could just give me another week . . .'

'Well, look,' said the woman behind the desk, 'you know that I'm supposed to report any delay in your rent payment to probation and parole, but if you could get me a copy of your police report, I'm sure I can persuade the owner to give you another week.'

'Thank you so much,' said Seren, struggling not to give in to the tears tightening her throat. 'I'm trying so hard. I can't believe someone would do this to another person.'

The woman averted her eyes for just a moment. Seren realised that the agent was probably thinking that she had a hide: she'd only been out of prison a couple of weeks and here she was complaining about thieves. She stood to leave. At least she now had a little more time to make up the money that had been stolen; support and understanding was not going to happen. That was fine by her. She was used to it.

She hurried back to the unit, reminding herself that she would need to go back to the police station after work tomorrow to request a copy of her statement.

The robbery was just more proof that she had to get her son out of this life. She hadn't wanted to ask Christian for any cash this early in the game, but she was going to have to now. She wouldn't be able to meet two rent payments with next week's wages, and she could not allow probation and parole to hear that she had fallen behind in her rent. She couldn't believe that they would throw her back in gaol for that, but an image of Maria Thomasetti pointing at her release conditions caused her to lengthen her stride.

Tonight Christian would take her to System; the club in which she'd previously seen him doing deals. It would be her first chance to get something recorded – something that would get her out of here forever.

35

Wednesday 10 April, 2.30 pm

'Here, have another one,' said Gabriel.

'No thanks,' Jill said. 'I'm stuffed. Why'd you bring so much?'

Gabriel, in the passenger seat of Jill's Magna, raised his eyebrows in answer. His mouth was full of one of the salad sandwiches he'd made before they left his apartment that morning. He'd seemed to just assume he'd come with her to stake out the Station Hotel. Mondays and Wednesdays, Skye and CK had told her, were the days that their dealers, Agassi and Urgill, did business at the Station. And Monday she'd seen them arrive at the hotel in a black, three-series BMW to do business with Nader. Would Nader show up again today?

She shook her head at Gabriel, who again offered her more food. 'Cashews?' he said.

'I don't want any,' she said, grabbing a handful.

Their car sat behind a van, parked adjacent to the cemetery. Jill noted that the van had been here Monday too; it didn't look

162

as though it had moved. Someone's probably living in it, she thought. The impossible housing prices in Sydney meant that some people lived wherever they could. She'd heard there was quite a demand for shipping containers: dropped onto someone's vacant land for a little rent each week, they could each house a small family.

The afternoon was murky and miserable. The hotel's trade – just a dribble of people in the couple of hours they'd been here – didn't appear to be picking up. A young man leaned against the wall near the entrance to the pub. Jill watched him zip his hoodie a little higher, the wind whipping his wispy blonde fringe into his eyes. The trees in the graveyard next to them rattled and moaned, skeletons shaking.

'Well, lookie here,' said Gabriel. 'Aren't they your boys?'

'That's them,' she said, recognising the BMW.

Gabriel smiled happily, popping cashews into his mouth and munching; he looked like he was at the movies.

The two men stepped out of the car. Agassi, Jill knew from his sheet, was the overweight, balding bloke in the suit pants and brown leather jacket. Urgill was probably around the same age, and would've weighed even more, but his weight was all in his chest and arms. He carried himself like a weightlifter, too, or maybe a boxer.

'Action,' said Gabriel.

Jill wasn't sure what Gabriel meant by that, but she also sensed something was about to happen. Maybe it was the way that Agassi dropped his cigarette, not even half finished. Or it could have been the set of Urgill's jaw, the tense carriage of his shoulders.

They approached the younger, blonde man and some animated conversation looked to be taking place. Agassi was doing the talking; Urgill kept his mouth shut and his fists clenched.

'Is this some kind of shakedown?' said Jill.

Gabriel unwrapped another sandwich, smiling, eyes on the show.

The youth waved his arms a little and vehemently shook his head. Finally, he threw his hands in the air and turned to walk away. Urgill exploded into movement. He grabbed the kid's hand and wrenched it up behind his back, swivelling him around in one action. Nice move, thought Jill. Single-handedly Urgill propelled the kid in the direction of the BMW. They could hear him yelling now, until Agassi stepped in front of him, momentarily blocking their view. The next thing they saw was Agassi aiding the kid to stand upright.

Agassi's eyes swept the street, spotted them, paused. Jill had her head in the map book; Gabriel took another bite of his sandwich, grinned at her.

'Couldn't you put your head down or something?' she hissed.

'Don't worry, he'd be expecting us to be watching; they're putting on a show. They never made us. It's cool.'

The gorillas shoved the young man into the back of the car. Agassi went in after him. Urgill folded himself in behind the wheel.

Jill started the Magna. Although there was clearly a crime in progress, she decided it was not of sufficient urgency to risk blowing her cover. Yet. The blonde boy in the BMW would likely have disagreed with her, but today was not his lucky day.

She waited until the target vehicle was a block ahead before she pulled out to follow them. The black car stayed just under the speed limit. Three cars behind, Jill indicated right to turn with them off Marsden onto the Great Western Highway. A minute later they signalled left.

'Hey,' she exclaimed, 'they're going to –'

'Merrylands,' said Gabriel. 'Told you it's the place to be.'

'This house ever come up on any of your radars?' asked Jill.

'Nope,' said Gabriel. 'Not any that come to mind, anyway.'

The Merrylands street was working class, a poster child for the multicultural melting pot that made up Australia. Jill saw a woman in a hijab bumping a stroller down the front steps of her home. The woman waved hello to her neighbour, an Asian woman wearing a conical sunhat, even on this drizzly afternoon. Jill spotted the Aboriginal flag displayed as a sticker in the front window of the house in front of which she'd stopped; and, cracking and billowing in the wind, on a flagpole in front of the fibro home across the road, was a one-and-a-half-metre-wide Australian flag.

'Who lives here, then?' she wondered aloud.

'The bloke they abducted,' said Gabriel.

'What makes you say that?'

He didn't respond to the question; said instead, 'Interesting that we're in *this* street in Merrylands, don't you think?'

She grunted in reply. She'd been here before: the Nader family home was a few doors down. Was Kasem connected to this kid?

They sat silently for a little while. Jill grew increasingly tense. The young man they'd seen forced into the car was clearly a dolphin. She believed in the saying that the world was divided into dolphins and sharks. This afternoon she had watched two sharks take down a dolphin, and she felt uncomfortable sitting here doing nothing. The fact that she wasn't in there helping him, that she was pretty much using him as bait, made her wonder which species she most resembled. It was a question she'd asked herself many times before.

'Here he comes,' said Gabriel. 'Nader.'

He was right. Jill had told her partner that Kasem had driven her and Jelly to his parents' house in a late-model silver Porsche 911. It purred around the corner and pulled up out the front of the dolphin's house. Jill was aware that the ride probably cost more than the house itself, maybe even more than it and the one next door combined. She would bet her own apartment that the Porsche had been paid for in cash.

Nader got out of the car. Jill held her lower lip between her teeth, watching him uncurl himself from the driver's seat and step into the street.

Gabriel watched her. 'Well, this is fun,' he said.

'We gonna leave this guy in there with the three of them?'

'Your call.'

Jill screwed up her nose. Trust Gabriel not to go all Rambo and decide to storm the house, rescue the victim. She'd have to make the decision, live with the results. She thought through Kasem's record. No murders she knew of.

Blondie, you're on your own for the moment. 'We'll wait,' she said.

Oh my God, oh my God, oh my God. Damien couldn't stop thinking it, over and over. He'd actually tried praying to Jehovah, but he couldn't get his thoughts straight, and had ended up just mindlessly repeating the mantra.

His gut ached. Even with all the bullying he'd copped at school, he didn't think he'd ever actually been punched. He'd definitely *never* been punched like that. Who were these guys? What did they call themselves? He forced himself to try to think what the fat one had said outside the pub. It was a tennis player's name – Agassi, that was it. The other one, who knew? Damien just wanted to stay away from his fists.

From the chair into which they'd pushed him, his eyes shot around his lounge room. Oh shit. They were moving over to the chemicals. Don't touch that, you idiot, he thought, trying not to panic.

He tried to find his voice. 'Ah . . .' Nothing. A beaker clattered to the floor. Oh my God. He tried again. 'Um?'

'WHAT?'

Shit. Agassi. Coming over.

Agassi stood over him, his bulbous gut at eye height. Damien focused on the man's shirt: black with red hibiscus. It seriously did not match the brown leather jacket and grey suit pants. Concentrate, you dickhead, he told himself. He forced himself to look up at the unshaven jowls above him. Agassi exhaled; a waft of sewer air buffeted Damien's face. He coughed, dropped his eyes back to the hibiscus and spoke.

'Ah, the anhydrous ammonia is really unstable at this stage,' he said. 'The reactivity point is pretty low.'

'What?'

'Um, the chemicals,' he tried, 'that your friend is fucking around with. They're pretty volatile.' He looked up. Agassi gave him a watery, red-rimmed stare. 'They could blow the house up.'

Agassi bawled, 'Urgill! You dumb fuck. Stop touching shit!' He turned back to Damien. 'Good little set-up you got here,' he said, and smiled. Some sort of cheese coated his lower teeth.

'You can have it,' said Damien.

'Why would you want to walk away from all this?' Agassi asked. 'Anyway, much as I'd like to, I can't take anything off your hands. You're going to need all your stuff.'

'Look,' said Damien, 'I don't understand what you want from me. If it's cash, I already told you, I can get it for you. If you want E, I've got a hundred tabs you can have right now. There's no ice cooked yet, so I can't help you with that.'

'You know,' Agassi said, looking around the room, 'even though you got all this shit in here, you got no fucking security. Anyone could get in here, man! I've never seen a shop like it. Damn, usually you got at least a couple of motherfuckers with guns on the door. I mean, *look* at your fucken door. You're going to have to get something that can take a bit of hammering. This is a dangerous business you're in, Damien.'

'I have to go to the toilet,' said Damien.

Agassi gave him a sidelong look. 'I'm trying to give you some business advice here, Damo, and all you can tell me is you gotta take a piss?'

'Number two, actually.'

'Yeah? See, here's the thing. I don't believe you. You're gonna try and run or maybe become a hero all of a sudden and bring some kind of weapon out here.'

Damien spoke in a small voice, to his lap, 'I always have to go when I get nervous.'

Urgill crossed the floor. 'Don't know what you're nervous for, son. We haven't done anything to you, yet,' he said.

Damien put his head in his hands. How the hell had he ended up here? He'd skipped a lecture to meet Byron at that pub. Fucking Byron! What was going on? Had he set him up? Damien should be studying. His half-yearly exams would be on him soon. He'd never failed an exam in his life. He was certain that he couldn't feel any more dejected.

And then his front door opened and Kasem Nader walked in.

Damien had been neighbours with this man all his life but they had never spoken. The schoolyard anxiety he'd experienced every time Nader or one of his brothers was nearby was magnified a hundred times. He thought he might cry.

Nader beamed at him and stretched out a hand. 'Stand up, Damien. I don't think we've properly met.'

Damien struggled to his feet. He had to reach out a hand to steady himself when his legs didn't quite agree with the standing up idea. 'Hello,' he said.

Nader looked around the room, taking in the cooking equipment in the corner. 'You know what's great?' he said. 'To see a local boy come good. You're doing real well, I'm told, Damien.'

'Who told you?'

'Well, Damien, you see, I make it my business to always know my competitive environment.' He smiled, reached out a hand and rested it on Damien's shoulder; he stood almost a head taller. 'I've got a running SWOT analysis. I daresay you've heard of SWOT, given you're a uni boy and all. Strengths, Weaknesses, Opportunities, Threats. SWOT. It's a business concept.'

'What's that got to do with me?'

'Well, everything, Damien. We'll start with Threat, shall we? I always think it's best to start there myself. You're selling ice and E on my turf, cutting into my profits. That's a threat to my business, you see,' he said, gestering to the cooking equipment. 'And that would be a Weakness for me. And I hate weakness.' Nader gave Damien's shoulder a squeeze so hard that his knees buckled again. He raised his hand to the shoulder being gripped and moaned.

'Sorry, brother.' Nader released his grip and gave Damien a

cuff on the arm. 'Just back from the gym. I'm a little pumped up. Do you work out?' He clutched Damien's bicep, giving it a press. Frowned. 'Never mind. You're a uni boy. You exercise that brain of yours.'

Damien felt a little faint. His mother had never really been a touchy-feely kind of person, and to date he'd not had a lot of physical contact with anyone at all. Nader handled him almost intimately, as though he really was his brother. Big problem there. Since they were old enough to walk, Damien had been watching the Nader brothers nearly kill each other in knockdown brawls in the street.

'Anyway,' said Nader, 'that brings us to the Opportunity part of the SWOT. You, Damien, are apparently an excellent cook. I like excellence in my business, and I propose a merger.' He grinned widely.

Damien stared at the pockmarked carpet. What with Whitey traipsing in with grotty feet all the time, and Byron dropping cigarette ash, the floor coverings were filthy, and he doubted he'd get his bond back on this place. This was his chance to get out of all of this.

'Look, Kasem,' he said, 'thanks for your offer, but I'd already made up my mind that I was getting out of this business completely. I never wanted it to get this far at all. I'm really serious about my studies. I'm thinking about going into medical research.' He lifted his eyes from the ground. 'So you see, I'm no threat at all. Byron told me that you were interested in joining us, but you can actually have it. The whole thing. As is, move in and take the lot.'

Kasem smiled and appeared to think it over. He spoke in a considered tone. 'You see, Damien, that's where we go back to the SWOT. You've forgotten all about the first category. Strength. This thing here,' – he swept his hand around, past Agassi and Urgill – 'this is what you call a hostile takeover. Now, we can do this real friendly; we can actually be best mates. Or we can do it another way. Any way you like it, Damo, but you're now my cook. You work for me. And I'm the boss.' He gave Damien's arm another cuff. 'You'll be right, brother,' he said. 'I'm a pretty good employer. Shit, you'll get good wages, and I'll even give you study leave.'

He put his hand back on Damien's shoulder, looked him in the eye. 'I like having educated staff,' he said. 'We're going to get on fine, uni boy.'

'Well, I don't see any blood,' said Gabriel.

Jill gave him a hard glance, and turned back quickly to watch Nader, Agassi and Urgill stroll from the blonde youth's house. She kept the rim of her cap angled low.

'What do you reckon they did to him?' she said.

'Whatever they wanted,' he replied. 'Those fuckers could've been playing one-handed strip poker and still have given that kid the flogging of his life without getting up from the game.'

Jill rubbed balled fists up and down her jeans. Part of her wanted to go inside and make sure the kid was okay. The other part thought it would be better to leave and get some intel before they approached him. He could prove to be a very useful link to Nader if they went in with their eyes open. The dolphin–shark thing again, she thought. As a cop, it probably wasn't a bad thing to be a bit of each.

She stared at Gabriel. He raised his eyebrows.

She cracked the car door. 'Let's go, then,' she said.

They walked quickly and quietly up the street, and approached the home by crossing the lawn, hugging close to the house so as not to be seen from inside. It was difficult to know what they'd find in there. Jill saw Gabriel reflexively check the firearm in the holster under his arm. She'd done the same thing with the .45 at her ankle before leaving the car.

He stopped, and she saw him peek through the window. He flattened himself against the siding, and whispered, 'He's in there. He looks okay. But be very careful, Jill. Don't touch anything and be ready to leave fast if we need to.' He paused. 'It's a clan lab.'

She could smell it now. Meth had been cooked here. She gave

Gabriel a worried look. They should definitely call for back-up. They needed a Hazmat team out here. Plenty of cops had been injured by toxic fumes or explosions in these places.

Gabriel shrugged. 'On your go,' he said.

Jill took a deep breath and moved around Gabriel to enter the house ahead of him. She tried the door. And walked in.

36

Wednesday 10 April, night

The rain thrummed against the balcony doors; Darling Harbour showered at the same time as Christian. Seren stared through the juicy colours of the wet twilight; with her eyes unfocused, the scene ran together like water drizzled into a paintbox.

She leaned her forehead against the glass, peering down at her reflection, at the gorgeous new underwear purchased this afternoon by her lover. Three years ago, this moment would have been perfect. Today, she knew that it was as flimsy as the French lace of her knickers. At any time, all of this could evaporate and she could be sharing a cell with semi-naked women looking to kill each other. Or worse, she might be finally beaten into submission by a man who had decided that she was his bitch, and that she'd better get used to it. Like her mother.

But much worse than all of that would be Marco living through it. When Marco was laughing, when he'd just woken up, when he ate cereal, Seren saw the light. It kept her going. It was light she'd seen in his eyes when they put him on her chest as a tiny baby; when he'd first tasted a strawberry; when he'd found that he could talk and stand up by himself. She'd seen the light in other children fade to a glimmer, a dull pulse, and finally, a staggering flicker, before blinking out forever. She'd seen kids with eyes as old as a digger. Seen much too much; their eyes told you that there was nothing they were going to live to see that would make all right what had already come to pass.

Every day since she'd got out, she'd searched her son's eyes for the light. It hid, crouched, waiting, marking time, trusting that she would pull them through. And she would pull them through.

Seren snapped the garter of her suspenders and straightened at the window. She sauntered towards the master bedroom, steam leaking from the ensuite. She began to dress in the clothes purchased this afternoon by Christian. The man who had taken her away from Marco for three *hundred* and forty-eight days.

She dressed with particular care.

Seren watched the writhing press on the dance floor. Maybe she'd stayed away from these places because she'd never learned to dance like that, she considered. She'd been partying since twelve, but never in places like this.

Without any particular pride or happiness, she knew that she looked better than any other girl in System. Every man told her that, without speaking, as soon as she'd walked in. But it was the women who confirmed it. She copped three types of looks from the other girls; the most common, hate. The message? Come near my man tonight and I'll tear your eyes from your head. Usually, these women had had a few; they'd have wanted to if they'd known where Seren had spent the last year. The next most common stare was neutral. A kind of I-don't-even-notice-you-there Teflon glance that slid across her body as though she were nothing. She knew that the studied nonchalance was well-rehearsed, and it had probably always stabbed deeply at the other girls in high school. The third look was from the desperate, or particularly enterprising. They knew they had been beaten, and figured that maybe if they could hook their claws into her coattails they could soar up with her into the heavens they thought she occupied.

As she watched the beautiful people of Sydney throb to the beat of the DJ du jour, the irony of her situation shuddered to life with an image: Tready masturbating into her bra in the elevator of her unit block. The picture quickly evaporated in the lights.

Where the hell had Christian gone? She manoeuvred through the crush to find him holding court in a dim corner booth. The low table in front of the group was covered in glasses holding multicoloured drinks. All of the seats were taken. Two men made out on one side of the nook. Seren had seen the couple here before with Christian. Two near-naked girls sitting next to Christian spotted her crossing the floor towards them, and with their eyes clearly told her to piss off. Instead, when she reached them, she wriggled between them and the table to plonk herself onto Christian's lap. The hem of her teensy black dress rose up and she left it there, suspenders and long legs on show.

'God! Make yourself comfortable!' growled one of the girls.

'How rude!' muttered the other.

Christian laughed and kissed her. His eyes glittered. 'You want to dance?' he asked.

'No, I want to party. I'll have whatever you're having,' she told him.

He raised his hand and within moments, a uniformed boy materialised.

'We'll have a bottle of tequila,' he said. 'Some lemon, salt, shot glasses. And can you clear some of this shit away?' He gestured to the table.

With her arm hooked around Christian's neck, Seren leaned backwards, and bent her head down to the face of the redhead next to them. She whispered, 'I think he means you, sweetie.' She gave the woman her back again and snuggled into Christian. 'What else have you got for me, baby?'

He locked eyes with her and reached into his jacket pocket. The left pocket, Seren, she mentally noted.

'Open wide,' he said, something small between his fingers.

Oh fuck. She had just wanted to know what he was carrying tonight. She didn't want to take it! She couldn't take it – she had a urine test at P&P after work tomorrow. Christian's eyes had not left hers.

'Not a whole one, darling,' she said. 'You know I'm not used to it.' She prised her fingers between his thumb and forefinger and removed the little white tablet. 'Ooh, lovely,' she said, checking out the little tiara figure stamped on the front. Her heart thudded.

Still curled into Christian's body, she snapped the tablet between her fingers, and made a show of dropping half into the little clutch purse at her feet; instead, she deliberately missed the purse and ground the pill fragment to dust under her stiletto. She swivelled on his lap to find him staring at her.

'Here. You can take it with my drink,' he said.

Fucking hell. Seren gave Christian a luscious smile and licked her finger, leaving the half tablet there on the tip of her tongue. She turned and faced the others at the table. The redhead had been sipping a luminous lime concoction from a tall glass and now Seren picked the drink. She took a deep sip. 'Mmm, yummy.' she said.

'*Thank* you!' the redhead said, snatching her glass back.

Seren beamed at her. ''Scuse me again, everyone, for just a mo. Be right back.' Once again she traversed the dance floor; this time blood rushing in her ears. She found the ladies and pushed past the gaggle of girls at the sink, all caking on more make-up. She slammed the cubicle door and bent face first over the toilet, thrusting her fingers down her throat. Please God let it come out. She heaved.

When she saw the tiny white pill swimming in a pool of fluoro green in the bowl, Seren began to cry. She turned and sat on the toilet, holding her hand in front of her, her fingers dripping in vomit and saliva.

'You know you can get help for that, honey.' The voice came from the next cubicle. 'You should see a counsellor or something. Bulimia is a serious illness.'

Seren wiped her hand on some paper and waited for the toilet next door to flush. She waited some more. Finally, she rose and made her way to the sink to splash her face and rinse out her mouth. She ignored the two women pretending not to stare and faced herself in the mirror.

Go and get that fucker, she told herself.

Back at the table, the redhead had gotten too close to Christian again. Seren plopped down between them.

'I'd like five please,' the girl said to Christian, glowering. 'To go.' She stood to leave, tugging at her friend's arm, encouraging her to also rise.

Seren almost snorted in frustration. She was too close to record this drug deal safely. She reached under her feet for her bag while Christian stood and moved to say goodbye to his friends, to give them their parting gifts. She turned the camera on, but missed the whole transaction.

'Actually,' she said, 'I do feel like dancing now, Christian.' Seren rose from the chair and smoothed her dress. She stood a foot taller than Redhead, who quickly made her exit.

She dragged Christian to the dance floor. Within moments, a crowd of people surrounded them. Seren moved closer to her man.

Weary, but satisfied, Seren stepped out of the cab and walked quickly towards her unit block. She'd not yet heard whether Tready was out of hospital, and although she was dubious that he'd be in the mood to tangle again so soon, she didn't want to be out here any longer than she had to be. Especially tonight: Christian had given her enough money to cover her rent and she had to get it inside; she couldn't afford to lose it again.

Leaving the lift on Angel's floor, she smiled. A couple more nights like this one, and she should have enough evidence to convince Christian that he had to pay up, and then she and Marco could get out of here forever. She'd already thought about asking Angel to move with them. She'd easily have enough money to cover rent for a place for her too.

Thank goodness for Angel, she thought, making her way along the balcony that led to her door. It had turned out to be a lot more convenient to have Marco fall asleep in Angel's unit, and then bundle him back to his own bed when she arrived home. It was awful spending all this time away from him when she'd ached for so long to be near him. Despite her impatience to finalise her plans to blackmail Christian, she determined to stay home tomorrow night and spend time with Marco.

A small frown appeared as she made her way along the balcony. The light was on in Angel's unit. It's after one, she thought. I hope Marco hasn't kept Angel up this late. She tapped quietly at the door. When Angel opened it, Seren could see that she'd been crying.

'Angel, what's wrong?' Seren moved around her, into the small unit. Marco wasn't curled up on the lounge. 'Where's Marco?'

Angel hid her face in her hands. 'I tried to stop them, Seren,' she said.

'Who? What are you talking about? Marco!' Seren moved through the unit. 'Oh my God, Angel! Where's Marco?'

'DoCS took him, Seren.'

'What are you *talking* about?'

'Your P&P officer, Maria Thomasetti. She came here with this bitch from DoCS. Someone must've told them Marco was down here with me.'

'What's wrong with him being here? There's nothing wrong with that!' Seren stared around the room wildly, and then turned to face Angel. 'Why did they take him?'

'Thomasetti said that you were behind in your rent and that was a breach of your parole. She said they might lock you up tomorrow.' She glanced at her watch. 'Well, today. They said that Marco would stay with them until they knew whether you had to go back inside. I'm so sorry, Seren. I couldn't stop them.'

Seren put her face in her hands and screamed.

37

Thursday 11 April, 2 pm

Damien moaned on the toilet. He hadn't moved from the bathroom since the cops had left his house. He hadn't been joking when he'd told Agassi that stress sent him straight to the toilet. He'd had a lot of time to think in here, and he'd come up with a few possible explanations as to why this was happening to him.

The main one had to do with the curses.

Probably the main reason he hadn't been able to get into the whole Jehovah's Witness thing, he considered now, was his mum's double standards. When the God Squad were around, she was all sweetness and light, but if no one was there to see her, she would give you a flogging with anything that came to hand. He thought he had been more frightened of her words, though. Since he'd been old enough to understand, and probably before, she'd been placing curses upon him, damning him to the devil to burn for anything naughty he'd done. That's what's going on, he realised now. One of those curses. That had to be it.

He tried to clear his head and think more rationally; to sum up his situation. I'm a drug manufacturer working for a gangster. Great. Even better, I am now also supposed to spy on this gangster and report to a nark and the Feds. If I fuck around with Kasem Nader, he'll kill me. If I don't do what the cops ask they'll lock me up. And if I don't pass my half-yearlies, I won't get into Honours next year. *And* I've got a class presentation due next week.

Damien's stomach insisted that he evacuate his bowels. Problem was, that process had finished twenty minutes ago, and there was nothing left with which to oblige.

He bent double on the bowl, moaning in agony.

'Well, that went well,' said Gabriel. 'Our own little double agent. Fun.'

'You reckon he's going to be okay?' asked Jill.

They sat in Gabriel's car beside the park near Merrylands McDonald's. Her Magna waited in the spot next to them. Jill had another half hour before she had to be back to pick up Ingrid and Mrs Dang.

'Well, that depends on what you mean by okay,' he said. 'I think you're going to get enough on Nader to put him away for a long time, so from that perspective, Damien will be great. The thing about doubling someone is that the more you make them do, the deeper in they get, and then you can make them do even more again.' Gabriel stretched his neck from side to side and turned to face her. 'But the suicide rate's above average.'

Jill gave him a hard look.

'I'm kidding,' he said. 'We'll look after him.'

'I'm thinking that I'll arrange to meet him for debriefs at his uni,' she said. 'I don't want Nader to see me with Damien. I guess there would be nothing really wrong with Damien knowing someone like me – as Krystal Peters – but we don't need to complicate this any further.'

'Agreed.'

Jill took her time with her next comments. She realised that she was growing used to having Gabriel to rely upon again and she really wanted him involved in this case. More than that, she wanted to spend time with him generally, and she had spent a good deal of last night wondering why. Was she just lonely for close contact after three months of false and potentially treacherous relationships?

'I wanted to thank you for helping me out with this, Gabe,' she said.

'You already did.'

'Yeah, I know. It's just that you've been so great in helping me set all this up. I just wish there was some way we could formalise it, so we could work this Nader thing together.'

'Well, I was meaning to say something about that.'

She did a double take. Waited.

'I was hoping you wouldn't mind,' he said. 'When I got home yesterday, I called Last and asked him to get me written into it.'

'What'd he say?'

'He's hooking it up.'

Jill did a mental fist pump. 'So how will that work?' she asked.

'I'm not going to go undercover with you,' he said. 'I'd get made as a cop. It takes me a while to get into that zone; your people would be able to tell that I'm not one of you guys. We'll just keep it as it is. We'll meet, do this kind of thing. I'll stay in the loop with you and Damien.'

'That's great,' she said, smiling.

'There should be a Fed connection in here. It could be that Nader's just a blow-arse and he's spinning shit to Damien about having a big operation. But it could be real and maybe he's linked in with others that we can round up with him. The Pacific islands thing also needs to be followed up. Why's he been visiting? Could be that he likes a good suntan, or little brown boys; but on the other hand it could be that he's importing precursor chemicals.'

'Okay, sounds good,' she said. 'I talked to Last too, last night. He didn't say a word about you, but I did get him to okay me buying a private mobile phone to use only to take Damien's calls. I don't want Damien calling me on my work phone; I don't want to get confused about whether I'm Krystal or Jill, and I want to know immediately if it's him when he calls.'

'Good thinking.'

They watched a cyclist fly by. 'What's that, his fifth lap?' said Gabriel.

'Sixth,' she said. 'Listen, I was thinking last night about what I'd say if anyone from the block saw us here together.' Her cheeks felt suddenly hot. She reached out and started to pick at the registration sticker on Gabriel's windscreen. 'I kind of told Ingrid and some others that I was seeing my boyfriend again. So we can use that.'

'So, I'm your boyfriend?'

'Well, I know you're not coming in undercover. I know we're not going to deliberately get noticed or anything, I just figured that if anyone saw us . . . And also I have to explain why I'm away from the unit block more than usual. You have to talk a lot about stuff with these people. They want to know everything.' She was rambling. Was she rambling?

'So if we get noticed, should we kiss?' Gabe suggested, with a grin. 'Maybe we should role play a little.'

'Would you stop fucking around, Delahunt?'

'I'm just thinking maybe we should practise, that's all. I mean, we've got to look authentic if someone sees us. We're talking about some heavy people here.'

'I have to get back to the shops,' she said. 'I'll set a time to meet when Damien calls in. I'll get back to you.' She pushed the door open, stuck one foot out.

'Okay, darling, we'll talk soon then. I love you.'

'Idiot,' she said, and ducked her head to hide her smile.

38

Thursday 11 April, 2.30 pm

Seren thrummed her fingers against her thigh and waited. Hurry up and wait. She'd heard that war veterans described deployment that way. Lots and lots of waiting for the action; as a recent ex-con, she felt she could relate.

She'd been in this room twice now, and already she could close her eyes and describe every feature. Diarrhoea-coloured walls and industrial carpets, the latter always some hideous classroom-blue, or synthetic-grass-green. These places all looked the same. She could've been waiting in the emergency department of St Vincent's Hospital, the visitors' reception at Silverwater gaol or her local medical centre. How did they get these places so dispirit-ing? Was there some sort of secret awards ceremony, where designers could submit their best effort at creating urban depres-sion? If there was, she could nominate a good MC. *Welcome everybody, if you could please take your seats, I'd like to intro-duce your host for the evening, Ms Maria Thomasetti!*

'Seren Templeton.' Flat, dead-fish voice.

Seren opened her eyes and looked over at the people in the cage.

'Yo,' she said.

Muster. She was still in gaol, and now her son was in lock-up too. You're a total fuck-up, Templeton, she told herself, walking over to meet her probation and parole officer.

'You realise, Ms Templeton,' said Maria Thomasetti, 'that I could be transporting you back to Silverwater right now?'

'Yes, Ms Thomasetti, I do. And I'm eternally grateful that you have chosen to give me a pass, given that I managed to pay my rent first thing this morning.'

'Yes, well, there's that,' said Thomasetti. 'Another P&P might have given you a hard time about how you could come up with a hundred and ninety-five dollars at such short notice, when all of your cash was supposed to have been stolen from your flat.'

'So good of you not to do so,' said Seren. 'Of course, another P&P might have at least found out what was going on before handing someone's kid over to DoCS.'

Thomasetti coughed.

'And I'm curious,' said Seren. 'Did Fiona from the real estate call you? It's just that I did explain to her that I'd get her the rent this morning.'

Maria Thomasetti studied a crease in her skirt; she smoothed her chubby palm across it, and then looked up. 'Why no, Ms Templeton. I'm your P&P. I told you that I'd look after you. *I* called Fiona to make sure that you were keeping up to your obligations. I've got a job to do – and I'm doing it. She told me that things had gone awry, and, of course, I had to take action. You'll find that I do things like that pretty swiftly around here.'

'Oh, I can see that.' Seren smiled sweetly across at the woman who could lock her up with Crash and Little Kim for the next hundred days. 'It's obvious you're more than up to your job.

But you'll excuse me if I'm in a hurry to piss into your cup? It's just that I need to go and pick up my child from DoCS.'

I guess it makes sense, Seren thought, sitting in yet another waiting room. Why wouldn't they put a DoCS office in the middle of a suburban shopping centre? Go to where the people are. That way, you can visit your kid and pop into Franklins to pick up some Coke and Doritos at the same time.

She clutched her arms to her chest, pretending that she was holding Marco in her lap. She didn't mind at all what Maria Thomasetti thought of her, and she couldn't care less about what the woman behind this desk was thinking. What Christian felt about her would matter not one iota in a couple of weeks from now. Truth be told, she could even live with it if Angel was disappointed in her. No, when Seren stared into someone's face, there was only one person whose appraisal mattered to her: a ten-year-old's.

The door opened and Marco emerged with his school backpack over one shoulder, his eyes on the floor.

She rushed forwards. 'Baby, I'm so sorry! Come on, let's get out of here,' she said.

Marco sidestepped every attempt she made to touch him and she decided not to push it. Of course he was furious at her, but not as angry as she was with herself. How could she keep hurting this little boy when she would do anything to make him happy?

'I thought maybe we could pick up some yummy things and go back home for a feast,' she said. 'Or maybe we could go to see a movie?'

They stopped outside the DoCS offices, opposite a chicken shop. Marco just stood there.

'You don't have to worry about the money,' she said. 'I got a loan from a friend. We'll be fine until payday next week.'

Marco stepped backwards to allow a woman pushing a trolley to roll past them.

'So, what'll it be, honey? Movies?' she said.

When he didn't answer again, Seren knew she'd have to try something different. The woman behind the counter in the takeaway shop openly stared; this was her afternoon's entertainment. Seren imagined she'd witnessed plenty of drama in this food court.

'Marco, baby, I'm really so sorry,' she tried again. 'I don't know what they told you in there. They were going to lock me up because I didn't pay the rent, but what was I supposed to do? We'd been robbed! I can't believe they took you. I got the rent to them first thing this morning. That's why I'm working so hard, baby, to try to keep this all together. It's not going to be much longer; things will be better soon, I promise.'

Seren thought she saw her son's shoulders relax a little. She held her breath, praying he was coming around, would forgive her just one more time. Her knotted stomach loosened a little in hope when he raised his eyes to finally meet hers.

'I just want to get to school,' he said. 'I've got to get some sort of education. I don't want to end up some dumb slut like you.'

39

Thursday 11 April, night

'So, what'd *you* get up to today, Krystal?' Ingrid asked.

Jill glanced over from the stove, where she was helping Jelly make dessert. She pushed his hand away from the saucepan. Again. 'I saw Gabriel,' she answered.

Ingrid blew smoke. She had no problem wearing her pyjamas when she had houseguests. In fact, unless she had to run an errand, Jill had noticed that it was her standard attire. Ingrid sat at her kitchen table, playing solitaire while Mrs Dang watched. Every now and then, Mrs Dang would crow with laughter and slap at the cards, scattering them, bawling out something unintelligible. Ingrid would re-deal patiently, call her neighbour a silly old bat or somesuch, and take another sip from the mug next to her.

'I fucken *told* ya!' said Ingrid. 'I told everyone you were gonna take him back. Didn't I tell you that, Mrs Dang?'

Mrs Dang tried to smack again at the cards; she threw her head back in hysterics when Ingrid blocked her with an arm.

'So when do we get to meet him, Krystal?' asked Ingrid.

'Yeah,' said Jelly. 'Who are we talking about?'

'Gabriel,' said Ingrid. 'Krystal's boyfriend.'

'SHUT UP!' bellowed Jelly.

'What's *your* fucken problem, Jelly?' screeched Ingrid.

This is another thing about this undercover job, thought Jill. It's so bloody loud. It's ten o'clock on a Thursday night, and here I am making honeycomb with an alcoholic, a schizophrenic and a hundred-plus-kilo man with the mind of an eight-year-old.

'Look,' she said to Jelly. 'This is the important step.' She added bi-carb soda to the concoction in the pot. 'You've got to stay alert, Jelly. You've got to tell me when it all starts to bubble up. Reaaaady – look!' The mixture in the saucepan fizzed and seethed; it frothed to the top of the pan faster than she had anticipated. She whipped it from the stove just before it spilled over.

Jelly cavorted madly around the kitchen, causing a mixing bowl to clatter to the ground. 'Honeycomb! Honeycomb!' he shouted.

Jill transferred the caramel-coloured sludge to a tray she'd purchased that morning for this purpose. 'It's got to go in the fridge now,' she said.

'We don't need the fridge!' Jelly held a spoon ready.

She had prepared for this eventuality. 'Okay, okay,' she said. 'But just stand back, Jelly. We can cool it faster, but it won't taste the same.' She grabbed a saucer from Ingrid's cupboard and dolloped a big spoon of honeycomb into the centre. She smeared it across the plate and turned to the freezer, blocking Jelly and his spoon with her body. 'Three minutes,' she said, 'that's all.'

'Oh, come *on*,' said Jelly, jogging from foot to foot.

'What kind of a name is Gabriel, anyway?' asked Ingrid.

'He's an angel,' said Mrs Dang. 'Archangel Gabriel,' she said. 'He watches over all of us. He's a soldier. He came to me last night. He told me he found my cat.' She cupped her hands together and made a rocking motion; tears sprang to her eyes. 'My little baby, my little kitsy, kipsy-cat. Archangel Gabriel will get my cat back from the government.'

'An angel, eh?' said Ingrid. 'I don't know about that. Seems to me that there ain't many angels that go around beating up women.'

Jelly hurled his spoon at a cupboard door. The crack was like a gunshot. 'WHO FUCKING DID IT?' he hollered.

'Jelly! Jelly. It's okay, it's okay. No one hurt anyone,' Jill picked the spoon up and moved to Jelly's side, stretching her arm around his huge shoulders to hold him close. 'Shh,' she said. 'You want to wake the little baby next door? You know he's only been home from the hospital two days.'

Jelly shuffled his feet. 'Sorry,' he said. 'I don't like Archangel Gabriel.'

'That's okay, Jelly,' said Jill. 'What's really important is whether or not you like honeycomb.' The bell sounded on the microwave and Jill pulled out a bowl of melted chocolate. She opened the freezer and pressed her finger into the honeycomb mixture. It was set. Just. She drizzled the liquid chocolate over the plate and handed Jelly his spoon.

'Tell me what you think,' she said.

40

Friday 12 April, 11 am

Seren made her way through the blood-sloshed gutting hall to her supervisor's office, her tiny camera tucked into her pocket. It was insurance. It's only a matter of time until this guy tries it on, she thought. Or maybe he's just gonna give me some more hell about having yesterday off. She sighed. She was definitely not in the mood for either option today. Marco hadn't said anything to her for the rest of the day, and that was fine by her after the words he *had* said at the supermarket. God, is that really what he thinks of me, she wondered.

She stepped into the office. Zeko sat behind the desk he was entitled to use when on duty. His thinning hair, translucent and moist, was carefully positioned over his bald spot, as though he'd just found a moment to comb it, slick it down.

'Please, have a seat, Seren,' he said.

She sat waiting, her hands in her lap. What would it be this time?

'It's your son,' he said.

When she lurched to her feet her chair toppled backwards and crashed to the floor. 'What?' she said.

'Hey, hey, hey,' said Zeko, waving his hands. 'Your son, he is all right. He's all right, now. Shh. Sit down, sit down.'

Seren slammed hands flat on the desk. 'What's going on?' she said.

'Your son's school called here. There's been some trouble. Your boy's in trouble.'

'What happened?' she demanded. 'Would you just tell me what's happened?'

'They would not tell me. I told them you were working and that I was your good friend, but they would not tell me. They only said he is all right and he has been bad, and would you come to get him.'

Seren thought quickly and turned to leave the room. She'd just grab her things and catch a cab over there.

'Wait, Seren.'

She turned back to Zeko, her brow creased.

'I think you should let me go to get your son,' said Zeko.

'You?' she said.

'I can go and pick him up in my car and bring him back here before the boss notices. You can call the school and tell them I am on my way. I can drive you and your son home when the shift finishes.'

'I don't think so.' She again moved to leave. 'Thanks, anyway,' she said.

'Seren, I think you had better think more carefully about what you do,' he said.

'What are you talking about?' Would he just bloody shut up? She needed to get over there.

'This will be your second day away from work. You cannot afford this. I am your supervisor. I can be your good friend. You don't want there to be a mark on your record.'

'Thanks, Zeko,' she said, meeting his eye. 'But I need to go and get him myself. You'll have to do whatever you think is right about my record.'

He moved around the desk. With his step forward, she took one back.

'I got you a good job here in D Squad, didn't I?' he said. 'I think you owe me a little bit more. I think you should try harder to be friends with me.'

'What do you want?'

'You don't have to be so mean to me. This would be a start.'

'And . . .'

'And I would like to maybe meet with you in here each day, for a progress meeting. I think we should keep up to date with your training, make sure you are settling in with me.'

'What would we do in here?' she said.

'You will like what we do in here, Seren. Very much. All the girls do. They call me the rooster, the cock. I'm going to be reviewing your performance just as I have for every girl here on my team. To work here on my floor all girls must give satisfactory performance to the cock.' He grabbed at his crotch. 'Come a little closer, Seren. I'll show you why you will enjoy our meetings.'

'I can't, Zeko. I have to go. We'll have to talk about this later.'

Zeko angled his head to the side, placed his hands on his hips. 'Yes, Seren,' he said. 'We will have to talk about this later. With that, I agree with you. We can talk about this while you're sucking my balls. Now go and get your stupid bloody brat.'

41

Friday 12 April, 11 am

Bluesy kind of weather again, lamented Jill, peering through the tiny bathroom window in her unit. Of course, any kind of weather was going to be depressing viewed from here. The cheerless courtyard, surrounded by unit blocks like this one, rarely captured any sunlight; it was as though even the sun wouldn't hang around here if it didn't have to. A queasy-looking tree drooped in a caged garden bed in the middle of the asphalt. Fed on cigarette butts, piss from the drunks and screams in the night, the tree looked to have given up, waiting to die. Jill knew that many of the residents who woke to see it each morning felt the same way.

Autumn blasted frost into Jill's soul at the best of times. Even the glow of a brilliant Maroubra autumn felt poignant, painful, like happy times were on the way out, leaving for good. The problem was that autumn dragged winter along after it. Winter: the anniversary season of being kidnapped as a twelve-year-old. The cold always snapped her memories of being raped and tortured into sharp focus.

192

Flicking the thoughts away, she decided she'd bling it up today; attempt to simulate cheer where there was none. A pink velour tracksuit and push-up bra should do it. She grinned as she pulled on the pants: spray-on, sitting just below her navel, with a little diamante appliqué of a star stuck on the hip. You *are* a star, Krystal Peters, she told herself, smudging extra kohl around her lashes and maxing out the mascara. It surprised her to be kind of having fun with this. She had never dressed this way in her life, had always been careful to play down her femininity, feeling frightened or aggressive when drawing male attention.

And she rarely wore her blonde locks down from a tight ponytail. Now she bent her head forward and backcombed her hair, teasing it at the crown to give it height. She flicked it back in front of the mirror. Whoops – she smoothed it down a tad. A little less porn queen. She smirked at herself, kind of shocked by the girl who stared back at her. She looked as though she could be in a magazine shoot. She looked like her sister. Like Cassie.

Jill shrugged into her jacket, her smile suddenly gone. It was time to get to work.

She decided that she'd try to get some more dirt on Agassi, Urgill and Nader if she could. Damien could have this first day off. She would let him adjust to his new life a little and then have him report in tomorrow.

She knocked on Ingrid's door, and waited a while. Nothing. Could be too early for her. Before two was pretty much too early for Ingrid.

Jill headed down to the ground, but left the car where it was for the first time since Last had delivered it to her. She'd done pretty well the last few months on foot patrol. You learned a lot when no one was going anywhere in a hurry.

She stopped in at McDonald's and bought a coffee. There was no one of interest in there so she headed over to Orbit.

'Krystal!' Jelly put his head down and ran straight for her. Oh fuck. Ooof.

'Jelly,' she said, winded. 'We've gotta work on your greetings.'

'I told Kasem about the honeycomb. He wants some,' said Jelly.

Kasem? Jill glanced around Jelly's massive shoulder and saw Nader headed in their direction.

'Hey there, little hoodlum,' said Nader, dropping his arm around Jelly's shoulder and facing Jill. Nader and Jelly stood at the same height, with similar shoulder spans, but the similarities ended there. Jelly's body was refrigerator-shaped all over, while Nader appeared to have spent more than a bit of time in the gym.

'Hi, yourself,' she said.

'I heard you're a good cook,' he said.

I heard you just got a new one, Jill thought. 'It's only honey-comb,' she told him. 'With chocolate poured all over it. Lollies. We are talking about Jelly, here.'

He laughed. 'True. You could pour chocolate over snails and Jelly would call you a good cook.'

'But I am a good cook,' she said.

He stepped a little closer. 'Oh, I bet you are, Krystal. Arse-kicker by day; chef by night. I, for one, want to know what other talents you have.'

'We'd be here all night.'

'And who wants to be here all night?' he said. 'I want to get some lunch. Hungry?'

'I'm hungry,' said Jelly.

'I'm shocked,' said Nader.

Jill and Jelly laughed.

'Can I take you two to lunch?' asked Nader.

Jill followed Nader and Jelly out to the car park. Jelly stopped in front of a shiny new-looking sedan, hopping from foot to foot. Jill whistled. Scotty would kill someone to have this car. Well, not literally; unlike, perhaps, the current driver.

So Nader has a Porsche and an HSV, she thought. Both were current models. Business must be booming. Still, he didn't seem to be working too hard today. She climbed into the leather cockpit and strapped herself in for the ride. These cars could give the chasers a run; cops were told to call in the chopper when they were pursuing a vehicle like this.

'We'll go for a ride,' said Kasem. 'Got something to pick up in Bondi. Steak all right with you guys?'

'STEAK!' roared Jelly from the backseat.

With the day steel-grey and the table set way back in the restaurant, Jill and Jelly sat in shadows. Despite this, the atmosphere was relatively cheerful. The busy tables were draped with chequered red cloths, crowded with condiment bottles of every description, and a slim vase in front of Jill's place setting held a single red orchid.

'I wonder where he's gone,' said Jill.

'Don't worry, Krystal,' said Jelly. 'Kasem always does this. He's never gone long. And he said we can order whatever we want.'

That turned out to be rather a lot. Nader appeared through the dimness of the restaurant as Jelly was still speaking to the waitress. Kasem added a porterhouse steak to their list, which included steaks for Jill and Jelly, buttered corn on the cob, mashed potato, fresh bread rolls *and* beer-battered steak fries, tomato bruschetta, rocket and roast pumpkin salad (Jill had to get something green in there), and a shared plate of olives and dips.

'Beer or wine?' Kasem watched Jill.

'Coke,' said Jelly.

'Of course,' said Kasem. 'Krystal?'

'Um, red wine?' she said.

Kasem scanned to the bottom of the wine list, held it up to the waitress, and pointed to the priciest red; he bundled up the menus and handed them up to her. Jill wondered whether Nader had had the wine before, or whether he'd just chosen on price. For some reason, she thought the answer would say a lot about him.

Jill took another look around the room and then faced her dining companions again. She smiled, but her senses were pinpoint-focused. She couldn't afford to relax for a minute. She'd just set up an operation to take this man down, and here they were having lunch. More than ever she had to ensure she kept her worlds apart. Still, this was a great opportunity. She'd gather anything she could when she had this kind of access to a subject. The way he spoke on the phone, people he might interact with, changes in emotion around particular topics, the way he handled frustrations. Some of these behaviours could give her an indication of how high on the totem he might be in a criminal enterprise, while others could be used later in interrogation, as leverage points, should it come to that.

This train of thought reminded her of Gabriel. An expert on body language and kinesic interviewing, she'd learned a lot from him that had contributed to her success over the past few months. She was realising more than ever that although you might not be able to pick the truth from someone's words, you could tell from their actions if they were lying.

A waiter approached with their drinks and the bread and olives.

'Why are you smiling, Krystal?' asked Jelly, smiling too.

'I'm happy to be here,' said Jill.

'I'm happy we're all here,' said Kasem. 'A toast.' He maintained eye contact with Jill as they clinked glasses. 'To new friends.'

'To new friends,' she said, and took a deep sip.

'Do me! Do me!' said Jelly, holding up his glass.

Kasem clinked glasses with Jelly and toasted in a singsong voice:

> *Here's to you,*
> *Here's to me,*
> *And should we ever disagree,*
> *Fuck you,*
> *Here's to me.*

Jelly collapsed with laughter. 'Again!' he said.

42

'So what happened, Marco?' Seren asked.

Suspended. At ten years old, for godsakes. Even younger than she'd been the first time. A storm cloud darkened his face, his fists were clenched and his arms hung rigid at his sides.

Seren felt the pull again. Fate. *Just give up*, it whispered to her. *You know this is how it works. Did you seriously think your child could ever amount to anything? You just got out of prison! You're a loser – born that way. Stop struggling; just relax, let go and let the current carry you down to where you're supposed to be.*

'Why should I tell you anything?' said Marco. 'You don't care about me anyway.'

See! There! Take that!

'Marco, I love you more than anything, more than anyone.'

'Except Christian.'

'Marco, I don't love Christian.'

'Why do you always lie to me? I know that's where you go.

197

Who else would give you all that money? Pay for taxis? Buy you clothes? That's what he did before. And you'd rather be with him than me.'

'Okay,' she said. 'All right.' When did he grow up? How could he know these things? 'You're right. I have been seeing Christian, but I don't love him.'

You see, he was right. You are a slut.

'I'm doing some work for him,' she said. 'It's only for a little while. That is the truth, I promise you.'

'Is the work against the law?' he said.

Ha ha! Tell the truth? Tell a lie? Either way, I win, laughed Fate in her head.

'Baby, you shouldn't have to worry about things like that.'

'No, I shouldn't,' he said. 'But I do.' The storm build-up broke, and Marco's face crumpled. He pushed his fists into his eyes, but they couldn't hold the tears. 'I hate it in DoCS!' he cried. 'I hate it! You're going to go to gaol again. You're going to leave me.'

Seren dropped to her knees. She could physically feel his suffering. She remembered, now, how it felt when he was pulled from her arms when she was led down to the cells; how she had left him standing, helpless, at the mercy of strangers. Powerless to do anything other than what he was told. Eight, when she went to gaol. He was eight years old; the top of his head did not even reach their waists. And when he cried at night, alone, for her, she didn't come. And when he wondered what would happen to him, what would happen to her, if they would ever see each other again, she couldn't console him. No one reassured him; no one could. That was her job. Marco had been fed, housed and clothed while she had been locked up. She did thank the State for that. But Marco had been completely alone; she felt it more than ever, right now.

She wrapped her arms around her son. They stayed there, on the floor, for a long time.

Seren shut her thoughts to Fate. She concentrated on Marco.

43

Friday 12 April, 10 pm

Jill smeared at the mascara with a cottonwool ball. She looked like a panda. Kasem wouldn't be so keen to take her out again if he saw her like this. Then again, remembering the intensity in his eyes as he'd leaned into her to say goodbye, her spine pressed hard against his car, she figured he wouldn't notice a bit of smudged make-up. She wondered what would have happened if Jelly hadn't chosen that moment to lose it, shouting at them that he wanted to go home. Actually, she knew what would have happened, and it freaked her out. Intimate contact with any man could panic her, send her nervous system scuttling back down memory lane to when such a touch meant terrible pain. How would she react if Kasem Nader tried to kiss her?

She brushed her teeth and stared into the bathroom mirror, beyond her reflection. It was strange, but pinned against the car she hadn't felt distressed at all. She thought back to the moment. The street and all its sounds had seemed to disappear, and she'd felt cocooned with him in a trancelike state. When he'd inclined further towards her, she'd felt her hips tilt up to meet his.

199

Oh fuck, Jill thought now. That wasn't good. She turned on the cold tap and doused her hot cheeks. It was the Krystal Peters thing, she decided. It had started this morning, putting on the costume, becoming another woman with another life, another history, who had different predilections and attractions. Who hadn't been defiled by two men in a basement.

Or maybe it was the wine. She shouldn't have had anything to drink.

She turned from the mirror. What the hell. What's done is done, she thought. She'd better call it in.

She took her mobile into the centre of the apartment, furthest away from the insubstantial walls, and dialled Superintendent Last's number.

'Jill, I'm pleased you called,' he said. 'Did you pick up a mobile phone to take Damien's calls?'

'Yes sir. I'll be meeting him at Sydney Uni tomorrow. Gabriel will be there.'

'Excellent. You're okay with working with Delahunt again, I trust.'

'Yep.'

'Good. Good. Now, I want to let you know what we're doing on our end,' he said. 'As you know, we can't afford to leave a drug lab in operation in the suburbs for too long. They're okaying it for the time being, but it's going to be a day by day thing, and we could be told to shut it all down at any time.'

'I understand,' she said, 'but it would be a pity if that meant losing the networks associated with it. We could take down the whole web.'

'I know. I'm keen to do that too, and if Gabriel is correct in his hunch that this Kasem Nader is importing precursor chemicals, it would be a particularly important takedown.'

Jill paused a moment. She should tell her commander what she'd been doing today. Before she could, he spoke again.

'The commissioner wants a listening device in there, Jill. We're going in tomorrow.'

'What about Damien's accomplices?'

'We'd like you to ask him to do something about that. We'll need twenty minutes to install the LD. Half an hour would be good. We want to do it tomorrow after nine pm. Damien will have to think of a way to get them out of there for at least that amount of time. But the problem is Nader,' he said. 'Damien has no control over him.'

'Well, actually,' said Jill, 'I went out to lunch today with Kasem Nader.'

'To lunch.'

'Yes,' she said. 'To Bondi. He told me he had to pick something up. He left me for around fifteen minutes, so I couldn't determine what that was. He took and made around ten to twelve calls. Very brief conversations, often just yes or no. Sounded maybe like deals being made.'

'That's good work,' said Last. 'And you felt safe enough with him?'

How do I answer that? she thought. 'It was fine.'

'You went to lunch as Krystal Peters, of course?'

'Of course.'

'Okay. Well, that's a new development,' said Last.

Here we go, she thought, no backing out now. 'I can keep him away from the house tomorrow night,' she said.

'You can?'

'He's asked me to dinner. I'll accept, and make sure we don't go anywhere near Merrylands.'

Last was silent for a few seconds. 'You haven't had a situation like this come up while you've been undercover, Jill,' he said finally.

'A situation like what?'

'Well,' he cleared his throat, 'a potential love interest for Krystal.'

'I'll be right,' she said.

'And if Nader wants to . . . develop the relationship?'

'I'll handle it,' said Jill.

44

'What do you even need me for, then?' asked Damien.

Jill smiled at the young man in front of her. He had a scattering of pimples across his chin, and his cheeks still had that adolescent chubbiness. 'What are you, nineteen?' she asked.

'Twenty,' he said.

'What'd you get mixed up in this shit for?' she wanted to know.

'I was cursed,' he said.

'What?'

He shook his head. 'I don't know why. Because I'm a dickhead, that's why. Because I thought just because I can, then maybe I should. I really was going to get out of all of this, concentrate on my studies, and then Nader showed up. And now you guys.'

'That's right,' said Gabriel, his boots up on the seat in front of him, his hands in the pockets of his black cargoes. 'Now us. And to answer your question, the reason we need *you* is to cover all our bases.'

Jill couldn't see Gabriel's eyes as he spoke; his trucker cap sat low on his brow. He didn't look like one of the other students around here, but he didn't look like a cop either. She realised that he seemed to blend in wherever he went; no one seemed to pay him a lot of attention, but she was pretty certain she'd have noticed him in a crowd, even if they'd never met.

'Like we said,' Gabriel continued, 'we are going to put a listening device in your house, and we'll also have one on your landline and your mobile, but you could be in the street when Nader tells you something important. You could be in a pub; you could be in a car. Our line could go down. Whatever. So you need to call in twice a day and tell Detective Jackson what you know.'

Gabriel reached across for a handful of chips from a packet on the table in front of them. Three soft drink cans shared the space, and Damien had ordered a vegetarian burger he hadn't even unwrapped.

'You're going to report anything Nader tells you about deals coming up,' Gabriel said, 'about how much he wants you to cook, how quickly he can get you the base ingredients.' He paused. 'You could be even more helpful, if you like. You could ask Nader where he gets the chemicals; act interested, you know, you're a chemist, you would be interested in that sort of thing.'

Damien sat there, his face sour. 'If I want to be helpful?' he said. 'Do you think it's fair to ask me to interrogate a gangster? You're using me as bait! Why should I go out of my way for you people?'

'Well,' said Gabriel, popping chips into his mouth and then licking his fingers, 'you should go out of your way for us because you're jammed up, that's why. We can lock you up now, today, and you'll get five to eight years. We'll shut down your lab and get Nader another way. If you do like we say, though, Damo, we can get you off.' Gabriel continued to stare straight ahead. 'But if you snake us, Damien, we'll get you an extra ten years on top for being an arsehole.'

Jill noticed that the couple of pimples on Damien's chin stood out livid red against his ashy pallor. She hoped he wasn't going to throw up.

'Anything else?' Damien asked.

'Yeah,' said Gabriel, raising his face. Jill was always a little distracted by Gabriel's eyelashes when he wore that hat; they were so long, and the brim seemed to frame them. She mentally shook herself, refocused. 'If you happen to see Detective Jackson here when Kasem Nader is around, you will act like you don't know her.'

'Well, obviously,' said Damien. 'You think I want to get killed?'

'If you do see Detective Jackson outside of this university campus,' Gabriel continued as though Damien hadn't spoken, 'she will be presenting as someone named Krystal Peters. Is that clear?'

'Yes.'

'And if you think Nader is someone to worry about,' said Gabriel, 'you have no idea what'll happen to you if you blow this operation. Not only will we lock you up, Damien, you need to understand that you won't make it out again. Gaol's a very unsafe place for rats.'

'I get it. I fucking get it, all right. I'm fucked, every which way, sideways and up against the wall. I get it, okay?'

'There's another thing,' said Jill.

'Of course there is,' said Damien.

'We need you to get your friends out of there tonight,' she said. 'You're to be out by eight-thirty at the latest and you can't return until ten at the earliest.'

'Is that when you're going to bug the place? Whitey won't just let me go out and leave the place unlocked for someone to walk in.'

'We won't be worried about the locks,' said Jill.

'Lock it up,' said Gabriel.

'Can I go now?' said Damien.

'One last thing.' Gabriel took his feet from the chair and leaned forwards.

Damien made an are-you-serious face, but he waited.

'You should relax a bit,' said Gabriel. 'Have you tried yoga?'

'Yoga,' said Damien, his voice fracturing around the word.

'Did you say *yoga*? I have been literally shitting myself for three days straight, and you think I should do yoga?'

Gabriel grinned and clapped the boy on the shoulder.

45

Saturday 13 April, 11 am

Westfields shopping centre; a theme park for the poor. Seren finally lured Marco from home with the promise that she'd watch him play his favourite arcade game at least twice, and that he could choose what they ate, no matter how greasy or sodden with sugar.

They strolled together through the sprawling mall, Seren aware of the dozens of other struggling parents who spent their Saturdays here trying to keep their kids entertained. It was fine for the littlies – the free kindy gym, two-dollar rides on mechanical Disney characters, lollies or chips purchased from Franklins all worked well enough to keep a smile on their faces for most of the day. But from age eight or nine, appeasement cost a lot more. Brand names called siren songs to the children, recruiting the next generation of insatiable consumers. No-name noodles from the supermarket would absolutely not do, when McDonald's, KFC and Pizza Hut stalls beamed like beacons across the food hall floor. From nine am until closing, a throng invariably queued for service at those places, like the faithful praying at shiny altars, kids with their pocket money first in line.

Seren's eyes glazed over watching the tattooed thug on-screen steal yet another car and tear screaming away from the cops. Marco sat in the driver's seat, making the stolen car race with his joystick controls, completely focused, hungry for the action. His favourite game. Great. She wondered whether boys born to a life of privilege loved the same game. Probably, she reasoned. Only *their* parents didn't have to worry that in five years' time their son would become the real-life role model for the latest version.

She planned her strategy for the evening ahead. First she had to find a DVD that Marco would love and that Angel could bear, and then bribery food to try to make up to him for leaving him again tonight.

She couldn't stop now. And Saturday night was certainly not the night to kick back at home with her best friend and her little boy. Right now, just eleven o'clock in the morning, thrumming beneath the city was Saturday night, waiting to be released. It pulsed and throbbed, biding time, emitting sub-threshold vibrations that caused apprentices to focus for once, to hurry to finish their morning shifts. Fifteen-year-old schoolgirls drilled each other on the elaborate fairytales they'd created for their parents, about who was sleeping at whose house, and what to do if the oldies actually checked. The beautiful people sipped coffees in cafés, waking slowly, apparently languidly, but Saturday night waited beneath them and the beat started an itch they knew would not be scratched until the dark came again.

Saturday nights in the city. A knife-edge. From the pavements outside, the clubs would seem to breathe, to writhe to the orgy within. The night's beat was like a dragon in the streets, insatiable, gorging itself on stomping partyers, blood in the alleys, fucking in the toilets and in the dark up the back of the clubs.

And to ramp it all up further, for the gluttonous who just could not get enough, there were the drugs. The drugs that made everyone beautiful, that made the world a better place, that made the boss bearable five days a week, or that faded the memories of what Daddy used to do when Mummy fell asleep. Saturday night was the night to binge, to blow, to party, to score. And in the middle of it all was Christian. The candyman, spreading the love.

Seren felt Saturday night breathing beneath the concrete, waiting. She waited with it.

Cassie nursed an espresso at a table on the pavement out the front of Palermo Café. When her mobile sounded, she nudged it deeper into her handbag, drowning the ringtone.

'Aren't you going to get that?' asked Adele, sitting opposite her in white-rimmed sunglasses that completely swamped her face. The very latest release. She looked ridiculous.

'I would have thought that was obvious,' said Cassie.

'Mmm, snotty little biatch this morning, aren't we?'

Cassie gave her companion a saccharine smile.

The call would be from her mother. Wanting to know whether she'd spoken to Jill, if they were talking again. Fat chance. Her supercop sister could go stuff herself, she thought, lighting one of Adele's cigarettes and then grinding it out again almost immediately.

'Sorry,' she muttered to Adele, who'd shot her an irritated look when she wasted the cigarette.

That morning she'd woken again with The Promise uppermost in her mind: I won't go out tonight. I won't drink. I won't smoke. I definitely won't use. I'll just have fresh fruit juices all day. She stared down into her triple-shot espresso. It was hardly juice. The syrupy coffee here was so strong she felt she'd hyperventilate for a half hour after it. Why did she have that craving for her senses to be altered, heightened? she wondered. Even if it was only from coffee? She felt beaten already. Powerless. Who was she kidding? Tonight would end the way last night did – not that she could remember how that was, precisely. When she woke tomorrow, it would be to the guilt again. She cradled her head into her hand, hot tears forming behind her Aviators. This was no fun anymore.

Cassie raised her eyes. Maybe I need to be around people who make me feel better, she thought. Adele was becoming a bore. She was between jobs, which pretty much meant it was Cassie's shout twenty-four-seven.

She considered her options. Saturday night was not the night to try to be a nun. She had a much better shot at that on a Sunday. No, tonight, she'd dress up, make herself feel better, and go find someone who treated her right.

Christian, she thought, it's time to thank you for those beautiful flowers.

Byron shook his head at the loser in the Commodore next to him. Don't bother, he tried to tell the family man with his eyes. You're definitely outclassed.

The Commodore's engine growled. Oh, you want a go, do ya, fuckwit? Byron asked Family Man with his eyes.

Byron focused on the traffic lights; his foot hovering above the accelerator. He knew he didn't need to worry. He could give this prick half the intersection and he'd still thrash him. He tried not to smirk – it ruined the image. That's why he bought this car, an electric-blue Subaru WRX – a Rexie. He'd wanted one since they first came out. A Rexie could beat almost any street-legal car from a standing start, especially with the right driver. And he knew he was the right driver. Family Man, you're about to be humbled, he thought.

The lights changed and the Rexie screamed off the mark, hurtling through the intersection as though ratcheted through a spear gun.

'*Fuck* yeah!' yelled Byron, hurled back by the speed against the headrest. He saluted out the window to the Commodore behind him, middle finger held high and proud. 'Suck me off, Family Man!' he shouted.

Byron continued to smile as he rolled up Woodville Road, elbow out the window, blowing smoke in the breeze. Oh yeah, this is a sweet ride, he thought. He laughed, remembering the conversation he'd had with Damien when he'd paid his deposit on this car. What a knob.

'I told you, Byron,' Damien had said to him, 'you shouldn't go buying things that can create a paper trail.'

'What paper trail?' Byron had countered. 'I'm paying cash.'

'Well, it's a figure of speech,' said Damien. 'It means that you're acquiring assets that you can't afford. Anyone looking into your declared income and purchases will see that you can't afford to buy that car.'

Byron had waved the order for the Rexie in front of Damien's face. Proof that he could.

'*Legally*,' said Damien.

'You ever heard of horse races?' said Byron. 'The casino? I'm a lucky cunt is all. That's what I'll tell 'em.'

'They've heard that before, Byron. They've got ways of figuring that shit out.'

'Look, chef. You worry too much, man. You just do what you do and I'll do what I do so well,' Byron had told him.

Byron cut into the left lane without indicating. Business had already picked up, he thought. With Nader in, they had new orders coming out of their arseholes, even just over the past couple of days. And Damien would have to cook the shit to fill those orders. Byron knew that pretty soon Damien was going to be too busy to worry about anything other than the stove.

He punched in the cigarette lighter on the dash and thought about asking Kasem if he could hire a runner. He knew that he was supposed to be the runner, but there was a lot of shit to move; he could use a hand. Still, this new contact Nader had given them might be enough without getting anyone else involved.

He considered the delivery waiting in the wheel well in the boot. That's a lot of eccy, he thought, and our whole batch of ice. Nader reckoned this new prick would take them into lounge rooms all over the Eastern suburbs; he'd said they'd be turning over a lot more than that soon.

He pulled onto the M4 and opened up the Rexie a little, scaring the bejesus out of some nanna who'd wandered into the right lane. He laughed at the woman's ashen face as he shot past. That'll teach ya, he thought. You bitches should keep to the left! He glanced at the time on the dash. He'd better get a move on for real. As the streetlights winked to life, Byron raced his Rexie into the city to meet their new distribution partner.

Who'd have fucken believed it, he thought, shaking his head and lighting another smoke. The hot new connection was Mr Pro Bono himself. Christian fucking Worthington.

46

After leaving the uni, Jill and Gabriel spent the rest of their Saturday at Central in Surry Hills, the Sydney headquarters for the New South Wales police. Superintendent Last had organised for them to meet up with two of the most senior drug investigators in the country. Cameron Genovese and Olsen Lanvin were at the pointy end of the Australian Crime Commission's Special Intelligence Operation into amphetamine type stimulants.

Last had insisted that Jill take the basement entrance to the multistorey building and had arranged for Genovese and Lanvin to meet them in a secure interrogation room. Jill noticed that the CCTV cameras in the corridors were not operating. She appreciated it. It had been three months since she'd had such regular contact with other police, and she was antsy. She couldn't afford any slip-ups. Even this far from Fairfield, she could still be made as a cop by a civilian.

But meeting Lanvin and Genovese actually worried her more than being recognised on the street. Her cover could be blown in

212

here just as easily as out there. While Last had promised her these were the good guys, the ACC had been brought almost to its knees a couple of times by its own double agents. Parasites within, who'd been hooked up to the highest-level intel in drug enforcement, and who'd used it to get really rich, really fast. The most recent scandal had involved one of the ACC's senior operatives, caught mid-shipment trying to import six hundred kilograms of pseudoephedrine.

Jill paused at the door to the closed room. You've got to trust someone sometime, she told herself, and turned the handle. Gabriel followed her in.

The guy who stood when they entered seemed somehow see-through to Jill, kind of transparent. His suit and wire-rimmed glasses, his hair and even his skin, seemed all the same shade of featureless fawn.

'Olsen Lanvin.' He reached his hand across the table to Jill.

'Jill Jackson,' she said, with a quick grip of his hand. She stepped to the side to introduce her partner. 'And this is –'

'Delahunt,' said the third man in the room. He stayed where he was, seated on the table, his big feet in black boots resting on a chair. He wore a blue police jumpsuit tucked into the boots, and even sitting he seemed to take up most of the room.

Jill reached forward to shake his hand; hers was completely lost in his. 'I see you know Gabriel,' she said, maintaining eye contact, but unable to prevent herself taking a small step backwards. The guy was huge. 'So, you'd be Genovese?'

'Cameron,' he said.

'Jill,' she said.

Gabriel just waited.

Lanvin cleared his throat, gestured to the chairs. 'We should get on with it, then,' he said.

Jill and Lanvin took a seat. Gabriel and Genovese didn't move. Jill sighed inwardly. The boy thing. Again. Lanvin gave Genovese a neutral glance and inclined his colourless eyes to a chair. Genovese dropped into it. Gabriel took the remaining seat.

'Our brief,' said Lanvin, 'is to give you both a rundown on precursor substances used in the production of ATS.'

Lanvin continued. 'You're going to have to forgive me if I cover shit you already know. But stop me on points that require clarification.'

Jill pulled her notebook and a pen from her bag. Straight into it, then. Suited her fine.

'You'd be aware that the precursor substances used for illicit ATS production are also used by the chemical industry for licit purposes,' he said. 'Because of this, it's been difficult to control the production and importation of many of these substances, and criminal elements actively exploit the holes to get their hands on this stuff.'

'Could you tell us a bit more about these holes?' said Jill. 'Last probably told you we're watching a clan lab now, and we'd like to know where they might be sourcing the precursors.'

'Well, everyone knows about the pseudo-runs, of course,' said Lanvin. 'Buying or stealing cold and flu medications from multiple pharmacies and then extracting the pseudoephedrine. That's harder for them now since we got the chemists to put this stuff behind the counter and restrict bulk purchases.'

Genovese spoke for the first time. 'Which has increased the number of stick-ups and smash-and-grabs in chemists,' he said.

'True,' said Lanvin, 'but those are only the small-time cooks, anyway. If you've found yourself a big player, you want to be looking for someone who's importing. They'll be channelling shipments through countries with poor control systems.'

'Like Papua New Guinea,' said Gabriel.

Genovese raised his eyes.

Lanvin said, 'Yeah, maybe. Your boy got links there?'

Gabriel shrugged. 'Not sure yet,' he said.

'How do they get it through these countries?' Jill asked.

'There're a number of methods,' said Lanvin. 'Some Pacific island nations are not party to the international control convention on these chemicals, so there is some trafficking to and through these nations. There's also bribing of corrupt officials, product mislabelling, falsification of authorisations or official documents and misuse of free trade zones and bonded ware-houses. Of course there's also traditional smuggling in private vessels or in seemingly innocuous shipments.'

Jill listed the methods as bullet points in her notes. She felt Genovese watching her, sizing her up. She met his eyes.

'You're gonna need our help with this, if you've got yourself an importer,' he said.

'We're not sure what we've got right now,' said Jill, eyes on her notes as she spoke. 'The clan lab's pretty small-scale to date, but there is a new entrant and we don't want to move too quickly and lose him now.'

'Agreed,' said Lanvin. 'Last has sketched in some of the details, so we're giving you a little leeway at the moment. I understand you have a direct line of communication with this new entrant?'

'That's right,' said Jill. *I'm having dinner with him tonight.* She ignored the nervous thrill that came with the thought.

'It sounds to us,' said Genovese, who still hadn't looked away from her, 'that what you've probably got here is a boxed lab being muscled in on by organised crime.'

'Ah, you *think*?' said Gabriel.

Jill ignored Gabriel's sarcasm; these two obviously had a history. And she, for one, hadn't heard the phrase before. 'Boxed lab?' she said.

'It's just a term for a small, local enterprise,' explained Lanvin. 'They can be mobile within a few hours, box the whole kitchen up and find somewhere else to cook. They're particularly prevalent in southeast Queensland at the moment. You often find that the cooks don't even have a criminal record. Sometimes it's just a group of friends who got together and came up with what sounded like a good idea at the time.'

Jill nodded. Sounded familiar. She pictured Damien's miserable face and his untouched falafel burger at the university cafeteria.

'What we're noticing lately, though,' continued Lanvin, 'is that the professionals are locating and muscling in on these pigeons. They just buy the job lot and subsume the whole operation. You got the usual suspects involved. Outlaw bikies are probably still number one, especially with the speed. The Triads and Middle Eastern crime gangs slug it out over the ice and the eccy.'

Jill wondered how much they knew about Nader. They seemed to have a very good picture of what was going on in this particular investigation. She dropped her eyes to her notes and chewed her bottom lip. She wondered whether this was a stitch-up. Was she being used? It suddenly occurred to her that these guys might not be here to help with her investigation, but to check them out to make sure she wasn't compromising theirs. Organised crime gangs weren't the only people known to muscle in on small, promising operations and take over.

It never changes, she thought; bull elephants at the edges of the clearing, dicks in the wind, preparing to take out their rivals. She sighed. When it comes right down to it, she thought, they could have the bust – lord knew they needed some good PR, and she wasn't going to raise her hand for a media interview. The main thing that worried her, though, was the potential for casualties of war. She glanced at Lanvin and Genovese – the invisible man and the armoured tank. When they went in, she knew it would be heavy. She caught Gabriel's eye. He raised one eyebrow, smirked just a smidge. Yeah, the whole thing could be considered pretty funny, except that caught up in the middle of it all was Damien, a kid in way over his head. She wasn't sure what kind of punishment he deserved, but she knew it wasn't death.

And then there was Kasem Nader. Right at the heart of the web. He'd be preparing for their dinner tonight, and here she was briefing the exterminators.

47

Saturday 13 April, 7 pm
Seren left Marco and Angel with homemade plum pork ribs and
store-bought fried rice. Before she walked out the door, Marco
had let her kiss the top of his head without ducking away. He was
pretty happy with the food. Angel smiled at her from the kitchen,
one arm draped around his shoulders. *Thanks*, Seren mouthed at
her friend as she pulled the door closed.

She just hoped that the smells wouldn't entice any hungry
neighbours. One in particular. Angel had told her that she'd seen
Tready this morning, limping back from the mailboxes.

'Did you say hi for me?' Seren had asked, falsely bright. Her
stomach had dropped into free-fall at the mention of his name.
'How'd he look?' she'd asked, not wanting to know.

'*All* fucked up.' Angel had laughed. 'His nose! Oh my God!
And his eyes are completely black. Remind me, bitch, not to get
on your bad side.'

'*You're* talking!' Seren gave a flat laugh. She and Angel shared
a look. They joked about the violence, but they both knew it
wasn't funny.

Within a week of meeting Angel in gaol, Seren had shocked herself by telling her new friend about her stepfather's violence. She hadn't told anyone since Alexandra, her best friend in Year 7. She even told Angel what happened to Bradley, her little brother, and she'd never told anyone that. How she used to hear him screaming and could do nothing. How she'd tried, smashing at her stepfather's back with her fists, as he leaned over her little brother's bed. How he hadn't even turned around while backhanding her across the room, before going on with the beating. How her mother's pleading and screaming had drawn his attacks back to her. Holding her stomach in the prison laundry, hunched forward with the pain of talking about this for the first time, Seren had told Angel how she hated her mother for not leaving that man, her heart tearing as she admitted it, because she had also loved her mother so much.

Finally, Seren had told Angel how she hated herself – more, even, than she hated that pig. She hated herself for not killing him while he slept. Any night would have done; she'd planned it a thousand times, lying frozen in her bed, so taut with tension and fear that she felt her teeth would shatter in her mouth. But she'd never acted; not even when the cops had carried Bradley out of the house and into the care of the state. Not even the night she'd spent an hour trying to wake her mother from unconsciousness, pink fluid drizzling from her ear after yet another bashing.

Angel had held her, quietly, while the washing machines sloshed and whirred around them. Somehow, Seren had known that Angel would understand. As it turned out, she did: Angel had repaid Seren's confidence by telling her about her husband, Danny. She'd loved him once; all she'd ever wanted was to have his children and look after a family. She told Seren about the miscarriages – giving birth, howling, to jellied globs, after being head-butted in her pregnant stomach, or rammed, belly first, into the corner of a lounge. She'd told Seren how she'd screamed for her babies to stay with her, not to die. And how Wayne had snored through it all, sleeping off his drunken slugfest. Angel had told Seren that she'd had the same murderous fantasies, every night. And how now she felt his brains on her hands, every night. And that she wasn't sure what was worse.

Now, in a taxi yet again, on the way to meet Christian at his office, Seren closed the door on those memories. She checked her glossy, barely-pink fingernails, and angled her bare legs towards the door, away from the cabbie's eyes in the rear vision mirror. Every now and then, a spear of brightness from the streetlights lit up the shadows around her feet. Her patent stilettoes glinted like blades when they caught the light. She was a long way from her gaol-issue tracksuit in this outfit. And yet, so close. If Maria Thomasetti knew where she was going right now, and why, she'd be bunking with Crash and Little Kim tomorrow night.

As the cab idled in traffic near Chinatown, she wondered why she hadn't told Angel about her blackmail plot. As far as her friend knew, while she was babysitting Marco, Seren really was working. Seren was aware that Angel didn't buy the whole story. Angel knew that Seren wasn't off to waitress, dressed like this. She knew what Angel thought she was doing: the kind of work most girls got into when released.

Seren stared out into the dusk. She figured that Angel wasn't that far wrong. After all, Seren actually *was* giving Christian sex in return for money. But the cab vouchers, clothes and petty cash would only temporarily dull her self-disgust for sleeping with the man who'd sent her to gaol.

Seren held her mobile phone up in front of her face and in the reflective screen checked her lips for shine. Oh well, she was pretty sure that the million dollars he was going to pay would have a more lasting effect at cheering her up.

48

Saturday 13 April, 7 pm

'You know, I really don't have time for this.' Jill angled her face towards Gabriel and her hair snagged on a twig in the grass. She tugged, and it snarled further. She snorted in frustration and sat up.

'No! Lie back down,' said Gabriel. 'It's going to happen soon.'

'But it's getting cold.'

'Shh. Wait.'

Jill scowled and reclined into the almost damp grass under the canopy of a massive Port Jackson fig tree. She had to admit that the fading autumn light around Mrs Macquarie's Chair was gorgeous. As she watched, the transparent oranges blushed into reds, bruised into purple, and then slipped, almost imperceptibly, into inky wine.

And then it happened.

The skies erupted. Hundreds and hundreds of pieces of the night exploded from the trees above her, and swarmed across the sky. She tried to exclaim, but found she had no breath, as though it had been sucked from her by the downdraught of the countless bat wings. The little bodies spun and circled, careening and twisting, silent, but for the shushing, breathy noise of their wings. Her hand on her heart, Jill stared as suddenly, almost as one, the bats soared away from the harbourside park and headed across the water for the city. She sat up on the grass, peering after them, her eyes straining against the darkness. When the cloud approached the lights of the skyline, it seemed suddenly to shatter, to splinter apart.

The thousand dots of darkness spread out across Sydney to hunt for smaller, more defenceless things on Saturday night.

49

Saturday 13 April, 7.40 pm

Feeling as though his shoulder would pop out of its socket, Damien reached even further into the manhole in the ceiling. Balanced on tiptoes on his bed, one arm shoved in up to his neck, he splayed his fingers, and scrabbled about with increasing desperation. There! Something. How had he pushed it so far in there in the first place? He scraped with his fingernails until he could feel the chain hooked around his finger. He pulled it carefully forward and grasped it in his fist before flopping back down on the bed.

This would be his last night in this room. He sat back against the headboard of the only bed he'd ever owned. He hadn't seen any need to buy a new one when the money started rolling in. Whitey's room, on the other hand – Damien's mother's former bedroom – resembled a furniture warehouse. The first thing Whitey had bought was a waterbed, too big for the room even without the heavy matching side tables and mirror. Very Whitey: it never occurred to him to measure up the room before laying down the cash for a bedroom suite.

What would Whitey do without him? He'd lived here since Damien's mother left when they were both fifteen. Far as he could tell, Whitey's parents hadn't even noticed him go; they'd certainly never been over here to visit him.

It was possible that Whitey might stay on if Kasem left him alone. Damien reasoned that when he left, there'd be no reason for Nader to keep muscling in when he realised that Whitey couldn't cook. Well, not properly anyway. Damien knew it would be better for everyone when he just disappeared. And he couldn't even afford to tell his friend where he was going. Whitey just didn't think ahead – he might tell someone and then Nader could find out. He'd have to tell him something about what was going on, though, why he had to leave. It wasn't just that he felt he owed Whitey that much before dropping out of his life forever – his friend had to know just enough to keep him safe.

He sighed deeply, thinking about the worst part of all of this. Leaving uni. Of course, that would be the first pace they'd show up when he went AWOL. All he'd wanted since age twelve was to study at the University of Sydney. When he'd logged onto their site the January after his HSC and learned he'd been accepted to study chemistry, he'd put his face in his hands and cried. The notion that he would ever drop out had been preposterous until this week. He'd completed every class assignment, never handing a thing in late, and while some people didn't even open the core texts for the course, he'd read them cover to cover *and* borrowed every book on the recommended reading list from the library. After he was rolling in cash, he'd just gone out and bought them all.

Damien shook his head and stared morosely at the huge stack of textbooks in the corner. He'd have to buy most of them again. In Oxford. The thought sent a thrill hurtling up his spine, but he bit back his smile. He had to get there first. He should have no problem being accepted as far as his grades were concerned. He'd topped every class except one, and that had only been because his lecturer's nephew was in his year, and she hated that he thrashed her sister's boy in everything. Bitch. No, the problem lay in potential background checks. He knew that he had no formal criminal record. Yet. Detective Jackson had told him his charges would depend upon his cooperation over the next couple of days. But he knew they'd throw everything at him when they found out he'd left the country. He had to just pray that the administration at Oxford wouldn't check with the police over here. He'd thought it through a hundred times. There was no reason that they should – his transcript from Sydney Uni was flawless. They should be able to just proceed with that.

He tried to push the other worries from his mind – like the thought of taking that much cash on the plane. Had to be done. He had to get to Oxford and disappear quickly, pay for everything upfront.

He straightened on the bed, took a look at his watch. Almost seven forty-five. He had to get out of there. If he was going to buy his ticket when he got to the airport, he needed some time to make sure he could get on the next flight. He reached for the backpack under the bed. It had been packed for the last week. Just his uni stuff, some awards from school, a few scraps of paperwork his mother had bothered to hang onto. All he really needed to keep from his life so far. Everything else he could buy on the road.

He opened his other hand. The necklace sat like a small, golden puddle on his palm. This was the only thing his mother had left him before taking off to work for Jehovah. And even this was almost an afterthought, he thought, twirling the chain around his index finger, rummaged from her handbag before she left him at the customs gate at the international airport. Jehovah will take care of everything else you need, she'd told him.

Yep, he's doing a great job at the moment, Ma, he thought, sliding the necklace into an envelope and dropping it into his backpack.

Whitey had said he would be here just after eight pm, but he'd never been on time in his life. They'd arranged to meet Byron in the city at ten.

Damien wondered if he'd ever see them again.

50

Saturday 13 April, 7.45 pm

Cassie waited in Christian's office wearing a belted white trench coat and white knee-length leather boots. And that was it. It was a cliché, she knew, but she didn't think anyone would be complaining.

Another lawyer, leaving for the night, had no problem letting her wait in Christian's office. He'd seen her there with Christian plenty of times. And Cassie generally got what she asked for. She sat now in Christian's recliner with her feet crossed on his desk and thought about greeting him with a Sharon Stone moment. Now that would really be a welcome-to-Saturday-night-I've-missed-you-baby greeting. She laughed aloud, and stood to look out at the view.

Nope, I can't do it, she thought, that's just too slutty. At least it is without any party favours on board. And that's why she was here after all.

Cassie's mood plummeted. She leaned against the glass and thought about her motives for coming here tonight. It wasn't to see her boyfriend. She'd known when she woke up at St Vincent's that this guy was not the love of her life. No way did she want to make babies with a man who would dump her, overdosed and naked, at a hospital.

Now where did the baby thoughts come from, she wondered. She'd always been certain that she'd never have kids; could never imagine herself giving her life over to someone else so completely. Not to mention what popping out a baby did to the figure.

But is this all there is, she wondered, watching the night winking into life in the eastern suburbs below her. Since the fight with Jill, she couldn't shake this glumness, or the guilts. It wasn't so much regret about their argument, but more just feeling bad about the way she lived. It was so weird. She'd always loved her life, or pretty nearly always. And when she didn't, there was always a friend on tap to tell her why her life was so great.

Usually at a time like this she would go home to make herself feel better. A weekend in Camden at her parents' house was always good for the soul. She saw such breaks as like a detox retreat: she never took along more than a handful of Valium – well, a girl's gotta sleep, and it was so quiet out there, who could sleep with all that nothingness? But isolation aside, there was her mum to feed and fuss over her. And little Lilly, her niece, squealing over the make-up she took for her to play with. Best of all, she'd always put in an appearance at the local supermarket: that was as good for the ego as a school reunion. She'd play Spot the Former Classmate. Most of them did a runner when they recognised Cassie. She guessed she wasn't too hard to remember; she hadn't changed a whole hell of a lot. But whenever she'd spot a panic-stricken, big-bottomed woman dragging a couple of kids down an aisle, she'd be willing to bet that she'd gone to school with her.

And the guys! Most of them close to bald at thirty, and not letting go gracefully. Shave it off, she wanted to shout at them. Bald can be sexy. But those guys would need more than a Vin Diesel haircut to salvage them. Too much sun, too many beers and no time in a gym. And she could see the effect of their mort-gages stooping them forward at the shoulders. She pictured them almost as snails – it seemed as though they carried their house and kids on their backs. These cocksure boys, once so full of life and so certain of themselves, were now well on their way to their fathers' cynicism and a midlife crisis.

But this time she didn't want to go home. She felt too embarrassed to face her family just yet. They knew her lifestyle was glitz and glamour, but she didn't think they would ever have suspected that it also included cocaine and meth. Ugh! She couldn't believe she'd smoked that shit.

And yet here she was, alone and pretty much naked, waiting for the drug dealer.

Her stomach turned at the thought, startling her. It wasn't just a feeling of guilt this time, but also of disgust. She wanted to cry, but the thought of being a junkie, a whore, *and* a snivelling wimp dried her tears.

You can always walk out of here, she told herself. It was finally sinking in that she couldn't beat this shit alone. There's always rehab; she remembered her father's words in the hospital.

She moved away from the window, walked towards the door. Towards nothing. There's nothing out there for me, she thought, and took a step back. But there's nothing in here for me either. Cassie waited on the threshold of her future, feeling empty and cold.

A couple of blocks before Christian's building, Seren checked her digital recorder again. It had become a stupid ritual. She had to press record, capture something, rewind and play it back; she'd watch the tiny screen with the sound off. Then she'd do it again. She always operated the camera using the most minute of movements, hooking her thumb into the pocket just inside her bag and depressing the button. The tiny device pointed its little glass nose out through the zipper and captured everything surrounding it in surprising detail. She knew exactly where it was by feel. But if something distracted her, if she even suspected that there'd been a break in her concentration, she'd have to do the ritual again. Twice. Lately, if she'd had a negative feeling during the process, she'd do it three times. One extra to counteract the bad thoughts.

You're losing it, Templeton, she told herself in the cab. Obsessive Compulsive Disorder. An intern psychologist at the gaol had told her about the term, and she wished now that she'd never agreed to go along with the stupid test. Some uni girl had arrived at the prison, shining and brand new, bubbling along behind her supervisor, the burned-out prison psych, Eleanor Carnegie. Carnegie had asked if anyone would be willing to become a subject for Naomi Willis. She was already a full psychologist, and was studying for her masters, the psych had told them. Poor old Carnegie, Seren had thought at the time. The girls had told Seren in her first week that Carnegie was a soft touch. Had more days' sick leave than she showed up, and if you had a session with her, well fuck knew, you'd be handing *her* the tissues before she passed them across the desk.

Some of the prisoners had signed up for the sessions because it got them out of duties. Seren had signed up because that girl could be her. If her dad hadn't died. If her mum hadn't hooked up with that motherfucker. If she hadn't had Marco at fifteen.

Marco was another reason she'd signed up. Because Seren signed up for anything in there – anything that would keep her from thinking about her little boy and how the hell he was coping without her.

She'd completed hundreds of questions for Naomi. And after all the psychobabble, Uni Girl had told her what she already knew. That Seren was traumatised by her childhood – yay, Naomi, top of the class – and that she had a tendency to be obsessive. Seren had never heard most of the terms before Post-traumatic Stress Disorder, Obsessive Compulsive Disorder. Fucked up, is how she'd interpreted them. Well, fuck them, she'd thought. If they can break it, I can fix it.

She'd told Naomi thanks but no thanks for the ongoing therapy sessions and went back to her revenge fantasies. No point forever living in the past. Seren had a son. He had a future, and she was going to make sure he got there with less baggage than she'd dragged into hers.

Now, she stepped out of the taxi and handed the frothing driver a cab voucher without even looking at him. The longer she did this, the dirtier she felt. She shrugged off his leers, squared her shoulders, and stalked into the lobby of the impressive building as though she owned it.

Christian waited by the lifts. Always on time. Always the gentleman. Thirty metres of gleaming granite stretched between them, and as she sashayed towards him, she remembered crossing the same floor holding her little boy's hand on the way to visit the eye specialist. She clenched that hand now, as though his chubby fist was still in her own, giving her strength as it had that day, each of them then overwhelmed by the sophistication of the city.

No wonder she had been completely bowled over by this guy, she thought. Christian Worthington leaned against the wall, spotlit by points of illumination embedded in the floor, the ceiling and the wall around him. As though surrounded by magic. He might as well have been from another universe. Any man caught in her housing estate wearing a scarf like that loosely draped around his neck would find himself bent over a public toilet servicing Tready and the other boys who'd done a lot of time; and doing it old-school, using a plastic bag as a condom, just like inside. But call one of those blokes a poofter and you wouldn't live another week – *they* knew they loved women; it was just that they had got a taste for the girly-boys in the lock-up, and it was fun to eat out for a change.

But in this world, Christian belonged. No – more than that. It seemed to Seren as though he stood above it, reaching down to manipulate things the way he liked them, so that everything was always perfect, for him.

Like he had written the software.

Seren crossed the last three strides between them, a knowing smile in her bottomless blue eyes. She snaked a bare arm around his shoulder and nuzzled his neck in greeting.

She wondered how he'd feel if he knew she was a virus in his system.

Byron slammed his hand against the steering wheel and screamed.

'For fucksakes, you fucking cunt, the light was orange, you coulda gone through that, you *piece* of *shit*!'

He thought about taking his wog-basher out from under the passenger seat and teaching this fucker in the Volvo that he should have learned how to drive before he dragged his arse out here tonight. Instead, he took a deep breath and tried to get himself together. Get a grip, Byron, he told himself. This is your step up in the world. He forced himself not to look at the clock as he waited. It had taken him twenty minutes to get around the Pitt–George–Market Street block. Why would anyone wanna come into this fucking city anyway, he wondered.

At the front of Worthington's building he pulled the Rexie into a no standing zone. Motherfuckers could give him a ticket: he didn't care. Worthington could take care of that too. He jumped out of his cockpit and popped the boot, pulled back the carpet and lifted out the gym bag. He glanced down at his shiny Nike tracksuit: it was the latest from the US. A little too cool for the couriers around here, but he figured he could pass. Besides, Worthington said he'd wait for him in the lobby, to get him up past security. Byron beep-locked the Rexie and jogged into the building.

Well fuck me sideways, he thought, spotting Worthington immediately, standing beside the security desk. That lucky motherfucker. Byron didn't think he had ever seen a chick that hot in his life, even with her short hair. Tall bitch, though, he thought as he got closer. She's as tall as Worthington. Bet she's a model, he thought. Bet she won't even look at me. But if she's hanging round with Worthington she's probably got a coke habit. Byron knew that only beautiful girls got coke habits – the dealers wouldn't waste the blow on the fat ones. Byron increased his swagger just a smidge. Well, he was a new player now. Maybe he *could* get this bitch to look at him. The height difference wouldn't worry *him* – it was all the same when they were on their knees.

'You're a little late, Byron,' said Worthington.

'Yeah, sorry, boss. Fucken traffic.'

'Yes. Let's get you out of here.' Worthington nodded at the security guard staring at them and turned towards the lifts. On the move, he said, 'Byron, this is Seren; Seren, Byron.'

Byron stared up at the girl, expecting her to stare straight through him. Instead, he felt suddenly as though he were falling, lost in her blue eyes. Rather than the vacant, soulless, is-someone-there-I-can't-see-anything look he got from most bitches, this chick's eyes seemed to tell a tale that went forever – speaking intensely to him. Byron couldn't understand a word.

He dropped his gaze back to the ground, as much as an instinctive avoidance of the cameras everywhere in this fucking building as a way to hide the way he felt. *How* he felt, he had no idea. He only knew he could never handle a bitch like this, on her knees or not, and he hated Worthington more than ever for being able to control someone like her.

All the way up in the elevators Seren prayed that the bag held what she thought it did. This Byron could not more stereotypically fit the part. Oh my God, that tracksuit! He had to be a drug dealer, didn't he? The size of the bag worried her, though. It was too big. There was no way all of whatever was in there was drugs. Could it be cash?

It could, Seren, she told herself, just be this wannabe's change of clothes for the night. He might just be Christian's client.

But there was something about the way Christian had introduced them, about the importance he'd placed on meeting this guy in the lobby, about the tension she perceived emanating from Christian's body.

Another thought occurred to her as they walked down the quiet fluorescent hallway past closed doors on the way to

Christian's office. If this was a major drug deal, why would he do it in front of her? But then again, why not? she answered herself. She'd seen him do plenty of deals; he trusted her. And even if he didn't, who was she to threaten him? He was Christian Worthington. She was a parolee.

A parolee with a digital camera.

Seren prayed tonight would be the night.

Byron didn't know what the chick was doing here.

Well, he got it that Worthington wouldn't want this one getting too far away from him on a Saturday night. Just on the way round the block out the front he'd seen two SL600s and a new Bentley. That was 1.5 mil right there. Plenty of money out there to snatch a girl like this right out from under a prick's nose. But surely Christian would make her wait somewhere else while they did the deed? Bitches shouldn't be involved in business: that was Byron's motto.

He let himself fall a couple of steps behind them, imagined himself holding that arse. He smiled – he was going to be imagining that picure a fair bit, he knew, starting later tonight.

Oh shit! Byron dropped his eyes to the floor. Blondie had seen him checking her out. His cheeks flamed. Did she just *wink* at him? Nah, Byron, you silly prick, he told himself. She must have had something in her eye. That is, unless she does know what's in this bag, and wants a little taste.

Just focus on what you're doing here, Byron. One thing at a time. Kasem's waiting at Merrylands, and I've gotta bring him back eighty grand. This is the start of something big. Finally, I'm gonna get some big-time action, he thought. He was getting tired of the looking-around-hands-in-pockets-quick-swap kind of deals done in alleyways. Pockets full of sweaty twenties and wads of little plastic bags.

This is the kind of work I want to do, he told himself. Proper business deals in places like this, with people like them – he watched the backs of the gods walking before him. Byron straightened a little, and then spotted the winking blue light at the end of the corridor and dropped his eyes again.

Knowing how badly she'd regret this later – leaving with nothing – Cassie forced herself again to the office door. She had to go. Right then, Christian's voice approached from the hall outside.

Her heart jumped to her throat. With no idea why she would do such a thing, she dived into the coat cupboard at the entrance to the room. She left the door open just a crack.

She stood there in the semi-dark wardrobe, feeling like a complete idiot. At least she had a few more moments to figure out how this Saturday night was going to play out. Would she wait until Christian left, find her own way out and telephone for a bed at a detox clinic? Or, would the need to quench this anxiety just one more time see her use this cupboard to check her own coat and go out to meet Christian wearing just the boots?

At least it's good to have choices, she thought.

51

Damien left the note for Whitey on his pillow and pulled the bedroom door closed. One thing he would not miss, he decided, would be the stench of this house. He made a face. When he got settled he'd have someone come and clean for him every week, and he'd make sure his place smelled great. He'd been learning about the chemical components and synthesis of scent this past semester, and he'd been thinking that he might try his hand at making perfume. There was money in that too. He smiled. He could make a signature scent just for Erin. Might not get him the same kudos as a handful of eccy, but he figured that any girl would like their own designer perfume, especially if it came delivered with a business-class trip to the UK.

'Hey, uni boy. Nice bag. Is that what the in-crowd carries around these days?'

Damien bolted for the front door, ripped it open and smacked straight into Urgill's chest. The bald man belly-charged him back into his lounge room and he tripped, falling backwards and landing spreadeagled, staring up at the ceiling.

234

'Where you off to tonight, uni boy?' Kasem Nader stood up from the lounge and prodded at Damien's ribs with a pointy-toed boot.

Damien just lay there.

'Not a lot of work going on around here,' Nader said. 'That's not what a business partner likes to see.' Nader stepped over Damien and walked towards the kitchen. Damien heard the front door close and saw Agassi follow Urgill into his house.

'You see, what you've got here, Damo, are a few mystery shoppers,' said Nader. 'It's a business term; not sure whether you're familiar with it. Anyway, basically, management – that would be me – sends in a couple of people to check on progress when their staff – that would be you – least expect it.' He smacked his hand down onto a large box on the counter that hadn't been there before Damien went to his room to get the necklace.

Prick must've let himself in while I had my head in the roof, Damien guessed.

'Now, I know Whitey's on his way over here,' said Nader. 'And I told Byron to get his arse back here after he makes some deliveries for us. But, you, you're the chef, Damo, and you can't just go clocking off whenever you want. There are no union hours in the drug trade, mate.' He moved back towards Damien. 'You bloody uni students. You're all left-wing unionists, I know.' He smiled widely. 'What are you still doing on your arse, you idiot?' Nader reached out a hand and Damien saw nothing else he could do but take it. Nader yanked him to his feet, and gave him a playful punch to the deltoid. He nearly hit the rug again. Fuck.

Damien rubbed his throbbing shoulder. There was obviously no way he could get out of here tonight, and the longer he stayed in Australia, the closer he was coming to copping formal charges. He didn't know what would happen then about travelling. Could they automatically stop him at the airport when he tried to buy a ticket? He didn't know how these things worked.

'So where were you going anyway, Damo?' Nader wanted to know.

'Just to get something to eat,' he said, his voice reedy and high-pitched. I sound like I've just been castrated, he thought. He stared morosely at the thugs who shared his lounge room and figured he pretty much had been. 'You scared the fuck out of me. I didn't know who you were, sitting there.'

'Yeah? You don't need to be scared of me, Damo.' Nader turned to Urgill. 'Go get some food,' he said. 'What do you want, Damien? Chinese? KFC? What about Lebo?'

'Whatever,' said Damien. As if he'd be able to eat anything. What the hell would happen with the listening device now? Would this mean the cops would say he hadn't cooperated? They couldn't! Detective Jackson said she'd make sure Kasem Nader wouldn't come over here tonight. Great job there.

'What's that?' Damien asked, walking towards the kitchen and the box that took up most of the bench. Nothing he could do about the cops now. He was stuck here with these pricks until they decided they were ready to go.

'Pseudo,' said Nader.

'What, *all* of it?'

Nader laughed. 'You think that's a lot? You toys. I've got a fucking warehouse of this shit. You'll get a box a day for starters until we can get somewhere bigger for a better production run.'

This time Damien laughed. It sounded as though he'd inhaled helium. 'Are you crazy! Where the hell did you get that much? And anyway, I can't cook that fast. We're not set up to turn around that much shit.'

'So we set you up,' said Nader. 'That's another reason that you're where you are, Damien, and I'm where I am. You see an obstacle; I see a solution. You see a problem; I see an opportunity. But that's okay. That's why there are soldiers and generals.' He moved to stand next to Damien and gripped his shoulder. 'I don't even know that I'd call you a soldier, Damo. Agassi, over there? Now, he's a soldier. Urgill, soldier. What are you? Maybe you're in the engineering corps? Is that what they call it? Whatever. You're my little uni boy, and you're finally gonna learn what it means to work.'

Nader turned to face his friends. 'Hey, Agassi, you heard that joke about the uni student who goes for a job in a deli to pay his way through school?'

'Nuh,' said Agassi. He didn't sound as though he especially wanted to.

'The deli owner tells him he's got the job and to go mop out the back. The uni boy goes, "Mop! I've got a Bachelors Degree and I'm studying for my Masters!" So the deli boss comes from around the counter and grabs the mop. "Oh yeah?" he says. "Gimme the mop then and I'll show you how to use it."'

Agassi barked out a laugh. Urgill smiled at Nader expectantly, waiting. 'I don't get it,' he said, after a pause, big, confused smile still in place.

'Nah, you wouldn't, Urgill,' said Nader. 'But that's okay; you'd know how to use the mop, right?'

Urgill turned away, dropping the smile, his face indicating that he was pretty certain he'd just been insulted, but he was not exactly sure how. Damien figured he'd get that a lot.

'What do you pricks want to eat?' Urgill said.

'Are you still here, fuckwit?' said Nader. 'Get some kebabs. Use some initiative. Everyone wants food.'

Damien moved carefully towards his backpack and surreptitiously nudged it under a chair with his foot. He glanced sidelong in Nader's direction. Thank God he hadn't noticed. I've just got to get through tonight, he told himself. I can still be out of here first thing tomorrow.

Oh fuck! Damien dropped suddenly onto the lounge. The goodbye note. He had to get it before . . .

'What's up?' Whitey let himself in to join the party.

Damien put his head in his hands. Again.

This isn't good, Jill thought, trying to appear nonchalant.

'Shove over and let us in, Krystal,' said Ingrid. 'Now you're not going out, you can hang around with us for a change. You've hardly been around here at all lately.'

'Yeah, sorry, come in,' said Jill. She stepped back inside her unit and Jelly bowled through. Ingrid walked straight to her fridge.

'Not much in here,' said Ingrid, pulling out the cask. 'What are we gonna eat tonight?'

'I don't know. I was supposed to be eating out, remember?' she said. She turned to Jelly, who now had his head in the fridge. 'Did Kasem say why he can't take us out, Jelly?' she asked.

'Nope. Just called and said he'd take us another time. There's nothing in here,' he said, his mouth full of ham. 'I say we get pizza!'

'You're looking a little peed off, Krystal, babe,' said Ingrid. 'I reckon your man Gabriel might have something to worry about. Looks as if you might have seen the light, and you're thinking about taking a trip on the Nader train. I wouldn't mind me a ticket on that ride, I can tell you.'

'What are you talking about, Ingrid? Kasem's loss. I couldn't care less,' said Jill.

'Oooh, *denying* it! You got it bad, baby, and I don't blame you.' Ingrid held up Jill's cask and expertly squirted wine into a glass. 'Now me, if I'd been stood up by that man, I'd go find him, I would. See what else I could be doing to keep his attention away from all the other distractions out there.'

Jill forced a smile. 'He's not all that, Ingrid,' she said, wondering how she was going to let work know that Kasem was now unaccounted for. She checked the clock built into the stove. Eight. An hour till they moved in to install the listening device in Damien's house in Merrylands. If they couldn't get that thing in there, the ACC would shut the whole thing down before Jill had what she needed.

Damn, where was Nader?

52

Saturday 13 April, 8 pm

In the cupboard, the gnawing feeling in Cassie's stomach told her to put rehab off until Monday. Wasn't that what you were supposed to do, anyway? Someone had once told her that the intake line was choked Mondays and Tuesdays at every rehab in the country, but come Friday and Saturday it was tumbleweed city. Everyone knew you were supposed to binge before a diet – not that Cassie would risk gaining weight by bingeing on food – but the principle was the same if you were going to kick drugs.

I'll definitely do it Monday, she thought, loosening the belt on the trenchcoat as she heard Christian's voice draw closer. This'll be my last night.

She re-buckled her belt when she realised that the person Christian was speaking to was also going to enter the room. Great.

Make that the *people* Christian was speaking to. Cassie silently moved as far to the back of the small cupboard as she could, and peered from the gloom into the brilliant light of

Christian's office. Who the fuck was that? The short guy in the tracksuit barely registered. A mere annoyance; one of the hangers-on who flocked around Christian, although they usually dressed a little better than that. But the girl? Cassie's eyes narrowed in the darkness. He moved on pretty quickly, she thought. At least he appeared to have chosen a worthy successor. She searched her heart for jealousy – got nothing. So, she really didn't care about Christian at all. Huh. While she was pleased that at least she wasn't going to get her heart broken by this guy, she experienced more bitter awareness that it really was all about the drugs. She wondered whether she even had the capacity to feel love for a man. Maybe I've got more in common with Jill than I want to admit, she thought.

She prayed Christian would not find a need to use the cupboard. She could handle looking silly in front of the bloke, but she did not want to meet that female at a disadvantage.

Cassie tried to slow her breathing and shifted her weight a little, settling in for the wait.

53

Saturday 13 April, 8.05 pm

Damien decided he should try to get a call off to Detective Jackson. He had to seem as though he was cooperating. The cops might bring the whole house down tonight because they figured they couldn't trust him, and then there wouldn't even be a deal, let alone Oxford.

Now would probably be the best time. Whitey was over in the kitchen with Nader, dollar signs in his eyes as they opened the box. Urgill was still out collecting food, and Agassi sat in a lounge chair, eyes closed. He reminded Damien of a computer waiting in sleep mode: a blank screen until it sensed movement and then instantly became fully operational.

He rose carefully from the couch and decided he'd try to retrieve the goodbye note at the same time. Whitey laughed from the kitchen; he gave a nervous giggle at pretty much everything that came out of Nader's mouth. Agassi didn't move.

Damien made it to the hallway.

'Off to shit yourself again, uni boy?' Nader called from the kitchen. 'Something's seriously wrong with those guts of yours.'

'Yeah, thanks for that,' answered Damien. 'Very helpful.'

He walked straight past the toilet and carefully opened the door to his mother's old bedroom. He thought he could still smell the 4711 perfume she used to wear. She used to buy the jumbo bottle from the chemist warehouse and sprinkle it around liberally. The smell fired emotions through his scent memory – fear, loss, hate.

He could see the letter propped on Whitey's pillow. Earlier Damien had smoothed the doona back and pushed the tangle of sheets away from the bedhead to make the envelope easier for Whitey to spot in the mess. Damien didn't think he'd ever seen Whitey's bed made. He negotiated the tight path to the bed without knocking anything over, and snatched up the letter; he shoved it down his pants, blood surging in his ears.

He retraced his steps and reached the door again, relieved. That was one less problem.

Now, should he make the call from the toilet or his room? Nader would be less suspicious if he heard him in the toilet, but therein lay the problem: Kasem might be able to hear him speaking. Fuck knew he'd had to endure five years' of Whitey's farting through his morning shit while he ate breakfast every day. Dickhead – it suddenly occurred to him – send her a text!

He walked into his bedroom, removing from his jacket pocket the phone Jackson had given him. He pressed the on button and squashed the phone into his chest to muffle the sound of the welcome chime. Moving to the point in the room furthest from the kitchen, he faced the wall and began messaging: '*Nader's here. Call it off.*' There was only one number stored, 'Krystal'. He hit send.

On the way back to the lounge he decided he needed the toilet after all. He entered quietly and took what had become his favourite seat in the house since this mess began. 'Oh fuck!' he whispered, when his phone sounded. A return text from Detective Jackson. It read: '*Meet me at uni tomorrow. Same place. Ten. Are you OK?*'

'*Fine.*' He texted back. Yep, just fine and dandy. Ecstatic. He switched the phone to silent and shoved it back into his pocket, his hands shaking. He stood up and opened the door.

'What've you got there, uni boy?' Nader stood in the doorway.

'Nothing,' he tried, but Nader had his hand out.

'Give us the phone, fuckwit.'

Damien's perspective suddenly shifted and he felt quite calm. Weird. It was like he was watching the whole scene from the ceiling, looking down on an interaction going on in his bedroom as though he had nothing to do with it. The tableau rippled and shimmered, as though he watched it through water. He saw himself walking towards Kasem Nader. He saw Nader pull him close, put an arm around his shoulder. He saw Nader use the other hand to reach into his jacket pocket and pull out the phone. He saw his hands hanging, useless, by his sides.

From his vantage point near the ceiling, Damien watched Kasem press a couple of buttons on the phone and draw him in closer, into a cuddle, Kasem's arm firmly around his shoulders. Kasem held the phone up, close, near both of their heads, so they could both read the display. His messages to Krystal.

Still holding him tightly, Nader hit dial and raised the phone to his ear. Damien was close enough to hear Detective Jackson's voice on the other end say, 'Hello.'

Nader said nothing. His face a mask, he spun Damien around with one hand and mashed his face against the wall. Is this it, Damien thought, is this how I die? His mind raced, scrabbling through the contents of the text. He could explain it somehow. What could he say – he was going to meet a girl here, but had to call it off? Think. Think.

Nader said nothing, and with one hand still plastering his face to the wall, he began to pat Damien down.

'Oh fuck.' Did I just say that out loud? thought Damien. My pocket!

'Now what's this, uni boy. Is this a note?'

54

Seren had been in this office maybe fifty times, but she could feel tonight was going to be different. Her slim shoulder bag was tucked tightly in under her arm, her hand hooked through the strap as though she just rested it there. She stood back slightly from the men, remaining as still as possible, hoping that Christian wouldn't ask her to leave at the last minute, send her on some bogus errand.

This was going to be a drug deal, she knew it now. Two years in prison had taught her the signs of villainy about to go down – the atmosphere of nonchalance contrasting with intent; tension with feigned ease. She watched Christian relax a little when he closed the office door; he turned to face the little guy with a big smile.

'So, Byron,' he said. 'Can I get you something?'

'Nah, boss. I'm sweet,' said Byron. 'Fucken traffic, man. I told Nader I'd be back by nine. We probably should just get this done.' He swung the sports bag up onto Christian's gleaming desk.

Seren held her breath. Without shifting position, she hooked her thumb into her bag and felt for the record button.

Christian moved behind his desk and sat down in his big leather chair. She pushed the button on the camera, and almost gasped. It would not depress. Something's wrong, she thought. She pushed again, firmly, knowing it was not going to work: it never felt this way. Then it suddenly came to her – the record button would not depress when the power switch was off. Somehow, she must have unconsciously switched the camera off during her last ritual.

Mouth dry, she watched Christian reach into his jacket; glimpsed a small object between his fingers – a key, she guessed. He swivelled a little in his chair and bent forward, his head briefly below the line of the desk.

Fuck, fuck, fuck, she thought. I have to get this on tape. She snuck a look at Tracksuit Man. He appeared focused on Christian, the desk, and especially his bag: he seemed to have forgotten she was even there. She brought her other hand up to her handbag, forcing herself to make slow movements. She reached in, slid the little camera from its nook and palmed it quickly, the action taking perhaps five seconds.

Christian's head was still below the desk line. She opened her hand and found the tiny black switch, set to off. Shaking her head, she slid it into the on position and raised her eyes.

Christian's eyes bored into her own.

Cassie couldn't take her eyes off this girl. It wasn't just about how gorgeous she was. Something was going on here. She seemed almost like two people. She had this cat-that-ate-the-cream smile when the men watched her, and a deer-caught-in-the-headlights grimace when they did not. And she seemed to be fiddling with something in her bag.

And what was in that sports bag on the desk?

From her vantage point, Cassie could see Christian jiggling a tiny key in the lock in the largest drawer under his desk. He seemed to be having difficulty opening it.

The girl had something in her hand now. A tiny flash of green light, and then nothing, but Cassie could see that she now held her hand by her side, her fist clenched. What was she holding?

Cassie watched the girl look up; she stared at Christian. She looked freaked.

'Are you all right, babe?' Christian asked Seren.

At twelve, when she'd finally learned that her stepfather got off on pain and fear, Seren had mastered an indifferent stare, an unconcerned façade that more often than not saw him turn his attention back to his beer, or to someone else he could make cry. She dropped that mask into place now.

'Of course, darling,' Seren said. 'Are we going to be much longer?'

'No,' he said. 'Just about done.' He slapped a thick envelope down onto his desk and turned to Byron. 'Let's have a look, then, Byron. Come check this out, Seren.'

Seren pressed the record button and moved towards the desk, the camera nestled easily in her palm. She didn't know what was going to happen next, but she was going to get it all anyway.

'That's eighty grand, is it?' said Byron, eyes on the envelope. 'Doesn't look that much.'

'It's all there, Byron. Fifties. Surprising how compact that much cash can be, isn't it?'

Byron gave a short laugh. 'Shit yeah,' he said. 'Well, here's your bag of mixed lollies.' He unzipped the sports bag and Seren stepped back, partly in shock and partly to ensure that the camera got the widest angle. Jammed into the carrier were ten or so clear plastic bags, most of them full of hundreds of pills; others contained the little opaque rocks that had sent her to prison.

'Could you give me a hand over here, Seren?'

She snapped her head up to find Christian watching her closely.

'Would you mind doing a quick count of these bags, with me?' he said. 'I'll just make sure Byron's right with the cash and we can wrap this all up.'

She smiled into Christian's eyes, questions scudding through her mind. Why is he looking at me like that? Does he know? How am I going to get the camera back in my bag while he's watching me like this? She couldn't move. Christian waited, expectant, staring straight at her.

'Seren?' he said.

Byron glanced up from the money. His eyes moved from her to Christian, then back again. And stopped.

Certain her cheeks must be flaming, she knew she had to do something now. The camera was so tiny. Maybe if she pretended to sneeze, she could bring her hand up and somehow push the camera down her shirt, into her bra? No, she'd feign an itch. But what the fuck were they staring at her like that for? She turned the tiny camera around in her palm, readying for the move.

And she dropped it.

Seren watched the little device bounce once on the floor and begin to tumble over itself. It rolled slowly away from her, losing momentum on the carpet, and came neatly to rest next to Byron's shoe.

55

Saturday 13 April, 8.10 pm

All right, all right, Jill thought. It doesn't have to be anything too bad. Damien's probably okay.

She knew she was kidding herself. In the stairwell of the housing commission unit block, she punched in Gabriel's number. Waited.

Suddenly, she whipped her head around to a sound. A baby gangster, his undies protruding from the top of his jeans, sized her up as a mark.

'What?' she shouted in his direction. He took off.

Gabriel answered. Thank God. 'Gabe. I think we've got a problem. Nader's over at the clan lab. I think something bad is going down. Nader missed our date and I just got a hang-up from Damien's phone.' She listened a moment and answered, 'Okay, I'll see you there.'

She ran back into her unit.

'Make yourself at home, you guys,' she said, forcing herself to walk to her bedroom. 'I've gotta bail.'

'Where are you going?' Ingrid wanted to know. 'Not that Gabriel again? I told ya you should stay away from him.'

'I hate Archangel Gabriel,' said Jelly, his face darkening.

I've gotta get out of here, thought Jill. 'Jelly, it's okay,' she said. 'It's just that an old friend of mine is sad, and I'm gonna go and keep her company tonight.'

'I'll come too,' said Jelly. 'I'm good company. We could teach her how to make honeycomb.'

'Next time,' said Jill. 'Promise.'

She gave Ingrid a wave and bolted for the stairwell.

'Come on, Damo. Let's go tell your mate, Whitey, about the trouble you've got him into.'

Damien could feel Nader's arm draped across his shoulder, but remarkably very little else. He knew that he should be shitting himself – quite literally, given his dicky stomach – but he couldn't seem to process things properly. He had an intellectual knowledge of what was going on: Kasem Nader now knew he was working with the cops to try to bring him down. But the fear of what Nader would do to him seemed to be missing. He was faintly aware of a mosquito-like drone of worry somewhere at the back of his consciousness, but he very deliberately swatted at it every time it grew too loud.

Now he waited in the lounge room, staring blankly at Whitey.

'Now, Damo,' said Nader. 'Tell Whitey and Agassi what you've done.'

Damien stood up quietly.

'I'll start, shall I?' said Nader. 'And look, here's Urgill, back with the food. Just in time. Good man.'

'What's going on?' said Urgill.

'Well, that's just what we're about to let everyone know, Urgill. Have a seat.'

'But the food . . .' said Urgill.

'Sit your fucken fat arse down!'

Still unperturbed, Damien watched Nader walk over to the kitchen and pick up one of the many porno magazines Byron was always bringing over. Nader flicked through a couple of pages, then looked up.

'Damien,' said Nader, speaking calmly again, 'is a police informer.'

The room erupted. Urgill shot up from his seat, a plastic bag full of food dumping from his lap onto the floor. A container bearing some sort of yoghurt-like substance hit the ground hard and splattered white goop across the rug and onto one of Agassi's shoes. Agassi stood and rhythmically clenched and unclenched his fists.

'What the fuck!' yelled Whitey. 'What are you *talking* about, Kasem? As if Damien would do that! What's going on?'

'Damien,' said Nader. 'Your turn.'

Damien watched the white stuff drizzle down Agassi's shoelace. One fat droplet seemed to be gaining on another. He wondered whether it would catch up and form a superdrop before the first one hit the ground. His concentration was broken by the magazine waved in front of his face. He raised his eyes. Nader had rolled the porno magazine into a cylinder.

'Wake up, uni boy!'

Damien felt the magazine smack into the back of his head. His neck jerked forward and he bit his tongue.

'Now, get in here,' said Nader.

Damien remained silent as Kasem dragged him across the floor using his earlobe to steer. They stopped at the stove. Damien took in the glass beakers, crusty saucers and pans, the chemicals everywhere laid out in his carefully chaotic style.

'Now, are you gonna talk, Damo?' said Nader, 'or just stand around here like some deaf fucking mute?' He smacked the magazine into the back of Damien's head with each of his next four words. 'Because. I'm. Getting. Impatient.'

Damien knew he was fucked; he knew he should be trying to talk fast to try to get himself out of this mess. But this knowledge did nothing to help to reconnect whatever wire had tripped in his brain. And the fucking slapping to his head didn't help.

He stared at Whitey morosely. He felt a tear slip down his cheek.

'Kasem, man, what are you doing?' Whitey put his hand onto Nader's to block the next blow with the magazine. 'You've got something wrong. Damien and I started this thing. Why would he go to the police? Let's talk about this!'

'Get your fucking hand off me, cunt.' Nader's voice was low.

Whitey didn't move. He tried again. 'Kasem . . .' Damien noticed that Whitey was using his reasoning voice. He'd tried the same thing with Damien's mother once when she'd skitzed out in front of him. Nader drew back his arm, and, magazine still in hand, cracked his massive fist into Whitey's face. Damien thought he could feel the crunch of his mate's nose, breaking. Whitey hit the kitchen floor, smacking the back of his head on the bench on the way down. The reasoning voice hadn't worked on Damien's mother either.

'You, uni boy, are pissing me off,' said Nader. 'So we're gonna do this differently.' He turned the gas lever on the stove. 'Okay, now we're gonna talk.'

56

'What the fuck is going on here?' Byron shouted.

Cassie kept the luscious smile up, even when the little bloke reached a hand into his tracksuit jacket. Christian exploded from his chair, sending it rocketing backwards into the wall of windows behind him. She sashayed slowly across the carpet from the wardrobe, tottering on her heels. Before opening the cupboard door, she'd once again loosened the belt on the trench-coat, smudged at her mascara and smeared a little at her lipstick. She flicked her tousled hair and flung her arms into the air.

'Surprise!' she said, and giggled. She bumped against an armchair and pretended to topple, tripping forward, one hand reaching out to the seat of the chair as though to stop herself falling all the way to the floor. She laughed again, and as she was righting herself, she angled her face towards the girl. What had Christian called her? Seren? Cassie's sheet of honey brown hair hid her face from the men. She dropped the smile, mouthed

252

'Shh', and told the girl with her eyes to just play it out. She prayed she'd done the right thing.

When Cassie had seen the device fall from Seren's hand she'd immediately guessed what it was. A camera. This girl had this whole drug deal on tape. She didn't know whether Seren was a cop, but she immediately felt she had to help her. The thought of Jill, out there undercover and vulnerable somewhere, suddenly flashed through Cassie's mind. She simply couldn't hide here and watch these men bust this girl. She prayed that there were people out there looking out for her sister.

She had to hand it to this Seren, whoever or whatever she was. The girl slipped seamlessly from total panic into the role of an outraged lover.

'Who the fuck is this, Christian?' Seren demanded, at exactly the same time as Christian said, 'Cassie! What the hell are you doing here?'

The bloke in the tracksuit started to zip up the bag, his bulging eyes darting all over the room, particularly towards the door. 'I don't know what the fuck this is, Worthington,' he said. 'I don't know what the fuck you think you're doing here, but I'm getting the fuck outta here.'

'Who is she?' Seren demanded, hands on hips.

Cassie laughed and continued staggering towards Christian's desk. 'Yeah, baby, tell me who I am,' she said, and laughed again. 'No. Did that come out wrong? Tell me who she is.' She stopped at the man with the bag and smiled widely. She twirled her fingertip close to his face. His eyes followed, as though hypnotised. 'And. Who. Are. *You*?' she said, huskily, touching the tip of his nose with her last word. The top of his head came just to her chin, and she knew his view down her coat was a wonderland.

Christian suddenly gave a shout of laughter. 'Cassie Jackson. You idiot! Where did you come from? What are you doing here?' He came around from behind the desk; put a hand on Byron's shoulder. 'Look, everyone, just calm down, okay? Cassie's a very dear friend of mine. And she's cool. Way cool. I don't know what she's doing here, but she looks a little worse for wear this evening, and I think we should all just chill a little bit.'

Byron looked up at Christian, his eyes glazed. 'Where did she come from?' he said.

'Cassie?' asked Christian.

'Don't be mad at me, baby,' she said. 'I've been waiting ages for you. I wanted to surprise you. I hid in there,' she gestured vaguely behind her, 'and fell asleep. What time is it anyway? Is it still Saturday?' She dropped her eyes briefly and spotted the camera on the floor near her foot. She nudged it carefully with the toe of her boot into a little nook beside the leg of the table. Then she turned her back to the skyline and plonked down on the desk. Three pairs of eyes watched every single move she made, two of them on her tits. She crossed her legs, slowly; the trench slipped open to the top of her thigh. The man in the tracksuit made a woofing sound, as though he'd just been punched in the gut.

'Who's a girl gotta do to get a drink around here, Christian?' she said. 'I'm thirsty.'

57

Saturday 13 April, 8.15 pm

Jill's back wheels lost traction on gravel taking a fifty-kilometre bend at ninety. She hammered the Magna down Woodville Road, weaving through the traffic as though the other vehicles stood still. I wish I had a siren on this bitch, she thought for the tenth time, overtaking a Honda in the breakdown lane.

She had to assume Damien had been busted. Why would else would he make a call and say nothing? He'd already told her Nader was in the house. Was the call a silent warning to her that something else was going on? Some kind of message because he couldn't speak? Had someone else got hold of his phone? The kid was in trouble; she knew it. She slowed for a red light ahead. Cars waited in both lanes. Damn. She steered into the empty right-only turning lane and carefully crossed the intersection, ignoring the bleating motorists behind her.

How bad could this get? she wondered. If the whole thing was blown and these guys bolted with the goods before she could get there, she and Gabriel would look like fools, especially to the

ACC. But Superintendent Last would be the one to really cop it: passing up the opportunity to take down a known clan lab with offenders in custody, on the off chance that they might get something bigger. And they didn't even have any firm leads on whether Nader actually was importing precursors. It was all just speculation, and Last had believed in her enough to ask the ACC to back down while they ran the show. Fuck. Last would never trust her again.

And Damien. She thought about the kid's reaction when she and Gabe had detailed his role in this operation. Every emotion was painted across his face as he experienced it: fear, anger, guilt. Why had she ever thought he'd be able to pull this off?

She picked up her phone to call Last. He could get the local boys to go over there right now. But what if the plan was still intact? Or what if everyone overreacted and someone got hurt? The cops would have to be told about the chemicals inside and they would cordon off the street, go in with the megaphone. It'd end up a standoff. They wouldn't go in until everyone came out and if Nader chose to take hostages, the whole thing would go to shit.

Call. Don't call. What would be best here?

She dropped her mobile back onto the passenger seat for the third time. When a truck ahead suddenly slowed, she stood on the brakes. The phone flew forward, smacked into the footrest and skidded somewhere under the seat. Well, that decides that, she thought.

A couple of streets from Damien's she backed the speed off a little. She knew Gabriel couldn't have got here ahead of her. She planned to do a recce and decide what to do when she had some more information. If all seemed quiet in there, she'd wait for Gabe and talk through their next steps. If she discovered Damien was being hurt, that would be another story.

Jill ditched the Magna out the front of a redbrick home at the top of the street. The lighting for this road was brighter than most of the others around here, and fortunately it was a pretty dark evening. She hoped to be able to get as close as possible to the house to see whether she could hear what was happening inside.

Risky, she knew. If Kasem didn't know what was going on and spotted her out here, she'd be hard pressed trying to explain what 'Krystal Peters' was doing hovering around a house in Nader's parents' street in Merrylands. She figured that she could pretend to be a lovesick stalker, disgruntled at his blowing off their date, who had come to his house to find him, and then spotted his car down the road. Whether he'd believe her or not was debatable. Whatever: any way she played this, he would not be happy to see her here. Best that he doesn't, then, she told herself.

She stopped jogging three houses from the clan lab and kept as close to the property boundary as possible, out of the pools of light glowing over the road. It all seemed pretty quiet. The tension in her shoulders scaled down a little. She hadn't known what to expect – a shootout on the lawn, a body on the front steps? But the house squatted silently, windows lit behind blinds: just another home in the suburbs.

No lights were on in the house next door, and Jill took the chance that no one was home. She stepped through the gap in the low brick wall that partitioned the home from the street and crept across the well-tended lawn. Shrubs and another low-lying fence now lay between her and Damien's house. She wriggled closer, the branches of a straggly bush raking through her hair, clutching at her clothes. She thought she could hear voices now and wondered whether she should climb the fence.

Men shouting. She couldn't make out what they were saying, but something was going down in there. Jill stepped up onto the lowest rung of the fence and cartwheeled over into the dark yard next door.

Whitey lay still at Damien's feet, blood oozing from his nose.

Someone had to say something. The gas was already shimmering the air around the stove, the sweet, distinctive smell setting off an alarm in Damien's head. Finally, he found his voice. 'Kasem.'

'Ah, you *can* speak, uni boy.'

'I don't know what you're trying to prove here,' Damien said, 'but can you do it some other way? The shit in this kitchen is already reactive enough without the gas going. I'll tell you whatever you want, but can we just shut the gas off and open some windows?' He reached out to turn off the stove.

Nader smacked the rolled-up magazine across the back of Damien's hand. 'Actually, mate,' he said, 'you can tell me what I want to know right now. Who is Krystal?'

Damien gave it his best shot. 'A, um, a girl from uni.'

'FUCKING LIAR!' screamed Nader. Then, in his reasonable, calm voice, he said, 'It's Krystal Peters. She's a fucking cop, isn't she, uni boy?'

'Yes.'

'Real name?'

'Detective Jill Jackson.' Damien watched the air shimmer.

'Urgill, Agassi, get over here.' Nader waved his hand above the benchtop. 'Pack up whatever shit you can carry and get it out of here now.' He turned back to Damien. 'Never bullshit a bullshitter, isn't that what they say, Damo? You chose the wrong side.'

Damien's brain threatened to piss off somewhere again. He forced himself to focus. 'Look, we can get this shit sorted out, Kasem, but you've got to turn the gas off now. Even if you get the chemicals out of here, there're a lot of by-products and gases that remain. You'll blow us all up!'

'Thanks, Damien. That's a good point. I just need the gas going another coupla minutes.'

Damien stared open-mouthed at this lunatic. What the fuck was he going to do? He nudged Whitey with his foot. Wake up, he wanted to scream. He could try to bolt for the door, but he couldn't leave Whitey here like this, in a house full of gas with Kasem Nader. Nader smiled back at him, seemingly amused by his desperation. Damien scrambled for the right thing to say to this idiot to make him stop.

'What do you want me to do?' he asked.

'Just what you're told in future, thanks, Damo. Remember our little talk about soldiers and generals? Well, I need you to stop trying to pretend that you have a cock, and just do whatever the fuck I tell you to do.'

'Okay, okay! Just turn the gas off.' Damien started to cough. His eyes streamed. 'Whitey's out cold, man. You're gonna kill him.'

'Actually, you'd better hope you can wake your little friend up pretty quickly, Damo, or that just might be the case.' Nader rolled the magazine in his hand into a tighter cylinder, and to Damien's mushrooming horror, shoved it into the toaster next to the stove and depressed the lever.

'I'll be outside waiting, Damo,' he said. 'We'll relocate this little enterprise and you'd better do as you're fucking told next time.'

Damien forced himself to be calm and careful. He might have three minutes, if he was very lucky and the place didn't go up even before the magazine ignited. He grabbed a beaker off the sink and jetted water into it from the cold tap. If this didn't wake his friend, he'd have to drag him out. He dashed the water into Whitey's face. Whitey coughed and moaned, and Damien started dragging him.

'What the fuck? Get off me!' Whitey struggled and thrashed.

'Whitey,' said Damien, bending close to his friend's ear. 'If you want to live, please get the fuck up and run.'

58

Saturday 13 April, 8.20 pm

Jill felt like screaming. From the shadows at the side of the house, she watched Agassi and Urgill carrying out what had to be drug paraphernalia. She pictured her phone, wedged somewhere under the seat in the car at the top of the street. Please, Gabriel, get here soon, she thought.

She was sidling closer to the dark underbelly of the house when another man emerged onto the relative brightness of the porch. Kasem Nader. He too carried a box. So, would Damien be next? Or was he in there somewhere, hurt, or worse?

She began to breathe deeply, pumping herself up for action. No way could she just sit here and watch. These men were packing this thing up. They were going to get away with it. Back-up or not, she had to do something. She couldn't just squat here in the dark while they removed all the hard evidence and moved on, leaving her, Gabriel and Lawrence Last to take the crap.

She wrinkled her nose. That smell. What . . . ? The odour

suddenly registered and she sprang from the ground, launching herself onto the fence using it as a hurdle.

And the world went white.

It jarred back into technicolour with a roar of sound. Jill found herself sprawled eight metres from the fence on the lawn next door to the clan lab, unable to breathe.

Am I dying? she wondered.

She made an O with her lips, as though sucking through a straw, sipping for any tiny breath of air she could get. Nothing. Her vision darkened, bruised purple, cleared, then faded again.

'You all right there, Krystal?'

Nader. He reached a hand down. Jill heard the Maroubra surf in her ears.

'You're just winded, I think. Here, sit up a bit,' he said. She could barely hear him.

He carefully hooked an arm around her waist and helped her sit up. Air streamed into her lungs and she sat quietly with her head between her knees, drinking it in. The sweetness quickly gave way to the acridity of smoke.

She coughed and turned her head to the left. The wall of the clan lab she'd huddled against was gone. A mouth-like opening now yawned, revealing blackened furniture and a sputtering fire within the house. She lifted her eyes to Nader. They seemed to be the only part of her body she could move without pain.

'Little Krystal,' he said, smoothing her hair from her eyes. 'Such a talented little soldier. I would have made you an officer.'

Jill wasn't certain she was hearing any of this right. The ocean still rushed inside her head. She blinked up at him.

'But that's not going to happen now,' he said. 'I'd say your cover is blown, ah, Jackson.'

Their eyes met and they both looked back at the house. Nader winked and walked away.

Jill lay down in the cool grass and waited for Gabriel.

59

Sunday 14 April, 12.30 pm

Seren leaned back on her elbows on the picnic rug and watched Marco kick a soccer ball with some kid he'd just met. The midday sun had been almost too hot today, which was surprising for April, especially this close to the harbour, which usually cooled things down a lot. She tilted her head back further and studied the intricate underbelly of the Sydney Harbour Bridge, almost directly above her. She sighed, and just as they had all night, her thoughts flip-flopped backwards and forwards. Should she let go of the plan and try to make the most of what she had, or should she just go ahead with the final step – confront Christian with the evidence and demand a million dollars?

Seren knew Christian had that much money and more. On several occasions before going out for the night, he'd traded shares online; she'd seen his portfolio. Before she'd been imprisoned, he'd even offered to give her some tips for online trading, and she'd almost slapped him, even then, when she'd loved him madly. Like *she* needed to know how to do that. What was she going to buy shares with? And she knew his Darling Harbour apartment was worth more than a million alone. Late one Saturday morning, two Asian men had knocked on Christian's door and offered him $1.8 million to buy it. He'd later explained that they owned the apartment next door and, like him, had bought their unit off the plan when it was worth half as much. He told Seren that his neighbours knew he owned the apartment outright, and they'd been trying to buy the property for their relatives ever since they'd moved in. She knew Christian had the money, and she believed he'd pay it rather than risk exposure and gaol, but she was no longer certain that she could bear the strain of the risks she was taking.

By eight this morning she'd had to get out of her flat. She didn't think she'd slept even one moment last night. She couldn't believe she'd got out of that office alive, let alone with the camera, and that evidence. With hands that still shook, when she had arrived home she'd carefully downloaded the footage onto the laptop, transferring it to the folder she'd hidden in her system files. She had re-set the password and shoved the computer back under her bed. She thought about the girl – whoever Cassie Jackson was, she'd saved Seren's life. She had a feeling that Tracksuit Man wouldn't have let her just walk out of there if he'd seen the camera. But now, what did she owe Cassie? No one gives you something for nothing – her stepfather had taught her that one useful thing at least.

Surely last night was a sign of how dangerous this whole thing was. She looked back at her son, saw him laughing, his too-long black hair flopping into his eyes, then streaming back from his forehead as he ran. How could she be so selfish as to put him at risk again? She knew there were three ways their life could now pan out. One: Marco having her there to protect him as best she could in that unit block – well, at least for the foreseeable future. Two: she and Marco, rich and safe, away from there forever. Option three was Marco, all alone in the world again, with her in gaol or dead. What right did she have to take the gamble?

She turned to Angel, sitting on the rug next to her, carefully peeling a mandarin. Should I ask her advice? she wondered again.

'Whatcha thinking, hun?' said Angel, startling her.

'Ah, just how I wish I could hang out with Marco more and that I didn't have to go to work tomorrow,' she said.

'I hear that!' said Angel, who worked a probation-and-parole-ordered job in a mail-sorting depot, with an hour's commute each way.

'Angel . . .' began Seren, at the same moment that Angel said, 'Speaking of which . . .' They both laughed, and Seren said, 'You go first. What were you going to say?'

'Nothing exciting,' said Angel. 'I was just going to say that maybe we should pack up and start heading back. I've got to get a few things sorted before work tomorrow.'

'Yep, okay, we should,' said Seren. 'As long as you come over for dinner tonight. I've decided I'm going to make chicken lasagne. I'll shout a good red.'

'Hey, good red or shit red, you don't have to ask me twice. I'm there.'

They packed up the remnants of their lunch and Seren called Marco over. Angel bent to pick up a bag and winced.

'Angel! What are you doing?' she said. 'Marco, take that bag from Aunty Angel.' She watched with concern as Marco hurried to take the bag from Angel's bandaged right hand. A prickling of blood welled through the large cloth bandage. 'That hand isn't getting better very quickly, is it?' Seren said. 'You never did tell me how you hurt it.'

'Oh, just cooking, like I said before,' said Angel. 'There's no big bloody story.' She grabbed the rug from the grass with her left hand and shook it out, favouring the right. 'Let's get going. I've got nothing washed at home, and I'm not gonna get anything dry if we don't hurry up.'

60

Monday 15 April, 12.40 pm

Jill could glimpse sunshine in Belmore Park to the right of the Central Square building, but none of its warmth reached her. She stepped out of Gabriel's car into Castlereagh Street, a strong wind from the railway tunnel behind her blasting straight up her shirt. She wrapped her arms around her body, and hurried after Gabriel towards the multistorey building. The street noise muted instantly when the glass doors shooshed closed behind them, and they crossed the lobby to the bank of elevators that would take them up to the Sydney offices of the Australian Federal Police.

Two jump-suited federal cops, necks like front-row forwards, stood beside a desk and studied their approach when they got out of the lift.

'Help you?' one of them said. He looked to Jill like some monstrous teenager; she wondered how the hell his parents had kept him fed.

'It's all right, Moose. I've got 'em.' Jill watched Cameron Genovese make his way across the room – it took him maybe two strides. He and the other two footy players dwarfed her and Gabriel, and looking up at them she suddenly felt her throat constrict. She automatically scanned the room for every exit point and for something to use as a weapon. Her eyes closed involuntarily but she could still picture where everyone stood, heard every movement in the room. She forced herself to open her eyes, furious with her body for assuming this ridiculous defensive reaction every time she perceived male threat. Having trained herself for years to fight blindfolded, her first instinct was to close off the visuals when she perceived danger.

You're in the copshop, stupid, she told herself, following Gabriel and Genovese from the lobby. Whatever greeting they'd exchanged when shaking hands had not registered. But she was certain she wouldn't have missed much of a love-fest between these two.

Genovese led them down a narrow corridor and into a clinically-outfitted office. A desk, a few high-backed office chairs, and that was it. But there was no need for decoration in the room; the entire wall facing the door was made of glass. She walked across and stood looking over the park to Central Station, the ornate sandstone clock tower registering twelve forty pm. A train to the left of the tower snaked silently towards the city; she watched it until it disappeared at the corner of the window, then turned when she heard footsteps approaching the room.

Olsen Lanvin knocked once at the open door and walked in. Jill could see the clock tower reflected in his wire-rimmed glasses, with no eyes visible behind the reflection. She crossed the room to shake hands. Gabriel and Genovese had already claimed their seats. She took the one closest to the window and swivelled her back to the view.

'Would anyone like some coffee or water, before we begin?' asked Lanvin. When everyone responded in the negative, he too sat.

Jill steeled herself for the lecture. She knew that the ACC would badly have wanted the clan lab bust, and she was certain that Lanvin and Genovese would've copped heat from their superiors for not taking the Merrylands operation down as soon as they knew about it. She rubbed at her neck, which was still stiff and sore from the blast. Sore she could understand, but she could not believe that she still felt tired – she'd spent the whole day yesterday asleep in her bed, in her *real* bed, in Maroubra. After being checked out by ambos at the explosion site in Merrylands, and making her formal report to Superintendent Last, he'd instructed her to go home, informing her that her undercover operation would be shut down.

'So, Jill,' said Lanvin. 'We got your report from Last. You doing okay?'

'Fine, thanks.' Let's just get this done, she thought.

He glanced down at a typed document in his hand. 'So, just to clarify, Jill, after the explosion, you believe that Kasem Nader, Francis Agassi and Ralph Urgill forced Damien Rose and Peter White into a black Holden Statesman?'

.'Yeah, well Agassi and Urgill did, anyway,' she said.

'While Nader was speaking to you,' said Genovese.

'That's right,' she said, her voice hard. 'After I came to.' And I was on my arse trying to breathe, you prick. She already felt like shit that she hadn't been able to do anything. Genovese was trying to make sure she felt that way a while longer.

'And then Nader drove the vehicle away from the site?' said Lanvin.

Jill nodded.

'I don't really understand why you think White and Damien were forced into the car,' said Lanvin. 'Could it not have just been that these men knew you were on to them, blew up the lab and moved on together?'

Jill paused at his words – *knew* you *were on to them*. They were already trying to extricate themselves from this mess. If the Feds had closed the operation, she knew she wouldn't have even got a mention, but now things had gone south, her name would be inserted at every opportunity. She let it ride. It was more important at the moment that these guys understood that Damien and Whitey had been abducted. If she didn't make that point clear right now, there'd be no mercy in the takedown when they caught

Nader and co. She knew that in most cops' eyes Whitey and Damien were nothing but drug dealers, and if they got caught in the crossfire, then so be it. She didn't think it was as simple as that.

'No,' she said. 'As I indicated in my report, it was obvious that there was something wrong with White. Damien was supporting him, helping him to walk. I didn't see them leave the house, but they'd almost made it across the road when I came to. Damien was looking around and he called something out to a neighbour. There were plenty of spectators by then. It looked like Damien wanted someone to help him: he waved his arm. Agassi opened the back door and Urgill pretty much threw Whitey into the back seat. Damien tried to run; Agassi pursued, caught hold of his jacket. Damien twisted out of the jacket and ran again. By that time, Urgill was there, and he brought Damien down in a tackle, then a knee to the back. He hauled him up again and into a wrist hold, hand up behind his back; frogmarched him back to the car. Delahunt and I have seen him use the same hold on this kid in the past.' Jill paused, remembering the frustration of being unable to move or find her gun, knocked from her hands in the explosion. 'By that time Nader was back at the vehicle. He got in the driver's seat and took off.'

'And waved to you first, I think it says in here.' Lanvin flourished the report in his hand.

'Well, you read that part all right,' said Jill. 'Why'd you make me go over it again?'

'Just clarifying, Jackson,' he said. 'You know the deal.'

'Well, it's pretty clear now, isn't it?' said Gabriel. 'We've got two people taken by force, one of whom was a cooperative police informant, and neither of whom has a criminal record. Yet.' He stood and walked over to the window. 'So we got the site cleaned up out there as much as possible, and we now need to get these guys back again. You got the techies to do an interception on the whole grid, didn't you?'

Genovese and Lanvin locked eyes, then looked at their shoes.

'To do what?' said Jill.

'Monitor their mobile calls,' said Gabriel.

'We planned to talk to you first and get on it,' said Lanvin.

'Well, let's move then.' Gabriel walked as he talked, then stood at the door waiting. 'Coming?' he said.

Jill grabbed her leather jacket from the car, and hurried back to Gabriel, who was waiting for her at the front of the building. As she jogged into Hay Street, she spotted him, surrounded by pigeons. He was breaking small pieces of bread off a roll and scattering them to the cooing birds, oblivious to the irritated stares of the office workers having to negotiate around them.

'Where'd you get the bread?' she asked him.

He held the roll out to her.

'No, I don't want to eat it,' she said. She shook her head, and took the roll from his hands, shredded it quickly and threw the pieces to the birds. 'I just wondered . . . oh, don't worry. Come on, let's go.' She began the walk down towards Chinatown.

'I always bring bread over here,' he said, catching up. 'The pigeons here are always hungry.'

Aren't pigeons hungry everywhere? she wondered. Whatever. 'So, what was all that in there?' she asked. She had stayed quiet for the past hour, feeling out of place as Gabriel, Genovese and Lanvin had hit the computers and given orders to a series of personnel.

'We put keyword telecommunications intercepts on the whole Sydney grid. We're blanketing the metro to find him.'

At the next intersection, she let another pedestrian hit the button at the lights to get the walk signal. Those things were filthy. She didn't touch them unless she had to. 'So how does that work?' she asked. She had a pretty good idea about telecommunication surveillance, but she wanted to understand exactly what they were doing to try to find Damien. And Nader.

'Easy,' Gabriel said. 'We assign key words to a watch list and then red flag them when they come up.'

'So you listen to everyone's conversations to try to catch them saying Nader's name, or a word associated with him?'

'Sort of. And not just his name. Nicknames and aliases of known associates, street names, discussion about the explosion in Merrylands, slang terms for drug deals, especially amphetamines.'

Jill noticed the woman next to them staring openly at Gabriel. She felt relieved when the traffic stopped and they could cross the road. Nothing he'd said was really confidential, but she hated the thought of anyone listening in on this conversation. She considered her discomfort and smiled at the irony.

'So a name comes up, and then what happens?' she said. They'd outstripped the office workers and had a clear run down to Dixon Street.

'Well, a program prioritises the mentions and someone brings it to our attention when it reaches our set level of importance,' he said.

'Computers monitor the calls?'

'Yeah, it's a word recognition program. It recognises the word, records the whole conversation, our techies review it to see if it's got a connection to what's going on, and if it does, they pass it to us. We'll be the first to know.'

'What are we meant to do while we're waiting?' she said.

'Eat.'

'After that.' Sheesh.

'If we're lucky, we'll go pick 'em up. They'll come to us. We just need to wait.'

She stared at Gabriel's back as they descended a couple of stairs into a Dixon Street food hall. It was single file from there – the place was packed.

'You sure you wanna eat here?' she yelled, close behind him, eyes on her shuffling feet. The sight of so many people around her jump-started palpitations in her chest.

'Yeah. I'll order. You get us a seat,' he called over his shoulder, and peeled away into the crowd.

Ah, shit, she thought, all appetite evaporating.

Rows of long, rectangle tables stretched through the centre of the hall. Dozens of steaming food stalls lined the walls in a riot of colour and noise. Throngs of people pushed along the narrow corridors between them. Jill stood still.

'Get out of the way, would you?' A sweating man pushed past her, balancing a tray. Having spotted a seat at a table ahead, the man was missile-focused on the spare chair. She watched him, forcing herself to concentrate on one thing at a time. He plonked down and unloaded an impossible amount of food. It appeared all of the bowls were for him: none of the surrounding diners acknowledged him, or even glanced up.

Pushed and jostled at every turn, Jill stepped in between two rows of tables, and stood awkwardly as all around people ate and talked. Then, miraculously, two diners right in front of her finished their meals and she dropped gratefully into a seat. A dreadlocked youth carrying shopping bags aimed for the chair next to her, saw her face, and turned around again.

'Taken,' she said, unneccessarily.

The spicy smells seemed to have a soporific effect, and by the time Gabriel found her, she was surprised to find herself feeling much calmer and even hungry. He carried a plastic bag in each hand and balanced a tray tottering with bowls and two soft drink cans.

'I got a mixture of things,' he said.

'Yes,' she said. 'You did.'

He spread the food out in front of them and handed her some chopsticks. She pulled a bowl of short soup towards her. She tasted it; it was delicious.

'You don't need to eat that,' said Gabriel. 'It comes free with the real food. Here, try this.' He scissored a glistening piece of meat from a still-sizzling dish in front of him and held it to her mouth.

'What is it?' she said. He sighed and put the meat in his own mouth, answering while chewing. 'Garlic beef. Extra garlicky. You gotta eat it while it's hot.'

'Are you crazy?' she said. 'We have to work. You're going to stink.'

He raised another piece to her lips. 'Yep,' he said. 'So you have to eat some too, so you don't complain all afternoon.'

The morsel smelled so appetising that she accepted it. She pulled the dish closer and they ate for a while without speaking.

'What if he doesn't use a phone for some time?' she said finally, taking a sip of Pepsi Max. She liked that he remembered what she usually drank.

'He'll make a call, or send a text,' said Gabriel. He gestured to her to try some of the steamed vegies, but she was stuffed, and shook her head. 'That's what these dickheads do,' he said. 'It's how they live. They can't help themselves. Some of them think that if they buy a clean phone they'll be sweet. I've heard that some dealers buy a new pre-paid mobile every week, and dump the old one. They don't understand that if we wanna trace them it's not just the phone they use, but what they actually say. Then, when we think we have a hit we isolate the area and find out exactly where they are. And as long as their phone is switched on, we have a mobile tracking system. It's a beacon.'

Jill nodded. She'd heard before that these things could be done, of course, but she hadn't realised it could be put into place so swiftly. And *she'd* never caught a crook that way.

'What if he leaves Sydney?' she said.

'Well, we'll widen the catchment if we don't get a hit soon,' he said. 'But if Nader's who we think he is, he'll have another place close by. These guys usually have multiple properties fairly close to each other. They like to keep their operations separate. That way, if one of the labs blows up, or there's a bust at one property, they can get operations up and running again relatively quickly.'

Gabriel leaned back in his chair and stretched his arms above his head.

Jill started stacking plates. The table looked like a crime scene.

Gabriel rubbed his belly. 'You want dessert?'

She gave him a look.

'Then let's go,' he said. 'I bought extras and I want to drop them back at my house before this thing takes off again.'

Jill stood and joined the thinning stream of people next to her. She felt a finger hook into the waistband of her jeans and spun on the spot.

'Just keeping up,' said Gabriel. 'Chill.'

She wondered what the hell to say to that when she heard his mobile sound.

'Yep,' said Gabriel. 'Five.'

She felt him nudge her a little, hurrying her along.

'I told you I shouldn't have bought extra stuff,' he said. 'They think they've got him. All this food's gonna be wasted.'

61

Monday 15 April, 3.30 pm

'So how're you feeling about being out from undercover?' asked Gabriel, as he steered the car through the traffic effortlessly. Jill had noticed before when driving with Gabriel that he seemed to sense a gap or a slow-down up ahead before it materialised, and they seemed always to end up in the fastest lane.

Although they believed they had a confirmed location in Riverstone for Nader, Gabriel wasn't using the siren. She thought about his question for a moment before answering him.

'Pretty good, I guess,' she said.

'You're supposed to feel weird,' he said.

'Weird,' she said.

'Well, technically, you shouldn't be here. You're supposed to have a mandatory debrief with the psych, and then you're meant to have a couple of weeks off.'

'Mmm. Well the New South Wales police service is *real* good about ensuring that we all get access to counselling. Last count, I think they've got one psych on staff, and she's been on sick report for about six months.'

'They could call someone in, like last time.'

'Yeah, and as if I would go,' she said. 'Bloody useless, that woman.'

'Okay, so I'll debrief you.'

'Shut up.'

'How do you feel about not getting to say goodbye to Ingrid, and what did you call him – Lolly?'

She laughed. '*Lolly*! You're an idiot. It's Jelly.'

'So? How do you feel?'

She wrinkled her brow. She'd thought of them constantly since Last had pulled her out. They would worry about her. They'd worry a lot. And she couldn't believe she cared. She tried to remember her last real girlfriends: both of them she had left behind at age twelve, with the school carnival and her childhood, when she'd been dragged into the car by paedophiles. And *Ingrid* had been her first choice since for a new girlfriend? Ingrid: alcohol dependent, the confidante of junkies, foster mum to adults who could never survive out there alone. Jill knew that in her role as a cop she would have had some time for Ingrid, but she would mainly have seen her as another victim, someone to be pitied. She would never have imagined that she could have found her so funny, so warm. She smiled a little, thinking of all the laughs she'd had with Ingrid. Jill could count the number of times she'd laughed like that over the past twenty years.

She turned her face to the window and stared into her recent past. Since her kidnappers had died, she'd felt herself changing, and at first she'd grasped desperately at her old self, clinging to it frantically, as though to a towel being yanked from her naked body. She'd always believed that without all of her rituals and rigidity she'd splinter into pieces, irreparably fractured. But the opposite had been the case. She felt more whole; more real. She actually felt things.

She felt sad. Why did it take so long to get here? I'm thirty-two, she thought. She shifted her whole body around in the seat, angling herself as far from Gabriel as possible, her face wet with silent tears. The last time she'd spoken to her mum, she'd sounded old.

She'd never thought of her parents ageing, of her siblings becoming adults. Everything had changed all around her while she'd been frozen, the largest part of her still a shivering girl in the basement.

And Cassie. The tears were streaming now and she brought her hand up to her mouth. Her little sister had grown up without her, shut out completely. Cassie had been ten when the real Jill had left and never come home. Tim, her brother, had been an older adolescent, at the point anyway of beginning to separate from family into adult connections. Cassie had been on her own, their mother obsessed at first with keeping Jill alive, and then with keeping her at school. She and Cassie had been so close once. Their whole lives they'd shared the same room, all their secrets, their clothes, their toys and their friends. Until that day.

Jill pulled her feet up onto the seat, and huddled into the door, crying quietly. She finally got it. She hadn't been the only one snap-frozen twenty years before. Ten-year-old Cassie Jackson still waited alone somewhere, her adult self blocking out the sound of her cries with drugs and alcohol.

Jill barely felt Gabriel's hand on her shoulder.

62

Monday 15 April, 3.30 pm

Seren tried to slap the thoughts away as they flew forward from her consciousness. She just focused her eyes on the road and willed the next bus to come. Unable to stand still, she paced the pavement – up to the post box, back to the bus stop sign. Turn around, begin again.

She'd arrived early at the bus stop this afternoon, so she'd crossed the road to buy Marco a chocolate milk. When he didn't get off his regular school bus, a toaster-sized block of ice had dropped into her stomach. When the second bus had sailed past without even stopping, the ice had spread into her lungs and limbs. Her hands now freezing, she dumped the milk carton into the bin on the way up to the post box. One more bus and I'll go home. If he's not on this bus, he'll be there. If he's not on the next bus, he'll be at home. *Our Father who art in heaven, hallowed be thy name . . .*

Seren spotted danger crossing the road. The bloke from the convenience store who'd tried to convince her with his eyes that he could take her to heaven. She'd told him with hers that she'd see him in hell first. It didn't help that he was pissed. She'd smelled him as soon as he'd walked into the shop. Cheap bourbon and cigarettes. The scent had exploded the mental photo-album of her stepfather, raining images of him through her mind. Used to it, she'd shut them out with a shake of her head.

But now, stuck on the island in the centre of the four-lane road, the pisspot wasn't going to let it go. Did they ever?

'Hey you stuck-up fucken giant!' he yelled, spit flying from his mouth. 'Why do you think you're so fucken good. Stuck-up fucken giant.' He laughed at himself, mumbled something incoherent and tottered. 'You're gonna have a drink with me.'

Seren kept doing laps, looking for the bus. She glanced over her shoulder when a car braked hard and beeped, the drunk giving the finger and attitude to the driver who'd almost collected him. He made it to the gutter near the bus stop sign just before she did, and straightened himself up, preparing to use his best pick-up line.

'FUCK OFF!' she screamed directly into his face. And he did.

The bus! She spotted it at the top of the hill two hundred metres away, before it had even breached the crest. He'll be on the bus, she told herself.

The next two sets of traffic lights and six minutes, forty-eight seconds took forever. Seren felt she'd aged ten years.

Marco was not on the bus.

She started to run.

Before she even opened the door Seren could *feel* that Marco wasn't in the unit. She screamed his name anyway as she yanked it open. She bolted through their couple of rooms and straight back out again, still running, down to Angel's. No one was there either. Moaning and panting, she ran back to her unit and collapsed into a chair. She dropped her face into her hands.

I've got to call the police, she told herself, knowing, even as she reached for her phone, that Maria Thomasetti would hear of this almost immediately and would find a way to lock her up for breaching parole. One of her conditions for release was that she care adequately for her son. Trying to steady her breath so that she could at least speak when the police answered, she punched in the first zero to dial emergency services, and heard a key in the door. She flew from the chair and ripped the door open, to find Marco, school backpack in hand, staring at her blankly. She dragged him to her and slammed the door, holding him close. He shivered.

'Baby, what happened?' She struggled to keep the scream from her voice. He wasn't just late home from school. Something was very wrong.

He stared at her.

'Are you hurt?' she said. 'Here, sit down.'

She turned the kitchen tap on and splashed water into a glass. Put it in front of him. He drained it, and seemed to gather himself. His eyes filled with tears.

'What?' she said.

'Aunty Angel,' he said.

Oh God – was Angel hurt? She shook Marco's shoulder, once, to keep him talking.

'She took me,' he said.

'Took you where, darling?' What the hell? Where is Angel?

'She took me from school,' he said. 'At lunchtime. She told me you had to go back to gaol and she was gonna take care of me now.' Tears streamed down his cheeks.

'She told you . . .' Seren couldn't make sense of any of his words. She stood. '*Angel* said . . . What are you *talking* about, Marco?' Her voice bounced off the walls and he flinched.

'We got on a bus to Queensland. She was all weird, Mum. She's been real weird to me lately, like calling me her boy and stuff like that. And she told me she's my mum now and we'll be okay together.' He cried and she held him. He looked up at her. 'I got off the bus when we stopped for a toilet break and I ran.'

'But how did you get here, darling?'

'I told this man at the servo what happened and he drove me back here.'

'You . . . He drove you . . . Where is he? Did he hurt you?'

'No, Mum. He was cool. He just dropped me here and said good luck and he drove away.'

Oh. My. God. She gathered him up again. 'I'm here, baby, it's all right.'

Seren rubbed Marco's back reflexively as her thoughts scudded. Suddenly her hand stopped and she raised it to her mouth. Horror mushroomed in her chest and a chill raised the hairs on her arms. An image of Angel's hand, bandaged since the night her unit had been robbed, flashed before her. The thief had broken her window to get in. *Angel* took her rent money? Angel had wanted her locked up again?

'Marco.' She struggled to keep from screeching. A siren blatted ceaselessly in her mind, and she felt certain she must be shouting. 'Try and remember, honey. It's really important. Did Angel leave you alone in her unit for a while on the night we got robbed?'

He wrinkled his brow. 'I don't know, Mum. I always fall asleep after dinner over there. I'm not going there anymore. I don't care what you say!'

'No, baby. You're not going there ever again.' She stood and checked that the front door was locked. 'In fact, you're never going to have to see her or this place again. Go pack up some clothes and your games. You don't need everything – I just want you to hurry. Only grab your favourites. We're getting out of here.'

The Christian plan was going ahead. No way was she going to sit here and wait for Tready or some other prick to rape her and move in; or for some deranged woman to snatch her son. She'd fight her fate or die trying. She rushed into her bedroom and hauled out a duffle bag, shoved a few things in and then kneeled down by the bed to grab the laptop.

It was gone.

She flattened herself on the floor and swept her hands wildly under the bed, reaching as far as she could.

'I've got it, Mum.'

She snapped her head up, smacking it against the underside of the bed.

'What?'

'I've got the laptop. It's in my room. Don't be mad. I was playing games before school.'

She jumped up and hugged him again. 'I love you, Marco.'

'You're not very good at hiding things, Mum.'

63

Monday 15 April, 3.45 pm

'Sorry about that,' said Jill. She straightened in the passenger seat and wiped her face on her sleeve. She felt oddly calm, even peaceful.

'You all right?' said Gabriel.

'Mm-hmm. Where are we?'

'Approaching Blacktown. We should reach Riverstone in fifteen, twenty.'

'How'd they find him?'

'Techies got multiple hits from a thirty-second conversation. Most important word was "Urgill".'

'Huh. Dickheads. And then what?'

'Satellite navigation triangulated the call to the exact location. Have a look in the folder.'

Jill had intended to go through the information as soon as they'd begun the drive. But her outburst of emotion had come as a complete surprise. She pulled the folder from between the seats, flipped it open, and took out three stapled pages. The first contained an address in Riverstone and five or six bullet points about the area immediately surrounding the target property. She turned over to find a full-page colour aerial photograph of a sprawling, fenced homestead. The detail was amazing. She could see a rusted car, dead grass and missing roof tiles. She flipped the page again.

'Oh my God! Are you kidding me?' she said.

The picture had been zoomed in multiple times. She stared at another aerial shot, this time of a man sitting on a back porch. A child's pink bicycle, missing the back wheel, lay discarded at the bottom of the concrete steps. The man was smoking, and was unmistakably Francis Agassi.

Gabriel smiled.

'When was this taken?' she asked.

He glanced at the clock in the dash. 'Ah, around thirty minutes ago,' he said.

'But how'd they get it? Google Earth can't do *this*.'

'Well, they could if they wanted to, but they're not permitted. Google Earth can't get these shots – privacy issues. The mapping software's called Global Discovery; all our intelligence organisations have access to it. Google gets delayed feed. Ours is live.'

She turned back to the front page to read the bullet points. 'So the Feds will be running this one, then?' she said.

'Oh, we'll be there, all right. And so will Hazmat, the riot squad, and the local boys. Last'll be called in because you're involved, and I'm sure he'll bring a couple of the people you've been working with at Fairfield. It makes us all look stupid when the crooks use the suburbs to cook meth and then blow the place up when they're done. Everyone will want in. And half of them will be hoping for another bonfire.'

The show started on the main road leading into Riverstone. Detours were in place, with officers diverting traffic from entering the suburb. As the uniformed cop waved them through, she saw a female motorist out of her vehicle and having a stand-up argument about being denied access to her street. Jill knew that if the road was blocked this far out, they'd already have all exits from the homestead locked up tight. Any one of these cars being turned away could have made a call to the target property, warning them to get out.

They motored smoothly along their side of the traffic-free streets. Every motorist on the other side of the road, heading back towards the main highway, gawked at them. A few people nodded or even waved.

'They're evacuating the houses?' said Jill.

'I'd imagine it would just be a couple of neighbouring properties,' said Gabriel. 'This would just be the local traffic being moved out. The only spectators in there will be cops.'

They turned a corner and both sides of the street suddenly became a parking lot for government vehicles.

'Look: Lanvin and Genovese,' she said.

Gabriel grunted. 'Yep. They're in charge.' He parked next to another unmarked vehicle and turned to Jill as she was getting out. 'You know they're not gonna let you anywhere near the house, don't you, Jill?' he said.

She waited, her hand on the door.

'And you know that Damien and White could get hurt?' he said.

She gave him another look.

'And that if that happens, it's not our fault,' he continued. Waited for a response; got nothing. He began again. 'Because they got themselves –'

'Are we getting out of the car some time today, Gabe?' she said.

He smiled. They left the vehicle and headed over to Lanvin and Genovese.

The takedown of the homestead at Riverstone was textbook. Riot squad approached with loudspeakers first and told the occupants they had sixty seconds to evacuate before the gas went in. Jill and Gabriel had close viewing access, but were warned not to take any part in the operation.

Almost immediately following the loudspeaker directions, Jill watched Urgill walk out expressionless, hands in the air, palms forward. He lay down lithely on the parched lawn. Whitey was next, looking a mess; his nose was plastered all over his face, his eyes were barely slits and there was bruising up to his hairline and down to his mouth. Francis Agassi came out next with a big smile: the genial gangster, pleased with the show. He squinted through smoke, a newly lit cigarette hanging from the corner of his mouth. It took him a lot longer to get to the ground than Urgill, although it appeared a knee gave way mid-squat and in the end he hit the dirt like a sack of shit.

Come on, Damien, thought Jill. Where are you? The squad had their masks on; the gas canisters would be fired in within seconds.

Finally, Damien emerged, his face a portrait of misery. Jill knew he felt like everything he'd ever wanted in life was ending today. She knew he'd be taken into custody and charged. There was no getting around that. But she and Last would do everything they could to let the prosecutors know that he'd been cooperative, and hopefully they'd come up with something fair that most involved could live with. She knew that what he'd done was stupid, but she doubted he'd ever again have anything to do with something like this.

The moment Damien was on the ground, the gas went in, but no one else emerged. The riot team secured the house, and Hazmat followed for the clean-up.

Jill and Gabriel made their way over to Superintendent Last, who stood with Genovese and Lanvin.

'No Nader,' she said.

'Nope,' said Genovese.

'What next, then?' she said.

'Whatever,' he said.

'What does that mean?' said Jill.

'It means he'll show up. We've just gotta wait,' said Lanvin.

'We need to get you debriefed, Jill,' said Last.

Oh. Great. That's just what I need, she thought, another freaken debrief. She grimaced at Gabriel, who grinned widely, and together they walked back to his car.

64

Monday 15 April, 4 pm

Byron hit the horn in the Rexie as soon as the traffic slowed up on Richmond Road. It didn't do any good in terms of moving things the fuck along, but it made him feel better, 'specially since it was giving the shits to the driver in the three-series BMW in front. He watched the man eyeballing him through the rear vision mirror.

Byron wound his window down and asked the bloke if he wanted to talk about it. 'What's *your* fucken problem, cunt?' he screamed. 'You wanna have a go? Pull that piece of shit of yours over now!' He hung his whole arm out the window, and gestured the prick to the side of the road. The eyeballs dropped out of view in the mirror and the BMW's window buzzed closed. Fucken typical yuppie, he thought. No fucken balls at all.

'Ya fucken yuppie!' he shouted out the window for good measure. 'You've got no balls!'

He hit the horn a couple more times, but this time everyone minded their own business. Finally, the traffic began to move.

When Byron spotted the blue lights flashing ahead, he joined the other cars making U-turns to head the other way. Fuck that shit, he told himself. Nader would have to get someone else to do this pick-up. There was some sort of bust going down.

Sick of the pissants in front of him, who were obviously now lost because they'd had to change route, Byron peeled off onto a back road to take a short cut through St Marys. Fuck Riverstone. Who the fuck would want to move things out there anyway? Place was probably full of fucken hillbillies.

Byron opened the Rexie up and hammered it down the rural road.

65

Monday 15 April, 3.15 pm
Cassie woke up in Christian's bed with nothing left. Her mouth tasted of chemicals, cigarettes and semen. A perfect match for the way she felt – like an inanimate object: an ashtray or condom. So, this is what rock bottom feels like, she thought. She would have cried, but there were no tears available.

Instead, she stared at the ceiling. Pleaded. 'I surrender,' she said.

'Did you say something, darling?' said Christian.

'You're awake,' she said. Funny that a condom could speak, that an ashtray could converse.

'I'm worried,' he said.

'I'm past that,' she answered.

'What?'

'Nothing. What are you worried about?' she said.

Christian sat up in the bed. Surely he should resemble a cadaver, or something close to it. Shouldn't his teeth be rotten, his nails be black; shouldn't there be acne at least?

'Or horns?' she said.

'What did you say?' he said.

'I'm an idiot, Christian,' she said. 'Ignore me, darling. What are you worried about?'

The skin on his chest was hairless and golden. But she thought she could still smell the spray tan.

He spoke, and his teeth were so perfect. She remembered the plastic mouth moulds in the bathroom sink some mornings, gummy with spit and whitening gel. 'I've set up a deal,' he said. 'A big one. Same guys. Eight hundred grand.'

'Eight hundred thousand dollars?' she said. 'What are you, some kind of Colombian drug lord?'

He laughed. He shouldn't have, really, but she'd known he would.

'So, what are you worried about?' she said. No, really Christian, she wondered, what worries you about an eight-hundred-thousand-dollar drug deal? Which part of that concerns you?

'I'm scared they could try to kill me and take the money,' he said.

Well, there's that, she thought. 'Mmm,' she said. 'That doesn't sound good.'

'I was thinking you should maybe come with me.'

'You were thinking I should maybe come with you,' she repeated. 'To the drug deal where you might get killed.' Just to be clear here.

'You're so funny, Cass.' He smiled with his mouth only. 'To be honest, I know everything will be fine. I mean, I know this guy isn't a pussy, but it's not like he's a bikie either. He's in this for the business, like me. But just to be certain, I'm thinking that if there're a couple of us, it would be more of a hassle to take both of us out, and he'd be better off just continuing with the deal as arranged.'

More of a hassle, she thought.

'And I can trust you,' he added.

More of a hassle to kill two people than one, and he can trust me, thought Cassie. You slept with this man last night, she told herself. No, Cassie. You fucked him for drugs. You sucked his cock for cocaine and ecstasy.

She forced herself to stay in the bed. These were the moments she had to remember. Words she had to hear. Leaving now and pretending he was joking, that he was just talking three-o'clock-in-the-morning-drug-fucked-crazy-talk would just mean another day waking up just like this. Hating herself this much.

'I can't do it anymore,' she said.

'What do you mean "anymore"?' he said. 'It's not like I've asked you to do anything like this before. It'll be all right, babe. And when you see how many lollies that money'll get us, you won't regret it.'

'But what if he figures he really would like to keep his money *and* the drugs and decides that taking us both out is a hassle he could live with.'

Christian snorted with impatience. 'Look, Cass. I didn't want to tell you this because you didn't need to know,' he said. He sat up straighter in the bed, reached across and touched her shoulder.

Cassie just waited. She'd never seen him this serious before.

'I'll be bringing – now, don't freak out – I'm bringing a gun.'

'Are you crazy? Where would you even get a gun?'

'Remember Carl Davus?'

'Davus? The guy who murdered his wife?'

'Now, now, Ms Jackson. You know better than that. I got him off those charges and made myself famous. Do you know how I got him off?'

'I didn't follow the whole thing too closely. Wasn't it lack of evidence?'

'That was a big part of it. They couldn't find the murder weapon.'

'They couldn't . . . The gun! *That* gun? *You've* got the gun Davus used to murder his wife?'

Christian smiled beatifically. And suddenly, she really got it. This guy was truly despicable. Not just immature and insensitive, but completely devoid of any morals. Evil. For the first time in her life Cassie understood the AA saying that you have to truly surrender before you can let go of addiction. You have to really, completely realise that you can sink no further into filth, that you are powerless. Only then can rehab help, when you know that you have no control. That you must have help, that you will not just accept help, but beg for it. That, or die. The simple truth of this crashed down on Cassie and she wanted to cry with relief. Instead, she smiled. There were other people caught up in this shit. Seren. Seren needed help too, and Cassie knew the minute she saw her that somehow she had to do that.

'It makes sense,' she said, 'that it would create headaches for this guy if there were two people there rather than just one. It's not easy to get rid of a body.' She paused. 'Or so I've heard.'

'This is what I'm saying, Cass,' he said, smiling back at her, his eyes focused on her tits.

She tugged the sheet a little higher. 'But Christian, if two are a hassle, what if there were three? Maybe we should ask your friend, Seren, to come along?'

Christian laughed. Which she hadn't expected.

'You like her, don't you?' he said.

Oh that, she thought. Thank you, Christian. You're making this rock-bottom shit much easier.

'She's all right,' said Cassie. Actually, Christian, she's fine. She's got you on tape handing over eighty grand for meth and eccy. But eight hundred? Even you couldn't get yourself out of that one, Mr Bullshit.

Cassie scanned the apartment. The thing she'd always loved most here was the way the moving lights from the skyline danced around on the massive rug in the living room. She'd always liked the purple spots of brilliance the best; they seemed to sparkle most when the cocaine level was just right. She stared at the carpet. Nothing moved. Suddenly, her mum's image materialised, standing at the stove in the kitchen, patiently cooking up endless rounds of salami and cheese toast. It was when they were kids, of course; no one ate with that kind of enthusiasm after Jill came home. Then little Lilly, her niece, took her place on the rug – was she four or five now? Perfect little thing, eyes as infinite as the universe, staring up at her in awe. And then – was that? Yes, Fisher, her cat! Well, Jill's cat actually. Gone forever now, dead just before Christmas. Ancient, he'd been. He'd been Jill's until That Day. After that, Jill had never really looked at him again. Or her. Well, not properly, anyway.

'What's wrong with you, Cass?' said Christian. 'You want some wine, or something?'

Or something.

'Silly! I'm fine, baby!' she said. 'It *is* three o'clock in the morning. What did you say? Tell me again, I'm just sleepy. What'd I miss?'

'Sleepy? You're drug-fucked,' he said.

Rub it in, she thought.

'What I said,' he answered, 'is that when I saw you and Seren together, I couldn't help but think of you two . . . *together*. You know.'

'Oh, I know,' she said. Which is what he wanted her to say, after all.

'When that fucking Neanderthal saw you two together he must've spoofed in those tracksuit pants,' he said.

'Must've,' she said.

'So, you'll do it, Cass? Should I call and set it up?'

'If Seren will be there, I'll be there,' she said.

'One more thing?' He smiled that good-boy smile. The one that probably worked with his mummy and had been melting women ever since. The one that used to work with her. 'I was thinking,' he continued, 'that it might be best for you to carry the gun. You know, just in case he wants to pat me down?'

'So I carry the gun.'

'What do you think?'

'What the hell. Let's just get this done.'

'You see, baby, that's why I love you,' said Christian, reaching over to kiss her.

'Excuse me, sweetie,' she said. 'I'm going to be sick.' She rose from the bed. 'I've had a little too much.'

He pouted and blew her a kiss. 'Poor baby,' he said. 'Feel better.' He snuggled down into the pillows and rolled away from her.

Cassie got out of bed and went to the bathroom to vomit.

De rigueur.

66

Tuesday 16 April, 9 am

Seren warned Marco not to leave the room or open the door to anyone. She left him watching cartoons in the itchy, fifty-dollar-a-night hotel close to the unit block and went down to the car park to make the calls. She took a seat on a low brick wall alongside the building, out of the wind and out of sight of the road.

Her boss answered first ring. She'd hoped he'd be in his office. It was just after morning-tea time and there was always a lull before the new batch of freshly-slaughtered chickens was delivered to the gutting room floor.

'Hello, Zeko,' she said.

'Why aren't you at work, Seren?' he said. 'And why haven't you called me before now? I was becoming worried about you. Today is the day for your special performance review, have you forgotten?'

'Oh no, Zeko, I haven't forgotten. But I won't be coming in today.'

'Well, that is not satisfactory, I'm afraid, Seren. Your attendance here has been bloody bullshit! Now if you get your bloody backside in here now, sick or not, I won't have to call your bloody probation and parole.'

'Oh, you won't have to call them, Zeko,' she said, removing the tiny recording device from her pocket. 'I think you'll recognise this voice. It's a very distinct accent.'

While Marco had slept the night before, she'd downloaded the footage she'd taken of Zeko in their last meeting in his office. It was a pity Zeko wouldn't get the full impact of the visuals of himself fondling his prick, but she was certain that the audio of him telling her that her job description included blowjobs would do the trick.

And it did. Nicely. Zeko Slavonic would not find the need to call Maria Thomasetti today.

Christian was next. As she went to scroll to his number, the phone rang and she stared in astonishment at the number displayed on her ringing mobile.

'Christian!' she said. 'I was just this minute about to call you!'

'Serendipity!' he said.

'Exactly,' she said, with a fake laugh.

'So what's on your mind, beautiful? Why were you going to call me?'

'Well,' she said, then took a deep breath, 'I've got a day off today, and I wondered if you might want to meet for lunch?'

'Perfect!' he said. 'You see how in synch are we? I was hoping we could get together too. I've got a little business to take care of, and I was hoping you could help me out with it. And then after that we'll have a late lunch and dinner and breakfast too. I can be ready in an hour.'

Not on your life, she thought. Tonight, I'll be with Marco, and you'll be getting your finances together. 'Okay, great!' she said. 'Can you give me an hour and a half? You can pick me up back at . . . at my place. I'll be out the front waiting, just text me when you're close and I'll come down.'

First she needed to do a little shopping. Seren hurried down to the road to the ATM and withdrew a hundred dollars, which ate into her rent money, due in two days. This shit better work, she told herself. Next stop – Officeworks. She purchased two memory sticks, on sale – lucky again – and an envelope. Then it was off to Woollies, where she bought bread rolls and sliced cheese, the brand Marco loved – indistinguishable from soft, sliced rubber – a jar of Vegemite, a six-pack of juice boxes, a bag of Twisties, and a Mars Bar. Hopefully he'd only have time to eat the junk and she'd be back there with him. From the newsagents she bought a couple of comics, more lollies, and a skater magazine. Marco had a school reading book in his bag and the TV. Plenty to do. She wouldn't be that long.

Still, she felt terribly guilty as she watched Marco examining her purchases. She took the opportunity to quickly download the hidden files onto the two USBs, making certain to password-protect the folder again. Hidden or not, her little boy was smart.

She changed quickly, kissed Marco goodbye, and left the hotel.

Checking in last night, she'd seen the gym across the road and had the idea. She couldn't take the copied files with her to meet Christian. Although she couldn't imagine him becoming aggressive and trying to find the copies of the evidence she had against him, only an idiot would take that risk. And she couldn't leave them in the hotel room with Marco – if he found them he might find a way to open them, password-protected or not.

She smiled at the pony-tailed girl behind the counter in the gym.

'I'd like to use the pool, please,' she said. 'How much will that be? Oh, hang on, I'll rent a locker too.'

Five minutes later, after telling Ms Pony-tail that she'd forgotten something and would be back in a tick, she left the gym and headed home to wait for Christian.

67

Tuesday 16 April, 10.10 am

'Un-fucken-believable,' was Byron Barnes' greeting to the morning. 'What fucken cunt would call someone at this time of the morning?' Eyes still closed, he reached for his mobile and cigarettes from his bedside drawer.

'Man, what time is it?' he said when he answered the phone.

'It's past ten, you lazy cunt. Are you still in bed?' said Kasem Nader.

'Nah, man, nah. Kasem! Fuck, man. That thing at Riverstone. That shit was pretty close, man. I was almost fucken there.'

'Well, you weren't,' said Kasem. 'And the whole thing's a pain in the arse.'

'I know, man. Poor Whitey and Damo.' Still half asleep, he searched around with one hand for his lighter.

'Fuckwit. You're on the fucking phone. Stop with the names.'

'Yep, sure, bro. But this phone's sweet, don't worry. Some cunt donated it to me while he was taking a piss. Shoulda seen the prick when I took off with it. He swung around screamin' with his dick still in his hand and pissed all over the bloke next to him. It was fucken funny, man. You shoulda seen it.'

'I'm so sorry I missed it. Now shut the fuck up. I need you today. How long till you can get here?' said Kasem.

'Where, man?' Where's me *fucken* lighter? Byron was beginning to get the shakes. It'd been ten hours since his last smoke.

'My parents' place,' said Kasem.

Byron's hand found his lighter. Thank fuck. 'Sweet,' he said. He lit a cigarette, sucked it down hard. 'Can ya gimme an hour?'

'Don't be longer than that.'

68

'Jill, I'll meet you over at Central in ten minutes,' said Gabriel when she answered the phone.

'I can't, Gabe. I'm just about to go in to see the shrink,' she told him.

'Bail,' he said. 'Say you're sick. We got a hit on Nader. He's about to meet with Byron Barnes – associate of Damien and Whitey.'

'Shit! Well, Last'll know about it by now and he'll order me off it. He's not happy that I was out with you yesterday. I'm meant to get debriefed.'

'Last won't know. The techie told me, and I asked him to sit on it for a bit.'

'What about Lanvin and Genovese?' she said.

'No one likes them here. The tech called me first. Look, I'm on the way over. Just get ready.'

Jill didn't want to suddenly feel as great as she did. She was relieved they had a lead on Nader, and she was always happy

300

to avoid a conversation with a psych, but she was beginning to worry about how much she liked being with Gabriel, and how much she hated it when he wasn't around. She jogged out of the building to wait for him.

In his car, she kicked off her shoes to try to force herself to relax a little on the ride out to Merrylands. She agreed with Gabriel's decision that to take Nader in immediately would be a waste. It was possible that they'd be able to connect him with the operation at Riverstone, and that Damien's testimony might get him some charges for the Merrylands' gig, but they had very little evidence, really, that tied him into all of this.

Gabe was certain that Lanvin and Genovese would haul Nader in as soon as they found him. They wouldn't want to risk him taking off again like he did after the Merrylands explosion – they'd had to apply to get approval for the listening device and Nader's name had been all over the court documents. He'd made them look stupid.

But she knew they'd have very little time to get something on Nader before the Feds found out he'd been traced, or he showed up in another call. She just hoped that the pressure of the last few days had been enough to force him into trying to get some of his lost money back. And if he had to cook some more drugs in a hurry, he might lead them to his precursor supply.

She felt her fists clench when the traffic slowed to a crawl on the M4. There was nowhere to go. Gabriel hit the siren, but it was still slow going; half the civilians didn't know what the hell to do when the music started. She closed her eyes and forced herself to breathe slowly.

Byron cruised his Rexie past the Nader residence and took a quick tour of the bombsite. 'Damn,' he muttered.

Damien's house had been fenced off; signs proclaimed that entry was prohibited due to danger of collapse. He knew he should feel lucky – he was supposed to have been in there when the place blew, and he should also have been at Riverstone by the time it was busted. But instead, he had a real bad feeling. He couldn't pin it down, but he was thinking that maybe it had started with that bitch walking out of Christian's closet the other day, scaring the fuck out of him. Everything was too close for comfort lately.

He pulled into a driveway a couple of doors up from what was left of Damo's house, turned the Rexie around, and headed back up to Nader's. He left the keys in the ignition and walked up to the front door. No cunt would steal a car parked out the front of the Nader joint.

'You're late,' said Kasem when he opened the door. He stepped straight out of the house and into Byron's chest, forcing him to back up quickly.

'Sorry, man. Where we going?' said Byron.

'Just get in the car,' said Kasem. 'No, fuckstick, you go around the other side. I'm driving.'

Aw, fucken hell, worried Byron. No one had ever driven the Rexie but him. She was a virgin that way. Fucken Nader. He climbed into the passenger seat, and couldn't help but admire the view inside his car from this angle. Sweet.

'So what are you so shitty for, Kasem?' asked Byron when they screeched away from the house.

'Hmm, now, let's see. Why would I be shitty?' said Kasem. 'Well, one of my labs exploded. There's that. And the other got raided. That's pissing me off a bit. The cops got one of my best cooks, and probably half a million dollars worth of my drugs. Wouldn't that give *you* the shits a little, Byron?'

Nader took the next corner so fast that any other car would've lost it and rolled. Byron hurriedly plugged his seatbelt in, not sure whether to go with the anger he felt, or the awe that he had such a hot car. Either way, he had a hard-on. Take it easy, he wanted to say, but didn't. He knew that Kasem would only flog the car harder, and he might cop a backhander.

'So you and I, Byron, are going to make a bit of my money back today,' Nader continued. 'I've got a big sale with Worthington and he's expecting 800K worth of shit.'

Byron whistled.

'And what I've got *left* because of this *fuck* around,' Nader slammed his hand down onto the steering wheel, 'is around *500K* worth of shit. But I need all of this prick's money today to keep the supply chain rolling. You know what I'm saying, Byron?'

Byron nodded.

'You don't know what I'm saying, fuckstick, but that's okay,' said Nader. 'It's a business notion called the bullwhip effect. You see, if any part of the supply chain is stalled for even a while it has a flow-through effect on the whole system.'

'So you owe people the money,' said Byron.

'Well, there's that, too,' said Nader. 'So we're gonna meet with Worthington in half an hour and he's going to take the shit I've got, give me all the cash, and I'll get him the rest very shortly.'

'And if he doesn't like that?'

'Then he won't like it. But that's what's going to happen today. I want you there to help him see reason if that needs to happen. You seemed to understand the business behind the deal well enough. You can help me explain it to him if needs be.'

'So I bash him if you tell me to?' said Byron.

Nader sighed. 'Yes, Byron. If I tell you to.'

Seren stood on the pavement and stared down into the car.

'What is she *doing* here?' she said when Christian reached across from the driver's seat and pushed the passenger door open for her.

'Come on, babe, get in. Cassie's going to help us with something before we go to lunch. It won't take long, promise,' said Christian.

Dismayed, Seren didn't move. I can't blackmail Christian with her here, she thought.

'Darling,' said Christian, 'please – I'm in a no stopping zone.'

'I left you the front seat,' called Cassie from the back.

Seren folded herself into the sports car. This can't wait another day, she thought. I'll find some time alone with him.

***

'They're on the move,' said Gabriel, ending his call and handing Jill his mobile phone. The traffic had thinned considerably. He deactivated the siren. 'Can you answer next time it rings? It'll be Ajay, the techie. He's tracing Nader's phone and he said that he and Barnes are still together. He'll tell us where to head next.'

Jill took the phone and waited on the call.

'Who lives here, Kasem?' asked Byron as they pulled up at the front of a block of units in Merrylands.

'Plenty of people by the looks of it, Byron,' said Nader. 'It also happens to be where we'll be doing the Worthington deal.'

'Why here?'

'Why not? You don't need to know more than you need to know, Byron. You're the grunt. Now, hurry up. I want to get things set up before they get here.'

They climbed the stairs to the third floor of the block and Kasem unlocked the door to a flat. Byron took a walk around. Other than a dining table, a woggy-looking sofa and a few kitchen chairs, the place was pretty much empty. Not even a fucken fridge. Byron flopped onto a chair in the lounge room and shrugged. No point asking what the fuck they were going to deal from this empty shithole: apparently he didn't need to know.

Byron watched Kasem walk over to the linen cupboard built-into the wall. He opened it and pulled a box off a shelf. 'A hand here, Byron?' he said.

Byron walked over and peeked inside the box.

'Fuck me,' he said.

'Thank you, I'll pass,' said Nader. 'Take them over to the table.'

The three boxes, which had apparently once contained 'Golden Bananas from the Sunshine State' now held a few hundred bags containing thousands of pills.

'How can you keep that much shit in here, Kasem?' said Byron.

'Apparently you didn't inspect the door properly, Byron.'

Byron walked over to take a better look and saw that the front door was the newest thing in this place. And it looked pretty solid.

'It's iron, Byron,' said Nader, 'bolted at twelve points into the brick walls and the concrete floor, all with the turn of one key. They'd have to pull the wall down to move that door. You're the soldier, remember, and I'm the . . .'

'Boss?' said Byron.

'General, fuckwit,' said Nader. 'General.'

Seren couldn't believe it. Another deal? And eight *hundred* grand? Christian had explained the drug buy on the way over to this ugly-looking block of units.

'It'll be just like last time, Seren,' Cassie had said from the back seat of the car.

Did she mean what that sounded like? Seren wondered. What did Cassie want out of her taping Christian buying drugs? Why did she have to get involved? This was turning into a big mess. Every time there was a crisis in her life, the blackmail plan seemed perfectly logical, rational and justified. And then when things calmed down and she put herself again into situations like this, it felt like complete lunacy.

Exhausted by the constant doubts, Seren decided to just go with the path of least resistance. She didn't need any more evidence against this idiot, but she might as well go the whole hog. It wasn't like she could put the ultimatum to Christian with Cassie here anyway.

A couple of kids – who should have been at school, she couldn't help thinking – chased each other across the soil that served as a lawn in the front of the building. She prayed that Marco would stay put in the hotel until she got back.

Byron jumped up when the doorbell sounded. Scared the fuck out of him.

305

'Byron, get the door please,' said Nader. 'Oh, but make sure it's him before you open it.'

He must think I'm a fucken idiot, Byron thought, crossing the floor and peering through the peephole.

'It's him,' he said. And the supermodels. He opened the door.

Kasem jumped up and gave Byron a look that sent him stepping backwards out of fist-reach. What? he thought. How am I supposed to know who else you're expecting? I'm not meant to ask questions, remember?

'I'm sorry, ladies, I don't mean to be rude,' said Kasem. 'I thought, Christian, that we'd arranged for this to be just us? Why did you bring these women?'

'Yeah, what is it with you and these bitch . . . girls?' said Byron. 'Kasem, they're the chicks I told you about in the city.'

'Shut up, Byron,' said Kasem. 'Have we met?' he said, turning to the brunette.

'Yes, actually,' she said. 'My name's Cassie. I came to a gathering at your home, somewhere in this suburb, I believe it was.'

'Sorry, Kasem,' said Worthington. 'I didn't think you'd mind – the girls have done this before. We're going out to lunch after this, and I didn't want to leave them in the car.'

'Actually, I'd have much preferred that you did,' said Kasem. 'I'm afraid I have a bit of a peculiarity when it comes to business deals like this. It's a little embarrassing, I guess, and some people will not understand it.' He looked the blonde one in the eye. 'I don't do business like this with women. I happen to think it's beneath them.'

Byron wondered how this would go down. Everyone just stood in the entryway, a couple of steps inside the door.

'Well, we might have a problem, then,' said Worthington. 'You see, I have a certain way of doing business too. It's the lawyer in me. I don't make, ah, contracts without a witness.'

'We have Byron,' said Nader.

'He's yours,' said Christian.

'The problem remains,' said Nader. 'Maybe I haven't explained myself clearly enough. Do you like bacon, Mr Worthington?'

'Bacon?' said Christian.

'Yes. Bacon, spare ribs, sweet and sour pork?'

Christian stared.

Nader waited.

'A Muslim thing?' said Christian.

'A Muslim thing,' said Nader. 'The deal will not go ahead with the women present. I am sorry, ladies.'

'Well, what do we do here?' said Worthington.

'Well, we can't be here all fucking day,' Nader told him. 'Sorry. Pardon me, ladies. It seems we each want this deal to go ahead. Would it suit you if the women waited in the unit across the hall while you inspect the product and we talk?'

'The unit across the hall?' said Worthington.

'It's empty, much like this one,' said Nader.

Christian stared silently at the floor. Byron figured this whole thing had gone south and nothing good was going to happen today.

Finally Worthington spoke. 'Sounds all right,' he said.

Everyone in the room took a breath.

Nader cleared his throat. 'I hope I mentioned that this would be a *cash* transaction?' he said.

Christian stared. 'Oh, of course. The money. It's in the car. I didn't want to bring it in until I was sure you were here and everything was okay. It's a lot of money to just carry around.'

'It would've been better in your hands than out there, bro,' said Byron.

Worthington paled and left the room quickly. What a fuckwit, thought Byron. He couldn't understand how people that dumb got to be lawyers. No street smarts.

When Worthington returned he looked spooked.

'What?' said Nader.

'I think the girls should hang onto the money while I check out the product,' he said.

'You think I'm gonna fuck you up and take the money and the drugs?' said Nader.

'I just think the final transaction should happen in front of witnesses. That's the way I want to do this.'

Nader sighed. 'Whatever you want, Christian. If it was me, I wouldn't be letting that money out of my hands for anyone, but it's not like we'll be very long, anyway.'

'Oh, I trust Cassie and Seren,' said Christian. 'They know I know them and their *families* exceptionally well.'

'Very well,' said Nader. 'Let's get on with it, then.'

Byron stayed behind while Nader led Worthington and the girls out of the flat. He watched from the doorway as Nader unlocked the unit across the hall and let them in. How many places did this prick have? He hoped that this deal would hurry the fuck along. He didn't like his Rexie sitting out there this long in this neighbourhood.

69

Tuesday 16 April, midday

'I can't believe it,' said Jill. 'This is where Jelly lives. Nader's only come here to visit Jelly.' They sat in Gabriel's car in a shopping centre car park across the road from the unit block. She felt disappointed. She'd been hoping to catch Nader doing something wrong. Anything. 'Does Ajay know which unit he's gone to?' she asked.

'Nope,' said Gabriel. 'The software's not that specific, although they're guessing it's a centre unit rather than one on a corner. Let's just wait a bit, see if he comes out again.' He reclined his seat a notch, then commented, 'And, *that's* a car that definitely doesn't belong here.'

Jill stared at the late model silver sports car parked out the front of the units. 'What's that, an Audi?' she asked, dialling Ajay.

'Yep. R8,' he said.

She ended the call a couple of moments later. 'Car belongs to a Christian Worthington. Lawyer. Lives in Darling Harbour.'

'And that would be Mr Worthington right now, I would imagine. Leaving? No, he's getting something out of the boot,' said Gabriel.

Jill watched the young man take a large, expensive-looking shopping bag from the boot of the Audi. 'What do you reckon's in that?' she said.

'Could be anything,' said Gabriel. 'But Mr Worthington looks all wrong to me.'

'I understand that he might be nervous out here,' she said, 'but he's gonna put his neck out if he whips his head back and forth like that for much longer.'

'Something's going down,' said Gabriel. 'That's what I'm thinking. What do you say to having a look around?'

'Let's go,' said Jill.

As they crossed the hall to wait in the opposite unit for the drug deal to go down, Seren recognised the lettering on the shopping bag that Christian carried. *Christian Louboutin.* The same brand as the shoes that had helped send her to gaol. How about that? Was that a good omen or bad? All she knew was that she wasn't going to get this transaction on tape. It didn't matter, though: she had plenty to hang this guy. She just had to be patient a little longer.

'So,' said Gabriel, turning to face Jill in the car, 'I think we should approach the block from behind – cut through this car park, move up the street fifty metres and cross the road there. Stay close to the foliage at the rear of the property. What do you reckon?'

'Sounds good,' said Jill.

'Do you want to call it in?'

'Nothing to call in, yet.'

'Agreed. Let's go.'

They set off at a jog. When they reached the rear of the building, Gabriel pulled her down to a squat with cover from the building provided by a shrub. 'I think we should just have a look around in there, see what we can see. But Jill,' he said, 'if we encounter Nader, we're gonna have to arrest him. If he sees us here, he'll try to run.'

'Yep, and they'll hang us if we don't bring him in,' she said. She unclipped her firearm, and he did the same. 'Just don't terrify the civilians,' she said.

Byron stood up again from the couch and screwed up his nose. Friggin' thing smelled like old people. Nader must've got it from his oldies' house, he thought. You'd think a prick with that much money would buy some decent shit for this place. He glanced around the lounge room. I'd deck it out, he thought. Some cream leather lounges, the biggest wall screen plasma . . . What were they *doing*? He walked over to the doorway again and peered through the spyhole. Finally! He saw Nader and Christian closing the door of the unit opposite and heading back to where he waited.

As soon as Nader and Christian left the unit, Cassie decided to be open with Seren. She had no reason to trust this girl, but she'd passed the point of no return and she just hoped she was doing the right thing.

'Seren,' she said quickly, while they stood in the empty entrance to the unit, 'I know you don't know me from shit, but I just want to tell you that if you're taping these deals because you're a cop or you want to take this to the cops, I'll support you.'

Rather than expressing relief, the girl's face became even more pale.

'You don't look good, Seren,' Cassie said. 'Are you okay?'

Cassie lurched forward when Seren swayed and caught her before she dropped to the ground. Awkwardly she helped her to sit, right there on the floor, where she sat, staring.

'Seren?' she said.

Seren seemed suddenly to revive a little. She lifted her face and stared straight into Cassie's eyes. 'There's a lot I have to tell you,' she said.

At that moment Cassie felt that she'd believe anything Seren had to say.

Byron held the heavy door open with his foot and leaned against the frame, staring down the corridor.

Suddenly, all blood drained from his face, and he screamed, 'Motherfuckers!'

As Nader and Worthington crossed the hall to re-enter the room, Byron slammed the door in his boss's face.

As she rounded the corner, Jill skidded to a stop. A door slammed nearby and a man screamed at Nader and Worthington. Hearing her behind him, Nader turned to face her.

'POLICE! FREEZE!' Jill had her firearm out, pointed at his chest. She became aware suddenly that Gabriel was by her side, his gun also in firing position, legs spread.

'Don't move, Nader,' he said. 'Stay where you are, Worthington.' He dropped the volume and said to Jill, 'Forward.'

They moved slowly up the hall. A door opened on Gabriel's left and he whipped his head and gun to face the sound. A woman, a cigarette in her fingers, shrieked. 'Get inside,' Gabriel told her. She did.

'Up against the wall!' Jill yelled. 'Palms flat. NOW!'

The men complied, but Worthington quickly dropped his pissing-in-my-pants look and blustered, 'What is this? Point your weapons away from me. I am an officer of the court! I am here seeing a client. What are your names?'

They reached the men. 'Spread your legs,' Jill said.

Gabriel did the pat-down. Took a firearm from Nader's jacket. Disabled it quickly, shaking out the bullets and pocketing them. 'Open the door,' he said.

'What door?' said Nader.

'The door of the unit you were about to enter,' said Jill.

'Hi, Krystal,' said Nader.

'Open the door,' she said.

'It's okay, Jill, I've got it.' Gabriel reached forward and removed a set of keys from Nader's pocket.

'I want it noted that I have just arrived to see my client and I have not been in this room before now,' said Worthington.

'Noted,' said Gabriel, turning the key. 'Now get in there.' He drew Worthington forward by his coat sleeve and then put his palm flat against the middle of his back and pushed him into the unit.

'DOWN!' shouted Gabriel. 'There's a third in here, Jill. It's Byron.'

She shoved Nader through the entry and covered all three men. Byron was already lying face down on the ground. 'Get down with him,' she said to the other two. Nader locked eyes with her and smiled, but they both went down.

Gabriel swept the unit quickly and returned to the lounge room. 'Clear,' he said. He walked towards the dining table, glanced inside the boxes sitting on top. Big smile. He walked back and nudged Nader gently with his toe.

'Ha-ha. You're in trouble,' he said.

Jill carefully removed her mobile from her pocket, keeping her gun trained on the men on the floor. She'd call Superintendent Last first, and then Lanvin. Gabriel stood at the dining table, inspecting the contents of the boxes.

'How much you reckon is in there?' she said.

'Shitloads,' he answered.

And then the doorbell rang. Gabriel indicated that she should take a look.

'Oh, my God, Gabe, it's Cassie!' she said. She froze for a moment and then pulled the door open. Gabriel shouted. Suddenly Jill felt herself propelled forwards, shoulder-charged from behind, smacking her head into the doorframe.

'Jill!' screamed Cassie, as Nader barrelled past her, followed by Barnes.

'Get inside, Cass!' Jill shouted and took off after them.

Barnes overtook Nader in the hallway and cartwheeled over the stairwell banister, landing like a rabbit, jumping up and repeating the same move again, six stairs at a time.

By the time she reached the first landing Nader was already on the bottom stair. She leapt from the top step and landed on him, his shoulder cracking into her chest. They both went down and, once again, she found herself unable to breathe, with Kasem Nader leaning over her.

'Cunt,' he said, and smacked his fist into her face.

'KRYSTAL!'

The next series of sounds and movements shuddered and skidded, incomprehensible to Jill as she rolled onto her side and sucked in air. She turned her head and saw Nader, out cold.

Jelly was sitting on Nader's chest. Crying. 'Kasem. You shouldn't hurt Krystal,' he said.

70

Jill refused to let the paramedics near her until they let her speak to Cassie. She sat on the tailgate of the ambulance and waited.

Gabriel brought her little sister over. Handcuffed.

'What are you doing?' she shouted at Gabe, although she already knew. She'd seen Cassie at Nader's house. She must have been in on this deal somehow.

Gabriel's eyes were hooded. 'Cassie's made a confession, Jill. She's been very cooperative.'

Jill stared at her sister, desolate. A rhythmic, pounding ache surged from her stomach and tore through her heart. She doubled over and her vision darkened. A bright spot appeared, distant in the field of blackness, rapidly flickering closer. She saw two girls, laughing. Eyes impossibly bright, unguarded, exultant. Cassie at nine; Jill at eleven. Before the abduction.

Right now, Jill lifted her head and looked into her sister's eyes. She wanted to speak, to tell Cassie how sorry she was that she hadn't been there all those years. Of course, right when she needed them most, she had no words. What could she say? What could she do?

Suddenly Jill lurched forwards and threw her arms around her sister, held on, too tight, delaying the moment that Cassie would push her away, fight her off, gawp at her as though she were deranged. Instead, Cassie leaned into her, their tears merging. There was no sound. And suddenly, the white-eyed girl was there with them: a part of twelve-year-old Jill that had split off from her when the pain had become too bad during the torture she'd endured in the basement. The white-eyed girl stood and stared at them holding each other.

'I love you, Jill,' said Cassie.

The white-eyed girl disappeared.

'My face hurts,' said Jill.

They laughed, and peeled away from each other.

Jill tried. 'I . . .' It stuck. She'd never said it before.

'It's okay, Jill. I know,' said Cassie.

'No, you don't, Cass. I love you, too. I've always loved you. I just didn't know that because I didn't know that I had any feelings left. I know that sounds stupid, but it's the only way I can explain it. I've always known I loved you, and Mum, and everyone, but I only knew it in here.' She touched her head. 'I just couldn't feel anything in here.' She put her hand on her chest. 'I thought that part of me was dead, like rotten or removed or something. Anyway, I can feel it now.' She reached up and touched her taller, younger sister's face. 'I'm so sorry, Cass.'

Cassie's eyes and nose streamed. Jill dug for a tissue in her pocket and wiped her face for her.

'You could use one of those too,' said Cassie. 'You look like shit.'

Gabriel made a movement and Jill suddenly became re-aware that people watched them. Genovese leaned, arms folded, against an unmarked car. Lanvin had already left with Nader.

The lawyer, Worthington, stood at Gabriel's shoulder.

'Ah, Detective Jackson,' said Gabriel. 'May I have a brief word?'

'Just wait here a sec, Cass,' Jill said. 'Don't move . . . I mean, could you just stay . . .'

'It's okay, Jill,' Cassie said with a tiny smile. 'I'm not going anywhere.'

Frowning, Jill turned towards Gabriel. He indicated with his chin to walk with him a few metres from Worthington.

'What the fuck, Gabe,' she said. She looked back over her shoulder towards the lawyer. 'Why isn't that prick cuffed?'

Gabriel sighed, squinted into the sun. 'Look, he's coming in, Jill, but he's already making some big noises about our treatment of him during the bust. His story is that he's Byron Barnes's lawyer. Reckons he was out there giving legitimate counsel, and is as surprised as we are about the drugs. Reckons he'll prove all of it to us back at the house.'

Jill scowled. 'It's bullshit,' she said. 'You saw him, Gabe. He was shitting himself. He's involved in this deal.'

'I hear you,' said Gabriel. 'But Last wants him treated carefully. If he is Barnes's lawyer, we may have nothing on him. And Barnes is still in the wind. We're gonna have to wait and take this carefully. Apparently this fucker has some major connections. And he's already got his own lawyer lined up, waiting for us back at the shop.'

'Well, what's he doing now?' said Jill, speaking to Gabriel but watching Worthington, who was standing close to Cassie, whispering. 'What's he want with my sister?'

Gabriel shrugged. 'He asked for a word,' he said. 'Reckons he'll be representing her. He insisted on a couple of minutes. Because we haven't formally arrested him, there's nothing really we can do.'

Jill folded her arms and watched her little sister speaking with Worthington. He just seems like a smarmy scumbag, she thought, watching him lean over Cassie, speaking rapidly, assuredly. Suddenly, he stiffened, his head snapped back. He stared at Cassie as though she had just projectile vomited in his face. But her sister just stood calmly, smiling a little, her lips mouthing words Jill had no hope of hearing.

Worthington's shoulders slumped. He moved away from Cassie, back towards Genovese, his face ashen.

'What was that?' said Jill.

'Whatever,' said Gabriel. 'Time's up, anyway. You ready, Jill?'

'Yeah,' she said. She walked slowly back towards her sister, already dreading the next part of the process – taking Cass's statement, calling her parents.

But what is she thinking? Jill thought, watching Cassie beaming as she approached, genuinely smiling at her for the first time in a very long time. Doesn't she understand the shit she's in?

'Jill,' said Cassie, when she reached her side, 'could you reach into my top pocket?'

Brow furrowed, Jill reached in and removed a memory stick for a computer.

'In there,' said Cassie, 'you'll find multiple video and audio files documenting Christian Worthington buying and dealing commercial quantities of drugs.'

Jill stared at the USB in her fingers.

'And Jill,' said Cassie, 'this is very important. You won't *see* me in there, but you'll hear people talking to me a lot, especially Christian. But he doesn't call me Cassie. He uses a pet name of mine – Seren.'

'Seren?' said Jill.

'Yep. Nice, isn't it? It's short for Serendipity. You know, it means happy coincidence, lucky chance.'

71

Tuesday 16 April, 12.41 pm

Dirk McClintoff put his Coke in the cup holder and his smoke between his lips to take the corner. The traffic had been a freaken nightmare – an hour to get from Parramatta just to Petersham. He swore he could feel his ulcer bleeding a little more when he got stuck at every light. The petrol gauge dropped without mercy before his very eyes as he crunched the semi-trailer up through the gears after every holdup.

Finally, his turnoff. He didn't know why he was in such a hurry to get home, though. The place had been cold and gloomy since his bitch wife had left him. Not that it had exactly been all warm and fuzzy when she'd been there. She'd spent every waking minute on online forums or at the shops spending his money.

As always, he indicated from the centre lane to take the left turn. No way this rig could take the tight corner from the kerbside lane. As usual, he could sense the other drivers' frustration all around him as they waited for the heavy truck to negotiate the corner. Where were they gonna go anyway, he thought. The road was a parking lot ahead of him.

'What the fuck!' Dirk's cigarette fell from his mouth and landed on his balls. The blue WRX was flying in the empty left lane up the hill. This prick's gonna try to overtake in the left lane! Dirk ripped up the handbrake and stood straight up on the foot-brakes, but he knew there was no way he was gonna stop this thing before . . .

Dirk's forehead smacked into his window when the Rexie slammed into the side of his trailer. He shook his head, dizzy. He then shot out of his cabin and bolted through cars around to the left side of the truck. He stopped dead, knowing there was fuck-all he could do.

He rubbed at his forehead, feeling his fingers sticky with his blood. His head would hurt tomorrow. He took another quick look at what was left of the blue car jammed in under the trailer. Who was he to complain? At least he still had a head.

Epilogue

June

Seren used the remote to bump up the aircon a smidge. Marco would be home in an hour, and she wanted it toasty. She smiled and hugged herself, thinking of the trail of clothes he left as soon as he walked into the apartment each day. His private-school uniform. He began shedding bits and pieces in the lift – the hat, the blazer – and by the time he reached his bedroom, he wore nothing but jocks and socks.

'I hate it there,' he moaned every day, trying to hide his smile. She knew he loved his new school; saw the effort he was putting into his homework for the first time in his life.

She thumbed through a *Gourmet Traveller* and selected tomorrow's dinner. Slow-cooked salmon, she decided, poached in barely warm olive oil for an hour. It has to be seafood, she thought, staring out at the water off Birkenhead Point beyond the balcony.

She picked up the business card from the kitchen counter; flipped it over and back again, studying every letter, as though this could make its owner move things along faster. I wonder if he'll even *want* to stay with us, she worried. She read the name again – *Barbara McDougall, Department of Community Services*. Barbara had found her little brother, Bradley, within twenty minutes of her first call. He was eighteen now, and living in a share house.

She stared at the front door of the apartment, picturing Bradley walking in here on the weekend to visit them. Will he look like me, she wondered? Like Mum, like Dad? Will he forgive me? She wiped her cheeks with the backs of her hands and turned again to look out at the water. A monstrously fat pelican sat perched on a buoy in the winter sunshine, staring straight at her. He seemed to wink. Did he just wink?

She winked back, just in case.

And that reminds me, she thought. I must do more about maintaining this lifestyle. She hopped off the bar stool in the kitchen and padded, barefoot, across the thick carpet to her bedroom. She rebooted the computer and logged in to her bank. She electronically transferred funds to pay the rent on her old apartment, wondering who would have commandeered it. Probably Tready. She shuddered. He, or whoever else it was, would be the last person to tell anyone that she didn't live there anymore. He'd probably have moved right in and rented his own shithole out to the hookers on an hourly basis.

What else do I need to do to keep all of this going? she wondered. She was sure that Christian would never bother her again. He knew that Cassie had told her where to find the gun he'd hidden during a murder trial for his client. That would get him at least fifteen and up to twenty-five years for aiding and abetting, perverting the course of justice. He'd cop his five years sweet and forget he'd ever laid eyes on her.

She stretched her neck and stared at the ceiling. She'd thought she'd had the world figured out, people figured out. She knew there were good and bad people. She knew that some people were kind, could love, could be relied upon. She didn't know there were people like Cassie Jackson. She smiled, thinking of the last letter she'd received. Cassie still had another six months in gaol-ordered rehab. That'd make it summer before she could have her over here to thank her properly. She was already planning the menu.

And Zeko? What about Zeko? Was it time to call him again, remind him that it was best that he forget her name completely? She didn't think so. She knew as well as he did that his mortgage and his six kids relied upon that slaughterhouse wage, and that some skinny blonde bitch wasn't worth losing it all for. No, as long as she showed up to visit the lovely Maria Thomasetti for another few months, she was home and hosed.

Except that eight hundred thousand wouldn't last forever with these Sydney rental prices.

She did a quick Google search and leaned back in her leather office chair; she put her feet up on her bed and dialled the number she had found.

'Sydney Stock Exchange,' said a female voice.

'Oh, hi,' said Seren. 'I'd like to enroll in your beginners' classes for share trading.'

'You're not going to believe this,' said the woman. 'I was just closing off the enrollments for this session. I can just squish you in. If you'd called a couple of minutes later, you'd have had to wait another two months. How lucky!'

'That's me,' said Seren. 'Lucky.'

Acknowledgements

Once again, this book is inspired by the soldiers I've met in my day job. In this case, the veterans of wars taking place every day in homes, behind closed doors: survivors of domestic violence. If you're in one of these war zones, find someone to help you out. You can do it.

To the book sellers and everyone I've met within the book industry: thanks for welcoming me into your world. I'm still trying to find a baddie amongst you (sorry, occupational hazard). So far, no one.

To the whole team at Random House Australia: thank you. For everything.

To Josh: ∞

Dr Leah Giarratano has had a long career as a psychologist. An expert in psychological trauma, sex offences and psychopathology, she has had many years' experience working with victims and psychopaths. She has worked in psychiatric hospitals, with the Australian Defence Force, and in corrective services with offenders who suffer severe personality disorders. She has assessed and treated survivors of just about every imaginable psychological trauma, including hostages; war veterans; rape, assault, and accident victims; and has worked with police, fire and ambulance officers.

Leah is also the host of a prime-time television documentary series entitled *Beyond the Darklands*, in which she delves into the minds of some of Australia's most infamous criminals.

Galiano Island
Community Library